David Handler

"If I could get Stewart Hoag to ghostwrite my books they'd sell better, and I'd laugh myself silly. David Handler is a hoot, and his books are just the thing for what ails you. I find it hard to begrudge him his Edgar!"
Parnell Hall, author of *You Have the Right to Remain Puzzled*

"Some books deserve to go quietly into that good night, but the works of David Handler are not among them. Busted Flush Press has brought back to print a master of the mystery genre. Stewart Hoag, amateur private eye, has smarts and intelligence. Handler brings his characters to life instantly—the voices are original and real. Best of all, though, Handler treats his audience with respect. He doesn't write down. And Lulu will steal your heart."
Carolyn Haines, author of *Bones to Pick* and *Penumbra*

"When it comes to digging up dirt, there's nobody quite like natty ghostwriter Stewart 'Hoagy' Hoag and his neurotic basset hound Lulu."
People

"One of my all-time favorite series!"
Harlan Coben, *New York Times* best-selling author of *Promise Me*

also by **David Handler**

Stewart Hoag & Lulu Mysteries

The Man Who Died Laughing (1988)
The Man Who Lived by Night (1989)
The Man Who Would Be F. Scott Fitzgerald (1991)
The Woman Who Fell from Grace (1991)
The Boy Who Never Grew Up (1992)
The Man Who Cancelled Himself (1995)
The Girl Who Ran Off with Daddy (1996)
The Man Who Loved Women to Death (1997)

Mitch Berger & Desiree Mitry Mysteries

The Cold Blue Blood (2001)
The Hot Pink Farmhouse (2002)
The Bright Silver Star (2003)
The Burnt Orange Sunrise (2004)
The Sweet Golden Parachute (2006)

other fiction

Kiddo (1987)
Boss (1988)

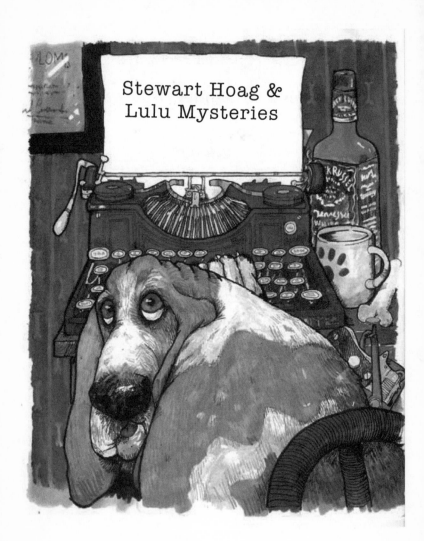

Stewart Hoag &
Lulu Mysteries

The Man Who Died Laughing

&

The Man Who Lived By Night

the first two
Stewart Hoag & Lulu Mysteries
by
David Handler

Busted Flush Press
Houston 2006

The Man Who Died Laughing

Originally published by Bantam Books, 1988

&

The Man Who Lived by Night

Originally published by Bantam Books, 1989

Published by Busted Flush Press

Trade paperback ISBN: 0-9767157-9-1
First trade paperback printing, September 2006

Layout & Production Services: Greg Fleming & Jeff Smith

BUSTED FLUSH
PRESS

P.O. Box 540594
Houston, TX 77254-0594
www.bustedflushpress.com

Introduction

to the first

Busted Flush Press
Omnibus Edition

Now the truth can be told . . . I never *intended The Man Who Died Laughing* to be the first installment of a murder mystery series starring celebrity ghostwriter Stewart Hoag and his faithful, neurotic basset hound, Lulu. I had no idea I'd ever end up writing a mystery series, let along go on to launch another series of five novels (and counting) featuring pudgy New York film critic Mitch Berger and the beauteous Connecticut State Trooper Des Mitry. It was all, as the great Ozzie Nelson used to say, one of those wonderful surprises that make life so interesting.

In the early '80s I was a young journalist scratching out a living in New York City. I had many gigs, among them New York cultural correspondent for the Scripps-Howard News Service. Truly, this was my idea of a dream job. I not only got paid to review the hottest shows on and off-Broadway, but to interview countless celebrities. Through the years I sat down with everyone from Betty Friedan to Jerry Lewis. Not that I was satisfied. Deep down inside, I yearned to write the Great American novel. Often, this meant setting my alarm for 4 a.m. and squeezing in two hours at my typewriter before dawn with a blanket thrown over my shoulders. My landlord didn't turn on the heat until 6 a.m. – if at all.

It took me, from start to finish, seven years to get published my autobiographical first novel, *Kiddo*. By which time two significant things had happened in my career. One was *Kate and Allie*, the hit New York-based sitcom starring Jane Curtin and Susan St. James. I was lucky enough to land on its original writing staff, and from then on to navigate my way through the roiling show biz seas, writing sitcom scripts and screenplays for Alan King, Stiller and Meara, Garry Marshall, Grant Tinker, Rob Reiner and others too numerous and psychotic to mention here.

The other thing that happened was that I'd experienced life as a celebrity ghostwriter. Helped someone whose daughter had been one of the most celebrated murder victims of the '80s tell her true story about what can happen to an American family when it is thrust unwillingly into the tabloid limelight. I wasn't prepared for just how different ghostwriting was from anything I'd done before. As a journalist, I was paid to tell it like I saw it. As a ghost, I was paid to tell it like *she* saw it. This was to be her version of what went on, not mine. Which isn't to say the book was a lie. It wasn't. But it is to say I wasn't an independent member of the press corps anymore. I was there to serve. I was also inside the palace walls, privy to dark family secrets that reporters on the outside knew nothing about.

In later years, I came to refer to myself as a thinking man's Kato Kaelin.

As my completed manuscript for *Kiddo* was inching its way around New York from publishing house to publishing house, I began turning over in my mind a moody suspense novel about a ghostwriter who gets in too deep with his celebrity and can't get out. I briefly considered doing *The Man Who Died Laughing* as an original screenplay instead of as a novel, but elected to try it as a book first. Since I'd spent so many years interviewing people, I decided to employ a Q & A technique several times throughout the book. It was what I knew and was comfortable with.

So was the world of comedy. I'd been working with comic performers for years. It was largely out of my experiences with them that I came up with Sonny Day, one half of the famous '50s comedy duo of Knight and Day. Sonny is also based in part on my father, Chet Handler, who grew up on Gates Avenue in the Bedford-Stuyvesant section of Brooklyn, worked in the Catskills as a youth, chewed Sen-Sen mints and paced around with his hands in his pockets when he got excited, jangling his coins.

As for my lead character, Stewart Hoag, I decided he'd be a taller, smoother, much more successful version of *me*. Someone whose first novel had been a huge smash. Someone who was such a hit with women that he'd married a movie star named Merilee Nash. Hoagy, quite simply, is the guy who I'd hoped to be someday when I sat there huddled in that blanket in front of my manual typewriter at 4 in the morning, dreaming and shivering.

Not that life has necessarily worked out for Hoagy. When we meet him in *The Man Who Died Laughing* he's washed up, bitter and blocked. Which brings me to the question I'm asked most often by readers: How did I come up with Lulu? Truth is, I was about four chapters into the first draft when I kept getting the nagging feeling that Hoagy was too alone. I decided he needed a sidekick. My girlfriend and I had recently spent a weekend in upstate New York with some friends who had a litter of basset hound puppies, one of whom was named Lulu in honor of Ed Norton's long-lost childhood dog on *The Honeymooners*. And so a crime-fighting duo was born.

Absolutely no one wanted to publish *The Man Who Died Laughing*. Several editors said they couldn't quite tell whether it was a "serious" novel or a thriller. Many were flat out unenthusiastic. One of the editors who rejected it, a young paperback mystery editor at Bantam named Kate Miciak, did say that she liked Hoagy and loved Lulu. But Kate identified two key shortcomings in the manuscript. One was that there wasn't a punchy enough plot to satisfy mystery readers. Not a surprise to me, since I hadn't intended it to be a mystery. The other was that there was basically no such thing as a one-shot mystery. There still isn't. So if I wanted *The Man Who Died Laughing* to work I had to do a better job of presenting Hoagy as a compelling series character. Make him a capable, self-aware pen for hire who goes from celebrity to celebrity, digging up secrets.

Not a bad idea for a mystery series, when I stopped to think about it. Pretty original. Not to mention fertile. There'd always be a fresh supply of real-life celebrity memoirs to draw upon, not only from my own world of entertainment but politics, business, sports. Plus the choice of locales was wide open. Hoagy and Lulu could travel the world together. I liked the idea a lot. And I can't emphasize this enough:

It was something that had never occurred to me.

I took Kate's advice, re-submitted the manuscript to her and she promptly signed me to a two-book contract. When *The Man Who Died Laughing* came out in 1988 it received encouraging reviews in several mystery publications and later that year I was stunned to learn had been nominated for an Anthony Award at the mystery world's annual Bouchercon convention. I didn't win, but I did learn something about myself: I was a mystery writer.

Which brings me to my second Hoagy novel, *The Man Who Lived by Night*. I guess every writer who has been toiling at the trade long enough has one pet book that he or she continues to absolutely adore even though no one else seemed to. Or maybe *because* no one seemed to. Each of us is a proud parent, and we feel a special attachment to that offspring that wasn't able to make any friends out there. The book that was misunderstood or shunned or, worst of all, just plain ignored. Mine happens to be this 1989 novel about the legendary '60s British rocker Tris Scarr, which was the only installment in the series that disappeared from American bookstores after a single paperback printing, never to be seen or heard from again.

I'm not sure the booksellers even unpacked this book. That's how fast it was gone from the stores. I've encountered very few Hoagy fans through the years who've even *seen* it, let alone read it. Oddly enough, *The Man Who Lived by Night* has always been one of the most popular Hoagy books overseas. The Japanese and Italian translations have sold steadily through the years. But here at home, only a prized handful of copies survive. I myself possess only three. I've received more letters from readers through the years about *The Man Who Lived by Night* than about any other book in the series. Truly, it qualifies as a crime fiction artifact – The Lost Hoagy. I'm grateful beyond belief that David Thompson of Busted Flush Press has finally returned it to print after so many years.

Honestly, I can't tell you *why The Man Who Lived by Night* suffered such an ignominious publishing fate. It features delicious English locales and my favorite climactic plot twist in the entire series. Most significantly, it marks the arrival of Hoagy as we've come know and, I hope, love him. Re-reading it now, I'm exceedingly aware that this is really the book when Hoagy *becomes* Hoagy. His passion for fine clothes and dining are on display for the first time here. Likewise his giddy and perilous relationship with ex-wife Merilee Nash, who we set eyes on for the first time. Lulu steps up to her first full-fledged starring role as the child who gets caught between her warring parents.

Nonetheless, *The Man Who Lived by Night* was dead on arrival.

Maybe it was the subject matter. In those days, not many mystery readers were also rock music fans. Possibly they were put off by this rather lurid tale of sex, drugs and rock 'n' roll. Possibly I should have waited until the Hoagy series had established itself more fully before I tackled the music scene. But at the time I wrote *The Man Who Lived by Night* I was a young mystery writer trying to make my contribution to the world of Chandler, Hammett and Macdonald. I happened to be a product of the '60s cultural revolution that the much heralded British Invasion helped bring about. Taking on a fresh subject that I felt a special generational affinity for seemed like a good idea to me. It still does.

Or maybe it was the rabies thing. When I sat down to write *The Man Who Lived by Night* I was still trying to learn the do's and don't's of writing a mystery series (which is not to say you ever stop learning). Always, I had question . . . Is it okay for Hoagy to age from book to book? Can I refer back to events that happened in previous books? But, believe me, no rules were harder to master than the ones for Lulu. When it came to Hoagy's four-footed sidekick, I was basically on my own – partly because I thought of Lulu more as a person than as a dog. She falls in and out of love. She gets her own place setting at restaurants, her own aisle seat at Broadway premieres, on airplanes, you name it. Everywhere Hoagy goes, she goes.

In this particular case, that somewhere is Great Britain which, as you may know, has very stringent animal quarantine laws designed to prevent the spread of rabies. In reality, Lulu would have had to leave for London six months ahead of Hoagy. This seemed totally unlikely to me. It wouldn't play. Nor did I want to leave Lulu behind and write *The Man Who Lived by Night* without her. She was too valuable a character. So I took a small liberty and let her into the country without quarantining her. After all, Lulu already did lots of things she couldn't actual do in real life, right? Well, yes and no. A couple of early readers, friends of mine, called to tell me they were a bit bothered by it. And yet others were totally fine with it. In hindsight, maybe I should have included an author's note to explain my thinking.

Still, nothing satisfactorily explains *why The Man Who Lived by Night* has been out of print for so long. I hope, after all of these years, that it will bring you as much pleasure as it brought me at the time. And I'm really sorry about the wait.

David Handler
Old Lyme, Connecticut
February 2006

The Man Who Died Laughing

the first
Stewart Hoag & Lulu Mystery

For Diana
who asks only for happy endings

Night and day you are the one,
Only you beneath the moon and under the sun

from the song by Cole Porter

"You know, I was thinking – that Rosebud
you're trying to find out about. Maybe that
was something he lost."

Mr. Bernstein to the reporter, in *Citizen Kane*

CHAPTER ONE

I was dreaming about Merilee when the phone woke me up. I don't remember the dream. I do remember my face felt all hot and I was having trouble breathing. Lulu was sleeping on my head again; a habit she got into when my landlord cut back on the heat. I pushed her off and tried to focus on the clock next to the bed. It wasn't easy. I'd been drinking boilermakers at the Dublin House until two-thirty, which was . . . exactly nine minutes before.

I answered the phone. Somebody was speaking in this gravelly Brooklynese. Somebody who sounded a lot like The One.

"You can write, pally. You can write."

I cleared my throat. "You read my book?"

"My people read it. They're impressed. They think you're vibrant and, whattaya call it, *resonant*."

"So did *Newsweek*. That's their quote off the back cover."

"So let's talk, pally."

"Sure. Read the book yourself. Then we'll talk. Also, never call me again in the middle of the night. It's rude."

"Hey, nobody talks to Sonny Day like that. Who you think you are, *me*?"

I hung up and burrowed back under Lulu and the covers. I didn't have much left anymore. Lulu and my pride were about it. I went back to sleep immediately.

The next thing that woke me up was this loud, steady pounding. At first I thought it was my head, but it was somebody at the door. Lulu was barking. I tried to muzzle her – she has a mighty big bark for somebody with no legs – but she leapt off the bed and waddled to the door and kept barking. I focused on the clock again. It wasn't yet nine.

"Who's there?!"

"Sonny Day!" came the reply.

I found my silk dressing gown in a pile of clothes on the chair. "How'd you get in the building?"

"Vic is good with locks!"

"Who's Vic?!"

"Open up, will ya, Stewart?!"

I opened up, and there he was. It was strange meeting someone I'd known since I was in kindergarten. He looked just like he did on screen, only more so. He was shorter. He was wider. The furrows in his forehead were deeper, the black brows bushier, the nose bigger. He was in his sixties now, but he still wore his hair in a pompadour and he still dyed it jet black. I think he dyed his chest hair, too. Plenty of it was showing. His fur coat was open, his red silk shirt unbuttoned to the waist. His heavy beard was freshly shaved. He smelled of cologne and talc, and he was tanned and alert. He stuck out a manicured hand. I shook it. His grip was a hell of a lot firmer than mine.

Behind him stood a sandy-haired giant in a chesterfield coat. He was maybe forty and balding and had a long scar across his chin. I figured him for six feet six, maybe 250.

"That's Vic Early," said Sonny.

Vic nodded at me blandly.

I stood there in the doorway shivering. "Don't you ever sleep?"

"Can we come in?" asked Sonny.

I let them in. The two of them filled my tiny living room. Lulu barked viciously and then ran under my desk.

"Good work, Lulu," I told her.

Sonny looked around at what little there was in the way of furniture, at the piles of newspapers, the dust, the beer bottles, the stack of dishes in the kitchen sink, which dripped. "Lemme see, the premise for this scene is poverty, right?"

Vic laughed.

I went into the kitchen, stirred two heaping spoonfuls of instant coffee into a cup of cold water, and swallowed it down with three extra-strength Excedrin. Then I smiled bravely. "Breakfast," I said, "is the most important meal of the day."

Sonny bared his teeth like a rat, found a box of Sen-Sen mints in his coat, and popped two in his mouth. "Get dressed," he ordered. "Plane leaves in an hour."

"What plane?"

"To L.A. You can have the guesthouse. Stay as long as you need."

"Whoa – "

"You better step on it if we're gonna – "

"Wait! What are you talking about?"

"I want you," he said. "You're it."

I sat down on the sofa, rubbed my eyes.

"I already told my people to take care of it. Whatever deal you want, you got it. It's done."

"I don't think you understand," I said slowly. "Nothing's done. I do your book if I decide I want to, and I haven't decided yet."

"Did I tell ya, Vic? Huh?" Sonny beamed at me. "You got moxie, kid. Talent, too. You're some kind of writer."

"Oh, yeah?"

"Yeah. I read your book last night after we talked. I apologize. I'm not used to working with New York talent. I forget. You people are very – what? – *sensitive.* Anyways, I stayed up all night and read it. Never went to sleep, I'm impressed. I don't agree with you. I mean, your conclusion at the end. But that's cool. Point is, you tell a good story, you have real smarts, and you're no phony with big words."

I had nothing to add.

"Ever sell that book as a movie? The father's a great part. I could play the hell out of it."

"Orion optioned it for Paul Newman."

"Yeah, he can act, too," Sonny kidded.

Vic laughed. Clearly it was one of the things he was paid to do.

"We'll have to have a literary discussion sometime, pally. Time I got plenty, of, now that I'm off the stuff. You like to run? Me and Vic do five miles every morning. We already ran in Central Park this morning. Vic used to play offensive line for the Bruins."

Vic looked down at me impassively. He didn't scare me. I knew in a fair fight I'd last at least one point two seconds.

I turned to Sonny. "Can we have a minute alone?"

He tugged at the gold chain buried in the hair on his chest. "Vic, wait down in the limo."

Vic headed out, which got Lulu barking again from under the desk, where she was still cowering.

Sonny cleared a space on the love seat and sat down. "What do they call you? Stu?"

"Hoagy."

"As in Carmichael?"

"As in the cheese steak."

He narrowed his eyes at me. "You kidding me?"

"No."

"Good. Never kid a kidder. You know why?"

"No."

"We bleed. On the inside. What's on your mind, Hoagy? What's the problem?"

"No problem. This is rather sudden, that's all. I have to decide if I really want to do it."

"What else you doing?"

"Professionally? Not much. But it means leaving town for a few months and – "

"Got a girl?"

"Not right now."

"I hear you used to be married to Merilee Nash."

"Yes."

He shook his head. "It's tough to get over. I know. I had two marriages fall apart. Deep down inside, you always figure it was your fault."

"It *was* my fault."

"Don't be that hard on yourself, kid. One thing my doctors at Betty Ford told me I'll never forget – take the blame, don't take the shame."

"They give you sweatshirts with that printed on it?"

"You're a sour guy."

"You noticed."

"You're too young to be so sour. I'm gonna have to take you in tow. See, I used to be a sour pickle myself, a real kosher dill. But I got a much more positive attitude about life now."

"About your book . . ."

"Yeah?"

"Why are you writing it?"

"Got a lot I wanna get off my chest."

"You'll tell the truth?"

"Only way to tell it, pally. I'm prepared to be totally upfront. And this is my top priority, if that's what you're wondering. I'm yours – for as long as it takes." He jumped to his feet, paced into the kitchen, prodded the dishes in the sink, and paced back again. "It's part of my healing process, see? It's very important to me. And I won't shit you – my career could use a shot in the arm, too. I need the exposure. The dough. But that's all secondary. True story."

"My agent said you're having trouble finding someone. Why?"

"Because those Hollywood entertainment writers are all liars and scum. All they care about is the bad, the negative. They print lies and everybody who reads that crap thinks it's true. And they expect me to cooperate with 'em. They're whores who hide behind the constitution.

You, you're a *real* writer. You dig into what makes people tick. That's what I want."

"Are you planning to use other sources?"

"What are those?"

"Can I talk to your ex-partner?"

Sonny stiffened at my mention of Gabe Knight. He didn't answer me for a second. Then he stuck out his lower lip like a kid – a trademark gesture – and said, "Gabe's off limits. That's the only ground rule. I hear you've spoken to him once and you're fired."

"Why?"

"Because I don't want him involved in it," he snapped, reddening.

"But you'll talk about why the two of you broke up?"

"Yeah. I'll do that. And you can talk to anybody else you want. Ask anything you want, of any of 'em. Connie, my first wife. We're getting friendly again. Vic, he's been through the bad years. There's my lawyer. There's Wanda. You can talk to Tracy, if you can find her. Last I heard she was off in Tunisia, shtupping some prince."

"Has she retired from the business?"

"Her tits fell, if that's retiring."

He waited for me to laugh. He expected me to laugh. It was a habit of his that came from thirty years of being a famous comic. But I've never been an easy laugh. That put him off, I think. So he turned serious.

"That broad almost destroyed me. I loved her, gave her everything. She was sweet, beautiful, my whole life. One day she just packs up and leaves me – not even a word of warning. Says she has to go find herself." He heaved a deep, genuine sigh of pain, then abruptly winked at me, man to man. "Not that it should be such a great fucking discovery, huh?" He looked around. "Jeez, this place is a real dump. Reminds me of the old neighborhood. Plaster falling down. No heat." He motioned toward the kitchen. "Roaches?"

"Thanks, I got plenty."

"That's hysterical," he said, not smiling. "You like living here?"

"As much as I like living."

"What's that, New York intellectual bullshit?"

"Of the highest order."

"So whattaya say? You'll do it?"

"I don't know if we'll be compatible."

He frowned. "Is that so important?"

"We'll be spending a lot of time together. We'll be like . . ."

His face darkened. "Partners?"

"Partners."

"Look, pally. Me, I make instant judgments about people. Always have. Sometimes it gets me in trouble, but I'm too old to change. I like you. I think you're talented. I think we'll be good for each other. Okay? Now throw some stuff in a bag. Plane leaves in – "

My head was thudding. "I'll have to think it over. If I decide yes, I'll catch up with you in a week. I have to straighten some things out here, board Lulu."

"Bring the dog with you. Space I got lots of."

"Really?"

"Sure."

"I don't think she likes you." Lulu was still under the desk.

"Nonsense. Kids and dogs love me. Know why? Because I'm one of them – an innocent. Only the critics hate me. I got no use for them either. My contract is with the audience. *My* audience. You a gambling man, Hoagy?"

"I am."

"Tell you what. I get Lulu to like me, you'll take the job. Deal?"

"She's never steered me wrong. If she okays you, I'll do it. Deal."

Sonny grinned. "My kinda guy." He snapped his fingers. "Get me a piece of candy or something."

I got him a doggie treat out of the cupboard. Sonny put it between his lips, leaving one end sticking out. Then he went to the desk and got down on his hands and knees in front of her. That started her barking again.

"Kiss Sonny, Lulu," he cooed. "Give Sonny a kissy-kissy." He crawled to her on his hands and knees, the doggie treat between his lips – just like when he tried to tame the lion in *The Big Top*, Knight & Day's circus picture and their first in color.

I couldn't believe it. Sonny Day, The One, was crawling around on my living room rug, trying to feed my dog mouth to mouth. Even more amazing was that it was working. Lulu stopped barking. Her tail began to thump. When Sonny got nose-to-nose with her, she took a tug at the treat. He held on to it, teasing her. She yapped playfully at him. He yapped back.

"Say," he said from the side of his mouth. "Her breath smells kind of . . ."

"She has kind of strange eating habits."

Lulu took another bite at the treat. This time he let her take it from him. She stretched out and began to munch happily. He patted her. Her tail thumped.

Sonny stood up, swiped at the lint on his trousers, and grinned at me triumphantly. "So whattaya say, pigeon? Plane's waiting."

Maybe you'd already heard of me before I got mixed up with Sonny. I used to be a literary sensation. In reviewing my first novel, *Our Family Enterprise*, *The New York Times* called me "the first major new literary voice of the eighties." I won awards. I spoke at literary gatherings. I got a lot of attention. *Esquire* was interested in what my favorite flavor of ice cream was (licorice, and it's damned hard to find). *Vanity Fair* wondered who my favorite movie actor was (a tie between Robert Mitchum and Moe Howard). *Gentlemen's Quarterly* applauded me as a man of "easy style" and wanted to know what I wore when I worked (an Orvis chamois shirt, jeans, and mukluks). For a while there, I was as famous as John Irving, only he's shorter than I am, and he still writes.

Or maybe you'd heard of me because of Merilee. Ours was a match made not so much in heaven as in Liz Smith's column. Liz thought we were perfect for each other. Maybe we were. She was Merilee Nash, that strikingly lovely and serious and oh-so-hot star of Joe Papp's latest Tony winner. I was tall and dashing and, you'll recall, the first major new literary voice of the eighties. We did London, Paris, and most of Italy on our honeymoon. When we got back, we bought a magnificent art deco apartment on Central Park West. I cultivated a pencil-thin mustache and took to wearing a Brooks Brothers tuxedo and grease in my hair. She went for that white silk headband that everybody copied. Together we opened every play and dance club and museum showing and rib joint in town. We were featured in the new Mick Jagger rock video (we were the couple he chauffeured through hell). We got a red 1958 Jaguar XK 150 for zipping out to the Hamptons, and a basset hound puppy we named Lulu. Lulu went everywhere with us. She even had her own water bowl at Elaine's.

I kept my old, drafty fifth-floor walk-up on West Ninety-third Street as an office and filled it with a word processor and a personal copier. I started going there every morning to work on book number two, only there wasn't one. They call it writer's block. Believe me, there's nothing there to get blocked up. Only a void. And a fear that you no longer know how to do the only thing you know how to do. My juices had dried up. I just couldn't get it up anymore – for the book or, it soon turned out, for Merilee. She met my little problem head on, so to speak. She was patient, sympathetic, and classy. That's Merilee. But after eighteen months she began to take it personally.

I moved back into my office. I kept Lulu and the mustache. Merilee got the rest. A dancer friend of hers called me and made it plain she was interested. That's when I found out it wasn't just Merilee I couldn't get it up for. The cocktail-party friends fell away fast. I managed to alienate the few genuine ones by dropping in on them unexpectedly, drinking all the liquor in their house, and passing out. The advance on the second book melted away. My check to the Racquet Club bounced. A few weeks after the divorce became final, Merilee married that hot new playwright from Georgia, Zack something. I read about it in Liz Smith's column.

It's amazing how quickly your life can turn to shit.

I'd fallen three months behind on my rent, and by the time my next royalty check filtered down, I'd be living in a shopping cart in Riverside Park. I was on my ass when I got the call from my agent about helping Sonny Day, The One, write his memoirs.

"Who cares about Sonny Day anymore?" I said.

"His publisher thinks plenty of people will, dear boy," she replied. "They're paying him one point three million."

"Well, well."

"The ghost gets a hundred fifty, plus a third of the royalties."

"Well, well, well."

All I knew about Sonny Day was what I had seen on the screen. Or read in the newspaper – which, of course, doesn't have to be the truth. When I was a kid, I thought he was the funniest man in America. I grew up on the dozen or so movies he and his partner, Gabe Knight, made together. Knight and Day. The critics never thought too much of them. After all, they did little more than make the same slaphappy, rags-to-riches picture over and over again, always with that same bouncy version of the Cole Porter song "Night and Day" as their theme song. But who cared? I didn't. They were funny. Everybody loved Sonny then, especially kids. He was a big kid himself, a brash, pudgy Brooklyn street urchin loaded with schemes and energy and no couth. Always, he was out of his element in the polite world, the adult world. It was Gabe who was Sonny's entry into civilized society.

Gabe was the football hero in *Big Man on Campus*, the ski instructor in *Alpine Lodge*. He sang the songs. He got the girls. Sonny got the laughs. Everything Sonny did was funny – the way he jabbed people in the chest with his index finger when he got excited, or whinnied when he got exasperated, or got the hiccups when he was nervous. Who can forget Sonny the klutz taking the wrong turn and going down the advanced slope in *Alpine Lodge*? Or Sonny the Romeo trying to act suave on his blind date with Joi Lansing in *Jerks*?

In the fifties, nobody was more popular than Knight & Day. Their movies made millions. They had their own hit TV variety show on CBS. They headlined in the top nightclubs and in Las Vegas, where they were charter members of the Rat Pack. They were gold. Of the two, it was always Sonny who got the acclaim. Sonny was the biggest of them all. Milton Berle was Uncle Miltie, Jackie Gleason was The Great One. Sonny Day was The One. Gabe Knight was a good-looking straight man who got very lucky, or so everyone thought.

"Here's the best part," my agent said. "He's agreed to tell what The Fight was about."

Knight & Day broke up in 1958. Their fight – The Fight – was probably the most famous in show business history. It happened in Chasen's in front of half the stars and moguls in Hollywood. Sonny and Gabe had to be pulled apart after actually throwing punches at one another and drawing blood. They split up the next day. They never appeared together again. Jerry Lewis tried to reunite them on his telethon twenty-five years later, but Sonny refused to show.

Ordinarily, there are no secrets when celebrities are involved. I know. I used to be one. But *nobody* knew the real reason Knight & Day broke up. Neither of them would tell. If anyone close knew, they kept quiet. It wasn't the most important secret around, like who really shot JFK or what's the mystery of Oil of Olay. But a lot of people did still wonder about it.

Especially when you considered what happened to the two of them. Gabe surprised everyone by proving that Sonny hadn't carried him all of those years. He starred in a Broadway musical. He recorded a string of easy-listening platinum records. He produced and starred in his own long-running TV sitcom, *The Gabe Knight Show*, in which he played a harried small-town portrait photographer with a wife, two kids, and a pet elephant, Roland. Gabe blossomed into a Beverly Hills squire. He was prosperous, dignified, well-liked – a man, in short, who had a Palm Springs celebrity tennis tournament of his very own.

The biggest charities and political fund-raisers sought him out as an after-dinner speaker. Most recently, the President had gone so far as to nominate him as America's envoy to France. Ambassador Gabriel Knight. It seemed an entirely appropriate choice now that the French were getting their own Disney World – though I personally would have gone all the way and named Annette.

Certainly it was Gabe's highly publicized stride into public service that had spurred some publisher's interest in a book by Sonny Day. Sonny, after all, went the opposite direction of Gabe after The Fight.

He became, as Lenny Bruce coined it, "the man who put the ick in shtick." Starting with *The Boy in the Gray Flannel Suit*, Sonny made a string of films on his own – wrote them, directed them, starred in them. He even sang. Horribly. His films were all disasters, not just because they were bad – and even his fans knew they were *bad* – but because he'd lost the sweet, naive charm that had made him so lovable. Sonny no longer wanted to be Sonny the klutz. He wanted to be Sonny the smoothie, too, down to the Hollywood tan, the nail gloss, the fancy clothes. He wanted to get the girl. His ego demanded it. The box office demise of his grand comic history of organized crime, *Moider, Inc.*, which he wrote, directed, and played five roles in, finished him as a filmmaker. I never saw it. Like most of America, I had stopped going to Sonny Day movies by then.

Nobody wanted to work with him after that. He was arrogant and difficult. He hosted his own short-lived TV variety show, and an even shorter-lived syndicated talk show. He became a regular for a while on *The Hollywood Squares*, always smoking a big cigar and wearing an obnoxious leer. He popped up on *Laugh-In*, dressed like Spanky Mc-Farland. He did a solo act in Las Vegas and grew into more and more of a monster. One night in Vegas he jumped off the stage and punched some guy who was heckling him. They settled out of court. Another time someone parked their car in his space at a TV studio and Sonny emptied a loaded revolver into it. He became an ugly kind of celebrity, the kind who thinks he can get away with anything. He clashed constantly with the press, which got even by reporting his stormy personal life in gleeful detail. In the mid-sixties he divorced his first wife, actress Connie Morgan, so he could marry Tracy St. Claire, a starlet barely out of her teens. She soon became an international film star. And promptly dumped Sonny. What little press Sonny got after that was mostly due to his daughter, Wanda, a model, an actress, and briefly, a singer, thanks to her hit bossa nova version of "Night and Day." Wanda appeared nude in a Roger Vadim film and in *Playboy*. Sonny called her a "slut" in the *Enquirer*, denied it, sued, and lost. Then she went on the *Tonight* show and told America she'd taken LSD more than a hundred times. She married a rock star and got her ankle tattooed, then she moved in with a member of the Black Panthers. Wanda was a wild and crazy gal. Seriously crazy. There were a couple of botched suicide attempts. When my agent called, Wanda had been out of the public eye for several years. Sonny had been getting less and less attention himself, other than for the odd celebrity roast, until a few months before, when it was revealed he'd checked into the Betty Ford Clinic. Turned out he'd been addicted to liquor and pills for a long time. Now he was on the road back.

"They say he's really picked himself up off the floor," my agent assured me. "He's supposed to be a changed man."

"Think he's looking to stick it to Gabe?"

She chuckled devilishly. "I'd say it's an excellent possibility."

"He'll be candid about the fight?"

"It's in his contract. Face it, Day has no career right now. An honest book will get him right back on the circuit – Carson, Donahue. Look what it did for Sid Caesar. He even has his own shape-up tape now. What do you think, Hoagy? Shall I tell them you're interested?"

"What made you think of me?"

"He wants someone serious and distinguished."

"Like I said, what made you think of me?"

"Stop it, Hoagy. Want to meet him?"

"I don't think so. I'm no ghostwriter."

"I know. But this might be just the thing to get you started really writing again. It'll get you out of the house, give you some focus. And it won't be hard work. All you have to do is sit by his pool for a couple of months with a tape recorder. You can even leave your name off. What do you think?"

I wavered. Sonny Day wanted America's sympathy and understanding. Sonny Day wanted to be loved again. I wasn't sure I wanted to help him. He was pretty much my idea of a pig. I also wasn't so sure I wanted to be a ghost. Ignore the blurbs on the book jackets – there's no such thing as an honest memoir. There's only the celebrity subject's own memory, and while memory doesn't exactly lie, it does preserve, protect, and defend against all painful truths. The ghost is brought in to make the celebrity's writing style, anecdotes, and various uplifting personal revelations seem candid and authentic, even if they aren't. The ghost also has to make the celebrity feel good about the book so that he or she or it will go on tour to promote it and the publisher will have some hope of breaking even on its seven-figure investment. I'd always equated ghosting with prostate trouble – I never thought it would happen to me. I wasn't even sure I could pull it off. I'm not very good with people. I became a writer so I wouldn't have to be around them. I'm also not very good at telling my ego to go on vacation. Actually, I tell it just fine, but it refuses to listen to me.

But it wasn't like I had much of a choice. I was on a first-name basis with the Ty-D-Bol man. I was desperate. So I told my agent it was okay to send Sonny a copy of *Our Family Enterprise*. She said she'd messenger it right over to the Essex House. Sonny was in town to roast Mickey Rooney.

"What could it hurt?" she said.

"What could it hurt?" I agreed.

CHAPTER
TWO

Lulu and I flew out to L.A. three days later. We rode first class. No matter what Sonny's financial situation was like, he always went first class. Lulu even got her own seat next to me, though she had to stay in her carrier. It wasn't much of a flight. The food was gluey, the stewardess ornery. Clouds covered the entire Midwest. Flying just doesn't seem as exciting as it used to be. But then nothing in the world does, except maybe baseball.

I spent most of the flight reading *You Are the One*, a gossipy, unauthorized biography of "those fun-loving, swinging partners who kept the fifties laughing." It had been written in the late sixties and was filled with the ego clashes, feuds, and jealousy that went on between Gabe and Sonny. There were lots of stories about money and how they blew it. Like how they went out and bought matching red Cadillac convertibles with their first big money – and paid for them with ten-dollar bills. Like how Sonny owned as many as five hundred pairs of shoes at a time and gave them away as soon as he'd worn each pair once. Mostly, I was interested in the reason the writer gave for The Fight. His theory was that Sonny, who was a compulsive gambler, owed somebody a lot of money and used the team as a kind of promissory note – forcing Gabe to work with him at a mob-owned Las Vegas casino for no money or be blackballed.

That didn't sound right to me. Maybe something like that had happened, but I didn't think it was why they fought. For one thing, that sort of dealing goes on all the time in entertainment business. Merilee told me stories about Broadway you wouldn't believe. Partners wouldn't roll around on the rug at Chasen's over something like that.

The other reason I didn't think it was true was that Sonny wouldn't be coming forward now with what actually *was* true.

I had a job ahead of me. It wasn't a particularly dignified one, but if I didn't do it well, I'd have to start giving serious thought to dental school. I needed to do more than just string together Sonny's funniest anecdotes. I needed to humanize him. That meant understanding him. And that meant getting him to really open up to me. There was the job. Still, the more I got used to the idea the more I believed I could make Sonny Day's book into something special. I

17

was, after all, no ordinary ghost.

Like I said, my ego wears earplugs.

Big Vic was waiting for me at the airport, wearing a windbreaker and a Dodger cap and holding a piece of cardboard that said "HOAG" on it, just in case I didn't recognize him.

"Sonny's at the therapist," he told me, taking Lulu's carrier. She growled softly. "Said he'll be back by lunchtime. Give you a chance to get settled."

We took the long moving sidewalk to the baggage claim area.

"So how long have you worked for Sonny?" I asked him.

"I've been with him eleven years now." Vic spoke in a droning monotone, as if he were reciting. "He followed me when I played ball at UCLA and read about how I enlisted in the Marines instead of playing pro ball. There was an article in the *Times* about me when I got back. He called me up and offered me a job. See, I got hurt over in Nam. I have a plate in my head."

"Bother you much?"

"Occasional headaches. On windy days I can pick up the Super Station."

I looked at him blankly.

"Sonny's joke," he explained.

"Of course."

"You make it over there, Hoag?"

"No, I was against it, actually."

"Me, too."

"Then why did you join the Marines?"

"To finish it," he said simply.

I got my suitcases and, with some embarrassment, the two cases of the only food in the world Lulu will eat – 9 Lives Mackerel Dinner for cats and very, very strange dogs. A gray Lincoln stretch limo with personalized plates that said "THE ONE" was parked at curbside. A ticket fluttered on the windshield. Vic pocketed it and put the stuff in the trunk. I got in front with him.

The L.A. airport had been redesigned for the Olympics, seemingly by an architect who had cut his teeth on ant farms. But it was a lot easier getting out than it used to be. Vic had no problems maneuvering his way to the San Diego Freeway, his big, football-scarred mitts planted firmly on the wheel, his massive shoulders squared. We headed north. It was the best kind of day they can have in L.A. There had been some rain, and then the wind had blown the clouds and smog out to sea. Now the sky was bright blue and it was so clear I could see the snow on Mount Baldy. The sun was warm and everything looked clean and shiny and new.

I rolled down my window. "Mind if I let Lulu out of her carrier?"

"Go right ahead."

I opened the carrier door. She ambled out happily, planted her back paws firmly in my groin, and stood up so she could stick her big black nose out the window.

"So you're what they call a bodyguard?" I asked, to say something.

"I do whatever he needs me to do. I drive. Run errands. Keep track of his appointments. And yeah, security. Course, Sonny doesn't go out that much in public anymore. It isn't worth it for him. He gets pestered too much. He needs a controlled environment. He stays in most nights now. He likes to read self-help books. He's a big fan of that Leo Buscaglia. Or we rent movies from the video places. Paul Muni is his favorite. John Garfield, Jimmy Cagney . . ."

"How about his own movies, the Knight and Day movies? Does he ever watch those?"

"Never. He has no interest in them. Or the past. He doesn't see his old friends, either. He used to entertain a lot. You know, dinner parties. The Dean Martins used to come by. Sammy and Altovese. The Jack Webbs. Jennings Lang. Sonny doesn't see any of them anymore. Connie, his ex-wife, drops by once in a while. That's it. He's kind of a recluse now, I guess you could say. And I'll tell you something, he's a heckuva lot more fun to be around now than he was before, when he was drinking and popping pills."

"What was he like then?"

Vic shrugged. "Take your pick – depressed, sentimental, suicidal, nasty, violent. He threw tantrums. A couple of times I had to belt him or he'd have hurt somebody. Most nights he'd drink his way through all of his different moods, then he'd pass out. I'd carry him to bed. Some nights he'd get hyped up and try to slip out the back door on me, take a car out god knows where. It got so I had to take off the distributor caps every night. It broke me up inside to see what he was doing to himself. See, I'm an orphan. I owe that man a lot. No, it's more than that. I love him like a father. You know where I'm coming from?"

"Fully."

"Sonny's a gifted man, real proud, real insecure. Things are a lot better with him now. He takes care of himself. We work out together. Run. Swim. Eat right. I give him a rub. We have a lot more fun now." He glanced over at me, then back at the road. "Listen, I think this book is a good thing for him. But you better not mess him up."

"Me? How?"

"You drink, don't you?"

"No more than any other failed writer."

"Well, don't try to get him started again. It's been a tough, hard road for him. He gets knocked off of it, I'll be very upset. Understand?"

"Yes, I do, Vic. And I appreciate your candor."

Vic got off the freeway at Sunset and followed its winding path into Beverly Hills, where it wasn't winter. Lawns were green. Flowers bloomed. The tops of the Mercedes 450SLs were down. Lulu kept her nose out the window. She seemed to like the smell of Beverly Hills. She's always had pretty high-class taste for somebody who likes to eat canned mackerel.

"So you live with Sonny?" I asked.

"I have a room downstairs, TV, bath, everything. There's also Maria, the housekeeper. A secretary comes in part-time. So does the gardener. Of course, Wanda's living with us right now, too."

That was news. The way I remembered it, father and daughter couldn't stand one another.

"She is?"

"Yeah, they're getting along much better. Boy, they used to have some fights. She was a real wild kid in the old days, I guess. That's before I came along. When she was an actress. Remember the scene in that French movie *Paradise* when she sneaks into the count's bed in the middle of the night, stark naked, and starts humping him, and he wakes up and doesn't know what – "

"I remember it, yeah."

"In my opinion, that's just about the most erotic scene in motion picture history." He said it respectfully.

"What is she doing now?"

"Studying for her real estate license."

Vic turned off Sunset at Canon, took that to Benedict Canyon, and started climbing. The road got narrower the farther up we went – and bumpier when we passed out of the Beverly Hills city limits.

"I think you'll like Wanda," Vic droned on. "We've had some good talks. She's been through a lot herself. She was institutionalized a couple of times, you know."

"I didn't know that."

"But she's got a pretty solid sense of where she's at now. She's pushing forty, after all. She's a survivor. She and Sonny are a lot alike. At least, that's my opinion."

"You seem to have a lot of them."

"This job leaves me plenty of time to think."

Sonny's house was off Benedict on a little dead-end road about five miles above Sunset behind a big electric gate. Vic opened the gate by remote control. It closed behind us all by itself. The driveway curved past a couple of acres of fragrant orange and lemon orchards, then a reflecting pool with palms carefully arranged around it. The house was two stories high and vaguely Romanesque. It looked like a giant mausoleum. Actually the whole place, with its neatly manicured grounds, came off like a memorial park.

Inside, there was an entry hall that was bigger than my entire apartment and a formal dining room with a table that could seat a couple of dozen without any knees knocking. The living room was two stories high and all glass. A brook ran through the middle of it, and there were enough trees and plants growing there to stock a Tarzan movie.

Vic pushed a button. I heard a motor whir and the glass ceiling began to roll back, sending even more sunlight in.

"If everyone lived in a glass house," said Vic, "nobody would get stoned."

I stared at him blankly.

"Sonny's joke," he explained.

Sonny's study was off the living room behind double hardwood doors. It was paneled and carpeted and had a big slab of black marble for a desk. There were plaques and awards and autographed photos hanging everywhere, photos of Sonny with three, four, five different U.S. presidents, with Frank Sinatra, with Bob Hope, with Jack Benny, with Groucho Marx. There were no photos of him with Gabe Knight. The lobby poster from *Moider, Inc.* hung over the black leather sofa. Over the fireplace there was a formal oil portrait of Sonny made up as his sad-sack clown in *The Big Top*. A single tear glimmered on his cheek.

"Very impressive," I said. "And the rest, I take it, is closet space?"

"Six bedrooms, each with its own bath, sitting room, and fireplace," replied Vic. "The guesthouse is separate. It overlooks the swimming pool and the log arbor."

"Log arbor?"

"For shade."

"Of course."

A flagstone path led across a few acres of lawn to the guesthouse. The bedroom was done in bright yellow and came equipped with a color TV, IBM Selectric, kitchenette, and bath. Sonny's health spa was right across the hall, complete with Universal weight machine, chrome dumbbells, slant boards, exercise mats, and mirrored walls.

"Very handy in case I get an urge to work on my pecs in the middle of the night," I said.

"Sonny'll be back around one," said Vic. "Why don't you unpack?"

"Fine. Say, is this place secure?'"

"Very. Private patrol cars, electrified fence, computerized alarm bell system on all doors and windows. Three handguns, one in my room, one in Sonny's room, and one in his study. All of them loaded." He chuckled. It wasn't exactly a pleasant sound. "Not that there's anything to be uptight about."

"Sonny's joke?"

He frowned. "No, mine."

"Actually, what I meant was, is there a fence all the way around, so Lulu can run loose?"

"Oh. Yes, there is. She won't tinkle in any specimen plants, will she?"

"Never has."

I let her off her leash. She rolled around happily on the grass and began to bark at the birds.

It was so quiet there in the guesthouse my ears buzzed. I unpacked my tape recorder, blank cassettes, notepads, and the quart of Jack Daniel's. There was ice and mineral water in my little refrigerator. I made myself a drink and downed it while I hung up my clothes. Then I said good-bye to my winter tweed sportcoat, cashmere crewneck, and flannel slacks and padded into the bathroom.

I looked kind of sallow there in the mirror. I was showing a little more collarbone than I remembered, and there were circles under my eyes. I certainly didn't look like the man who, fifteen years before, had been the third-best javelin thrower in the entire Ivy League.

I showered and toweled off and switched to California clothes – pastel polo shirt, khakis, and sneakers. I still had another ten minutes until lunch. I was going to celebrate that fact, but the Jack Daniel's wasn't on the desk where I'd left it. It wasn't anywhere.

It was gone.

Someone had, however, left me a small gift on my bed. There I found an old, yellowing eight-by-ten glossy of Knight and Day from the movie *Jerks*, back when they were still in their twenties and baby-faced. They were posed behind the counter in their white soda-jerk smocks and caps. Gabe wore a slightly annoyed expression and two scoops of melting ice cream atop his head. Sonny had the grin and the scooper.

The photo was autographed by each of them, and a very fine grade Wusthof Dreizackwerk carving knife was plunged through the middle of it and into my pillow.

Sonny had my Jack Daniel's in front of him on the glass dining table that was set for two next to the swimming pool. He wore a royal-blue terry cloth sweat suit and was reading *Daily Variety*. Lulu dozed at his feet.

He grinned as I approached him. "Welcome to L.A., pally. All settled in?"

I deposited my pillow on the table as I'd found it. "I'm not ordinarily one to complain about accommodations, but your better hotels leave their guests one individually wrapped chocolate on the pillow at bedtime. I prefer bittersweet."

"Jeez, where'd you find the old still?" Sonny asked, leaning over slightly, examining it. "Haven't seen one of these in twenty years. Signed, even. Must be worth sixty, seventy cents. But what's with the knife?"

"Someone left it for me when I was in the shower."

Sonny leaned back and squinted up at me. "You mean like some kind of gag?"

"You tell me."

"Hey, don't look at me, pally. I didn't do it."

"Well, someone did." I eyed my bottle before him.

"Ohhh . . . I see how it looks. Sure." Sonny winked at me. "Forgot to tell ya – Bela Lugosi's ghost lives here. I'll have Maria get you another pillow, okay? Sit."

I stood. Sonny was behaving as if this sort of thing happened routinely. Water lawn. Take out garbage. Stick knife in bedding.

He tapped my bottle with a lacquered fingernail. "I think we're gonna have to reach an agreement about this."

"You're damned right. I do what I want, when I want, provided it doesn't interfere with our work. And you stay out of my room or I'm moving into a hotel – at your expense."

"Calm down, pally. Calm down. I know what it's like. I been there." He fingered the bottle thoughtfully. "It's like somebody's taking away your security blanket. I'll let you in on a little secret though, pally – "

"You really don't have to."

"You don't need this bottle. You're fine the way you are. Know what I learned at Betty Ford? Your problems, your fears, your personal bogeymen – they're not unique. Everybody's got 'em. So don't hate yourself. Pat yourself on the back. And siddown, will ya?"

I sat down. He poured me some orange juice from a pitcher.

"Fresh squeezed from my own trees, no chemicals." He sat back with his hands behind his head. "Look, I went through a very bad time. I wouldn't reach out for help. I suffered because of it. I don't want you to make the same mistake I made, okay?"

"Let's get something straight, Sonny. I didn't come out here for therapy. I'm here to work on your book. Do a job. Just leave me be, or – "

"Or what? You'll quit? Let's put our cards on the table, pally. I checked you out. You *need* this book. You need it as bad as I do. Know what's on my calendar next week? I'm emceeing the 'Miss Las Vegas Showgirl Beauty Pageant.' For *cable*. That's it. One day of work. This pad is paid for from the old days, when it was coming in like you wouldn't believe. Otherwise, I'm out on the street. We've both seen better days, so let's not pull each other's puds, huh?" He softened, put a hairy paw on my arm. "Tell me if I'm butting in – "

"You're butting in."

"– but I want us to be close friends. It matters to me. And if it matters to me, it *matters*, understand? We're gonna be spending a lot of time together. I expect to tell you pretty personal things. If I'm gonna spill my guts to you, I need to feel you'll also confide in me. I need for us to have a relationship, okay? Drink your juice."

I hadn't been wrong – here was the job. But what was that knife all about? Had Sonny left it? If so, why? If not, who *had* left it? I sipped my juice and went to work. "Okay. Just don't push me."

He stuck out his lower lip. "I know. Sometimes I come on too strong. I apologize."

"No problem."

"I take it from your book you're not too close to your people. Or am I pushing too hard again?"

"No, that's okay. I . . . Correct. I'm not close."

"Brothers? Sisters?"

I shook my head.

"So who do you confide in then? Your friends?"

"My writing is my outlet."

"I don't get you book guys. Gag writers I'm used to. They're all nuts, but I can relate to 'em, because deep down they're performers, like me. But book guys – why would somebody want to spend their whole life all alone in a room, just them and a piece of paper?"

"Ever read Henry Miller?"

"Smut artist, wasn't he?"

"He once wrote, 'No man would set a word down on paper if he had the courage to live out what he believed in.'"

"What do you believe in, Hoagy?"

"Nothing much, anymore."

"Know what I believe in? Human beings. We're all in this together. We're all afraid. I believe in human beings. I love 'em. I even love you."

"You're not going to hug me, are you?"

"I'd like to, but I sense it would make you uncomfortable."

"That's very perceptive."

"Boy, you're gonna be a *project*." He grinned. "You are gonna be a project!"

The housekeeper brought us out our lunch. Marie was short, chubby, and in her fifties. Lunch was cold chicken, green salad, whole wheat bread, and fruit. Sonny ate with his face over his plate, shoveling with both hands.

"Do me a favor, Hoagy?" he asked, food spraying out of his mouth. "It's a personal request. You don't have to if you don't want to, but . . . how's about you join the exercise regimen me and Vic do every day? You'll feel like a million bucks. And it'll be good for the book, too, don't you think? The two of us, breaking a sweat together? I don't know. You're the writer . . ."

I sighed inwardly. What the hell, I hadn't been too crazy about how I looked in the mirror anyway. "Okay. If you'd like."

He beamed. "Great. You won't be sorry. And hey, while you're at it, it might be a good idea to cut back on the poison just a little bit.

You'll need the energy. Good thing you don't smoke. I quit totally. Tough, believe me. I used a cigar in my part of my routine – it was part of my rhythm."

"Poison?"

"A couple of beers after work feels good, I know. Wine with supper. Even a nightcap. But a bottle in your room, that's very low class, ain't it?"

"Think I need a haircut, too?"

He whinnied in exasperation, his famous whinny. "I'm very serious, Hoagy. Do you *have* to keep it there?"

"No, I don't *have* to keep it in – "

"Great! It'll be in the bar. Anytime you want it. You've made me very happy, Hoagy. I have a wonderful, wonderful feeling about us now. Really. We're gonna make a beautiful book." He sat back and belched, his plate clean. Even the bones were eaten.

A shadow crossed the table. Vic. He tapped his watch.

"Thanks, Vic," said Sonny. "Gotta go, Hoagy. Some folks at Paramount TV wanna talk to me about a part in a sitcom pilot."

I cleared my throat, nudged the pillow toward Sonny.

"Oh, yeah," he said, as if he'd completely forgotten it. "Hoagy found this in his room, Vic. Whattaya think?"

Vic checked it out, his face blank.

"Any idea who might have done it?" I asked him.

I thought he and Sonny exchanged a quick look. Maybe I imagined it. I'm not used to drinking that much OJ in one sitting.

Vic shook his head. "No idea, Hoag."

"Maybe I know," mused Sonny, scratching his chin.

"Who?" I asked.

"The tooth fairy," he shot back.

Vic laughed. I didn't.

"Hey, relax, Hoagy boy," Sonny urged me. "Enjoy the sun. Connie's coming by for dinner. She's anxious to meet you. We'll get to bed early. First workout is from seven to nine. Then we'll start on our book, okay?"

"Look forward to it," I replied. "Wait, what do you mean, *first* workout?"

"Are you Stewart?"

It was a woman's voice, a husky, familiar woman's voice. I was in a lounge chair by the pool with my shirt off, working my way through a collection of E. B. White essays, which is something I do every couple of years to remind myself what good writing is. I looked up. She stood before me, silhouetted by the sun, jangling her car keys nervously.

"Are you Stewart?" she repeated.

I nodded, squinting up at her.

"I'm Wanda."

We shook hands. Hers was thin and brown. Wanda Day was taller and leaner than she photographed, and her blonde hair, which she used to wear long and straight, was now cut short like a boy's, with a part on one side and a little comma falling over her forehead. She wore a loose-fitting red T-shirt dress with a big belt at the waist and high-heeled sandals. She still had those great legs and ankles – nobody had looked like she did in a microskirt. And she still owned that wonderfully fat, pouty lower lip that became so famous when she was the Yardley Lip Gloss girl. She'd painted it white then. Now it was unpainted. She wore very little makeup and no jewelry and looked just the tiniest bit knocked around. I guess twenty years in the fast lane and two nervous breakdowns will do that to a person. There were lines in her neck and crow's-feet around her eyes, which were dark brown, slanted, and at this particular moment, wary.

She sat down in the canvas director's chair next to me. It had Sonny's name printed across the back. "We have to talk, Stewart."

"Nobody calls me Stewart except my mother."

"What do they call you?"

"Hoagy."

"As in Carmichael?"

"As in the cheese steak."

Her nostrils flared. "I should warn you – children of famous comics have very little sense of humor. We cry too much to laugh."

"Why does everybody out here talk like a Barry Manilow song?"

"You're not very nice, are you?"

"Lulu likes me."

"Is she your wife?"

"I'm divorced."

"Girlfriend?"

"One and only."

Lulu was lying on her back on the pavement next to me, paws up, tongue lolling out of the side of her mouth. I scratched her belly, and she thumped her tail.

Wanda thawed a couple of degrees. "Oh, I see." She reached down and patted Lulu and spoke to her intimately in some kind of baby talk. Then she made a face. "Say, her breath smells kind of icky . . ."

"Lulu has strange eating habits." I noticed the thick textbook in Wanda's lap. "I understand you're studying for your real estate license."

"Yes. I may even go through with it, too. Ever find yourself envying terminal cancer patients, Hoagy?"

"No, not lately."

"I have. What a release, what a *rush*, not having to worry about how to spend the rest of your life. There is no rest your life. Your days are limited. You can just relax and enjoy them. And then die. That's so beautiful."

"It might not be so beautiful."

"Why not?"

"There might be tubes sticking out of you. It might hurt."

"It can't be any worse than this," she said quietly, looking around at Sonny's memorial park for famous comics of the fifties.

"I thought the two of you had sort of patched things up."

"Oh, we have."

"I'd like to interview you sometime."

"That's what I wanted to talk to you about. You should know I'm against this book. It's his thing, not mine. I don't want to be involved at all. In fact, I'd appreciate it if you'd leave me out entirely."

"That won't be possible. You're a big part of his life."

"I'd make it worth your while financially."

"No, thank you. I have a contract. But how come?"

"How come?" She took a cigarette and matches from her bag and lit one. "Because some things are better off left alone." She took a deep drag, let the smoke out slowly. "Look, Hoagy. I've done a lot of pretty spacey things with a lot of pretty spacey people. I'm not ashamed or anything, but I don't necessarily want the whole world reading about who I fucked, either. It isn't their business. Can you understand that?"

"Of course. I'm not interested in exploiting you, nor is Sonny. This won't be a sleazy showbiz book at all. You have my word."

"There are other people to think about. People who would be hurt."

"Who?"

She didn't answer me. She looked down at the cigarette in her fingers, which were shaking.

"I was hoping for your help, Wanda. Your insights."

"It's out of the question. Just forget it."

"Does Sonny know how you feel?"

"Yes, but one thing you have to learn about Daddy is how self-centered he is. If something matters to him . . ."

"It *matters.*"

"Correct."

"I'm sorry you feel this way about it. I hope you'll change your mind. This book is pretty important to him."

"Fuck him!" she snarled with sudden ferocity. "He's a dominating, manipulative *shit!*"

She jumped to her feet and stormed off to the house, high heels clacking on the pavement. Watching her go, I thought about how glad I was I hadn't been around when the two of them *weren't* getting along.

"I think it's wonderful that you and Arthur are doing this," Connie Morgan told me on the living room sofa before dinner, while we sipped white wine, nibbled on raw cauliflower, and listened to the brook babble. "He has come so, so far."

"Yes. He seems to have made a genuine effort," I said, smiling politely.

Connie Morgan was the sort of woman you were polite to. She was gracious and well-bred Virginia old money. She and Sonny had met when she played the gorgeous blond homecoming queen in *Big Man on Campus*, Knight and Day's second movie. In the movie, Gabe got her. In real life, Sonny did. She retired soon after they married to raise Wanda. She went back to work after the divorce. These days she was bigger than she'd ever been before. She played the proud matriarch in one of those prime-time TV soap operas. Connie was at least sixty, but she was well-kept, willowy, and she carried herself with style. She was exactly who she'd always been – the quintessential Hollywood good girl. She had on a khaki safari dress with a blue silk scarf knotted at the throat.

"I'm anxious to talk to you about what went on," I said.

"I'll make the time," she said. "You know, the set might be the best place. I have a lot of free time there, since I'm not one of the people hopping in and out of bed. Mostly, I get everyone together for a sensible breakfast. And do a lot of knitting."

Sonny put an Erroll Garner album on. The Elf was his favorite musician. When I think back on our collaboration, it's always set to Garner's sweet, fluid piano.

"Look at her, Hoagy," he said, sitting next to me on the sofa. "She's still the best-looking broad in town, ain't she?"

Connie blushed. "Now, Arthur . . ."

"It's true. The others can't hold a candle to you. Name one. Little Michelle Pfeiffer? Little Jamie Lee Curtis? They're Barbie dolls. This is a real woman, Hoagy. A very special woman. And I'll tell you why. I'm a comic, see? A performer. I'm trained to hide behind my professional personality. My mask. In fact, that's what I wanted to call the book – *Behind the Mask*. Publisher preferred *The One*. Anyway, it ain't easy to drop that mask for nobody, let alone a broad. Connie's the only one I could drop it for. Ever. She's the only one who ever knew the real me, who wanted to know the real me."

"Arthur, you're embarrassing me."

"Nothing to be embarrassed about. It's true. You stuck by me, baby. Always. I had to *drive* you away."

She swallowed and looked away. I gathered he was referring to Tracy St. Claire.

"And someday," he went on, "I'll earn your trust again, Connie. That's all I want." He took a piece of cauliflower. "You and Hoagy getting acquainted? This here is a talented boy. He and I have a lot in common, you know."

"We do?" I said.

"Sure. You're just like me. You hold back. You hide behind your own mask. I'm gonna pull it off you, though. Know why?"

"Let me guess . . . because you love me?"

"Right."

He started to crush me in a bear hug. I flinched.

"Gotcha!" He laughed.

Maria appeared to announce dinner was served.

"Not *served*," corrected Sonny. "How many times I gotta tell ya? The word is . . . *soived*."

She flashed him a smile and said it again in correct, south-of-the-border Brooklynese.

"That's more like it." He grinned.

He went to the foot of the stairs and called Wanda. She padded down barefoot in a caftan slit all the way to her thigh, and joined us at one corner of the giant dining table. Dinner was broiled snapper, rice, and steamed vegetables.

Wanda ate hurriedly and avoided eye contact with the rest of us.

Connie asked me what my novel was about.

"I'll handle that one," said Sonny before I could answer. "It's about the death of this small, family-run brass mill in Connecticut. See, it's been in the family for five generations or so, and now the father runs it, and he wants the son to take it over. Only, it's the last thing in the world the kid wants to do. See, he and the old man don't get along. Never did. So the mill dies, because the family has died. It's all like a . . . *metaphor* for the death of the American dream. Am I right?"

"Yes," I said. "Very well put.'"

"See?" He grinned like a proud child. "I ain't so lowbrow."

It seemed important that I think he was smart. I guess because he thought *I* was smart.

"Was it autobiographical?" Connie asked.

"Partly."

"Your old man ran a brass mill?" Sonny asked.

"My old man runs a brass mill."

"In Connecticut?"

"In Connecticut."

"Damned good story. Make a terrific picture. This kid can write, he's real *serious*. Hey, Wanda, you know a writer named Henry Miller?"

"Know him? I blew him."

Connie's eyes widened. Then she wiped her face clean of any expression and reached for her glass.

"Hey," snapped Sonny. "You know I don't like that kind of talk."

"So don't ask those kinds of questions."

"It's slutty and cheap and offensive. Apologize to your mother."

"Daddy, I'm going to be forty years old this year. I'll talk as I – "

"You're never too old to be polite. Apologize this minute or leave my table."

Wanda rolled her eyes. "I'm sorry, Mother."

"*And* to our company," Sonny added.

"No problem," I assured him.

"She's apologizing, Hoagy!" he snapped.

Wanda leveled her eyes at me. "I'm sorry if I offended you," she said quietly.

The matter closed, Sonny turned back to me. "I disagree with you in one area. I think the dream still lives. This is a great country. I come from nothing. Look what I got. How can you argue with that?"

"Kind of blew up in your face a little, didn't it?" I suggested gently.

He frowned. "I had a setback. But I'm on the road back."

"How did your interview go today?" Connie asked him.

"Total dreck. A lousy, two-bit sitcom about a a stupid Great Neck catering house. They wanted me to read for the old headwaiter. Three grunts per episode. Totally one-dimensional. I walked out. They don't write people anymore. They don't know how. All they can write is smut and car chases. And they wonder why nobody watches. Hey, Vic brought in a couple old Capra pictures for tonight. We'll pop some corn. I got celray tonic. Stick around, Connie."

"I'm sorry, Arthur. I have an early call."

"Wanda?"

"I'm going out."

"With who?"

Her body tensed. "Daddy, I'm *not* sixteen."

"So why don't you start making more sensible choices in men?"

"Mind your own – "

"Who are you – "

"It's none of your business!" she screamed.

"It's my business as long as you keep trashing your life!" he screamed back.

She threw her half-full dinner plate at him. Her aim wasn't much. It missed, sailed across the dining room, and smashed against a wall, leaving a splotch of rice. She ran upstairs. Emotional exits seemed to be a specialty of hers.

"Sorry, Hoagy," Sonny said, going back to his food. "She just never grew up in a lot of ways. And she never could stand me. That's no secret."

"I don't mean to be nosy . . ."

"Go ahead. You're part of the family now."

"Why does she live here if it makes her so miserable?"

Sonny and Connie glanced at each other. He turned back to me.

"Because she's even more miserable when she's not living here."

There was a plump new feather pillow on my bed, but I didn't fall asleep the second my head hit it. Or the hour. Anyone with the approximate IQ of pimiento loaf could see that that knife was meant

to scare me off. Yet neither Sonny or Vic seemed the slightest bit
ruffled by it. Had Vic done it? He *had* warned me not to mess
Sonny up. Maybe he seriously wanted me gone. Someone from the
immediate family did. The grounds were secure. The knife was from
Sonny's kitchen – I'd checked with Maria. I lay there, puzzled, uneasy,
wondering if I should just forget the project and go home. I'm the first
to admit it – trouble is not my business. But thinking about home got
me thinking about Merilee, and like I said, I was up for a while.

I had just dropped off at about four when this ungodly
wailing woke me. At first I thought it was sirens. But the more awake I
became the more it sounded like twenty or thirty wild animals. I put
on my dressing gown and opened the guesthouse door. It was animals
all right, animals howling away in the darkness.

Lulu nudged my bare ankle. I picked her up and held her in
my arms. She gave me very little resistance. Together we ventured
bravely forth.

Wanda was stretched out in a lounge chair by the pool, still dressed
in a shimmering dress and shawl from her night out. She glanced up
at me, then went back to the bottle of Dom Perignon she was working
on. "It's the coyotes."

"Coyotes? In the middle of Los Angeles?"

"They're miles from here – way back in the hills. The sound carries
in the canyons. Spooky, isn't it?"

"Maybe a little." I put Lulu down. She stayed right between my
legs. Wanda smiled at me. "You must think I'm an awful cunt."

"Don't worry about it."

"He just gets to me sometimes."

"My father and I don't get along either."

"I know he's right, about my taste in men. I have . . . I have a
kind of low opinion of myself. But I don't need for him to tell me,
you know?"

"Yes."

"Nightcap?"

"Don't mind if I do."

"Champagne do?"

"Always has."

I stretched out in the chair next to her. She filled her glass and gave
me the bottle. I took a swig. We listened to the coyotes.

"Don't get too taken in by him," she said. "He can seem nice, but
he's still as big a shit as he ever was. He's still crazy. He's just channeled
it differently. It used to come out as meanness and destructiveness.

Now it's peace and love. He's a bully. If you're nice to him, he won't respect you – he'll run right over you. The only thing he understands is strength. How did you get this job anyway?"

"By hanging up on him, I think."

"What exactly are you supposed to do?"

"Help him tell his story. Talk to him. Try to understand him."

She fingered the rim of her glass. "Good luck. It isn't easy to understand people when they don't understand themselves. I suppose he's trying, though. About before . . . I didn't mean to be so negative, I'll try to help you. We've mended a few fences, he and I. Certainly we're better than we were. That's something. I'll do what I can. Just don't expect a lot from me."

"Whatever you can do will be much appreciated."

The coyotes quieted down. It was suddenly very peaceful. We drank, looking at the moon.

"How do you like The Hulk?" asked Wanda, after a while.

"Vic? He sure seems loyal."

"He loves Sonny."

"He told me."

"And he's very protective of him."

"He told me that, too."

"He's a real sweetie – as long as he isn't angry. Then he can get . . . atilt."

"Atilt?"

"Yes. Trust me on this one, Hoagy. Don't ever let him get mad at you."

"I'll remember that." I looked over at her, stretched out so elegantly there in the moonlight, her lovely silken ankles crossed. She looked damned good. "How come you don't act anymore?"

"I never acted. I appeared in films."

"I always liked you."

"You liked my body."

"You have talent. You can act."

"I was no Merilee Nash." She raised an eyebrow. "What's she like? Is she as perfect as she comes off?"

"She has flaws, just like everybody else. I never found them, but I'm sure they're there." I drained the bottle. "You can act. Really."

"Well, thank you. I quit because it was making me too insecure and crazy. Stop, I know what you're thinking – crazier than she is now? You should have seen me before. You should have seen me when I was doing acid."

"Vic said you were . . ."

"Locked up. Yes, twice. Once during my famous psychedelic period. Once before, when I was a girl." She reached for a cigarette. "Why are you really here?"

"I'm writing your father's book, remember?"

"But this kind of work isn't very distinguished, is it? I mean, if you're such a serious writer . . ."

"I stopped writing."

"Why?"

"If I knew why, I wouldn't have stopped."

She smiled. "We're really quite a pair, aren't we? A real couple of exes."

"Exes?"

"Yes. Ex-famous. Ex-talented. Ex-young. Ex-married. We ought to become pals."

"Ex-pals?"

"For real."

"I got the impression you didn't like me."

She turned. Her profile, in the pale light, was very like her mother's. "I was just being difficult. Look, you're going to be here for a while. We can be friends, can't we? I'm not such an awful person. I'll help you, if I can. And we can have dinner sometime."

"I'd like that. I'll buy."

She gave me a slow, naughty once-over. She was hamming now, playing a game. "Where will you take me?"

"You'll have to pick the place," I replied coolly, playing along. "I don't know this town very well."

"Would you like to know it better?"

"I'm beginning to think I would."

"How much do you want to spend?"

"How much are you worth?"

"More than you can afford."

"Sorry I asked."

"Don't be."

"I'm not."

We both laughed. That broke the spell.

"What's that from again?" I asked.

"From?"

"Yeah. What movie?"

"*Our* movie. It's much more fun to make one up as you go along. You'll see."

CHAPTER
THREE

(Tape #1 with Sonny Day. Recorded in his study, February 14.)

Day: Whatsa matter, pally? You look tired.

Hoag: I'm just not used to swimming a hundred laps before breakfast.

Day: Do ya good. Where do I sit?

Hoag: Wherever you'll be most comfortable.

Day: Mind if I lie down?

Hoag: If you don't, I will.

Day: I told Vic to hold all calls. We're not to be interrupted for anything. I'm all yours. Where do we start?

Hoag: Let's start at the beginning.

Day: Okay . . . I don't remember too much, except I cried a lot.

Hoag: Why?

Day: Some guy in a mask was slapping my butt around. *(laughs)* How come you don't think I'm funny?

Hoag: Why do you say that?

Day: You never laugh at anything I say.

Hoag: You never laugh at anything I say either.

Day: Comics never laugh at other people's material. We're too insecure.

Hoag: Can we talk about your childhood?

Day: Sure. Hey, this is just like therapy, isn't it?

Hoag: Except we're getting paid.

Day: Hey, this is better than therapy, isn't it?

Hoag: I'm interested in –

Day: How about I put a record on? You like Nat Cole?

Hoag: It'll end up on the tape. I think we're going to need some ground rules, Sonny. When we're in here, I'm the boss. That means no kidding around, no stalling, no role playing. When we work, we *work*. Understand?

Day: Yes, I do. Sorry. I needed to warm up.

Hoag: Now, what kind of childhood did you have?

Day: Shitty.

Hoag: You were born . . . ?

Day: February 23, 1922. My real name is Arthur Seymour Rabinowitz. I grew up in Brooklyn, U.S.A. The Bedford-Stuyvesant section. Bed-Sty. We lived on Gates Avenue between Sumner and Lewis. There was me, my old man, Saul, my mother, Esther. And my brother, Mel. Mel was four years older than me.

Hoag: I didn't know you had a brother.

Day: Mel died just before the war. Sweetest guy in the world. My idol. A tall, strapping, good-looking kid. Good student. Great musician. The girls loved him. Boy, did I look up to him. During the Depression he was like a father to me really. . . . He got a staph infection. It got in his bloodstream and bam, he dropped dead. We didn't have miracle drugs then. I still miss Mel. Sometimes . . . never mind.

Hoag: Go ahead.

Day: Sometimes, I wake up in the middle of the night and there's something I wanna tell him and I . . . I have to remember he's dead.

Hoag: That's interesting. Glad you mentioned it. Your family lived in an apartment?

Day: What? Yeah. Third-floor walk-up, in the front. Two bedrooms. One for the folks. One for me and Mel. No such thing as a living room in that neighborhood. Everything happened around the dining table. Or the kitchen sink. We did all our washing up and shaving in the kitchen sink. There was no sink in the bathroom, just a tub and a toilet. *(laughs)* People wonder why families were so much closer in those days. Winters we used to turn the oven on to keep warm. Summers me and Mel used to sleep on a mattress out on the fire escape. Listen to the trolley go by on Gates.

Hoag: What kind of people were your parents?

Day: You sure you were never a shrink?

Hoag: Positive.

Day: My old man was from Russia. Came over on the boat in I think it was 1906. His English was never great. The old lady was born and raised on the Lower East Side, West Broadway and Spring. Her father was a furrier for the Yiddish show people. Had a shop right across from the Second Avenue Theater. Her folks always thought she married beneath herself, marrying an *immigrant*.

Hoag: What did your father do?

Day: He had a candy store on Nostrand Avenue, not too far from the house. The candy store had belonged to an Irishman named Day. When my old man took it over, he didn't have enough money for a new sign, so he left it.

Hoag: That's where you got your stage name?

Day: True story. Half the people in the neighborhood thought we were named Day anyway. It was a long narrow place. Movie magazines, comics on one wall. Cigar stand. Candy. And he had a soda fountain in there, too. Did egg creams, malteds, coffee and sinkers. Mel and me both worked there after school and on weekends. That's how I got the short-order routine Gabe and I used in *Jerks*. Mel and I did it as kids. You know, one guy crouches behind the other and sticks his arms out, and the guy in front is waiting on customers, only it's not his hands he's using, so he keeps knocking everybody's coffee over.

Hoag: We used to imitate that in the school cafeteria.

Day: You watched my movies?

Hoag: I loved your movies.

Day: I didn't know that. Gee, now I think less of you. *(laughs)* Mel and I were always fooling around like that to entertain ourselves. Mel, see, was my first partner. My best partner.

Hoag: What do you mean by best? Most talented?

Day: I guess.

Hoag: That's not good enough.

Day: *(long silence)* There was real deep love and trust between us. I guess that's what I mean. Deep down, I was always looking for that from Gabe. And it wasn't there.

Hoag: Excellent. That's the kind of answer I'm looking for.

Day: Do I get a cookie?

Hoag: Did you have friends?

Day: Friends? Pally, I had a *gang*. Bed-Sty was a tough neighborhood – half Jewish, half black. We used to beat the crap out of each other. Of course, nobody had guns or knives in those days. Just your fists. And your feet. You had to be in a gang, to protect each other. I went to Boys High, you know. It was a badge of honor graduating from Boys High with all your teeth. Yeah, I got in plenty of fights. Won some of them, too. I didn't get pushed around by nobody. That's also where I learned to lip.

Hoag: Lip?

Day: When I was maybe twelve this big black kid used to wait on the corner every morning to beat the crap outta me on my way to school. "Hey, Jew boy," he'd say, "what makes you so fat?" And I'd say, "Eating your momma's pussy." Subtle stuff like that. Laughter was a weapon in the old neighborhood. As long as you're lipping, you're not punching. That's how come so many slum kids got to be good at stand-up comedy. Kept 'em alive.

Hoag: Did your gang have a name?

Day: Yeah, the Seetags. That's Gates spelled backwards, with an extra *e* because it sounded better.

Hoag: Did you have jackets?

Day: What do you think this was, Park Avenue? We *made* it to Park Avenue, though. You know who was in that gang? Aside from me and Mel, there was Harry Selwyn, who became chief of neurosurgery at Mount Sinai. Harry's brother Nathan, who's a violinist with the New York Philharmonic. Izzy Sapperstein, Dizzy Izzy, who was captain of the Long Island University basketball team. And Heshie Roth. Heshie was the brightest of all of us, and the only one who got in any real trouble. His old man was hooked up with the Jewish mob on the Lower East Side, with Meyer Lansky. Heshie kinda worked part-time in the family business. He got himself nailed for being part of some extortion racket in the garment district. But they greased a few palms and got him off. Took good care of him, too, because he kept his mouth shut. Put him through law school. Made sure he passed the state bar exam.

Hoag: Whatever happened to him? A guy like that?

Day: Heshie? He became my manager. Gabe and mine's. His associations came in handy, too. The clubs were all mob-run. And he got us into Vegas early on. We were among the first. He still handles me. Two kids from the old neighborhood.

Hoag: I'd love to talk to him.

Day: Absolutely. Heshie's the top entertainment lawyer in the country. Got an empire. His name is Harmon Wright now.

Hoag: The Harmon Wright Agency? You're kidding.

Day: True story.

Hoag: But I'm an HWA client myself – in the New York office.

Day: So he'll have to be nice to you.

Hoag: I didn't know he personally represented anyone anymore.

Day: He doesn't represent anyone. He represents Sonny Day. Hey, Maria made us a chicken salad. Let's take a break, huh? We can eat outside, read the paper. Unless you'd rather keep working . . . boss.

(end tape)

(Tape #2 with Sonny Day. Recorded in his study, February 15.)

Hoag: We were talking about your childhood yesterday. So far, it seems relatively . . .

Day: Happy? I was just like any other kid in the neighborhood. But that was before the Depression.

Hoag: What happened then?

Day: Loss and shame, pally. Unblocking it has been a big part of my therapy. My doctors tell me a lot of my problems – my insecurities, my fears – they date from this period of my life. For years I couldn't face it at all. Didn't mention it to nobody, except Connie. It still ain't easy.

Hoag: I understand. And I want to remind you I'm not a reporter, I'm here to help you tell your own story as honestly as possible.

Day: I appreciate you saying that. And I trust you. At least, I think I do. I don't really know you . . . *(silence)*

Hoag: This was when?

Day: It was 1933, '34. It was before I was Bar Mitzvah. I know because my old man was falling down drunk at my Bar Mitzvah. I never went near a shul after that. Haven't been inside one in fifty years. True story.

Hoag: Did he drink before that?

Day: Not a drop. Losing the store did it. That damn store was his dream. When it went under, he broke inside. Started to drink. He got angry, bitter. Beat up on the old lady, beat up on me and Mel, too. When I began to drink too much, when things were going bad for me and I started to lash out at people I loved, I thought of my old man a lot. I thought – *I'm just like him*. It terrified me. It made me sick. There was this pool hall on the corner of Gates and Sumner. Nice Jewish boys were always told to stay away from it. *Bums hang around there*, my father had always told me. I'll never forget the day I walked by there and looked in and saw the bums drinking beer and shooting pool in the middle of the day, and one of those bums was my old man.

Hoag: How did you feel?

Day: It was a *shonda*. I was ashamed.

Hoag: Did he work?

Day: No.

Hoag: How did you get by?

Day: My mother. She was the hero. She stuck by him. She kept the family together. Never complained. Took in wash. Ironed. She worked for a time as a housekeeper for a rich family on Central Park West. One year they gave her an old hand-me-down squirrel coat. It was real ratty. She knew it – her old man was a furrier, remember. But she wore that damn coat, and she wore it proudly. I swore to her someday I'd buy her the most beautiful sable coat in New York. And I did, with the first dough I made.

Hoag: I thought you bought a red Cadillac convertible with your first big money.

Day: That story's a lie! I bought my mother a sable coat. Ten thou if it was a dime. The old man was dead by then. Died when I was in the service, a shriveled old man. Forty-five years old. You know, I wanted to make a movie about my mother after Gabe and I . . . when I was on my own. You'd think after all the money I made for those sonsabitches – They told me no. It was too real. What the hell does that mean?

Hoag: She supported the family?

Day: *We* supported the family. Mel worked after school at a grocery store. I sold papers, shined shoes. Lots of shoes.

Hoag: Is that why you always give away your shoes after you break them in?

Day: You work a rag over so many crummy, cracked old shoes, worn-out shoes – some guy spits on your head for a lousy nickel. . . . I like new shoes. Can't help it. What size do you wear?

Hoag: Meanwhile, your father drank all day at the pool hall?

Day: No, when it was cold out he drank all day at the Luxor Baths on Graham Street. He'd sit in the steam playing pinochle, drinking buckets of beer and schnapps. It was one of those old-time places where the attendants beat you with the eucalyptus leaves. I used to have to go fetch him and bring him home. The smell of that eucalyptus still . . . it still makes me sick. When I built this house there were eucalyptus trees all over the property. I had each and every one of them yanked out of the ground and carted out of here. You'll find no eucalyptus on this property. Maybe, someday, I'll be strong enough to handle the smell . . .

Hoag: Did you know then what you wanted to be in life?

Day: Somebody who . . . somebody *else*. Hoagy, I . . . I – I can't talk about this anymore. Can we . . . ?

Hoag: I'm sorry. I didn't mean to make you cry. You done good. C'mon, I'll buy you a juice.

(end tape)

(Tape #3 with Sonny Day.   Recorded in his study, February 16.)

Day: You got good color today.   Getting rid of your New York pallor.   You also look . . . different.   Why is that?   I got it – you shaved off your mustache!   That's it!

Hoag: Got in the way of my tan.   *(silence)*   What do you think?

Day: You look young.

Hoag: I'm not.   I was walking down Columbus Avenue the other day, all of those yushies rushing by me, fresh, eager –

Day: What's a yushie?

Hoag: Young urban shithead.   Anyway, it hit me that I'm not one of them.   I'm too old to qualify.

Day: And how did you feel?

Hoag: I asked my feelings to get lost a while ago.

Day: And?

Hoag: And they did.

Day: Have you thought about finding them?

Hoag: I thought I was the one doing the interviewing.

Day: You forget, I used to have my own talk show.   Not that I was a threat to Carson.   Or Joey Bishop.

Hoag: How were you doing in school through all of this with your father?

Day: I did okay.   I had my buddies.   I was pretty bright.

Hoag: Did you know you wanted to be a comic?

Day: I wasn't a class-clown type.   Too afraid of the teacher, I guess. I liked math and science.   Mel, he was always the talented one.   A fine trumpet player.   By the time I was ready to take up an instrument, there was no money left for me.

Hoag: So how did you get into performing?

Day: The Catskills, pally.   That's how we all got started.   Mel played trumpet in the dance band every summer up at Pine Tree Manor.   All the resort hotels had dance bands – Kutcher's, Avon Lodge, Vacationland, the Parkston.   Comics, too.   These old-timers who'd been in burlesque since the year 3.   Mel got me work up there as a busboy the summer of '38, I think.   Yeah, I was sixteen.   Got me out of the city and away from the old man.   They had a lake there, rowboats.   I set up tables, cleared 'em.   That first summer I got up at five every morning to fresh-squeeze orange juice for three hundred people. My fingers are still wrinkled. All of us lived up in the attic of the main building. Twelve of us to a room. The girls were in the rooms right across the hall. They worked as chambermaids and mothers' helpers. Lots of hanky-panky went on. Not me, of course. I was still very heavy then, real shy with girls. But I had a good time up there. I was with Mel.

Hoag: How did you get started performing?

Day: I fell into it. *(silence)* That's a joke.

Hoag: Tell me about it.

Day: Okay. True story. Like I said, they had these lousy comics up there. The guy at the Pine Tree was named Frankie Faye. Real class – loud plaid jacket, accordion, bad Al Jolson imitation, flop sweat by the gallon, Jack Carter is Ricardo Montalban next to this guy, okay? So one night he's up there on stage dying. I mean, if anyone in the audience has a loaded gun, the man's long gone. I'm still clearing my tables and bringing out the desserts during his act. I'm carrying – get this – a tray with twelve orders of strawberry, cream pie on it. True story. So I'm on my way to my table . . . big tray on my hand . . . I'm right smack-dab in the middle of the dining room – and guess what? – somebody left a fork on the floor. You know what a header is, Hoagy? Well, I took the most beautiful header you ever saw. *Varooooom* – up in the air I went. And *bam* – I went *down* . . . dishes, silverware, and twelve orders of strawberry cream pie all over me. Well, this stops Frankie's act cold. It's also the only laughter that's been heard in the room all season. Now, dumb he's not. He milks it. He starts making fun of what a big fat klutz I am. I'm sitting there on the floor with this shit all over me, red-faced, and he's going, "Hey, Sonny. You oughta be in the ballet. You'd look great in a tutu. Only you'd need a three-three." The audience is eating it up. The biggest laughs Frankie's gotten since the McKinley administration. He won't let me go. For five minutes I gotta take it. It was humiliating. Anyway, after the show he finds me in the kitchen. I start to apologize, and before I can say a word, he slips me a coupla bucks and asks me if I'd mind taking a fall like that every night in the middle of his act. So I said okay.

Hoag: Even though it was humiliating?

Day: It ain't humiliating if you're getting paid for it. So every night I'd come through with a big tray, and he'd say, "Hey, Sonny, what kind of pie is that?" or "'Hey, Sonny, what time is it?" and I'd take a header and he'd make fun of me. That's how I got started in show business. I was Frankie Faye's stooge. How I got my nickname, too – Sonny. Fit together with Day pretty good. Sonny Day.

Hoag: You were how old?

Day: Sixteen. Now, while this was happening, Mel and me were still doing our old routines together for fun. We used to do 'em up in the room to keep the other boys entertained. Mel was the straight man. I was the clumsy kid brother. Just like real life. We did our old short-order routine. A dentist's chair routine. And some new stuff we picked up around Pine Tree. We did one where Mel's this very high-toned guest with a big cigar and I'm this nervous new waiter trying to light it for him, only I end up lighting it in the middle instead of at the tip. Jerry Lewis stole that from us. All he did was make it more physical. I guess if I had a nine-inch jaw span, I'd make everything more physical, too. He was always on roller skates, throwing cream pies. Did you know I never threw a pie? Ever?

Hoag: What about in *Suburbia*? At the wedding party when the punch got spiked and Gabe said, "Let me have it."

Day: Except in *Suburbia*. And that wasn't me. That was the gag.

Hoag: What's the difference?

Day: The script called for it.

Hoag: That's a genuine bullshit answer, Sonny. You appeared in a movie in which you threw a pie. Fact. Don't jerk me around, okay? This isn't a fan magazine piece.

Day: You're right. I apologize. I've made that statement so many times through the years I've started to believe it myself. Forget I said anything about pies.

Hoag: It's struck from the record.

Day: Where was I? Oh, yeah, me and Mel. We did another routine where I'm afraid to ask this pretty girl to dance, so he shows me how, with me playing the girl. Remember the scene in *Ship to Shore* where I don't have the nerve to ask Lois Maxwell to dance, so I go back to my stateroom and dance with an invisible girl? It still makes people cry, that scene. It was the old Pine Tree routine Mel and me did. Anyway, the social director at Pine Tree was this little putz named Len Fine. He liked Mel and he thought I was funny stooging for Frankie. So he started letting us *tummel* after lunch in front of the guests. No pay. Nothing formal. If people wanted to ignore you, they could. And they *did*. Then one night we got our big break – Frankie's car broke down on the way up from the city. So Mr. Fine put up a sign and suddenly it was the annual New Talent Night at Pine Tree Manor. We billed ourselves as Day to Day. And on we went after dinner, knees knocking.

Hoag: Did you bring down the house?

Day: Yeah. Around us. We *bombed*, pally. Baby, were we terrible. Total amateurs. I mean, we actually giggled at our own material. See, there's a big difference between being funny in front of your friends and being funny in front of a roomful of strangers. They don't already know you, or like you. Half of 'em don't even *want* to like you. So you gotta *make* 'em. That means every little thing you do up there has to work for you. You can't have no weak spots or you'll lose 'em. Standup comedy is just like being in a prize fight. One mistake and – pow – you're flat on the canvas. We grew up a lot that night. We learned you gotta throw stuff out, replace it with better stuff, polish it, polish it again, work on your pacing, your delivery, your mannerisms. It's a *performance* up there, and you're a *performer*. You're not *you*. You've got to find your stage personality, your –

Hoag: Your mask?

Day: Exactly. And once you put it on, you don't take it off. That's harder than it sounds, especially when your material is bombing. The temptation then is to break proscenium, wink at the audience, and tell 'em, "Hey, that shit I just did? That ain't me." Watch those kids on *Saturday Night Live*: They do that all the time – disown their material. Or get dirty, the easy way out. Professional comedy is very hard work. But you never let the audience see the work. If you do . . .

Hoag: Then you're Frankie Faye.

Day: You're catching on. Anyway, we bombed that first night. But Mr. Fine, he saw something. He encouraged us to keep at it over the winter. And we did. We added some new stuff. Refined it. By the next summer our routines were pretty funny for a couple of kids who didn't know what the hell we was doing. We were good. We didn't know *how* good, though, until one night the social director of Vacationland, a fellow named Don Appel, caught our act and offered us fifty dollars a week to perform there. That was good money in those days. We went to Mr. Fine and told him he'd have to match it or we'd be moving on. He matched it.

Hoag: Did you like getting laughs? Did you like the attention?

Day: It beat being a busboy or a shine. It was fun, sure. People came up to us. Patted us on the back. Told us to look 'em up if we was ever interested in getting into plumbing fixtures.

Hoag: Did you know this was what you wanted to do with your life?

Day: No, absolutely not. Mel was going to City College, saving up to go to dental school. Me, I wasn't old enough to think about anything but my face clearing up. We were a couple of kids. We were having fun. There were a lot of kids up there like us – Red Buttons was doing stand-up then at the Parkston, Sid Caesar was at Vacationland, playing the saxophone. Mel Brooks was up there. He was from Brooklyn. A real nudnick. A pest.

Hoag: And you honestly didn't say to yourself, hey, I've found my identity – I'm a comic.

Day: No. I had no idea there was a future in it for me. And then, don't forget, Mel died on me in 1940. That was a real traumatic thing for me. I've never known such a sense of loss. He was everything to me – father, big brother, best friend, partner. When he died . . . I-I really didn't know what to do with myself. One thing I knew for sure was I couldn't even think about performing. All it did was remind me of Mel.

Hoag: So what did you do?

Day: I finished high school and took a civil service exam. Got a job in Washington as a clerk for one of FDR's dollar-a-year men. I lived in a rooming house. Met a nice girl from Indiana along the Potomac one day. Judy Monroe. A stenographer. She had red hair and the whitest skin I'd ever seen. My first real girlfriend. We went to the movies. Ate Chinese food. I almost married Judy. Then Pearl Harbor was bombed. I went into the army. They shipped me down to Hattiesburg, Mississippi, for my basic training. Hot, muggy, the food was so greasy and awful I lost twenty-five pounds the first month. Also, it was not a terrific place for a kid from Brooklyn named Rabinowitz. I was the only Jew down there. A lot of the crackers thought it was our fault that the United States was in the war. So I got in a lot of fights. It was just like Gates Avenue all over again. Only I was all alone now. No Mel. No Seetags. The only guy in my barracks who was nice to me was this tall, skinny kid from Nebraska who had the bunk below mine.

Hoag: What was his name?

Day: Gabriel Knight. And da rest is showbiz history.

(end tape)

CHAPTER
FOUR

No one left me any more presents that first week. Someone did sort of move around the tapes and notes piled on my desk one afternoon, but I figured that was just Maria doing her dusting. At least I did when the sun was out. When night came and the coyotes started to howl, I became convinced somebody was trying to spook me and was doing a damned good job. I took to looking under the bed at night. There was never anyone hiding down there. Except for Lulu.

I kept thinking it couldn't be Sonny. He was being so cooperative and open. Our work was going great. I was thinking it couldn't be Sonny until he announced after our morning workout that he'd decided he wanted to leave Gabe Knight out of the book completely.

We were eating our grapefruit by the pool. He wore his white terry robe with "Sonny" stitched in red over the left breast. I wore mine, too. A gift. Mine said "Hoagy" on it.

"You're kidding," I said, nearly choking on a grapefruit section.

"I'm very serious, pally.'"

He was. His manner had changed from warm and expansive to guarded.

"We can talk about plenty else," he went on. "My philosophy of comedy, my theories of directing, my recovery from – "

"Wait. You can't do this."

"It's *my* book, ain't it?"

"Yes, but the reason people are going to buy it is to read about the two of you. They want to know why you broke up. Certainly that's why the publisher bought it. Face facts. Gabe is now a very big – "

"So I'll give 'em their dough back. I changed my mind. Project's off. You'll be compensated for your time. Vic'll book you a flight back to New York for this afternoon."

As if on cue, Vic appeared. He seemed somewhat short of breath, and was chewing on a thumbnail. "I . . . I called them, Sonny," he announced timidly. "I called the police."

Sonny bared his teeth. "You *what?*'"

"They said there really isn't m-much they can do," Vic plowed on, rubbing his forehead with the palm of his hand. "What with you destroying the evidence and all. But at least it's on the record now. It's better this way. I'm sure of it."

I cleared my throat. They ignored me.

"Vic, I *told* you I didn't want you calling 'em!" hollered Sonny, reddening.

"I know you did," admitted Vic. "But you pay me to protect you."

"I *pay* you to do what I tell you to do!"

"So," I broke in, "what exactly are we talking about here, gentlemen?"

Sonny and Vic exchanged a look, Vic shifting uncomfortably from one enormous foot to the other.

Sonny turned to me, brow furrowed. "May as well know, Hoagy. Not like it's any big deal. I got a death threat in this morning's mail."

I swallowed. "What did it say?"

"He won't tell me," Vic said. "And he flushed it down the toilet."

"Crapper is right where it belonged," snapped Sonny. "Vic, I want you to know that I love you, but I don't feel very good about you right now. I'm real, real upset with you for bringing the cops into this. They're bound to leak it to the press. I'll have 'em crawling all over me again. *Just* what I don't want. Next time you get a bright idea, do me a big favor and remember something – you're a dumb ox. Always have been. Always will be. Dig?!"

Vic blinked several times, nodded, swiped at his nose with the back of his hand. He was, I realized, struggling not to cry. "Sonny, I . . ."

"Get out of my sight!"

"Yes, Sonny." The big guy skulked back inside the house, head bowed.

Sonny watched him go, shook his head. "Dumb ox."

"He was just doing his job, Sonny."

"Hey, you don't even *have* a job, Hoag," he snarled. "If I want you to talk, I'll ask you to talk. Otherwise, shut your fucking mouth."

With that he turned his attention to that morning's *Variety*. I sat there for a second, stunned. Then I threw down my napkin and started around the pool to the guesthouse to pack. Then I stopped. Suddenly, Sonny's book seemed real important to me.

"So why'd you drag me out here?!" I yelled across the pool.

He looked up, frowning. "Whattaya mean?"

"I mean, why'd you waste my time? I've put a lot into this. I think what we've done so far has been damned good. I'm ready to start writing. My mukluks are unpacked. I'm set to go. Why the fuck did you drag me out here, huh?!"

He tugged at an ear. Then he laughed.

"What's so funny?!" I demanded.

"You are, Mister New York intellectual kosher dill. If I didn't know you, I'd swear you're taking this personal."

"Maybe I just don't like to see you back down."

"Sonny Day *never* backs down."

"Really? You said you wanted to tell this story. No, *needed* to tell it. You said it was part of your healing process."

"There's something you gotta understand about me, pally."

"What's that?"

"Don't ever listen to anything I say."

I returned to the table and sat down across from him. "Why are you balking, Sonny?"

"I-I can't help it. This thing . . . this thing with Gabe is too painful."

"More painful than talking about your father?"

"Much more."

"How so?"

"I can't. I just can't."

"Don't you trust me?"

"How can I?" he asked. "*You* don't *trust* me."

"Yes, I do."

"No, you don't. You won't let me get close to you."

"This is *work*, Sonny. This isn't personal."

"Work *is* personal with me."

Wanda came padding out from the kitchen in her caftan and sweat socks. Her eyes were puffy, her hair mussed. "What's all the yelling about?"

"Creative differences," Sonny replied.

"This is your idea of creative differences?" I asked.

"Just like old times," he acknowledged. To Wanda he said, "You're up early."

"Who's up?"

"What's the occasion?"

"I have a class." She yawned and poured herself some coffee.

He turned back to me. "Tell ya what, pally. I got that emcee job in Vegas tomorrow. Why don't you come with me? We'll have the whole drive out. We'll talk, have dinner. Maybe it'll help. If I still feel the same way when we get back, then we'll call it off."

"What about Lulu?"

"It's only for one night. Wanda can take care of her."

"Sure, Wanda can take care of her," Wanda said.
"Okay," I said. "We'll go to Vegas."
"We'll go to Vegas," Sonny agreed. "Just the two of us."

Just the two of us, of course, included Vic.

We left well before dawn in the limo, Sonny and I riding in the back along with the smell of his toilet water. Sonny slept. Asleep, with a blanket pulled up to his chin, he almost looked like that pudgy kid from Bed-Sty again, the one who slept out on the fire escape with his big brother on hot nights. Now he slept in an air-conditioned limo.

I watched him. There's an old saying – to really get to know a man you have to walk around in his shoes. A ghost, I was learning, has to wear his skin, too. I had no doubts now that Sonny Day was a colossal piece of work – unpredictable, confounding, maddening. Was I getting him yet? I still couldn't tell if he was being open with me or merely showing me the Sonny he wanted me to see. I couldn't tell if I was seeing him as he was or as I wanted him to be. Maybe I was trying to invent him, turn him into a sympathetic, vulnerable fictional creation. Maybe I never would get him. But I had to try.

At one point he shifted and the blanket fell away. He reached for it in his sleep, his manicured fingers wiggling feebly, a whimper coming from his throat. I hesitated, then covered him back up. He grunted and snuggled into it.

We cleared Pomona and Ontario in the darkness. The sky got purple as we climbed the San Bernardino Mountains and was bright blue by the time we descended to the desert floor. Sonny woke up around Victorville and announced he was hungry. We stopped at a Denny's in Barstow for breakfast. Aside from a couple of truckers at the counter, we were the only customers. The hash browns were excellent.

Sonny bought the papers on the way out. They were filled with stories about the Oscar nominations, and that got him going.

"See this, Hoagy? The comedies got aced out again. That really fries me. Did Stan Laurel ever get nominated for Best Actor? Groucho Marx? W. C. Fields? Me? No way. They think we're just fooling around. Lemme tell you, comedy has to do the same thing drama does. It's gotta tell a story, have believable people, make a point – and then on top of that it's gotta be funny, too. That makes it even harder.

But the snobs, the critics, they don't see it. For them, you gotta hold up a sign. Be solemn. Dull. They act like it's a crime to entertain people. You *gotta* entertain 'em. It's like Sammy told me one time: If you can't tap your foot to it, then it ain't music,"

"It's that way in my business, too," I said. "You're only taken seriously in literary circles if your stuff is torturous and hard to read. If you go to the extra trouble of making it clear and entertaining, then the critics call you a lightweight."

"They like you. You ain't dull."

"That's true, I wasn't. But I also never wrote a second book. They'd have gotten me then."

"I wish you wouldn't do that. It really bugs the hell out of me."

"What does?"

"The way you talk about yourself in the past tense, like you're eighty years old, or dead. You're young, you got talent. You'll write lots more books. Good books. You just gotta work on your attitude. Not I *was*. I *am*. Say it: I *am*."

I said it, I said it.

"That's more like it." He glanced at the newspaper story again, then bared his teeth, disgusted. "Screw 'em. We're the ones who have the talent. *We* know what we're doing."

He reached down and opened up the little refrigerator in front of us and pulled out two small bottles of Perrier. He opened them and handed me one.

"I just have one question," I said. "If we're both so smart and we know what we're doing, then how come we're on our asses?"

His eyes widened in surprise. Then he laughed. He actually laughed at something I said.

"You're okay, Hoagy. You're a no-bullshit guy. Glad we decided to do this. Hey, Vic, how ya doing up there, baby?"

"Fine, Sonny," he replied softly.

"Stop pouting already, will ya? So I blew. I take the blame. I apologize. You're not a dumb ox. You're my pally, and you meant well. I'm sorry, okay?"

Vic seemed to brighten. "Okay, Sonny."

"Now how about some sounds? Get us in the groove."

"You got it."

Vic put on some cassettes, uptempo Sinatra and Torme from the fifties, and we bopped along, sipping our Perriers, the heat shimmering outside on the Devils Playground. It wasn't the worst way to travel.

"Merilee used to get letters from cranks," I said. "Guys who wanted to buy her toenail cuttings. Wear her panties. Never death threats though."

Sonny shrugged. "After thirty years you get used to it. Part of the deal, at least it is for me."

"What did this one say?"

He gazed out the window. "It said that I'd never live to see our book in print."

"Oh?"

Sonny polished off his Perrier and belched. He stabbed a finger in my chest. "I know just what you're thinking – that's why I maybe want to pull out. Well, you're wrong. The two things got nuttin' to do with each other. I'm not that kind of person."

"What kind of person is that?"

"The kind who you can scare. If I worried about the cranks out there, I'd go outta my head. Besides, I got my Vic. Right, Vic?"

"That's right, Sonny."

We hit the first signs for the Vegas casinos when we crossed the Nevada state line.

"What exactly are you supposed to do for this pageant?" I asked him.

"Show up. Everything's already written for me. I just introduce the girls, eyeball their tits, wink at the audience. We walk it through this afternoon. Go on at five-thirty. You like showgirls?"

"What's not to like?"

"Red-blood American boy, huh?" He grinned, man to man.

I grinned back. "Type O."

He furrowed his brow. "What can I tell ya? I wish I didn't have to be doing it. It's cheese all the way. But I got no choice. If you've had personal problems like I have, you start at the bottom again. Prove you can deliver. In this business, you're a prisoner of people's preconceptions of you."

"Not dissimilar to life in general," I said.

"You can say that again."

"Not dissimilar to life in general," I repeated.

He gaped at me in disbelief.

"You forget something important about me," I told him. "I grew up on *you*."

"Yeah?"

"Yeah."

He looked me over and scowled. "Coulda done worse."

"You can say that again."

After so many hundreds of miles of pure barren desert, Las Vegas rose up before us in the hot sun like a gaudy, indecent mirage, the hotels and billboards so huge, so unlikely, I was sure they'd disappear if I blinked twice. I tried it – they didn't.

"Put in a lot of years here," said Sonny wistfully. "A lotta shtick under the bridge."

The third annual "Miss Las Vegas Showgirl Beauty Pageant" was being broadcast live from the MGM Grand Hotel, or so the billboard out front said. The parking lot, which must have spanned ten acres, was mostly empty except for some broadcast trucks. Inside, the vast casino was colder than a deli case and about as quiet. Most of the tables were covered. It wasn't noon yet.

Sonny got the royal treatment. The staff bowed and scraped and whisked us up to our rooms. He and Vic had a two-bedroom high-rollers' suite with a living room, kitchen, and complimentary fruit basket. Nice view of the purple mountains, too. I was billeted across the hall in a single room with no fruit basket. I had a view of the MGM Grand parking lot and way off in the distance, a view of the Caesars Palace parking lot.

They had, to quote Sonny, a real peach of a health club downstairs. We each pumped a round of irons, then did ten kilometers on the cycles, had a sauna and a cold plunge. Vic suggested we have our lunch sent up to their suite. Sonny insisted on eating in the coffee shop. So, bristling with health, we stormed the coffee shop and attacked man-sized platters of tuna salad.

We sat in a booth, Vic and me on either side of Sonny. A lot of guests came over to ask for his autograph and shake his hand. They were tourists, salesmen, ordinary folks – his people. He joked with them, kidded them, acted downright pleased by their attention.

Vic, on the other hand, never relaxed, never stopped scanning the room for somebody who looked like trouble. Vic was on the job now.

"You gonna spend some time in the casino?" Sonny asked me between autographs.

"Only as long as it takes to lose all my money."

"How much you bring?" he asked, looking concerned.

"A thousand."

He was relieved. "That's chicken feed."

"How about you?"

"Me? I can't go near a casino anymore. I gamble like I drink – can't stop. Used to drop fifty, a hundred grand in a night. You won't find me near a table now. Or the track."

At five minutes before two, Vic tapped his watch.

"Thanks, Vic," said Sonny, signaling for the check. "Don't wanna be late for rehearsal, Hoagy. That's exactly the kind of thing I can't afford now."

The waitress was slow in coming over. As the seconds ticked away, Sonny tapped the table with his fork. Then yanked at Vic's wrist to check the time. Then popped a couple of SenSens in his mouth. Then yanked at Vic's wrist again.

"Honey?!" he called out again, clearly agitated now. "Waitress?!"

"One minute!" she called back.

"Why don't I just let you out, Sonny?" Vic offered soothingly. "I can sign for it."

Sonny smashed the table with his fist, bouncing our silverware, our glasses, our keno holder. "*No!*" he roared. "She's gonna bring it right over and she's gonna . . . !" He caught himself, suddenly aware that people at neighboring tables were staring at him. He took a deep breath and let it out slowly. "Good idea, Vic," he said quietly. "Thanks."

Vic let him out. He rushed off alone, half-trotting, so intent that he bowled over two Japanese businessmen on his way out.

"Sonny's upset," Vic observed, as he signed the check.

"No kidding."

"Oh, I don't mean this waitress business. This was actually a step in the right direction. The new Sonny."

"What would the old Sonny have done?"

"Gotten the girl fired. After he turned the table over and smashed some plates. He's a lot calmer now. No, it was the way he acted toward his fans."

"How did he act?"

"Like he liked them. Wanted them to approach him. He was performing. He only does it when he's upset. Calms him down. Hasn't done that in a long, long time."

"I suppose he has a lot riding on this job."

"It's not the job. It's that letter. It's got him plenty worried. Me, too."

"You think it's for real?"

Vic shrugged. "Have to assume it is. You can't afford to be wrong."

"Think there's any connection between it and my little housewarming gift?"

Vic shifted uncomfortably. "No. No, I don't."

"Then who –"

"Let's go. I don't want him to be alone for very long."

A set had been erected on the stage of one of the headliner rooms, seemingly out of all of the Reynolds Wrap in the state of Nevada. A runway extended out into the seats, where it met up with the TV cameras and the monitors. Production assistants with clipboards scurried around. Pot-bellied technicians fiddled importantly with lights and mikes and eyeballed the showgirls, most of whom were seated in the first few rows, ignoring them. A few of them were up on stage learning their cues and marks from the stage manager. They wore tight jeans and halter tops. They were very tall and very well-built, but their features were coarse, their expressions stony. Sonny was up on stage shaking hands with the promoters and making them laugh. Vic and I slid into a couple of seats.

"I don't like this," said Vic. "So many people coming and going. Any of them could take a shot at Sonny."

The big guy was getting jumpy. Something about him being jumpy made me jumpy. "So why don't you call the police? Or hotel security?"

"You know why."

"Sonny's kind of rough on you, isn't he?"

"He's got to be rough on somebody. Better me than somebody he can really hurt, like Connie or Wanda."

"What happened to the 'big guys have big feelings' business?"

"Nothing. It's just that I can take it from him, Hoag. It's my job to take it, not theirs."

"Think he's going to pull out of this book?"

"I don't know."

"Do you want him to?"

"I want him to do what's best for him," Vic replied.

The director announced a technical run-through and called for quiet. He was a kid with a beard, a Hawaiian shirt, and an impatient, uptight manner. He was insecure. An insecure director, Merilee once told me, can get to be a very bitchy one.

And this one did, within minutes.

Sonny was reading one of his introductions off the prompter. A joke: "And now, here they are, Miss Aladdin Hotel."

It got a few snickers from the crew, but Sonny wasn't happy with it. This he indicated by clutching his throat and making gagging noises.

"Do you have a problem with the line, Mr. Day?" the director demanded.

"Kinda stale, ain't it? I mean, it was stale when Paar used it twenty years ago. We can do better than this."

"The jokes are already written, Mr. Day."

"Yeah, but I gotta say 'em. Gimme a minute. I'll think of something."

"We don't have a minute," said the director testily. "And frankly, people aren't turning this pageant on to listen to your jokes. Half of them will have their sound off and their pizzles in their hand."

Sonny laughed. "*Pizzles?* What, they teach you to talk tough like that in grammar school – last week?"

That got a lot of laughter, from both the crew and the girls.

The director reddened. "Are you going to be uncooperative and unprofessional, Mr. Day? Tell me if you are. Tell me right now. Because I want to get on the phone and see who's in town who can pinch-hit for you. I can't deal with this. I need a professional."

The room got very quiet. Everyone was looking at Sonny now. Everyone was wondering what The One would do.

He bared his teeth and went for his Sen-Sens. He popped a couple in his mouth and chewed them. And kept chewing them, until the anger and hurt had all but gone from his face. And then he said quietly, "I *am* a professional."

"And?" the director prodded.

"And you're the director," Sonny added softly, like an obedient child.

"Fine. Now let's run through this, shall we?"

They resumed.

"I'm going to have to split," I told Vic.

"I don't blame you," he said tightly, glowering at the director.

"Think he'd mind if I missed the performance, too?"

"Just tell him you loved it."

I fled up the aisle.

"How's my little girl?"

"Getting a little familiar, aren't we?"

"I meant the one with the short legs."

"Oh. She's fine. She's taking a nap outside."

"I knew it. She doesn't miss me. She doesn't even know I'm gone."

"I was trying to spare you. She's actually been woeful and droopy all day."

"You're just saying that to make me feel better." I sighed into the phone. "And I do. Did I remember to tell you when to feed her?"

"You wrote it all down. Does she really eat – "

"Did I tell you she might want to sleep with you?"

"No."

"Do you mind?"

"Not at all."

"She might want to sleep on your head."

"And I might like it."

"I thought you would."

She sniffled. "You didn't call to see how I am. You called about *her*."

She was hamming. That movie of ours seemed to be rolling again.

"And how was school today?" I ad-libbed.

"If you're nice to me," she replied, her voice a husky whisper now, "sometime I'll tell you about . . . *rezoning*."

"Tell me, how does a sexy, front-page kind of girl like you end up in real estate, anyway?"

"I was fucking a realtor."

"Was?"

"He blow-dries his body hair. Do you blow-dry your body hair, Hoagy?"

"No, I pay somebody else to do it for me."

She laughed. There was a pause, and then: "Hoagy?"

"Yes?"

"I'm starting to get a feeling about the two of us. Are you?"

I hesitated, not sure if she were playing now.

"Hello?" she said. "Silence isn't a great answer."

"I'm not quite sure how to answer that one."

"You'll do fine."

"Okay," I said. "I'm getting the same feeling. Only . . ."

"Only?"

"I make it a point to never mix business with pain."

Now it was her turn to be silent.

"Whew," she finally said. "You're good at this."

"You're in the big leagues now, kid."

"I guess I am. Is it because I'm so old and decrepit? Is that why you're rejecting me?"

"Let's talk about it when I get back. Over dinner. And you're not old and decrepit. You're about the most beautiful woman I've ever met. I'm flattered."

"You shouldn't be. I have terrible taste in men, remember?"

She hung up, laughing. End of scene.

As for me, I took a deep breath and dialed Winnipeg, Manitoba. It took me several calls before I found the hotel where the cast and crew of the new movie by the new genius were staying, but I did find it and the phone in her room did ring and she did answer it. My heart began to pound when she said hello. Briefly I forgot how to talk. She said hello again, a little suspiciously now.

"Hello, Merilee," I finally got out.

"Hoagy, darling, it's *you*. I thought for a second it was going to be a breather."

"Disappointed?"

"Never."

For years critics have tried to describe Merilee's voice. It is one of her strongest assets as an actress and as a woman – rich and cultivated, yet feathery and slightly dizzy sounding. To me, she has always sounded like a very proper, well-bred teenaged girl who has just gotten her first kiss. And liked it.

"Hoagy?"

"Yes, Merilee?"

"Hello."

"Hello, yourself. Something I needed to ask you. Hope you don't mind."

"Mind? I'm stranded here watching a hockey game on television. Blood is spurting."

"Where's Zack?"

"In New York, wrestling with his new play," she replied. "Was that your question?"

"No. Is Lulu two or is she going to be two?"

"It's on the back of her tag. We had her birthdate engraved there, remember? I wanted to put her sign there, too, and you wouldn't let me."

"Dogs don't have astrological signs."

"They do, too."

"I can't check her tag. She's in L.A. I'm in Las Vegas."

"You didn't stick her in some kennel, did you?"

"What land of guy do you think I am?"

"Gifted and tragic."

"You got that half right."

"Which half?"

"So tell me what Debbie Winger's like."

"I don't know, darling. She never comes out of her trailer. I'm playing her bad side. It's all very psychological, which I think in this particular case is another word for baked beans."

"I've missed your quaint little expressions."

"I actually have no idea what's going on. The director can't tell me – he's too busy listening to people tell him how brilliant he is. We wrap in a week. Hoagy, what on earth are you doing in Las Vegas?"

"I'm working on a book with Sonny Day."

"I saw something about that in *People*."

That was another thing I always liked about Merilee – she never denied that she read *People*. "What did it say?"

"That Gabe Knight isn't very pleased about their past being dredged up. And that you were doing it."

"Think it's sleazy of me?"

"I don't think you could do anything sleazy if you tried."

"Why, Merilee, that's the second-nicest thing you've ever said to me."

"What's the nicest?"

" 'Are you sure there aren't any other positions you'd like to try?' "

"*Mister* Hoagy, you're getting terribly frisky, hanging around with borscht belt comics. So let's hear all about The One. Is he as greasy and awful as he seems?"

"I honestly don't know."

She was silent a second. "What's wrong?"

"What makes you think something is wrong?"

She didn't bother to answer.

"I'm getting involved," I said. "I'm not sure it's a good thing. My role here is already so fuzzy. I'm not a reporter. I'm not a shrink. I'm not a friend. There's really no word for what I am – at least not a clean one."

"Let yourself go, Hoagy."

"Let myself go?"

"You always have to hold on to yourself. That's always been

your problem."

"So that's it."

"Give yourself over to the role. Enjoy it."

"It's too creepy to enjoy." I told her what had been going on, and how Sonny had been reacting.

"He's right not to make a big thing of the sickies," she said calmly. "I never do. Tell me, darling, is there a novel?"

"There's nothing."

"I'm sorry to hear that. Wait, there's somebody at the door. Hold on." She put the phone down. I heard voices, and the sound of Merilee's door closing. Then she returned. "It's tomorrow's pages . . . merciful heavens, I'm going to be in *mud*. It's twenty-four below zero outside. How does one get mud?"

"With a lot of very hot water."

"Lovely. I'd better hang up. I have a five-thirty call in the morning and I have to learn this."

"Take your rose hips."

"I promise."

"Merilee . . . do you ever miss us?"

"I try to not think about us. It makes me sad. I don't like to be sad."

We were both silent for a moment.

"It *was* fabulous, wasn't it?" she finally said.

"It was very fabulous."

"Hoagy?"

"Yes?"

"Lulu's going to be three. And she's a Virgo."

I hung up and lay there glumly on my hotel bed, staring at the smoke detector on the ceiling.

There was a knock on the door. It was a bellboy – with a bottle of Dom Perignon in a bucket of ice.

"I didn't order that," I said.

"Compliments of an admirer, sir." He parked it on the dresser.

There was a note. Of course. It read: *Challenge excites me – W.*

"Shall I open it, sir?"

"What an excellent idea."

I toasted Wanda in the mirror over the dresser with my first glass. To my surprise, there was almost a smile on my face. She was right. It *was* much more fun this way.

The bubbly gave me just enough courage to watch Sonny's pageant on TV while I got dressed.

He had a tux, a ruffled shirt, and his mask on. He seemed at home there under the lights – tanned, relaxed, in control. He was kidding around with Miss Tropicana, a big varnished redhead who'd just won the talent category for her impression of Carol Burnett.

"Tell me the truth," said Sonny. "Ever think you'd be up here like this tonight, honey?"

"Never, Mr. Day," she replied earnestly.

Sonny's face darkened for an instant. I could have sworn he was about to say "That makes two of us." But he didn't say it. He brightened and said, "Good luck in the overall competition, honey." The mask had slipped, but it had stayed on. You had to know him to notice it at all.

I put on a white broadcloth shirt, burgundy silk foulard tie, cream pleated trousers, and my double-breasted navy blazer.

The orchestra slammed into "Uptown Girl" by Billy Joel. After an introduction by Sonny, each showgirl strutted out to the edge of the ramp clad in bikini and high heels, stopped, smiled, placed hands on hips, swiveled, and strutted back. It was one hell of a testimonial to the wonders of silicone.

I doused myself with Floris and went down to the casino.

There were crowds at the tables now. The wheels were spinning, the dice landing. Winners yelled. Losers groaned. I slid onto a vacant stool at a blackjack table and snapped one of my crisp hundreds onto the green felt. The dealer gave me my chips. I lit the dollar cigar I'd bought at the newsstand.

I won twenty dollars on my first hand by sitting on thirteen. The dealer showed a four, drew on a fourteen, and busted. I let it ride and lost it with a seventeen to his nineteen. I upped my bet to twenty-five dollars, lost it, won it back, let it ride, lost it and three more like it. That took care of my first hundred. I laid down another one, raised my bet to fifty dollars, and lost it in two hands.

I like to gamble, but I'm lousy at it. I'm impulsive and I'm stubborn. I throw good money after bad. It's no way to win. But then, I don't expect to win.

I stayed even with my third hundred for a half hour, then got reckless and left it at a roulette wheel. By then it was time to put out my cigar and meet Sonny and Vic backstage.

Photographers and contestants were crowded in the corridor around the winning girl, who was sobbing. I squeezed past them and made it to Sonny's dressing room, which was stuffed with casino executives, backers, agents, and other forms of carnivorous animal life. They all had gleaming eyes and were shouting words like "wonderful" and "beautiful" at each other. Goblets of white wine were being passed out.

Sonny was shaking hands, patting backs, still very on. He wore pancake makeup. He spotted me in the doorway. "Hey, pally! Like the show?!"

"Loved it!"

"Beautiful!"

I grabbed a wine goblet and joined Vic, who stood impassively against the wall. We stayed there together like potted plants until everybody had gone. Everybody except the director, who was now trying to be buddy-buddy.

"Sonny, it's been a total slice of heaven," the kid gushed. "I gave you total shit. You gave me total shit. But that's cool. It's only because we both care so fucking much about what we're . . ." He trailed off, frowning.

There was this steady dribbling sound. It was my drink slowly being emptied on his Reeboks.

"Oops," I said. "Sorry."

Next to me, Vic began to shake from suppressed laughter. Sonny just stood there grinning at me like a proud parent. A feeling passed between us, and just like that I knew the book was back on, Gabe and all.

Red-faced, the director quickly shook Sonny's hand and ducked out.

Sonny let out a short, harsh laugh and clapped me on the back. Then he turned to Vic and ordered, "Lock that damn door!"

Vic did, and Sonny immediately slumped into the chair before his dressing table, exhausted. Vic helped him off with his tuxedo jacket. The ruffled shirt underneath was soaking wet under the arms. Vic toweled Sonny's forehead and the back of his neck for him, like a water boy on the sideline.

"God, that was awful," Sonny moaned. "But it's over. I did my job. That's all that matters. I did my job."

"You're a pro, Sonny," Vic assured him.

Sonny heaved a huge sigh and began to wipe the makeup off his face with a tissue. Vic helped him off with his shirt and his trousers.

He took his shoes, socks, and boxers off himself and stood before us naked. "Lemme hose off and we'll get the hell away from this place, okay?" He started past me to the stall shower, stopped, and crinkled his nose at me. "Hey, you been smoking?"

We ate at a quiet Italian restaurant on one of those dark, deserted side streets you land on when you fall off the bright lights of the Strip.

The maitre d' welcomed Sonny with an embrace and led us to a corner table.

"Food's great here," Sonny advised me. Then he winked and added, "Funny how there are so many good Italian restaurants in this town, huh?"

We ordered spinach fettucine and veal chops. Vic and I got a bottle of Chianti. Vic only sipped from his glass, keeping his eyes on the other customers and the door.

"So how ya doing, pally?" Sonny asked me, cheerful now.

"I'm down three hundred."

He patted my hand. "That's hysterical. A real Vegas answer. Glad you made the trip. I'm feeling better about us now. Of course, working that shit pageant helps. Boy, I need this book. Let's face it, I'm at stage four. No kidding around."

"Stage four?"

"You don't know the five stages?"

I shook my head.

"Okay. There's five stages in a performer's career." He counted them off on his fingers. " 'Who's Sonny Day?' '*You're* Sonny Day?' 'Get me Sonny Day.' 'Get me *a* Sonny Day.' And 'Who's Sonny Day?' I'm at stage four. Gotta get back to three. Who would have thought twenty-five years ago . . ." He shook his head. "I need a shot in the arm. I really do."

Vic was watching the front. He stiffened. "Trouble, Sonny."

"Who?"

"I think he strings for the *Enquirer*," Vic replied.

There were two of them. The reporter was a fat slob with a scraggly goatee and shades on his head. He carried a tape recorder that looked as if it had been run over by a car. It probably had been. The photographer was an old-timer with two cameras around his neck and a cigarette in his mouth.

"Ahh," I declared, inhaling deeply. "Nothing like a breath of stale air."

They pushed past the maitre d' and headed urgently for our table. He trailed after them, protesting.

Vic started to get up.

Sonny stopped him. "Relax. Stay calm."

The photographer began to snap pictures of us eating. He used a flash attachment. The other customers turned and gaped.

The reporter stuck his tape recorder mike between Sonny's face and Sonny's pasta. "Is it true you're going to tell all, Sonny? You gonna talk about why you and Gabe went at it?"

"I'm sorry, Mister Day," apologized the maitre d'. "I couldn't keep them out."

"That's okay, Carmine," said Sonny. "The plague couldn't stop 'em."

"Why now, Sonny?" the reporter persisted. "You looking to fuck over Gabe's political future? Pretty vindictive, isn't it?"

"Look, pally," Sonny said pleasantly. "I don't have nothing to say. We're trying to have a quiet meal. Show a little consideration. If you want pix, take 'em and leave, okay?"

"What about the death-threat rumor? Is that true?"

"What death-threat rumor?" Sonny demanded sharply.

The reporter grinned, smelling blood. "So it's true?"

Sonny reddened. "I got nothing to say."

"What does Gabe say about it? He trying to stop you?"

"You're not hearing me," Sonny said, an edge in his voice now. "I still got nothing to say."

The repeated explosions of the flashbulbs were becoming more than a little irritating. Sonny put a hand over his face to shield his eyes.

Vic took over. "You're bothering us."

"Come on, Sonny," pressed the reporter. "I need a statement."

"You're bothering us," Vic repeated, louder this time. "Leave!"

"I got a job to do," he insisted.

Vic shoved his chair back and stood up. The reporter's eyes flickered when he saw just how long that took.

"And you've done it." Vic stepped between the reporter and our table, arms out, a human wall. "You got your pictures. Now leave!"

"You have to answer me, Sonny," the reporter said around Vic's bulk.

"I don't have to do nothing, bub," snapped Sonny.

"You can't avoid me."

"I'm making a real effort not to lose my temper."

"So am I," said Vic, sticking a large index finger in the guy's chest. "Beat it."

"Okay, if that's the way you want it," said the reporter. "I got my story anyway: 'Sonny Day falls off the wagon.'"

"*What?!*" demanded Sonny angrily.

"There's wine on your table. You're drinking again. We have the pix to back it up. You even tried to cover your face. It'll be in every supermarket in America, Sonny. But it doesn't have to be. I'm perfectly willing to work with you. I'm on your side."

"You're scum," spat Sonny. "Do everybody a favor – get AIDS."

Vic, I noticed, had begun to breathe oddly – quick, shallow gasps, in and out, in and out.

The reporter shrugged. "Okay, Sonny. If that's how you want it." He nodded to the photographer. "Let's go. We got our story."

Vic grabbed the reporter by his shirt. The guy's feet dangled two inches off the floor. Vic was gasping for air now. "You're not . . . not gonna do this!"

"Try and stop me, dumbo."

And then I found out what Wanda meant when she said to never, ever, let Vic get mad at you.

He blew. He just plain went into a blind rage. He wrenched the photographer's camera from its strap, tore it open, and yanked the film out. When the reporter tried to wrestle it away from him, he punched the guy flush on the face, sending him backpedaling onto a neighboring table, where food and dishes flew. Blood splattered. A woman screamed.

"*No, Vic!*" cried Sonny. "*Stop, Vic. Enough!*"

But this wasn't Vic. This was a wild man, an animal growl coming from his throat. He pulled the reporter off the table, slugged him again, breaking his nose, sending him up against a wall. There he grabbed him by the throat with both hands and began banging the guy's head against the wall. The reporter's limbs began to flop helplessly. His face got purple, his eyes glazed over.

It took Sonny, me, and every waiter and busboy in the place to pull Vic off him. There's no question in my mind he would have killed him if we hadn't.

"*Vic!*" screamed Sonny. "*Look at me, Vic!*"

But Vic was still heaving and straining to get at the reporter, who had now slumped to the floor, bleeding from his mouth and nose, dazed but conscious.

Sonny looked around, grabbed a bucket of ice that had been cooling a neighboring table's white wine, and dumped it over Vic's head. The big fellow sputtered, and then abruptly, he came around. He shook his head a few times to clear it, then stood there dumbly, his chest still heaving, ice water streaming down his head.

"Everything okay, Sonny?" He was gasping, looking around at the damage like someone else had done it.

"No, everything's *not* okay," sobbed the reporter, who was dabbing at his bloodied face with a napkin. He pointed it at Sonny. "I'm going to sue your ass," he wailed.

"Get out while you still can, you piece of shit!"

The photographer helped him up. They left, the photographer clutching his ruined camera, the reporter snuffling and moaning. Everybody in the place watched them go, then turned to watch us.

"I'm sorry about this, Mr. Day," apologized the maitre d', as he and his staff scurried to clean up our mess.

"No, I'm the one who's sorry, Carmine," said Sonny, slipping him some bills. "Please give everybody another bottle of whatever they were having."

"Yessir, Mr. Day."

Sonny turned back to me. "C'mon, let's eat."

"Maybe we should go," I said, eyeing Vic, who was still standing there in a half daze.

"Nonsense," said Sonny. "We came here for dinner and we're gonna have it."

We sat back down at our table.

"Sorry, Sonny," Vic mumbled. "Just couldn't help myself."

"That's okay, Vic. He asked for it. Why don't you go towel off and comb your hair. You look a mess."

"Okay," he agreed meekly.

We watched him as he headed for the men's room. He moved slowly, like he was shell-shocked.

"He'll be fine in a couple minutes," Sonny assured me. "It's that damned plate in his noggin. He almost killed a guy in a club once. Cost me plenty to get the charges dropped."

I took a gulp of my Chianti. "Think that guy will sue?"

"He'll try. Make more of a name for himself that way. I'll call Heshie tonight. He knows the right people to lean on. Cash settlement ought to take care of it. Can't stop the story though.

Not with my rep. It's news. It'll be in tomorrow's papers. On *Entertainment Tonight*. Wires'll pick it up. By the end of the week they'll have it that I was drunk out of my mind and I punched the jerk. I guarantee it."

The waiter brought us our veal.

"Something a little different for *you* tonight, huh, pally?"

"Lot of fun eating with you guys," I said. "We'll have to do it again real soon."

"Look at it this way – you'll be famous now. You'll be in every newspaper in America."

"I will?"

"Sure. You'll be the unidentified third man."

"Terrific."

My luck at blackjack finally turned at a little past three a.m. Maybe it was just the odds evening out. Whatever, I kept on doubling my bets and I kept on winning. I won so many hands in a row that I actually climbed all the way back up to even for the night. Then I lost five straight. I decided it was time for bed.

Somebody was sleeping in my bed. She had blond hair and a nice shape and no clothes on under the single sheet. The light woke her up. She was pretty. She stirred, then sat up and stretched, the skin tightening across her breasts. Then she lay back on the pillow and smiled at me, all warm and cuddly and inviting.

"Are you in the right room?" I said.

"Are you Hoagy?" she purred, in a slight Southern accent. "Yes. Who are you?"

"Yours. For the whole night."

"Whose idea was this?"

"I wouldn't know about that."

"Put your clothes on," I said. "You just had an easy night's work."

I went across the hall and pounded on the door to Sonny's suite. After a minute Vic came to the door and wanted to know who it was. When I told him, he opened up. He wore a robe. One hand was rubbing sleep from his eyes. The other held a gun.

"Hey, Hoag." He yawned. "What's up?"

"Trouble?" I asked, eyeing the gun.

"All quiet. Routine precaution."

"I have to talk to Sonny."

"He's asleep."

Sonny appeared behind him in the doorway. "It's okay, Vic. Go back to bed."

Vic went back to his room and closed the door.

Sonny grinned at me. "Get your present?"

"Sonny, I – "

"She's supposed to be the best in town. A graduate of Tulane University." He winked. "Do ya some good. I mean, there ain't a whole lot of action around my house, except for Wanda. And for her you need a butterfly net. Enjoy."

"Sonny, I don't want her."

He punched me on the shoulder, cozily. "C'mon, she'll do anything you want, and she knows what she's doing. You'll feel like a new man."

"I appreciate it, but . . ."

"But what?"

"It's not my thing, okay?"

"Why didn't you say so? I'll pick up the phone. You don't have to be bashful. Different strokes, right? I used to dig *schwartzers*. Two or three of 'em at once – taller the better. Gabe went for little girls. Just tell me what you want."

"I don't want anything. I'm very tired and I want to go to sleep."

He frowned. "You still carrying a torch for your ex-wife? Is that it?"

"Not exactly."

"Then what? Talk to me."

I took a deep breath, let it out slowly. "There is no torch," I said quietly. "Okay?"

He glanced south of my equator, then back up. "You mean . . . ?"

"Physically, there's nothing wrong. I'm just . . ."

"Impotent. Say it. You're impotent. So what? It happens to lots of guys. Come on in and we'll talk about it. We'll brew up a pot of tea and talk all night if you want." He smiled warmly. He looked happier than I'd ever seen him. In fact, he looked positively thrilled.

He put an arm around me to usher me in. It sort of developed into a hug.

"Come on in, kid."

CHAPTER FIVE

(Tape #4 with Sonny Day. Recorded in his study, February 20.)

Hoag: So that's how you and Gabe met. In boot camp.

Day: Right.

Hoag: You're not enjoying this, are you?

Day: How do you expect me to enjoy it? The man broke my heart.

Hoag: How?

Day: Not now.

Hoag: When?

Day: When I can handle it. Don't push me.

Hoag: The good times then. Your impressions of him, when you first met.

Day: Okay. Sure. Gabe Knight was a square. He was from a place called Lincoln, Nebraska. He lived in a big white house on one of those wide, quiet streets with the big elm trees. They had a porch swing. His dad was a pharmacist, always wore a white shirt, and for fun he sang in a barbershop quartet. The old lady, she wore an apron and baked pies. The town held a fucking parade for him when *At Ease* opened there. First time he took me there, I swore I was on the backlot at Warners.

Hoag: What was *he* like?

Day: A Boy Scout. A milk drinker. He said shucks. Called his dad sir. Went to church. Wrote home every day to his girl, Lorraine, who actually, I swear to god, lived in the house next door. He married her. She was his first wife. That was before he got corrupted.

Hoag: And what did he think of you?

Day: He thought I was a Dead-end Kid, the kind who stole old ladies' handbags and opened fire hydrants on hot summer days. Not true. I have never opened a fire hydrant. Seriously, I was as foreign to him as he was to me. He never knew a Jew before. Let alone slept under one. The characters he and I played, those characters were really us. That's why it was so good.

Hoag: How did the two of you hit it off? Or should I say why?

Day: Show business. He was putting himself through the university there as a kind of entertainer. He worked as a DJ on the local radio station for a buck a night. Performed in summer stock, the straw hat stuff. He could sing, play the ukulele, and he was a pretty fair hoofer. Did a magic act, too, for kids' birthday parties. Juggled. Palmed. Used it in *The Big Top*, remember? He did a little bit of everything. None of it great, but what the hell did they know in Lincoln, Nebraska.

Hoag: Was he funny?

Day: He was clever. Comedy itself, the art form, he knew shit from. I taught him everything.

Hoag: You became friends?

Day: We'd both performed. It was something we had in common and talked about and kept talking about. He had the bug, see. He loved to talk about movies, radio shows. And he loved hearing about the Catskills. When we had a pass, we'd sit over Cokes and talk all night. Pretty soon I'm showing him some of the old routines me and Mel did, and he was laughing and chipping in. And then he was taking off. And so was I. Once we got started, we riffed all the time, like a couple of musicians. It was our release. Basic training was a pretty awful place, believe me. You were told where to go, what to do. And for all you knew, you'd be dead in six months. Most of the guys drank to blow off steam. With me and Gabe, it was humor.

Hoag: Did you compare him in your mind to Mel?

Day: Hard not to. He was a big brother type. A little older than me. Tall, solid, dependable. People liked him.

Hoag: Was he serious about wanting to become a performer?

Day: You mean, what would have happened if we never met? Hard telling. Gabe was a small-town boy, conservative, not the sort inclined to take the big chance. I think he'd have settled down and ended up behind the counter of that pharmacy. We weren't looking for something to happen. It just did.

Hoag: You make it sound like a love affair.

Day: It was, at first. And then it's more like a marriage. You spend all your time together, plan your future together. There's trust, affection, loyalty, jealousy. The only thing you don't do is fuck. Come to think of it, it *is* just like being married. *(silence)* Whoops, sorry, Hoagy. Old joke.

Hoag: When did you realize you were good together?

Day: Right off. The guys kept hearing us and wanted to know what we was doing, so we tummeled some routines and started doing them for 'em. In the barracks. In the mess hall. For fun like in the dorm at Pine Tree. We did a drill routine where this tough sergeant, Gabe, is drilling a clumsy recruit, me, who keeps dropping his gun. That was our first big routine. We did it in *At Ease*.

Hoag: I remember it.

Day: We did one where I'm the city slicker teaching him, the hick, how to play poker. I figure I'm conning him out of all his money, only the whole time he's conning me. We did two recruits trying to identify what they're eating at mess. Oh, we did the old dance routine from Pine Tree, too, except we made it a USO dance. I was basically the same character I had been. He was Mel. But from the beginning we got belly laughs. Mel and me never got laughs like that.

Hoag: What was the difference?

Day: Shared experience. We was all in this together, we was all frightened. Plus, there was Gabe. . . .

Hoag: What about him?

Day: (silence) He was a brilliant straight man. It's taken me a lotta years to admit that. When we were on top, I always thought it was *me*. Everybody said so. They said anybody could have played his part, that he was a stiff, that I was the reason for our success. I believed that. I was wrong. He was a brilliant straight man. Best in the business.

Hoag: That's a pretty big admission from you.

Day: It's the truth. We just clicked, that's all. I was very hyper, very New York, you know? Go go go. He was very calm and collected. Midwestern. Innocent. Handsome, too, though I always thought his Adam's apple was kind of prominent. . . . We had great timing together. Gabe had this instinct for knowing just when to push the right button to make me funnier. And he knew just the right moment to rein me in and move on to the next bit. Not a second too soon. Not a second too late. He could feel the moment.

Hoag: Did the two of you talk about the future? About sticking together?

Day: We dreamed about becoming big stars the same way the other guys dreamed about fucking Betty Grable. It was wartime. You took it one step at a time. Ours was to get up on a stage. They used to have these dances Saturday nights on the base. A band. Local girls. Nice girls. So one Saturday night when the band took ten, some of the guys egged us into going up there. First couple minutes, everybody thought we was whackos. But once we got rolling, making fun of the sergeants, the officers, the food – they dug us. We performed at the dances every week. We was the highlight of the show. It so happens that one of the guys who sees us one weekend – now we don't know this, mind you – is a recruiting officer who had been a talent scout at Warner Brothers. Al Lufkin. Went on to become a vice president there. Anyway, for every showbiz success story there's some kind of cockeyed, crazy coincidence. Here's mine- – Al Lufkin is about to get married in New York to Len Fine's sister.

Hoag: Len Fine from the Pine Tree?

Day: The same. So Al happens to mention to Len about seeing these two funny soldiers down in Mississippi, and Len says, Sonny Day, sure, he's a real talent. I discovered him.

Hoag: You don't know this is going on.

Day: I don't know a thing. All I know is we finish basic training, we take the train up to Fort Dix, New Jersey, and our unit is shipped out to Europe. Only, Gabe and me aren't on the boat. We're ordered to report to some special recruiting unit.

Hoag: What kind of recruiting unit?

Day: We don't know. All we're told is to report to a theater on West Fifty-third Street in New York City. So we find the theater. Gabe's getting a stiff neck looking at the tall buildings. We show the soldier at the door our papers, we walk in, and we're in the middle of some big-time show being rehearsed. There's chorus girls, musicians, a band leader who looks a helluva lot like Kay Kyser, and these three girl singers who I'd swear are the Andrews Sisters. But what the hell are the Andrews Sisters doing there? What the hell are *we* doing there? Turns out they're putting together a revue called *You're in the Army Now*, which is gonna travel around the country and put on benefit performances to help with recruiting and morale. They want us to do our act in the show – you know, a couple of genuine recruits showing the humorous side of army life. And that's how we broke into showbiz – courtesy of Uncle Sam. They assigned us to work with a writer who'd written for Edgar Bergen's radio show. A soldier, like us. He helped us polish our routines and he gave us a couple of new lines. Two weeks later we hit the road. The night before we left, I went out to Brooklyn and visited the old man in the hospital. My mom made me. Last time I saw him. *(silence)* He was really out of it, didn't even know me. I had so much hatred for him and anger, and it didn't go away just because he was dying there in front of me. I felt . . . I felt tremendous pain about that.

Hoag: Were you on the road when your father died?

Day: I came back from Cleveland for the funeral. It was just me, the old lady, a couple relatives. We went back to the apartment when it was over, had some schnapps, and I caught the next train. It was . . . well, I guess you could say it was an end for me, Hoagy. And a beginning.

(end tape)

(Tape #5 with Sonny Day. Recorded in his study, February 21.)

Day: You know what I could really go for? A Baby Ruth candy bar. Used to eat 'em by the dozen when I was zonked.

Hoag: Does that mean I can have the last piece of pineapple?

Day: Hell no.

Hoag: So tell me about being on tour with *You're in the Army Now*.

Day: It was the most fun I'd ever had. We started in Buffalo. Stayed a couple weeks. Then did Detroit, Cleveland, Chicago, St. Louis. Had our own train. Stayed in the best hotels. It turned out that Warners was financing the whole thing. They had plans to film it somewhere down the line. They'd send different contract players out to join us for six or eight weeks – Jack Carson, Joanie Blondell. They'd emcee the show, do sketches. The whole thing was like a dream. Gabe and me went on in the middle of the show for about ten minutes. Rest of the time it was one big party. The girls, Hoagy. We was traveling with two dozen fun-loving, man-hungry chorus girls. We had wild times, especially on those trains. PJ parties. Singalongs. Drinking. But they were nice girls. All they were looking for was some affection. They thought we were cute. I was twenty-one. Gabe was twenty-three. What can I tell ya, there was a shortage of men.

Hoag: Didn't Gabe have a problem with that, being so square?

Day: Gabe Knight turned out to be one of those guys who says he likes vanilla – because it's the only flavor he ever tasted. Once he started getting a little action, he had a permanent hard-on. I mean, girls coming and going twenty-four hours a day. He was always kicking me out of our room. I'd go find the girl's roommate. Didn't do too bad that way, either.

Hoag: Did you and Gabe get along?

Day: He snored. Whistled off key. Tasted food off my plate. I hate that. Ask anybody. But we were buddies. And we were going over real well. Audiences loved our stuff. They even wrote a new routine for us. Gabe is sitting on the steps of the barracks in the moonlight, playing his uke and singing "By the Light of the Silvery Moon." I come out and join him. I'm a dogface from Brooklyn, he's a dogface from Nebraska, and we're both homesick as hell and frightened. So we share a smoke and talk about home and Mom and our best girl. And then we finish the song together. Scared the shit out of me the first time we tried it. I kept saying, where's the laughs? We gotta have laughs. But the people loved it. Seemed genuine to them.

Hoag: Did you guys sense that you were about to become big stars?

Day: Mostly, I think we felt we were being swept along by something that was much bigger then we were, you know? Then we hit L.A. in – what was it? – winter of '43. Warners was ready to make a movie of the show. Me and Gabe, we were ordered to report there for a screen test. We met Jack Warner, we –

Hoag: Remember what he said to you?

Day: I remember I was so frightened I didn't know my own name. He asked us which one of us was Knight and we both said, "I am, sir." They filmed us doing our routines in front of a backdrop. We went back to the hotel. Next day they pulled us aside and told us we weren't being included in the movie. We were crushed. We figured that was it. End of party. But that wasn't it at all. See, Jack Warner had decided to give us our very own movie, *At Ease*. He *loved* us. It was a dream, Hoagy. I kept waiting to wake up. I didn't wake up for thirty-five years.

Hoag: What was it like being out here then?

Day: This was a great town in those days. Pretty. Weather was beautiful. And the studio was huge – not like now. Blocks and blocks of streets on the backlot. Castles. Jungles. Lakes. Extras walking around dressed like Bengal lancers, like Robin's merry men. And we were part of it. But on the other hand we weren't. Technically, we were still attached to the army. *At Ease* was considered a recruiting picture. It came off like Jack Warner was doing a great thing for his country. In reality he was making a low-budget comedy with two stars and a bunch of army training footage that he got all for free. But they put us up in a nice apartment building in Encino. Gave us per diem money. A car. Whatever we needed.

Hoag: Who thought up *At Ease*?

Day: It was concocted on the run. Warner handed us to Hal Wallis, who sent a couple of writers down to see us perform with the company at the Pantages Theater. They talked to us for about fifteen minutes backstage. A week later they'd built a standard plot around five of our routines. Gabe's a rich-kid momma's boy, used to the soft life. I'm a two-bit con man, used to being on my own. We take an instant dislike to each other at the induction center, then turn out to be bunkmates, then rivals for the same USO girl. In the end we become great soldiers and great buddies. Strictly formula. But they gave us a great cast of pros to work with. Bart MacLane was the drill sergeant. Ward Bond was the camp boxing champ. Priscilla Lane was the girl. Lucille Ball was the friend. We learned a lot about screen acting from those folks. It's all repetition. Start. Stop. Stand over here. Do it again. And the scenes are shot out of order. Hard to keep your level up. We worked our asses off fourteen hours a day on *At Ease*. Did what we were told. Conked out every night. We weren't having any fun at all until guess who comes up to me on the set one day and says hello – Heshie Roth.

Hoag: Of Seetags fame?

Day: The one and only. Very interesting life story, Heshie. If he wanted to tell it, he'd make a helluva best-seller. I mean, he knows where all the bodies are buried. But I guess he'd just as soon forget. He's a very upstanding guy now. A lot of the people he moves with now, they don't even know how he ended up out here.

Hoag: How did he?

Day: Bugsy Siegel brought him out. Remember I mentioned how Heshie ran around with the Jewish mob when we was in Bed-Sty? Well, Benny Siegel was the idol of every punk in New York in those days. Lived like a king in the Waldorf. Moved in the fanciest circles. Anyway, he took a liking to Heshie when Heshie was a kid. It was his idea to put Heshie through law school. So now it's 1944 and Benny Siegel – nobody called him Bugsy to his face – has moved out to L.A. to take control of the mob action out here. Know who his right-hand man is?

Hoag: Allow me to guess – a bright young attorney by the name of Harmon Wright?

Day: Correct, pally. There was a lot of independent action out here then – racetracks, nightclubs, offshore gambling. Bugsy came out here to take all of it over. Bumped off anybody who got in his way. Heshie concocted the controlling partnerships and shit like that to make it legal. And this was just for starters. The main reason Bugsy was out here, according to Heshie, was that the Mexican border was practically in L.A.'s backyard and the guys in the East wanted to set up a drug pipeline. Heshie, he was the juice man. He spread it around – police department, DA's office, attorney general. In the meantime, Bugsy Siegel became the toast of Hollywood. Screwed every starlet in town. Hung around with Cary Grant, George Raft, Jack Warner. Show people love gangsters. They excite 'em. So when Heshie comes up to me on the set, well, he's in a position to show a couple of soldiers a pretty good time. Gabe and I got very little sleep after that. We met starlets. We even got to meet Benny Siegel.

Hoag: What was he like?

Day: A movie star. Handsome, charismatic, and a real dandy, right down to his monogrammed silk shorts. And what a temper. He threw a big bash at George Raft's house one night, and Heshie brought us and introduced us. Benny said to us, "It's a fine thing you're doing for our country." I said, "Coming from you, Mr. Siegel, that's a real compliment." Suddenly, the man's eyes turned into hot coals. Lips got white. And he said, "What the fuck is *that* supposed to mean?!" I started stammering. I see my life pass before my eyes. Then all of a sudden he relaxes, throws an arm around me, and we were pals. Scary guy. Right on the edge. *(silence)* That was my first Hollywood party. Half the guests were upstairs with somebody they didn't come with. I made it with my first Oscar winner that night. On the diving board. *(silence)* Yeah, we had a good time after we met up with Heshie. Only, Gabe, he started feeling guilty for his sins. So he and Lorraine got hitched when we were in his hometown for the opening of *At Ease*. Made a great story for the papers. We went all over the country to promote it. Before we left L.A., Heshie pulled us aside and said, "Listen, I wanna handle you when the war's over – movie contracts, nightclubs, Vegas." I said what the hell's in Vegas. He said Benny's gonna make it into the biggest, most glamorous gambling resort in America, with top entertainers. Strictly legit. We said to Heshie, sure, sure, we'll talk. See, deep down, we believed this whole thing was some kind of happy accident of wartime. You know, that it wouldn't last. Until the numbers started coming. *At Ease* turned out to be Warners' second-biggest grossing picture of the war, right behind *Casablanca*. A smash. Right away, Warners was interested in putting us under contract. Lorraine, she wanted Gabe to finish college. She wanted kids and a white picket fence. Plus, she thought I was a bad influence. But Gabe, he'd gotten a taste. He wanted it. So when we was discharged in '45 we signed a personal services contract with Heshie and set him loose.

Hoag: Did you have any qualms about being hooked up with a gangster?

Day: None. I always believe in sticking with people you know. And Heshie, he had a personal stake in us. He was anxious to get out from under Bugsy's wing. Start his own business. For a couple of years he'd been tucking away a little juice money on the sly. A nip here, a tuck there.

Hoag: Are you telling me HWA was started with mob money?

Day: Mob money the mob didn't exactly know from. They thought the cops pocketed it after a raid, or Heshie paid it to some independent who ended up getting bumped off. The stuff disappears, who knows where.

Hoag: How much are we talking about?

Day: Fifty thousand. A hundred, maybe.

Hoag: Pretty gutsy, wasn't he?

Day: *(laughs)* Better Heshie should be my agent than somebody else's. Bugsy, he was too volatile. He wasn't gonna be around for long. Heshie knew that. As it turned out, Bugsy Siegel got shot in the eyeball one year later. By which time the Harmon Wright Agency was doing pretty damned well for itself.

(end tape)

CHAPTER
SIX

onny wasn't wrong. By the end of the week the newspapers did have it that he'd gotten drunk and slugged that reporter himself in the restaurant in Vegas.

There were lots of phone calls that week. It made me notice how seldom the phone had been ringing before. The *Enquirer* called. *People* called. Liz Smith and Marilyn Beck called. Sonny refused to talk to them. He tried to act as if the negative publicity wasn't bothering him, but it was. He paced a lot now when we worked, baring his teeth, chewing a lot of Sen-Sens, and on occasion, his expensively manicured fingernails.

I was putting in a lot of time at the typewriter now – shaping, fleshing out, and polishing the transcripts of our tapes. I was up to Sonny's first summer in the Catskills. I was enjoying the writing. It felt good to be back in the saddle again. And I was doing a helluva job of convincing myself that my effort was leading to more than another junky celebrity memoir. Here, I told myself, was emerging a rare insightful study of a showbiz legend.

I definitely needed a dose of reality. I didn't get one.

What I got, I discovered one evening after dinner, was another visit. This time I could be sure it wasn't my imagination. I came in to find my room trashed – selectively trashed. The tapes that had been on my desk were ripped from their cartridges and strewn all over the bed, spilling onto the floor. They were ruined, of course.

Fortunately they were blank tape – not that whoever did it knew that. I had gotten careful, Sonny's death threat and the rising interest of the oilier tabloids had made me aware that the original tapes of my sessions with him might be precious to somebody besides me and the publisher's lawyers. So I had numbered and dated a batch of blanks and left those piled on my desk. The real ones were snug and secure under my winter clothes in my Il Bisonte bag in the closet. The transcripts I kept sandwiched between my mattress and box spring when I wasn't working on them. And the typing service that did the transcribing was not one of the usual Hollywood typing factories, where bribery and thievery are always possible. The publisher's sister, a retired geography teacher who lived in Santa Monica, was doing the job.

I had also asked Vic for a key to the guesthouse and had taken to locking it, though clearly there was no point in doing that. Whoever had trashed the tapes had a key, too, or a real flair with locks. There was no sign of forced entry.

Sonny and Vic exchanged poker faces when I presented them with this, the latest evidence of less-than-positive vibes.

Then Sonny fingered the mined tapes, grinned, and quipped, "Don't make 'em like they used to, huh?"

"This is not funny, Sonny," I told him. "The police should be brought in."

"No cops," Sonny snapped.

I turned to Vic. "Do you agree?"

Vic stared at me, tight-lipped. He didn't answer.

I turned back to Sonny. "Why? Is it really because you're afraid of leaks?"

"I got reasons."

"What reasons?"

"*My* reasons."

"Now who's shutting whom out?" I demanded.

Sonny softened, jabbed at a tape with a stubby finger. "This fuck us over?"

"No, we're fine," I replied, not disclosing how or why this was so. "We're just fine and dandy."

The day Sonny turned sixty-three was a damp, drizzly one. He announced at breakfast that he felt like driving himself to his therapist's appointment. This didn't thrill Vic – he didn't want Sonny out of his sight for that long. But The One insisted.

"I'm the goddamned birthday boy," he pointed out. "All I really want is to pretend I'm a normal person for two lousy hours. I'll be fine."

He took the limo. Vic, it seemed, wanted to be my pally now. After Sonny left, he asked me if I felt like taking a ride in his Buick down to Drake Stadium at UCLA. I said why not. Vic still knew the coaches there, and they let us take some javelins out to the field to fool around.

A lot of people think spear chucking is a dull, one-dimensional sport. But when you train hard for it, learn the fine points of technique and form and timing, you begin to appreciate just how dull and one-dimensional it really is.

"We used to keep ourselves amused by 'pooning," I told Vic, as we let a couple fly.

Vic was much too heavily muscled to get any kind of extension. Mine sailed way past his, though a good fifty feet short of my distance in my heyday. They both landed with a soft plonk in the moist earth of the deserted field. We fetched them.

" 'Pooning?" he asked.

"You aim it at a target."

"You mean like a tree?"

"Trees are no good. They crunch the spear. No, you lay a hankie on the grass a hundred feet out or so and see who can get closest. Whoever's farthest buys the beers. I used to be a dead aim."

I took sight at a mudhole a way off and let it fly. Nailed it.

"Everybody," I said, "ought to be good at something."

"I'm sure Coach would let us borrow a couple," suggested Vic. "Sonny's got plenty of room. We can 'poon for beers in the yard, huh?"

"Okay. Sure."

"You've come around pretty good, Hoag, with your drinking and all. I think you're good for Sonny. Just wanted you to know."

"Thanks, Vic."

He fooled around with a sixteen-pound shotput for a while. He'd thrown it when he was a freshman. I let a few more spears fly. Then we took a few laps and headed for the showers.

"About that night in Vegas, Hoag. When I went a little crazy. Sorry I got you involved."

"The guy asked for it. Forget it."

"I . . . I just lose control sometimes. You know the old expression 'seeing red'? Well, I do. Everything in front of me goes red. And my head feels real tight and I can't hear anything except for this pounding. And then I black out. I'm okay most of the time. But, hey, if it wasn't for Sonny, I'd be living on tranks at the VA hospital on Sawtelle."

"I understand you once . . ."

He frowned. "Once what?"

"Went a little too far."

"Sonny tell you that?"

"Yes."

"You're not putting that in the book, are you?"

"Did it happen because of Sonny?"

"Sort of. This guy was making crummy comments one night at the Daisy Club about Wanda. Real awful stuff about that Black Panther she was mixed up with. I let him have it, and his head hit something by accident. That was . . . that was a very painful episode for me, Hoag. Can't you leave it out?"

He began to breathe heavily and to rub his forehead with the palm of his hand, rub it so hard I thought he'd make it bleed.

"I certainly wouldn't want to cause you any grief," I assured him. "Why don't I talk to Sonny about it. See what he thinks."

Vic's big shoulders relaxed. "That's okay. I'll talk to him."

"You sure? I don't mind."

"It's my problem, not yours. Thanks anyway."

"Okay, Vic."

He finished dressing before I did.

"I'm going over to the office to say hello to some people," he droned. "I'll put the spears in the car. Meet you there in a bit."

I told him that would be fine and sat down on the bench to put on my shoes. I was bending over to tie them when a shadow crossed over me, the shadow of a large human life-form. I thought Vic had come back, but it wasn't Vic. It was somebody else's bodyguard. It was Gabe Knight's bodyguard.

The French ambassador-to-be was sitting in the stands. Had been, I gathered, the whole time we were out there on the field. Gabe had aged very nicely. His sandy hair was still only partly flecked with gray, his blue eyes were clear and bright, his build trim and athletic. He wore a shawl-collared, oyster-gray cardigan, plaid shirt, gray flannel slacks, and tasseled loafers. He looked every inch the elegant Hollywood squire.

He shook my hand and smiled. It was a warm, reassuring, confident smile. It was the smile that always got him the girls in the old movies. And doubtless still did. "Stewart Hoag, isn't it?" He didn't wait for my nod. "Have a seat. Please. I won't keep you long. I wouldn't want Sonny's gorilla to miss you."

Gabe's own gorilla waited discreetly on the steps to the field. I sat.

Gabe gazed out at the campus. "Takes me back, being here. We shot the *BMOC* exteriors here, you know. It was the rainy season, just like this. Of course, Pauley Pavilion wasn't here. Nor were those dormitories. This was a sleepy little place." He turned his gaze on me. "I suppose you weren't even born."

"Not quite."

"I've been reading the newspaper stories, of course. Did he really punch that reporter?"

"No."

"Is he really drinking again?"

"No."

"I'm happy to hear that. I was concerned." He tugged at his ear. "I decided it was time we had a talk, young friend. I've known Arthur's been working on a book. Naturally, I'm all for it."

"You are?"

"Surprised?"

"Seldom."

"There isn't as much hostility between us as everyone thinks. Arthur and I simply went our separate ways. Life has been plenty good to both of us."

"Maybe a little better to you."

Gabe shrugged. "I bear him no grudge."

"The feeling isn't mutual. He told me if I talked to you, I was fired, actually."

"I'm sorry to hear that. I guess I shouldn't be surprised. I know he's had his problems. Isolated himself up in that armed fortress of his. I suppose he's still dwelling on the old days. More than is healthy, perhaps." He pursed his lips. "I was hoping to get some idea from you about how you would be handling me."

"Through his eyes," I replied. "So far it's a pretty flattering portrait. He said you were the best straight man in the business."

"He said that?" Gabe seemed startled, and pleased. "Well, I'll be."

"He also said he could never admit that before."

"That's rich." Gabe chuckled. "That is rich, isn't it?"

"I wouldn't know. I didn't know him in the old days."

"I did," he said quietly. Then he cleared his throat and said, "Let's cut the bullshit. I want to know about the breakup. How will it be portrayed?"

"I don't know yet. He hasn't said a word to me about it."

"You mean you don't know why it happened?"

"That's correct."

"You wouldn't by any chance be jerking me around, would you?"

"I am not," I replied. "Would you like to tell me about it?"

"That, there's very little chance of."

"I'm assuming it wasn't over Sonny's gambling debts," I ventured.

"I'll let him be the one to tell you. I'll be interested to see how he handles it. Very interested." His eyes were on the empty field.

"Nervous?"

"Not if I can avoid it," he replied sharply.

"All I know is, he's being very frank so far. It'll be an honest book." I glanced over at him. "Death threat notwithstanding."

Gabe raised an eyebrow. "Death threat? Oh, yes, there was something in the papers about that," he said very offhandedly. "What did this threat say?"

"Not to write it – or else."

"Any idea who . . . ?"

"I thought maybe it was you."

He chuckled, low and rich. "Was it a phone call?"

"Letter. Why?"

"What were the exact words?"

"I didn't see it."

"Did anyone? Aside from Arthur, I mean."

"No. He destroyed it."

"Hmm. Far be it from me to tell you your business, young friend, but you ought to bear in mind that Arthur may have made the entire thing up."

"Made it up?"

"I've known the man for forty-five years. Believe me, he is not above concocting fables to make people do what he wants them to do."

"What can he hope to gain by fabricating this?"

"Publicity," Gabe replied simply.

I turned that one over. It didn't sound totally wild. Sonny *had* told me he needed a shot in the arm. The threat *had* found its way into the papers. Could he have rigged it himself to hype the book?

"Then again," said Gabe, stroking his chin, "it's also possible he *believes* he has been threatened, only he *hasn't* been. Arthur and paranoia happen to be boon companions, you know." Gabe reached into his billfold and pulled out a card and handed it to me. It was his card. "I'd like for us to talk again. I'd like to be kept informed along the way. And I'd love to see a copy of what you're doing."

"I don't think it would be a good idea."

"Call it a professional courtesy. Perhaps I'll be able to do you a favor sometime."

"My own château in the Loire Valley?"

"My company is always looking for talented writers to do screenplays."

"I don't know how to do screenplays."

"If you can write a book, you can write a screenplay." He stood, stretched his long legs. "It's Arthur's birthday today, isn't it? I always remember it. Always. I don't call or send a card. But I do remember." He shook his blond head. "I still love that little son of a bitch, you know that? We went through heaven and hell together. Nothing can ever take that away." Gabe seemed very far away for a second. Then he glanced back down at me. "An honest book, you said."

"That's right."

"You might want to reconsider that."

"Another professional courtesy?"

"It isn't a pretty world we live in, young friend. Honesty is not always the best policy. Do I make myself clear?"

I went right back to the typewriter when Vic and I got home. It was peaceful working out there in the guesthouse, Lulu snoozing under my chair with her head on my foot. I was used to the quiet now. I was even getting to like it. What I didn't like was Gabe's popping up to issue his cordial, tasteful threats and his unsettling suggestions. *Had* Sonny made up the death threat?

I had been working about an hour when Vic burst into the guesthouse. He was perspiring heavily.

"He should be home by now, Hoag."

"Maybe his shrink was running late."

"I called there. He left over two hours ago."

"Maybe he went to visit Connie."

"I called her at the studio. She hasn't seen him." He paced back and forth, wringing his hands. Back. Forth. Back. Forth. "I should call the police. I'm *gonna* call the police."

"If it turns out to be nothing – "

"He'll kill me, I know. But I don't know what else to *do*, Hoag. I shouldn't have let him go by himself. I *knew* it."

Just then Vic's beeper sounded. Someone had triggered the front gate. He tore out of the guesthouse and double-timed it to the main house.

Lulu and I followed at a more gracious pace. By the time we got to the house, Sonny was pulling up in the limo, which seemed to be considerably muddier than it had been when he left.

He got out, wearing a nervous, boyish grin. "How you guys doing, huh?" he asked cheerfully.

Vic cried, "Sonny, where the hell have you – "

"Took a drive up through Topanga Canyon. Felt like being by myself for a while. Relax, I'm fine. Totally fine. Just lost track of the time, okay?" Sonny kneeled on the grass to rub Lulu's ears. There were small, fresh scratches all over the back of his hands, as if he'd been tussling with a kitten. "How *you* doing, Hoagy?"

"Other than having a caged lion in my room with me," I replied, indicating Vic, "I'm quite well."

"You should have called me, Sonny," said Vic.

"Who are you – my mother?"

"I was worried."

"You *are* my mother. Calm down. Everything's cool."

I went back to the typewriter, but I found it hard to concentrate now. Sonny hadn't fooled me. Not with his yarn about taking a scenic drive to who knows where. Not with his cheery front. Not with any of it. I knew him too well now.

Something had shaken Sonny. Shaken him but good.

Sonny kept the front up all evening. We spent it celebrating his birthday quietly at home. Wanda made it a point not to be around – she was off in Baja visiting friends. Connie came by and fixed him his favorite dinner – her Southern-fried chicken with mashed potatoes, gravy, and greens. He ate three platefuls, smacked his lips, and pronounced it the greatest meal he'd ever eaten in his entire life.

After dinner he opened his presents. Connie's wasn't ready yet. She apologized. He assured her that her belief in him was a greater gift than he deserved. Vic gave him one of those fancy new rowing machines. Sonny tried it out right there on the floor of the study like a gleeful kid on Christmas morning.

My gift was out on the patio – a small, potted eucalyptus tree, suitable for planting.

Sonny gaped at it for a full minute before he broke down and cried. "God bless ya, Hoagy," he blubbered, throwing me in a smothering bear hug. "God bless ya."

As a special treat, we got to watch Sonny's infamous 1962 tour de farce, *Moider, Inc.* I had never seen it before. Few people had – the studio pulled it out of release after only a week. I was sorry to see it now. It was juvenile, tasteless, and self-indulgent. Gabe hadn't been there to rein Sonny in. One of the five roles he played in it was that of a temperamental crime czar whose name was – I swear – Sudsy Beagle.

But it was his birthday, so I laughed all the way through it. We all laughed, and we all agreed with him when he said "the public just wasn't ready for it." Then it was time for Connie to head home. Sonny proclaimed this the greatest birthday of his entire life.

Lulu had finally forgiven me for not taking her to Vegas. She consented to curl up next to me when I climbed into bed to read some E. B. White. And when I shut off the light, she circled my pillow several times and assumed her customary position with a contented grunt.

Her barking woke me in the middle of the night. Followed by laughter. The laughter was coming from the foot of my bed. I flicked on the bedside light to find Sonny standing there swaying, red-faced, giggling to himself.

"What's going on, Sonny?" I mumbled.

"Have a drink with me, pally. Huh? All alone. No fun to drink alone. Not like it used ta be. Used ta drink with Francis. Dino. Ring-a-ding-ding." He laughed. "And Gabe." He stopped laughing. Now he looked sad. He began to hum their theme song. Then he went into an unsteady version of the soft shoe he and Gabe did when they played down-on-their-luck vaudevillians in *Baggy Pants*. He danced and hummed his way from one side of the bed to the other, clutching an invisible cane. Abruptly, he stopped. "Have a drink with me."

"I'm putting you to bed."

I started to get up. He shoved me back down with a hairy paw.

"Whassa matter, don't like me no more?" he demanded, sticking out his chin like a bullyboy.

"No, I just don't believe in pouring gasoline on a fire."

"Oooooh," he sneered, swaying. "Whassat, writer talk? Well, don't get upper crusty with me. I'm Sonny Day, ya hear me? I hired ya. I can fire ya, ya . . . ya dickless, washed-up son of a bitch!"

"I see you're very sensitive when you're sloshed."

"Don't like what ya see? Huh? Don't like it? Well, that's tough." He thumped himself on the chest with his fist. "I'm the *real* me now.

Take a good look. Time you see for yourself. See who I am."

"And who are you?"

"I'm trouble. I'm pain. I'm . . . I'm not a very nice person, is who I am."

"Could have fooled me the other night. That was a good talk we had in your hotel room."

"That was *bullshit*. Total bullshit. Need ya happy. Need a good book outta ya. Need a best-seller. Need this."

He sat down heavily on the bed. Lulu jumped off and scratched at the door. She wanted out. I didn't blame her. I got up and opened the door.

Sonny sat there, hunched, staring at his bare feet.

"What happened, Sonny?"

"The limo . . ."

"What about the limo?"

"Somebody . . . they left something in it when I was at the shrink. Freaked me. Freaked me good," he moaned.

"What was it?"

He stuck out his lower lip.

"Tell me," I ordered.

"Ages ago . . . I-I had this dummy made up, see? Of Sonny. Sonny-size. Sonny. Looked like Sonny. Just like him. Used to keep him behind my desk at Warners after they gave me and Gabe offices. A gag, see? Clothes and all. Only somebody, they ripped him off. And . . . and . . . today, there he was, waiting for me behind the wheel of the limo!"

"How do you know it's the exact same dummy?"

"His head. On his head h-he had on my beanie. My beanie from *BMOC*."

"The cap you wore. I remember it."

"That was ripped off years ago, too, see?" Tears began to stream down Sonny's face. "A cigar in his mouth, he had. A-A *lit* cigar. And . . . and . . ."

"And what?"

"Holes in his chest. Like from bullets. Fake blood all over him. I'm freaking, Hoagy. I'm freaking. Never been so . . ."

"What did you do with him . . . it?"

"Took him away. To Topanga. Pulled off on a fire road and found some twigs and sticks. Lots of twigs and sticks. And burned him. Had to. Couldn't look at him. Couldn't."

That explained the muddy car and the scratches on his hands. Maybe.

"Was the car locked when you were at the shrink?"

He shook his head. "Parking garage. People around."

"Sonny, why won't you call the police?"

He didn't answer me.

"Do you know who's doing all of this? Is that it?"

He shrugged the question off, like a chill. "Got anything to drink out here, Hoagy boy?"

"You took my bottle away, remember?"

He winked at me. "How about the ol' bottle in the drawer, huh?"

"There isn't one."

"C'mon, all you writers got a bottle in the drawer."

He stumbled toward the desk and started to rummage through the drawers, throwing out notebooks, tapes, transcripts, manuscript pages.

"Stop that, Sonny. There's no bottle in there." I put on my dressing gown. "Come on, I'm putting you to bed."

But he kept looking. He even threw open the shallow middle drawer and started digging around in it. That's when he found Gabe's card. I could tell when he spotted it. His body stiffened and then he recoiled from the drawer in horror, as if he'd just found a severed human hand in there,

"You son of a *bitch*!" he screamed, pelting me with flying spittle. "You been going behind my back! Telling him everything! Selling me out!"

"No, Sonny. I haven't."

"You *have*!"

I grabbed him by the shoulders. "Listen to me! Gabe approached *me* today. He wanted to know what the book was about. I told him nothing. That's all. Do you hear me? That's *all*."

"So why ya got his *card*?! Why ya hiding his damn *card*?!"

"I saved it for my files. Throw it away. Go ahead."

I took it out of the drawer and gave it to him. He stood there clutching it, frozen with rage. Then he fell to his knees and began to wail. Gut-wrenching sobs came out of him, ugly sobs of hurt, of self-pity. I couldn't tell if this was an act or not. If it was, it was better than anything he ever did on screen.

"I bared my soul for you!" he cried. "Gave you my love! And look what ya done to me! *Look what ya done!*"

"Sonny – "

"I wanna die! I wanna die! Oh, please. Let me die!" He jumped up and went for the bathroom. "Gotta have a razor blade! Gotta die!"

I ran after him. "Sonny, for God's sake stop this! You don't want to die!"

"Razor!" He grabbed the leather shaving kit Merilee had bought me in Florence on our honeymoon and dumped the contents on the floor. Bottles smashed. "Razor!"

"It's no use," I said. "They're Good News! disposables. The head pivots."

Frustrated, he tore the kit apart and hurled the pieces against the wall. Then he grabbed the shower curtain and yanked it off the rod and plopped down on the toilet amidst it, rocking back and forth like a bereaved widow, moaning.

I headed for the phone.

"Where ya going?!"

"To wake up Vic."

"No, don't!" There was fear in his voice now. "Please! He'll be mad at me!"

"He won't be alone."

"Do it and you're fired!"

I phoned Vic and quickly filled him in. Instantly alert, he said he'd be right out.

"Okay, Hoag," Sonny said, quietly now. "That's it. You're fired. I warned ya. Stay away from Gabe, I said. But no. Ya wouldn't. Get off my property. You and your smelly dog. Take your stuff and git. You're through."

"I *am* through. But you're not firing me. I'm quitting. You hear me? I quit."

Vic came rushing in now, brandishing a hypodermic. Sonny screamed when he saw him and tried to fight his way out of the bathroom cursing, flailing, sobbing. Vic wrestled him to the floor. Still he continued to writhe and thrash.

"Pin his arms, Hoag," Vic ordered, his face set grimly. "Pin 'em."

I did. Sonny rewarded me by spitting in my face. Vic gave him the injection.

"Doctor gave me this in case this ever happened again," Vic told me. "It used to happen almost every night. He'll quiet down in a few minutes. Sorry you had to see it."

I wiped off my face with a towel and began to pack.

I booked the last seat on the noon flight to New York. Said good-bye to Vic. Left Wanda a note, asking for a rain check on our dinner date. A cab picked me up at the gate.

I didn't say good-bye to Sonny. He was still out cold.

I made it to the airport. Got my ticket. Read the national edition of *The New York Times*. Got on the plane. Apologetically stowed Lulu under me in her carrier. Fastened my seat belt.

I'd had enough of Sonny Day and his creep show. I was going home. I really was. The stewardesses were even closing the doors.

Until The One bulled his way on board.

He wore terry sweats and shades. He found me immediately.

"Where the fuck you think you're going?!" he demanded. Heads swiveled.

"Home," I replied calmly.

"You can't. We're not done."

"I'm done."

"Nobody quits on Sonny Day!"

"I am."

"You son of a bitch! You're nothing but trouble. I wish I never hired ya!"

"I wish I'd never met you."

"You're a fucking coward!"

"You," I returned, "are a fucking asshole."

"I hate your fucking guts!"

"Fuck you!"

"Fuck you!"

We went on at this mature level – at the top of our lungs – for quite a while, everyone on the plane watching and listening. And most of them recognizing Sonny.

A jumpy steward sidled over to us and cleared his throat. "What seems to be the problem, gentlemen?"

"Creative differences!" I told him.

"This is your idea of creative differences?!" screamed Sonny. "Getting on a fucking plane?!"

"Gentlemen, perhaps you could deplane and continue this – "

"All right, I unfire ya!" shrieked Sonny, ignoring him. "Okay?!"

"You can't unfire me, Sonny. You didn't fire me in the first place. I quit. I'm leaving. Understand?"

"Uh, gentlemen – "

"You're not leaving! Nobody's leaving until you do. This plane is not leaving this goddamn airport until you get off it!"

"Okay. Fine. You want to make a jackass out of yourself, get yourself arrested for air piracy, go right ahead. You doubt me. You abuse me. You actually, literally, spit in my face. As far as I'm concerned, people have been right about you all along – you are a pig."

His face got all scrunched up. Tears formed in his eyes. "Please, Hoagy," he pleaded softly. "Come back. I need you."

"No."

"I panicked last night. I ran out of courage. I wish I had enough, but I don't. I'm a frightened man. A sick man. I lost control. Poison came out of me. Those things I said, I didn't mean 'em. That's not how I feel. I love you like a son. I'd never intentionally hurt you. It was the booze. It won't happen again. You got my word. It won't happen again. We're both vulnerable. We're both human beings. Human beings forgive. Come on. Come back."

When we got home from the airport, we planted the eucalyptus tree outside his study window.

CHAPTER
SEVEN

(Tape #1 with Harmon Wright. Recorded in his office on the 12th floor at HWA on February 25. It is decorated in French provincial antique furniture, which appears genuine. He is tall, wiry, tanned. Hair is white. Wears gold-framed glasses, Brooks Brothers gray flannel suit.)

Hoag: I appreciate your giving me this time.

Wright: Anything for Artie. He called, by the way. Told me to hold nothing back.

Hoag: Terrific. He's already filled me in on your old neighborhood, on the Seetags –

Wright: The what? Oh, our old club. Sure.

Hoag: And on your past associations . . .

Wright: Associations? Did he bring up that old Benny Siegel business?

Hoag: Yes, he did.

Wright: Take what Artie says with a grain of salt. I was never in jail, or technically in the actual employ of Benny Siegel. I knew him. But lots of people did.

Hoag: What about the money?

Wright: Money?

Hoag: He told me about the money you siphoned off to start this agency. Should I take that with a grain of salt, too?

Wright: (silence) When is this book coming out anyway?

Hoag: Next fall, probably. I'll take that as a yes. You *were* out here in Los Angeles when they were filming *At Ease*?

Wright: I was fresh out of law school and interested in getting into the field of talent management. Artie and I happened to bump into each other on the lot. Naturally, I was surprised as hell. I mean, Mel Rabinowitz's fat kid brother – who would have figured? But I watched some of the filming, and I was very impressed. They had something, those two kids. They were like Abbott and Costello, only with class. Gabe had the class. Artie . . . Artie was a comic genius. You know they never had a flop? Every picture they made together made money.

Hoag: What happened when they got out of the service?

Wright: I grabbed Jack Warner by the short and curlies and didn't let go. He wanted to sign them to three pictures at $25,000 per. I said one picture, for $50,000, then we cut a new deal. He called me a fucking greaseball a couple times and hung up on me. I waited for him to come crawling back. I waited one day. Two days. Three days. I was gambling with their future, but I figured, worse comes to worst, I'll put them on the nightclub circuit. I was about to do just that when Warner came crawling. Gabe and Lorraine rented a little house in Studio City. Lovely girl. Wasn't suited for the show business life. Artie took an apartment in Encino. And they made *BMOC*, their college picture. That's where he and Connie met. It was a good picture. First one to use their theme song. As soon as they wrapped it, I put them together with a top writing team and they came up with a new act. Civilian material. They did personal appearances to push the picture, then turned right around and did the nightclubs. As headliners, too. Only the top clubs – the Chase in St. Louis, Chez Paree in Chicago, Latin Casino in Philly. Sold out every night. Pulling down $3,500 a week. By the time they hit New York it was official – *BMOC* was outgrossing *At Ease*. People loved these boys. I booked them into the Copa for two weeks at $5,000 per. They stayed eight weeks. You couldn't get near the place. Even the big-timers had to pull strings to get in. Jack Warner was panting now. Wanted to sign them up for three pictures for $175,000. I tell him the price is now a half million. Again with the greaseball stuff. So I sent them to the Flamingo. They were one of the first name acts to play there – helped legitimize the place. They played four weeks at $10,000 per. Only, Artie left more than that in the casino. So I brought them back to L.A. and booked them into Slapsie Maxie's. Place was packed with movie people every night. Every studio in town wanted them now. I got the deal I wanted. And I got it from Jack Warner. Their third picture for him, *Jerks*, was another smash. From then on, for the next ten years, the sky was the limit for them. The money came in so fast they were, I think, overwhelmed by it. Remember, they were still boys. Just like today with the rock stars and the tennis players. One day they're a couple snot-nosed kids from some neighborhood. Next day they're pulling down what was the equivalent of twenty million a year today. And Artie, he was everybody's darling, could do no wrong. He started getting crazy with the ego stuff, the competition. They were telling him he was Charlie Chaplin, for God's sake. Whatever Gabe did, Artie had to do better. If Gabe built a new house with six bathrooms, Artie had to build one with seven.

Hoag: Did they socialize? Were they friends?

Wright: No. Gabe liked to move in the A crowd. Artie liked to have a lot of hangers-on around to laugh at everything he said. His boys, he called them. Then after they had their first big row, the blood was always bad between them. It was strictly business after that.

Hoag: Their *first* big row?

Wright: You don't know about that? Okay, this was 1949, I think. Maybe '50. Artie got into serious financial trouble. Big house. Cars. Gambling, like I said. Plus he supported his mom, his entourage, and he was a soft touch. If somebody needed help with hospital bills, you never met a more generous guy. Trouble was, he wasn't paying his taxes. The IRS nailed him for close to half a million. So you know what his solution was? He asked for sixty percent of the take. Everybody kept telling him he carried Gabe. So he figured he should make more. Gabe's response was – fuck you. Gabe had his pride. He was a professional. You think he liked reading in the paper that he was a stiff? You think he liked Artie rubbing it in? For a week the two of them didn't speak. Finally Artie backed down and apologized. Then he turned right around and said if he wasn't going to get more money, then he wanted his name first. Day and Knight. Again Gabe told him to fuck off. It was like that between them from then on. Always. During the whole TV series they were at each other's throats. I remember we were at dinner one night – I had to fly to New York to try to calm things down between them – and Artie ordered a steak and the waiter said, "And for your vegetable?" Artie said, "He'll have the same as me." Gabe walked out of the restaurant.

Hoag: This went on while they were working, too?

Wright: Artie was a monster on the set. Drove people hard. Made them crazy. Gabe was a nice, easy-going guy. Artie hated that Gabe was more popular on the set than he was. So he demanded more credit. He insisted on a head writing-credit on the series. He got it, too. And he would undermine Gabe. If they had a musical guest on, and Gabe was doing a nice duet with him, Artie'd come out on stage and heckle them. Ruin the number. For laughs, of course. But it made Gabe seethe. I remember he used to say to me, I won't go down to his level. Finally he recorded his own album of songs to keep himself sane. It did very well. That drove Artie crazy. After that, they only spoke to each other through the producers, or me. Each would cry his heart out to me. It went on for years. I earned my cut, let me tell you.

Hoag: But they stayed together?

Wright: Underneath, there was a deep relationship there. I don't know, they needed each other. Artie more than Gabe, actually. His work was never as good after they split up.

Hoag: He thinks the public just wasn't ready for it.

Wright: He's right. They weren't ready for total shit. *(silence)* Artie was trying to prove he never needed Gabe. Prove it to the world. Prove it to himself. He lost touch with his character. Lost his confidence. A comic without his confidence it's like a tightrope walker getting scared of heights. He drove his writers away. His friends. Drank too much. Saddest thing was when he broke Connie's heart with that no-good tramp Tracy. Every producer and leading man in town had jerked off on her chest. Sonny, he *married* her. I remember one night my lovely wife Ruthie and I went to dinner with them at Scandia. Through the entire meal he'd stop the conversation, cup Tracy's face in his hand like she was a three-year-old and say, "Is *this* a *face*?" After he did it for the thirtieth time I grabbed Ruthie's face and said, "Whattaya call this, Artie, a sack of shit?" He didn't speak to me for months. Not until she dumped him. Then he called me up in the middle of the night and cried. Artie and I . . . we've been through a lot together. I was never as close to Gabe. He was harder to get to know. And he left the agency after they split up for good. Financially, I got the short end. The joke was on me. A fucking ambassador . . .

Hoag: Can you tell me why it happened? What the famed, mysterious fight at Chasen's was about?

Wright: No mystery to it at all. They were sick to death of each other. They'd been together day and night – no pun intended – for more than fifteen years. They hated each other's guts. It happens.

Hoag: That's it? There's nothing more to it than that?

Wright: That's all it takes. When did you say this book is coming out?

Hoag: Next fall, probably. Say, you may not realize it, but I happen to be one of your clients myself.

Wright: You don't say. Small world. What did you say your name was again?

(end tape)

(Tape #1 with Connie Morgan. Recorded February 26 in her dressing room at the Burbank Studio, where she is filming the TV series Santa Fe. *She knits a muffler.)*

Morgan: It's Arthur's birthday present. I couldn't finish it in time. It's an exact copy of the scarf he wore in *BMOC*.

Hoag: He'll be thrilled. What happened to the original?

Morgan: Wardrobe took it back.

Hoag: I seem to remember he also wore a beanie cap in that.

Morgan: Yes, he did. That he kept.

Hoag: Do you happen to remember where?

Morgan: Where? In a trunk someplace, I believe. He'd know where it is, if you're really interested in seeing it.

Hoag: Do you remember his having a dummy of himself?

Morgan: (laughs) In his office, of course. Gabe threw it off a cliff. (silence) You've gotten awfully serious.

Hoag: Do you know what happened to it?

Morgan: Is it important?

Hoag: Possibly.

Morgan: Someone stole it off the lot. How are you two getting on?

Hoag: We have our ups and downs.

Morgan: One does.

Hoag: He's unpredictable.

Morgan: Arthur learned long ago that he can keep people off guard that way. Make them accommodate him. If you're wondering when you'll hit the core . . .

Hoag: I am.

Morgan: I've known him forty years and I'm not sure I have.

Hoag: You met on *BMOC*.

Morgan: Yes. I'd had a few bits, but it was my first real part. A scout had seen me in a play at the University of Virginia. I came out here for a test and Warners put me under contract.

Hoag: First impressions?

Morgan: I remember Gabe seemed very nice. He was a polite young man, very handsome, a bit stunned by what was happening to them. He was inclined to be modest about it. Arthur was the opposite. He never stopped bragging or jumping up and down or cracking a joke. He had as much energy as three people. He was almost like a little boy, the way he was constantly looking for approval. To this day, I've never met anyone who so badly needs approval.

Hoag: Were you attracted to him?

Morgan: It was more . . . You see, I was essentially playing myself in *BMOC*. I was a campus beauty queen at Virginia. Boys had always stammered when they talked to me. Or tried to put a move on me. Or just stared. Arthur, he teased me right from the beginning. Badgered me, called me names such as Bones and Stretch. He treated me like absolute garbage, in the sweetest possible way of course. I loved it. Finally, after about a week of shooting, he came up to me on the set and said, "Listen, Bones, me and Gabe and a few of d'udders decided youse is an unstable pain in the behind and somebody's gonna have to give ya a good fucking or the picture's goin' inta the toilet."

Hoag: You're kidding.

Morgan: It's true. I swear. He said, "So's we drew straws." I said, "And you won?" And he said, "No, I *lost*." If it had been anybody else, I'd have slugged him. But Arthur . . . it was his way of saying I think you're pretty terrific and I wish I had the nerve to ask you out.

Hoag: You went out with him.

Morgan: I hadn't met too many nice guys. One doesn't here. And I wouldn't go to the parties. He took me to Ocean Park. We went on the rides. We ate cotton candy. I felt as if I were back in high school. He was so nervous he never stopped talking. He talked about how much money he was going to make. He talked about how he was going to bring his mother out. He talked about –

Hoag: His father?

Morgan: No. Not for months. Not until he was absolutely positive I loved him. At the end of our first evening together he fell to his knees and proposed to me. He did that every single time we saw each other, which got to be more and more often. I finally said yes about six months later, when he and Gabe were on the road. Gabe was his best man.

Hoag: Were you happy together?

Morgan: At first, yes. He adored me. I thought he was the sweetest man in the world. Plus, life was more fun when Sonny Day was around. The problem got to be that he wasn't around enough. He and Gabe were either shooting a movie fourteen hours a day or they were on the road. And Arthur was very old-fashioned. Once Wanda was born, he insisted I quit the business and stay home to raise her. So I was stuck at home with his mother, who moved in with us when we bought our first house in Pacific Palisades.

Hoag: Did you get along with her?

Morgan: As well as anyone could. She was a nasty, horrible woman. I hate to say it, but it's the truth.

Hoag: I didn't get that impression from him.

Morgan: One wouldn't. But she never stopped picking on him, belittling him, telling him what a bum his father had been and how he was no better.

Hoag: When did the two of you start having problems?

Morgan: Pretty early on. I wanted more from him. I wanted a relationship. But I was little more than a trophy for Arthur. He preferred to spend his free time with his boys – playing cards, going to the racetrack. And when he was in Vegas with Gabe, they . . . they slept with women. Many women. I caught him once when he came back. He left a package of condoms out on his dresser. Maybe so I'd catch him. I was furious. He started crying. He said he didn't deserve me, that he was born in the gutter and belonged there. He offered to move out. He even started to pack. He made *me* beg *him* to stay. And I did, even though I was the injured party.

Hoag: The other women – you were jealous?

Morgan: Of course, though he insisted most of the time he didn't even want them, that *they* wanted *him*, and that he couldn't get over that. He's very insecure about his appearance. Gabe was the one who was conquest-minded. If he saw a pretty girl walk by in a restaurant – Lorraine sitting right there with him, mind you – he'd excuse himself, intercept her in the lounge, and get her phone number. Arthur would never do something like that. Lorraine didn't take it for very long. She divorced Gabe after two years.

Hoag: Did you consider divorcing Sonny back then?

Morgan: I was brought up to believe that if there were problems with a marriage, they were the woman's fault. It took me a lot of years to get past that. And then there was Wanda to consider. Do you know what he wanted to name her? Stormy. Stormy Day. I had to put my foot down. She was a happy baby. A beautiful baby. You've never seen a man love a child as much as he loved Wanda. When she began to walk, we moved down to Malibu so he could take her for walks on the beach in the morning before he left for the studio. He'd go down there at dawn and sprinkle shells along the sand for her to find – just so he could see the look of delight on her face. I think she was the only real joy in his life. He was devastated when she began to have problems.

Hoag: Which was when?

Morgan: After we moved back from New York. She was about eight. She became sullen and withdrawn. Cried a lot. The doctors thought it was from having such an unstable home life moving back and forth cross-country, her father gone so often, and such an up-and-down presence when he was around. Arthur was convinced it was his fault, that he was somehow getting what he deserved. Totally self-centered response, of course.

Hoag: Tell me about the move to New York.

Morgan: I was for it. I thought if he did the series he'd be home more. At least it meant thirty-nine weeks out of the year he wouldn't be on the road. Becoming a big TV star in New York was more a fulfillment of Arthur's fantasies than anything he ever did. He lived in the Waldorf. He got the best tables at the best nightclubs. He got his name in the newspaper columns right next to Caesar, to Berle, to Gleason. He was in heaven.

Hoag: And you?

Morgan: I didn't like living in a hotel. He suggested we get a place in Connecticut, where we could unwind. I found us a lovely little cottage on a few acres. The idea was he'd come out on weekends. Only there were no weekends. We owned the place for three years and he never saw it. Not once. Wanda and I lived there by ourselves. She started school there. He stayed in the city, working eighteen hours a day, nightclubbing the other six. And then when he and Gabe had their thirteen weeks off in the summer, it was back to L.A. to do a movie. I'd say to him, why don't you let up, why do you drive yourself so hard? He'd say, "I gotta grab it while I can, baby."

Hoag: So you hardly ever saw him.

Morgan: Or talked to him. When he called me at the farm, it was to ask about Wanda or kvetch about Gabe. They fought over money, over billing, over everything. Arthur never understood that Gabe had feelings. After four seasons, Gabe couldn't take doing the series anymore. Arthur couldn't keep up the pace either. He pushed himself so hard he put himself in the hospital. So they quit the show. We all moved back to Malibu. That's when things really started to turn bad.

Hoag: How so?

Morgan: Wanda, as I mentioned. And Arthur's mother died. That seemed to set Arthur loose. He started running with a rougher crowd. He became big pals with Frank Sinatra, who is not a positive influence on any man. And he had his first serious affair. It was with a young bombshell-slash-actress named Jayne Mansfield. He met her in New York. One thing led to another. This was different than what had gone on before. This was a steady thing that went on for several months. I read about their affair in a gossip column. He didn't deny it. We went through the ritual of his packing his bags again, only this time I didn't beg him to stay. He moved into a hotel for a while. Until they broke up. Then I took him back. For Wanda's sake. But by then our marriage was a complete travesty. We went more than two years without having sex.

Hoag: He told me.

Morgan: You're referring to the talk you two had in Vegas about your sexual dysfunction. He's very excited and proud that you confided in him. He hasn't many close friends anymore.

Hoag: He said you had become more of a mother to him.

Morgan: He rebelled against me. Began to run around with the trampiest girls in town. For a long time I put up with it. So many other things kept us together. There was Wanda's condition. There was his breakup with Gabe. He worked even harder after that – writing, directing. Then he took up with Tracy. She was that year's hot sex kitten – 1965, I think it was. He flaunted it. He had his picture taken in the newspaper, nibbling on her ear in some nightclub. He took her to Vegas with him. That was it for me. I wasn't going to pick up the pieces for him anymore. I moved out. I offered a home to Wanda, but we'd lost control of her by then. She moved in with that French director and began to support herself as a model. She was all of eighteen. I went back to work. It was a frightening, difficult time for me, but I survived. I enjoy my work. I guess it's my life now. *People* magazine voted me America's favorite mom last year, did you know that? It's silly, I suppose, but it's the biggest honor I've ever gotten.

Hoag: About Sonny and Gabe. Can we talk about their breakup?

Morgan: What about it?

Hoag: The fight in Chasen's, to be specific.

Morgan: *(silence)* I've given that a lot of thought.

Hoag: And?

Morgan: My feeling is if Arthur wants to put it in his book, it's his decision. But he'll have to be the one to reveal it. I'm not going to talk to you about it.

Hoag: Why?

Morgan: Because I'd rather it never come out.

Hoag: Harmon Wright said it was nothing more than the fact they were sick of each other.

Morgan: Harmon Wright is paid to say things like that.

(end tape)

(Tape #6 with Sonny Day. Recorded in his study, February 27.)

Day: Vic keeps bugging me about the time he clocked that guy in the Daisy Club. Whattaya think, should it go in the book?

Hoag: Not if it will hurt him. Why? Do you have a strong feeling?

Day: I wanna use it. I got a lot of bad press over that. I don't wanna hurt him, neither. He knows that. Just gotta know how to handle him. So what'd Heshie and Connie say about me?

Hoag: Want to hear the tapes?

Day: No, I'll wait for the paperback.

Hoag: I got the impression you were pretty crazed.

Day: Not *pretty* crazed. *Crazed.* Work. Booze. Pills. Girls. I'll tell you something though – know what drove me the most in those days? Fear. Fear that it would disappear and I'd be right back where I was before the war. So I pushed, pushed, pushed. Everybody started calling me Little Hitler. Cussing me out behind my back. Sure, I started getting involved in the writing. Why not? It was my ass on the line. Sure, I wanted credit for it. Who wouldn't? Sure, I wanted more money than Gabe. Why not? I was there all day, knocking heads with the writers, trying to make it work. He was playing golf. Or recording an album behind my back. They said I kept a lot of my boys on the payroll. Bullshit. I was giving some young writers a break. Three of 'em have gone on to win Emmys so far. They said I *needed* to be surrounded by stooges. Bullshit. Who says I can't pick my own friends? Give some putz a newspaper column and he thinks it gives him the right to psychoanalyze ya. Judge ya. I was living out the American dream. What's wrong with that? Okay, I built this huge place. I owned twelve cars. A few extra pairs of shoes. So what? I earned 'em. I didn't hurt nobody. I didn't judge nobody. But *they* judged *me.* They said I was ego mad. They said I was a fucking nut. They said I couldn't get along with Gabe. Sure, Gabe and I fought. Who doesn't? Abbott and Costello fought. The Ritz brothers fought. Martin and fucking Lewis fought. Anytime you care, anytime you got something at stake, you fight. It's easy to get along when you're both going nowhere. It's a breeze. Ya can sit around together broke and agree about everything. Every single fucking . . . *(silence)* Sorry, Hoagy. Whew, all I need is the two metal balls, huh?

Hoag: Next birthday.

Day: Plant looks great out there. Love sitting here and looking at it.

Hoag: I'm glad.

Day: Besides, me and Gabe didn't fight all the time. Especially early on. That first public appearance tour, after *BMOC* came out.

The kids went crazy. They'd rush the stage. They'd hang around outside the hotel, waiting for us to come out. We'd put on disguises and slip right by 'em. One time I dressed up like Marlene Dietrich. Some salesman tried to pick me up in the elevator. I clobbered him with my purse. Knocked him right on his keister. Gabe, he'd dress up like an old man. White wig. Cane. It was fun. But the real fun was Vegas. Vegas was always laughs. No wives. Gambling. Booze. Broads. We'd go up to the rooms and have horror shows like you wouldn't believe. You name it, we did it. And on stage, we was dynamite. We came up with some new routines – about our childhoods, about being young fathers. Whatever we tried, it worked. And the movies just kept pulling 'em in. *Jerks*. Then *Hayride*. *Ship to Shore*. We couldn't miss. Except at home. Lorraine dumped Gabe. Connie kept complaining I wasn't around enough, that she felt stifled and ignored. And I didn't get to see enough of Wanda. She was such a joy to me, a little blond bundle of joy. She was so lovely, in such a *fragile* kinda way. I was afraid she'd crack if I squeezed her too tight. I wished I could be around her more.

Hoag: That's partly why you did the TV show in New York?

Day: That was for blood money. I owed the IRS. What the hell – I had it, I spent it. Gabe got socked by Lorraine for an alimony you wouldn't believe. They gave us a fortune to do that show. We never saw a dime of it, neither of us. But I had this thing in my mind – you wasn't a real success until you licked New York. And the guys who were big in TV there – Caesar, Berle – they was taken a lot more seriously by critics than me and Gabe. Us, we was considered lowbrow. Anyway, we was approached in – I guess it was '51 – about doing this comedy-variety thing for Lucky Strikes on CBS. It was a helluva deal, so we went back East and we licked New York. Did great stuff on that show. Better than Broadway, and a new one every week. Got great ratings, too. Only problem was the critics still hated us.

Hoag: It was done live?

Day: No retakes. You wanna talk pressure? Hoo, boy. Know where we did it? The same theater on West Fifty-third where the army sent us when we joined *You're in the Army*. That was home for the next four years. We had suites at the Waldorf where we'd pass out for a couple of hours, but we lived at that theater. I'm still proud of that show. We had top people. Goody Ace was our head writer. We hired him away from Berle. Later on, we brought in John Grant when he split up with Abbott and Costello. We had Selma Diamond writing for us, god rest her soul. I bought the first sketch Woody Allen ever sold to TV – about a guy with a mother complex who's in love with his lady analyst. Peggy Cass played both parts. Fucking hysterical. What a troupe we had. Me, Gabe, Peggy, Dick Van Dyke – who was practically still in diapers – Freddy Gwynn, Morty Gunty, god rest his soul. And guest stars like you wouldn't believe. Basil Rathbone. Ronald Colman. I remember one time we had Charles Laughton and Elsa Lanchester on, and we made 'em do a nursery-school sketch with us where we all crawled around on our hands and knees. We'd have a musical guest, too. Ethel Merman, Patti Page. Gabe'd do a couple of numbers with 'em. We'd work 'em into the sketches if we could. It was wild. We'd have a format, but this was *live*. Halfway into the hour the format went right out the window. A couple of times we ran out of time right in the middle of something. Mitch Miller, our bandleader, he'd go into our theme song and that was it – off the air we went, still talking. I'd want to collapse, but I was too wired. So I'd hit Lindy's. Everytime I walked in I'd spritz Gleason with a seltzer bottle. Pretty soon it got so he's carrying a water pistol so he'd be ready for it. We'd go at it right there in the restaurant, like kids. Then Silvers got one. We were like gunslingers. The three of us even talked about doing a western picture together – *Last Stand at Lindy's*. After Lindy's we'd all hit the Copa, the Trocadero, the Stork, finish off with a steak at Danny's at about five a.m. I'd pass out for two hours, show up Tuesday morning – exhausted, hung over – and guess what? We got a whole new show to do, and nothing but blank pages staring at us.

Hoag: Your relationship with Gabe deteriorated?

Day: We didn't talk. It bothered both of us, but we couldn't seem to live any other way. Then he met Vicki, his second wife. Suddenly, he don't want to work so hard. We *did* fight about that. The staff and the crew took Gabe's side, even though I was the one putting food in their mouths while he was off making records. This happened – let's see – this was the third season. I was seriously crazed by then. Drinking a bottle a night. Taking pills to sleep, to wake up. Eating like a horse. I was totally excessive. In everything. It finally broke me in the fourth season. I collapsed right on the air. People laughed. They thought it was a gag. I was dying. Had to be taken to the hospital. I was in bed for a month with double pneumonia. Gabe went on every week with a pinch-hit costar – Jimmy Durante did one, Red Skelton. When I came back, I swore I'd take better care of myself, but right away I was back to my old habits. And me and Gabe, we'd had it with the grind. We just couldn't keep it up anymore. That was the only thing we could agree on. So we went out with our heads high. Moved back to California.

Hoag: According to Connie, that's when your life . . .

Day: My life turned to shit.

(end tape)

CHAPTER
EIGHT

Wanda said she was up for having some fun. I said that would be fine with me as long as I didn't have to wear roller skates.

We started out at that year's favored celebrity eatery, Spago. The chef was a fellow named Puck, and you had to know him, or know someone who knew him, to get a table. Ours was right by the windows, which looked down on the traffic and billboards on Sunset Boulevard, and on the city beyond. The sun was setting soft and pink in the smoggy sky. It made everything out there look fuzzy, as if the whole city were made of Necco Wafers.

We ordered champagne – our drink. Brooke Hayward and Peter Duchin stopped by for a hug and a hello while we waited for it to arrive. So did a former wife of Richard Harris, who was with a guy with nineteen-inch hips who spoke only German and couldn't take his eyes off his own reflection in the window.

Lee Radziwill was eating there that night, too. So was a former U.S. senator, who was not with his wife. None of those people stopped by.

Wanda wore skintight black leather pants, high heels, and a little red silk camisole that could very well have qualified as underwear in many parts of the country. Her face was made up and she was acting very up, very gay. A little too gay. I wore a starched tuxedo shirt with a bib front, mallard suspenders, and gray pleated flannels. I also had a little something greasy in my hair. It was fun to be out again.

The waiter popped our cork and poured.

"To exes," Wanda said, raising her glass.

"To exes," I agreed.

She drained hers and leaned over the table toward me, showing me most of what was there under her camisole. "I think I should warn you," she said, her voice husky and intimate. "I'm not as tough as I look."

She was off and rolling again, playacting her ass off.

I refilled our glasses and charged right in. "I don't think you look very tough at all."

"You see right through me, don't you?"

"It's easy. Your despair is showing."

She looked hurt. "You go right for the bone, man."

"Nothing personal. I'm in the same place, remember?"

"There's very little I'm sure about," she said, "but that's one of the things – *nobody* is in the same place I am."

We ate a pizza that was covered with some sort of rare, aromatic fungus that only grows in a tiny region of the Alps, following it with grilled tuna and a second bottle of champagne. Wanda only picked at the food. She was much more interested in the champagne. When the waiter took our plates away, I ordered a third bottle and lit her cigarette for her.

"About you and Merilee," she said. "What happened?"

"Not much. I lost interest."

"Someone else?"

"No one else."

She took one of my hands in hers. Her fingers were smooth and cold. "Tell me about it, Hoagy."

"I'm rather hung up on myself and on my work. That doesn't leave enough for other people. At least that's Sonny's theory."

She dropped my hand. "Sonny's hardly one to talk."

"How come you and he don't get along?"

"I don't want to talk about him. I want to talk about you and me. Why won't you fuck me? You promised me you'd tell me. Are you involved? Are you gay?"

"When I say I lost interest, I mean . . ."

"You lost the urge."

"That's right. I suppose I just have to – "

"Meet the right woman?" She raised an eyebrow. I felt the toe of her shoe toying with the cuff of my trousers under the table. "How do you know I'm not her?"

"I don't."

"How long has it been?"

"Four years."

"Whew. I wouldn't want to *be* her."

"No?"

"At least, not on the first night. Or the second. Or the . . . christ, you really know how to issue a sexual challenge, don't you?"

"I didn't intend to."

"Too worried about what *Sonny* would think." She shook her head. "You've been taken in by him, haven't you?"

"I'm doing a job. I don't want to mess up the relationship he and I have going right now. It's important to the book, and it's shaky."

"So what are we doing here tonight?"

"Having dinner. Being friends. I like you. I want to get to know you better."

"So you can use me?" Her voice rose.

"Absolutely not."

"So you can find out who I've *fucked* and put it in your *fucking* book?!"

Heads began to turn.

"Maybe you'd better say it a little louder," I said. "I don't think everyone heard you."

"You *cocksucker*! All you care about is that book! All you want is some juicy dirt! I won't tell you a thing, you motherfucker! Not a thing!" She jumped to her feet. "*Motherfucker!*"

She liked scenes and she got one. Everyone in the place was staring at her now in stunned silence, avid for her next move.

Wanda turned on her heel and marched for the door. But she wasn't done. When she got to the bar she stopped and screamed at me again, "*Motherfucker! Motherfucker!*"

Not wanting to let her down, I chipped in with what I thought was a marvelous ad-lib. "Does this mean we're not going dancing?"

In response she grabbed a platter of duck ravioli from a passing waiter and hurled it across the restaurant at me. It didn't come anywhere near me. Lee Radziwill took most of it, if you want to know.

Then Wanda ran out the door and slammed it behind her. Sonny was right. They should have named her Stormy.

I'll grant her one thing – she didn't drive off and leave me stranded there. She was waiting for me in her Alfa after I paid the check and strolled leisurely out to the parking lot, toting our half-full bottle of champagne. She had on a soft doeskin jacket and racing gloves. The top was down, and she was revving the engine and flaring her nostrils. I took a swig and hopped in. She took off with a screech before my butt hit the seat.

She headed up into the Hollywood hills, her foot to the floor. Wanda drove exactly the way you'd expect Wanda to drive – like a nut. She shifted gears with fury, skidding around the hairpin curves, the little car barely holding on to the road. Actually, it did leave the pavement completely when we cleared a hump at the top of the hill and started flying down. That was when we really picked up speed. Houses and parked cars flew by. We tore down the narrow canyon road, Wanda accelerating blindly into the curves. If anybody happened to he coming up the canyon, we'd all be raspberry jam.

I held on and enjoyed the ride. I knew what she wanted me to do. She wanted me to tell her no, tell her bad girl. She would have a long wait.

When we got back down to Sunset she pulled over and wept in my arms. I gave her a linen handkerchief and she blew her nose in it. Then she took several breaths in and out and ran her fingers through her hair. I passed her the champagne bottle and she drank deeply from it. Then she lit a cigarette. I finished what was left of the bubbly.

"Get all of that out of your system?" I asked.

"Yes. Where to?"

We had to make seven stops before we found an ice cream parlor that sold licorice. It was a place down in Ocean Park on Main Street, and it was good licorice, though she thought it tasted "icky." I suggested she was too old to keep using a word such as "icky." She told me to get fucked.

We walked for a while, eating our ice cream, looking in the windows of the antique shops and galleries. It had turned chilly and foggy. No one else was out walking.

Suddenly she stopped and stared at me long and hard with narrowed eyes.

"What is it?" I said.

She just kept staring. Then she turned and strode away.

"Where are you going?" I called.

"I want to take you somewhere," she called back over her shoulder.

She took me to Malibu, to the beach. *Their* beach, where she and Sonny had gone for those morning walks when she was a little girl. We walked a long time in the damp mist, not talking, the waves pounding. She was a lot smaller in her bare feet. And when she started talking, her voice was higher and more girlish than I'd ever heard it before. She wasn't playing a role anymore.

"We used to come down here every morning when he was in town," she said. "He'd hold my hand and he'd point out the prettiest shells for me. He always knew exactly where to find them. I don't know how, he just did."

I cleared my throat, but I kept my mouth shut. I didn't have the heart to tell her.

"I – I couldn't cope, Hoagy. I never could."

"With what?"

"What was going on around me. Any of it. I'm like him – I've got thin skin. Only, he grew up in Brooklyn. Brooklyn is real. I grew up in Hollywood. It's not. It's all make-believe here. Make-believe is real. Sly Stallone isn't acting. He actually thinks he *is* Rocky. He really does. People here become whatever they want to be, and as long as they stay hot enough, nobody turns the lights off on them. Would you like to hear the benefits of my twenty-eight years in therapy?"

"Yes, I would."

"Okay, here goes: In the absence of a rational, ordered reality, people sometimes create one of their own, one that has the values and standards they require to survive. I grew up in a household that didn't make sense to me. Daddy was either crazed or bombed or trying to be Mister Macho – fucking around, beating up on people. And Mommy never tried to change him. He was Sonny Day. The One. She gave in to him. He treated her like total shit and she just came back for more. I couldn't deal with that. I just couldn't. It was wrong. So, when I was little, I started my own world. My make-believe place. My . . . my movie. And sometimes I still live in it. Partly for fun. Partly because I need to. See, I never outgrew it."

"I never outgrew wanting to play shortstop for the New York Yankees."

"Most of the time, I'm okay. I'm aware that it's make-believe. But sometimes . . . sometimes I'm not. I kind of lose touch with the so-called real world, and I . . . I'm what they call a borderline schizo."

"What's it about, your movie?"

"Me. What's going on around me. Only things make sense. They turn out the way I want them to."

"You seem okay right now."

"I always am when I'm down here."

She flopped down on the sand. I flopped down next to her. She snuggled into me. She smelled good against the sharp salt spray.

"I'm telling you all of this," she said, gazing out at the water, "because I think I'm falling in love with you."

I put an arm around her and she pressed her head against my chest. I was seeing her now for who she really was – a sweet, sad, vulnerable, and messed-up little girl who happened to be thirty-nine years old and all mine, if I wanted her. If I could handle her.

"And what about Hoagy's Little Condition?" I asked.

"I don't care about that. The real problem for me is this book. It's like a barrier. I keep wanting to trust you. Wanting to open up to you. But I'm afraid."

"I'm glad you trusted me."

"Are you really?"

"Yes."

"How is it going?"

"You really want to talk about it?"

"Yes, I do."

"It's hard work. He's a complex man. And it's his own memory of his life. Memory is really another form of make-believe. But I'm getting there. I'm starting to feel like I comprehend him and what's gone on. I spoke to your mom. She helped a lot."

"Did she tell you . . . ?"

"Tell me what?"

She placed her hand behind my head and brought my face down toward hers. I thought she was going to give me a kiss, but she had something else to give, a far greater token of her love.

She put her mouth to my ear, and in an urgent whisper Wanda told me why Sonny Day and Gabe Knight got in that fistfight in Chasen's.

CHAPTER
NINE

(Tape #7 with Sonny Day. Recorded in his study, February 28.)

Hoag: Okay, so you quit your TV series and moved back here.

Day: Right away, I feel different. Like something has gone out of me. Nowadays, they call it burnout. All I knew was I felt like I was just going through the motions. With Gabe. With Connie. I was very unsatisfied by my life all of a sudden. I was down. Gabe and I started a picture, *Alpine Lodge*. It was the same damned picture as *BMOC*, only with snow. Nobody seemed to notice. Or care. We did a couple of specials for NBC that season that were stale as hell – top-rated shows of the season. We did our six, eight weeks in Vegas. Again, stale. Again, sold out. It was fucking depressing.

Hoag: Did Gabe feel the same way you did?

Day: He did.

Hoag: Did you talk about it?

Day: Nah. We were like two people with a marriage that didn't work anymore. Bringing out the worst in each other. But the love was still there. And so was the dough. We flat out couldn't afford to break up, and we knew it, and it made us resent each other even more. I drank more and more. Took pills. Then my old lady died, and I don't know, I felt like nobody was looking over my shoulder no more. I started kicking up my heels. But I was still low. Show you how low, Francis calls me up one day and says, "We're doing a caper picture in Vegas together – Dean, Sam, Peter, Joey, everybody. Who do you and Gabe want to play?" And I said, "I don't know. I'll get back to you." I never did. It didn't sound like fun to me. We never did appear in *Ocean's Eleven*.

Hoag: I understand you had an affair with Jayne Mansfield.

Day: Connie told ya, huh? She was a sweet kid. Hottest new piece in town. Everybody wanted her. For a while, I had her. And I felt, for a while, a little bit fulfilled. Until Connie threw me the fuck out. That's when Wanda started to give us trouble. Stopped doing well in school. Got very quiet. Didn't want to be around me anymore at all. I figured God was punishing me for fucking around. We put her in a special school. Sent her to a shrink five days a week. She just kept getting worse. Anyway, Connie and me decided I should move back in. Give Wanda as stable an environment as possible. So I did. So one morning we're having breakfast, and I'm complaining to Connie about not wanting to go to the studio, not wanting to work, and it hits me.

Hoag: What hits you?

Day: This isn't Sonny Day. If Sonny Day is unhappy, he should do something about it. I needed to stretch. It took me a long time to realize that. See, people were constantly telling Gabe to branch out so he wouldn't be hanging on to my coattails. But nobody ever said that to *me*. This was a breakthrough for me. I started tummeling an idea with Norman Lear. It was a kind of satire on Madison Avenue, but it was a real statement on modern morality, you know, with depth and sophistication and a message . . .

Hoag: This would be *The Boy in the Gray Flannel Suit.*

Day: Warners thought it was brilliant. But they said, where's the part for Gabe? I said there isn't one, and they said put one in. They wouldn't let me do it by myself. They also wouldn't let me take it elsewhere. I was under exclusive contract – *with* Gabe. There was nothing I could do. Studios still ran things in those days. So I got drunk. Then Norman and I put in a part for Gabe. And guess what?

Hoag: He didn't want to do it.

Day: He said it was stupid and one-dimensional. He wanted us to do a big musical, a *Guys and Dolls* kind of picture. Only, that didn't interest Warners. Or me. He ended up by doing one on Broadway. And he was a smash. But my little movie he wouldn't touch. The studio said to him, you don't do this picture, we'll make it without you. Give Sonny a new partner. Which they did – they gave me a kid named Jim Garner. I made him into a star. Anyway, it was a standoff. Gabe wasn't bluffing. Warners wasn't bluffing. They gave him a few days to think it over, but it was over. In the meantime, we kept on the happy face. Connie threw me a huge birthday party here at the new house. Must have been three hundred people. She invited Gabe and Vicki and they came. We hadn't socialized in ages. And what a performance Gabe put on. All hugs and kisses. Even got up and made a birthday toast. He said, and I'll never forget this as long as I live, he said, "Here's to my best friend, Sonny Day. The man who gave me everything." We hugged. He sang me our song, "Night and Day." Henry Mancini played the piano. Then we sang it together. Everybody sobbed, it was so fucking moving. Nobody knew we was gonna bust up. Nobody but Heshie. The rest of them, the industry people, they thought Gabe would back down. Not even the wives knew.

Hoag: So Gabe was really the one who ended it? It was his decision?

Day: That was one helluva birthday party. We drank and danced and sang and cried. Next day, Knight and Day was history.

Hoag: Next day you had your fight at Chasen's.

Day: Yeah.

Hoag: You're saying it had to do with *Boy in the Gray Flannel Suit*?

Day: That was part of it.

Hoag: What else was?

Day: *(silence)* There was bad blood.

Hoag: It was alleged in the book about you, *You Are the One*, that the fight was over your gambling debts. That you sucked Gabe into debt with you.

Day: That's not even worth discussing.

Hoag: At the time, you said the book was garbage. Now is your opportunity to refute it.

Day: All right, all right. Sure, I got in money trouble from time to time. So what? Gabe got in deep with his divorce. I bailed him out. He bailed me out.

Hoag: I see. *(silence)* Sonny, there's also been an allegation concerning Connie. That she was . . .

Day: She was *what*?

Hoag: That she and Gabe Knight were lovers. Secretly, and for a number of years. And you found out about it. And that's why the two of you fought.

Day: *What*? Where'd you hear that crap?!

Hoag: It isn't important.

Day: It's a vicious lie! No truth to it. Who told ya that crap?

Hoag: Sonny, I know this isn't easy for you to deal with. I understand. But you've got to deal with it. I'm going to ask you again – is that what the fight was about? Be honest.

Day: What, you think I'm lying?

Hoag: No . . .

Day: Then why'd you say that?

Hoag: I'm simply trying to get at the truth.

Day: You *do* think I'm lying. I can see it in your eyes. You don't believe me. You believe some lie somebody told ya. Just like that, the trust between us is gone. This is something. This is really something.

Hoag: Don't do this, Sonny.

Day: Don't do what? Get sore at ya? Wanna punch ya? For slandering my wife. For saying she'd fuck around on me with that . . .

Hoag: I'm only doing my job.

Day: Stirring up garbage? No. Forget it. I won't discuss it.

Hoag: You must.

Day: Or what? You'll print your lies anyway? Don't try to bully me, pally. I been bullied by the best, and they're still picking up their teeth all over town.

Hoag: Sonny, I'm not the *Enquirer*. We have to deal with this thing. Get it out in the open. Now, you mentioned to me once that Gabe broke your heart. Is this how? By sleeping with Connie?

Day: Turn off the tape. This interview is over.

Hoag: All right, then let's address ourselves to the fight itself. It took place at Chasen's the afternoon after your birthday party. What happened?

Day: Turn it off, damn it!

Hoag: Sonny, we've done a lot of good work so far. Won a lot of battles. But this is the big one. I know it's tough. It's hard on your ego, your pride. But you've got to take it on. We have to deal with it.

Day: You're not dealing with anything, pally. You sure have knocked me for a loop. After all we've been through, the love I've given you. . . .

Hoag: I'm fired again, right?

Day: Clear out. You're through. And that's no lie.

Hoag: I see. *(silence)* You know, I *do*. I really do.

Day: You see *what*?

Hoag: Just one more question and I'm out of here – how did you figure to get away with it?

Day: Away with *what*?

Hoag: Not telling. I mean, this whole project has been nothing more than a publicity stunt, right? You wanted to get some attention, revive your career. You even made up the death threats. The truth is, you were never going to talk about the fight. You figured . . . hell, what *did* you figure? You'd get *more* publicity for clamming up? Is that it?

Day: You're dead wrong, Hoagy. I acted in good faith. I just can't do it. Don't you understand? I thought I could. Now that I'm face-to-face with it . . .

Hoag: Face-to-face with what?

Day: I made a mistake. I'm a human being.

Hoag: You're a master, is what you are. You suckered everybody. The publisher. The newspapers. And me. And that's the part that hurts, Sonny. See, I came around to your side. I started to think there was more to you than all that bad press you've gotten through the years. I cared about you. And you've been wearing your mask this whole time. You've been working me, just like I was an audience in Vegas. Giving me what I wanted. Using me.

Day: You're wrong about this, Hoagy. Believe me.

Hoag: Why should I?

Day: Because I'm telling you the truth, damn it.

Hoag: Tell it to somebody else. Put an ad in the paper: "Wanted – one stooge. No experience necessary." That's what you need. That's what you've always needed. Good-bye, Sonny.

(end tape)

CHAPTER
TEN

I t was still winter in New York. The raw wind off the Hudson cut right through my trench coat when I got out of the cab in front of my apartment. Old, sooty snow edged the sidewalk.

My apartment was even smaller and dingier than I remembered it. I gave Lulu her dinner and her water and slumped into my easy chair. There was unpacking to do. Bills to pay. It could all wait. I wasn't in the mood.

Lulu was down, too. She only sniffed at her mackerel before she curled up on the sofa with a disagreeable grunt. There, she glowered at me.

I couldn't just sit there. I decided to take her out on the town. I changed into a black cashmere turtleneck, heavy wool tweed suit, and oiled hiking shoes. I got out the fur-lined leather greatcoat I bought in Milan. Then I found my cap, my gloves, and my walking stick and we headed out. It was night. There was noise and activity and energy out there. Enough to get lost in. We headed down Broadway. I strode briskly. Lulu waddled along beside me, her low-flying ears catching bits of the sooty snow. Down around Lincoln Center I discovered a Tower Records that hadn't been there before. We went in and browsed. I treated myself to several Erroll Garner albums. Then we headed over toward Central Park West.

It's a very small town. Just like that we found ourselves standing right across the street from the very building we used to live in. The windows with their $895,000 view of the park were all lit up. Zack was no doubt throwing her a little welcome-home bash – something smart and trendy and assholey. Lulu whimpered. She wanted to go up and say hello. I growled at her and started downtown. She didn't budge. I yanked on her leash. She still didn't budge. I yanked harder. I won. I'm bigger.

At Columbus Circle we cut east along Fifty-ninth Street and made for the Racquet Club. I wrote a check for all of the dues I owed and left Lulu in friendly hands at the desk. A masseur worked me over for an hour. Then I sat in the steam. Afterward, flushed and relaxed, I led Lulu down Park to Grand Central. I resisted the temptation to swing over to Madison and look in Paul Stuart's window, knowing I'd end up blowing whatever settlement I got from Sonny's publisher on clothes.

It wouldn't be enough for another Jaguar.

At least I had learned something from this experience – I wasn't cut out to be a ghost.

We stopped in at the Oyster Bar for a dozen bluepoints and a Bloody Mary. Then it was over to the Algonquin. The maitre d', who has a veddy English accent that he came to by way of Bensonhurst, greeted us like old chums and gave us a corner table. Michael Feinstein was doing a nice quiet Gershwin medley on the piano. A split of champagne sat neatly on top of the oysters. So did the prime rib and the médoc. As always, there was a little cold poached salmon on the side for my girl. It perked her right up.

Strangely, I was thinking about Wanda. I hadn't said goodbye to her. I should have, but my feelings were still too jumbled. It wasn't as if anything had awakened down below. It hadn't. She was crazy, no question. Still, she wasn't a bad person, and she sure as hell wasn't dull, and I sure as hell wasn't happy sitting here by myself.

I had a big slab of chocolate cake, coffee, and a Courvoisier. I thought about a second Courvoisier. Instead, I got a cab, had it drop us at the liquor store around the corner from my apartment, and I bought a whole bottle of the stuff.

It was sleeting now. Some of it landed on Lulu's nose as we headed home. She snuffled at it and speeded up the closer we got to our door.

The Courvoisier and the Garner went down very well together. I sat back in my chair and let them have their sweet way with me, the sleet tapping against the kitchen skylight, Lulu dozing in my lap. I particularly liked the way he handled "I Cover the Waterfront." It fit my mood. Blue.

The Elf and the sleet were still tapping away a few hours later when I drifted off there in my chair.

The phone roused me at about four a.m. Someone was sobbing into it. I guess I don't have to tell you who.

"Can't *stand* it, Hoagy. Can't stand the pain."

"So take an aspirin, Sonny."

"Not that kind of pain. And you know it. It's . . . it's . . . "

"It's what?"

"I lost your respect. Can't stand it."

"You should have thought of that before you got me involved in your sham."

"Don't do this, Hoagy. Don't shut me out."

"Sonny, it's the middle of the night."

"I know. I know. Sitting here in the study. Looking out at your plant. Got a floodlight on it. Just sitting here."

"You been drinking?"

"Some," he admitted. "You?"

"Some."

"So whatta we do, Hoagy? Huh? Whatta we do?"

"We go to bed. In the morning, we wake up. You get on with your life, I get on with mine."

"Mine seems awful empty, Hoagy."

"Yeah."

"Come back, Hoagy. Come home."

"I *am* home."

"We could tummel some other ideas, huh? A movie, maybe."

"Forget it."

"You can have your old room back."

"Sonny, my life is here. I have a career to get back to, such as it is."

"So write your next novel here. Stay as long as you want, huh? We can still have breakfast and talk and – "

"Sonny, I'm hanging up now. Good-bye." I started to put the phone down.

But then he blurted, "We can talk about the fight."

I stopped. "About *what*?"

"The fight with Gabe. My fight with Gabe. We can talk about it."

"You'll tell me?"

"I'll tell you."

"The whole truth?"

"And nuttin' but."

"I've heard this before."

"I swear it."

"I'm sorry. I don't believe you."

"It's the truth. Come out. You'll see."

"Why the change of heart?"

"I have to."

"Why?"

"Things . . . they've gotten too out of hand. I-I'll tell you when you get here."

"Tell me right now. Why did you and Gabe fight?"

"I . . . I can't tell you over the phone. I need to be with ya, to see the look on your face. I need for you to see why it's been so hard for me. Then you'll understand."

"This sounds like more bullshit. Good-bye, Sonny."

"It's *not*. Believe me. I need to tell it. It's gotta be told. It's the only way things will change. The demons won't go away. I *gotta* tell you."

"If you're lying . . ."

"If I'm lying, I'll give ya the entire advance. My share. All of it. It's yours. Just come."

"If I come, it won't be for money. It'll be because I want to finish what we started. Finish your book."

"*Our* book. Come back. We'll do it together. Just like we been. Catch the morning flight. Vic'll meet ya at the airport. Come back to me, Hoagy."

Lulu and I were on that morning flight. I know just what you're thinking – as soon as Sonny sobered up he'd clam up, and there I'd be, on my way back home to New York again, pissed off. I knew that. I knew there was only a slim chance that he was really going to tell me the whole story about Connie and Gabe. But I had to take that chance.

Besides, I hadn't said good-bye to Wanda.

I should have known something was wrong when Vic wasn't at the airport to meet me. I waited half an hour before I figured Sonny was still out cold and had never told him to pick me up. So I flagged down a cab and gave him Sonny's address. We got on the freeway. Lulu stood on my lap and stuck her nose out the window and wagged her tail, happy to be back in L.A.

The television news vans and press cars were backed up a full block down the canyon from his house.

"What's going on?" I asked the cabbie.

"Hey, this must be the Day place!" he exclaimed, excited.

"Yes, it is. What about it?"

He checked me out in his rearview mirror. "You a friend of his?"

"Yes, I am."

"You don't know then, huh? He's dead. Been on the radio all morning. Somebody shot the poor fucker. Sorry to be the one to tell you. That'll be twenty-five dollars, please. Plus gratuity."

And that's how I learned Sonny Day had been murdered – from a polite cab driver.

Reporters, photographers, and camera crews were milling around the front gate, chatting, smoking, waiting. I squeezed through them with Lulu and my bags. The cop on the gate wouldn't let me buzz the house. That happened to be his job. So I identified myself and let him do it. He spoke into the intercom and listened. Then he nodded to me. A minute later the gate clicked open and I slipped inside, the reporters shouting after me for my name, my business, my connection, my . . .

I headed up the driveway. As I rounded the curve where the orchard ended, I saw a cluster of people by the reflecting pool. One of them spotted me and ran toward me.

It was Wanda. She was still in her caftan and her eyes were red and her hair mussed.

"He's dead, Hoagy," she wailed. "He's dead."

She threw her arms around me and clung to me. I dropped my bags and held her.

I looked over her shoulder at the estate and began to realize how different it looked. Police cars were parked over by the garage. The log arbor was roped off. Uniformed cops, plainclothesmen, and technicians were talking and making notes.

Connie was there by the reflecting pool. So was Harmon Wright. And Vic. As Wanda and I made our way toward them, my arm still around her, Vic spotted me. His face turned red.

"You did it!" he screamed at me. "It's your fault! I'll kill you! I'll kill you!"

An animal roar came out of him. He charged. He came at me full speed, like I was an opposing linebacker. My first instinct was to freeze. Then, as he got closer to me, I tried to sidestep him. I failed. He rammed me straight on and down we went, my head cracking hard against the pavement. The inside of it lit up like a pinball machine. My memory is a bit fuzzy from there on. I remember him snarling. I remember him punching me, pummeling my mouth, my nose, my ears. I remember it hurt. And Wanda was screaming, and the cops were running toward us. And he was right on top of my chest with both hands around my throat, choking me, me gagging, not being able to get any air. And then nothing . . .

Until I heard the coyotes wailing again. Only this time it wasn't coyotes. It was an ambulance. I was in it, and somebody was putting something over my face. And then I was out again.

I came to in the hospital. I felt numb all over and very thirsty, and Detective Lieutenant Emil Lamp of the Los Angeles Police Department was sitting at the foot of my bed sucking on an ice cube.

C H A P T E R
E L E V E N

Emil Lamp didn't look more than sixteen. He was a fresh-scrubbed, eager little guy with neat blond hair and alert blue eyes. He had on a seersucker suit, button-down shirt, and striped tie. A bulky Rolex was on one wrist, an Indian turquoise-and-silver bracelet on the other.

"Lulu . . ." I gasped, my throat parched.

"She's okay, Mister Hoag," he assured me. He didn't sound much more than sixteen either. "Miss Day . . . Wanda, she has her. Nice dog. Breath smells kind of – "

"C-could I have a drink?"

"Sure, sure."

He jumped to his feet, all action. There was a carafe on the table next to the bed. Lamp poured some ice water into a styrofoam cup. I started to reach for the cup, only I got stabbed in the side by what felt like a carving knife. I yelped and clutched at the spot. My fingers found tape wrapped there.

"You've got a cracked rib," Lamp informed me, handng me my water. "Had one once myself. Hurts like heck. Take it from me, whatever you do, don't laugh."

"Shouldn't be too hard." I drank some of the water. It angered my throat going down. Vic's hands had left it sore and swollen.

"You've also got a mild concussion. Your face looks pretty raw, but it's just cuts and bruises. You're lucky you didn't get a fractured skull. That guy's an animal. You're in Cedars Sinai hospital on Beverly Boulevard. Doc says you'll be here for a couple of days."

I looked around. I was in a private room with a bath, color television, and window. Outside, it was dark.

"I'm not insured," I told him.

"Your publisher is taking care of everything."

"They do have a heart after all." I tried to sit up a little, but my head started to spin. I surrendered to the pillow.

"You're supposed to call them, when you're up to it." Lamp checked his watch. "Which I guess will be tomorrow. You've been out almost eight hours."

"What happened to Vic?"

"We're holding Early over for questioning and psychiatric observation. It seems he's had a history of violent episodes since he got back from Nam. Beat a reporter half to death in Las Vegas just a couple of weeks ago."

"I was there."

"Know of a reason he'd have wanted Mr. Day dead?"

"Vic? He loved Sonny."

"He doesn't seem to love you much."

Gingerly, I explored my face with my fingers. My lips were pulpy and tender. My nose felt like a soft potato.

"Could you tell me what happened to Sonny?" I asked.

"Sure, sure." He sat back down and pulled out a notepad and opened it. "Sometime around three a.m., Pacific time – while you were still waiting for your flight at Kennedy Airport in New York – "

"You checked?"

"You bet I checked. When a dead man's bodyguard screams 'You did it! It's your fault!' and beats the crap out of some guy, I always check his whereabouts at the time of the murder. That's how I got to be a lieutenant. Anyway, at approximately three a.m. Sonny Day took three shots in the stomach and chest from close range. It happened in the log arbor. He died before the ambulance got there. Massive internal hemorrhaging. He was in the yard, in his robe. Bed hadn't been slept in. It was his own gun, a snub-nosed thirty-eight-caliber Smith and Wesson Chief Special. No prints. The bodyguard, Early, says he kept it in the study, loaded at all times. There were two others around the place. Also loaded. Not fired."

"Somebody broke in?"

"We can't find any trace of a break-in. Nothing missing. He had darned good security there. Electrified fence, the works. We examined the grounds and the outer wall pretty carefully this afternoon. I don't think anybody broke in. No sign of a struggle. His hands, nails, the grass, nothing. I think he was shot by somebody whom he let in, or who was already there. You know, somebody he knew. That's why we're thinking about Early. He phoned it in. He, Miss Day, and the housekeeper said they were awakened by the shots." He closed the pad. "You know, Mr. Hoag, this is a real honor for me."

"First case?"

"Gracious no," Lamp chuckled. "Oh, heck, no. I mean, my job has brought me in contact with Hollywood celebrities before, but I've never met someone like you. I mean, I was a big, big fan of *Our Family*

Enterprise, Mr. Hoag."

"Thanks. And make it Hoagy."

"As in Carmichael?"

"As in the cheese steak."

"I went to the library to see about checking out some of your other books, but they didn't have any."

"Go ahead, kick me when I'm down."

"When's the last time you spoke to Sonny Day?"

"About four in the morning New York time. Yesterday. No, I guess it's still today, isn't it? Sorry, I'm kind of fuzzy."

"That's the concussion."

"No, I'm always kind of fuzzy."

He grinned. "What did you two talk about?"

"The book we were working on together."

"Did you often talk in the middle of the night like that?"

"Seemingly."

"Hoagy, you can be a big help to my investigation. I need your cooperation."

I swallowed. My throat didn't like that. "You've got it."

"Good. We have a report on file of a death threat Mr. Day received a few weeks ago. Early phoned it in. Evidence was disposed of. Mr. Day requested no intervention on our part. Know anything about it? What it said?"

"Supposedly it had to do with the book. I never saw it."

"Uh-huh. I read the newspapers. I know Mr. Day was supposed to come out with some pretty choice dirt in this book of yours. Can you talk about that?"

"No reason not to. He was going to reveal the true story behind his famous Chasen's fight with Gabe Knight. Only he backed out at the last minute. He wouldn't tell me. Maybe he never intended to. I don't know for sure. That's why I went back to New York. And why he called me in the middle of the night. And why I came back. He relented. Said he would tell me. *Promised* me he would. Of course with Sonny, you could never be sure."

"Either way, it's something," Lamp declared enthusiastically. "It sure is. Yes, indeed." Lamp jumped to his feet again and began to pace around my bed. He sure had a lot of energy. "Could be that somebody didn't want him to tell you what really happened. Stopped him before he got a chance. Somebody who heard him talking to you on the phone. Or somebody he informed about it. Maybe somebody dropped by for a nightcap. Somebody who figured in this thing, this fight. Yes, I'm starting to like this theory. This walks around the block nicely. Very nicely indeed."

Not for me it didn't. If Lamp was right, then so was Vic – Sonny got killed because of me. My head started to spin again, and a wave of nausea washed over me.

"You okay, Hoagy? You look a little green."

"I'm just dandy."

"I won't keep you much longer. Do you have any idea what this fight of theirs was about?"

I shook my head.

"Theory? Speculation?"

I hesitated, then shook my head again, which hurt. I wasn't ready to go that far with him yet.

Lamp eyed me. "So what's your next move?"

"I thought I'd try standing up."

"And then what?"

"Talk to the publisher. See what they want me to do."

"They've stopped a bunch of calls at the desk for you. Newspapers. Television. This one's a real circus. I guess Mr. Day was still a big, big star to a lot of people."

Clearly, Lamp was too young to be one of them. I felt particularly ancient all of a sudden.

"Anybody else call to see how I was?"

"Like who?"

I shrugged. That hurt, too.

Lamp opened his notepad again. "There *was* a call from a woman who said she was Merilee Nash."

There. My heart was beating again. "Any message?"

"Uh . . ." He checked his pad. "Let's see . . . 'Don't die, you ninny.'"

All right. I wouldn't. "When's Sonny's funeral?"

"Friday. Miss Day mentioned that you're welcome to move back into the guesthouse when the doctors release you. She assumed you'd want to stick around for it."

"She assumed right."

With great difficulty I raised myself up. My bare feet found the cold floor. I sat there on the edge of the bed for a second, my ears ringing. I was wearing a shortie gown and nothing else.

"You supposed to be up?" Lamp asked.

"Only one way to find out. Give me a hand, would you?"

He stuck a hand under my armpit and helped hoist me up to my feet. I wavered there for a second like a newborn colt. Then I pointed to the john and he helped me stagger toward it. He was a little guy, but strong.

"She seemed real concerned about you, Miss Day did," he commented, most delicately. "Are you and her . . . ?"

"No."

"Don't mean to be nosy. Nice lady. Pretty. Heck, I'll never forget her in that French movie *Paradise* when she crawled into that guy's bed and started to – "

"Yeah. You and Vic will get along well. It's on his top-ten list, too."

I looked for my reflection in the bathroom mirror but found Frankenstein's monster instead. My face was mottled several glorious shades of blue and red. All I needed was the bolts sticking out of my neck.

"Listen, Hoagy," Lamp said from the doorway. "What I said about your being a big help, I meant it. You may know something. Something he told you that nobody else knows. When your head clears, could be it'll come back to you. Don't give it out to the press first, okay? Work with me. I'd appreciate it."

"That's no problem."

"Great. Well, I'll be going now."

"Time to watch *Lassie* and hit the hay, huh?"

He laughed. "You've got quite a sense of humor." Then he cleared his throat. "Listen, I think I'd better keep somebody outside your door."

"What for?"

"I like to be careful. Chances are it's Early. He probably got mad about something and grabbed the gun from the study and shot his boss. But you never know. There's still our little theory to consider. And if that's correct, you may be in danger."

"I told you I don't know anything."

"The person who shot Sonny Day wouldn't necessarily know that. Not for certain." He grinned reassuringly. "Hey, not to worry, Hoagy. You're in good hands. Haven't lost anybody yet."

"I feel better already." In fact, I was starting to feel seriously dizzy.

"I still can't believe I'm actually talking to *the* Stewart Hoag. Maybe . . . maybe sometime you'd autograph my copy of your book?"

"Love to."

He started to go. So did I. He caught me just before I hit the floor.

I slept off and on through the night, never fully awake. A nurse woke me once to feed me a pill, a doctor to peer into my eyes with a bright light. In the gray light of early morning I had a little juice and hot cereal and two sips of the worst coffee I'd ever tasted in my life. The dizziness was starting to fade, but I still felt lousy. The kind of lousy that comes with losing a good friend and feeling like maybe you were partly responsible for it.

Overnight I'd become a hot commodity. The *Enquirer* offered me $50,000 for my story of Sonny's last days. The *Star* offered to top it. *Good Morning America* wanted me on as a guest. They'd even come to my hospital room for the taping. So would *Today*. So would *Entertainment Tonight*.

I was hot again. Everybody wanted me, just like in my glory days. Only this time I told all of them no. That confused them. They didn't get me. To them, I was one lucky son of a bitch – a has-been writer who stumbled into a major-league showbiz murder and had a golden opportunity to clean up on it. That's what I would have thought, too, if I was on the outside. But I wasn't.

I got hold of the dignified old gent who ran the publishing company. He didn't sound so dignified right now. There was too much greed in his voice.

He informed me they'd decided to rush Sonny's book into print as soon as possible. It would be made up of the one hundred or so pages of fleshed-out transcripts I'd turned in, plus what I could make out of the remaining tapes. There would also be photos and a lengthy postscript – by me – detailing the circumstances and aftermath of Sonny's death.

He coughed uneasily. "I have one very important question for you, young man," he said.

"No, he didn't," I said.

"No, he didn't what?"

"No, he didn't tell me what the fight in Chasen's was about."

"I see. Too bad. Well, find out as much as you can. Continue your interviewing. See if you can talk to that fellow they're holding, that bodyguard. He knows you. Maybe he'll confide in you. And make yourself available to the press as an authority on the subject. It'll be a big help for you when it comes time to go on tour. Just don't give them too much. We can't have them stealing any of our thunder, can we."

"I'm afraid you'll have to get someone else. I have no interest in continuing."

"You're under *contract*."

"My contract was with Sonny."

"But . . . but we've acted in good faith. We've taken good care of you."

"I'll pay you back for the hospital bills."

"Money is not the point, young man."

"Really? Then what is?"

"There *will* be a book, with you or without you. If you don't finish it, someone else will. A stranger. Is that the way you wish to see this project end for you? I can't believe it is. Stay out there. Stay and finish what you've started."

"I'm not interested."

"I simply can't believe that," he said, sounding genuinely puzzled. "You must not be yourself. That head injury. Why don't you think it over? We'll talk again tomorrow."

I hung up and called Wanda. I had to go past the head of my agency to get to her. Harmon Wright was there at the house screening all calls. He didn't ask how I was.

"How are you?" she asked me, out of breath. She sounded lot like that little girl on the beach again.

"Groggy. You?"

"Every time I hear footsteps I look up and expect him to come walking through the doorway. I guess I . . . I still can't believe it happened. Mommy's here. Heshie. Gabe even came by for a few minutes."

"He did?"

"He was crying, Hoagy. He said Sonny's murder was a crime against all Americans. They . . . the police think Vic maybe did it."

"Maybe."

"And after all Sonny did for him."

"Vic's just a suspect. Nothing's for certain."

"When can you leave the hospital?"

A nurse came in with more pills. I swallowed them with water.

"Tomorrow, maybe. Listen, Wanda, I want you to know I'm . . . I'm sorry I didn't say good-bye."

"Forget it. You're here. That's all that matters. Lulu's fine, but she misses you. And so do I. Come home."

"They want me to finish the book."

"So do I."

"You do?"

"Absolutely. He'd have wanted you to. Besides, if you don't, some sleaze will write one. You have to finish it, Hoagy."

"Say I did. It would all have to come out. Chasen's. The affair. I wouldn't be able to fudge anything. I'm not made that way."

"Good."

"But there's your mother to consider. It would hurt her and . . . wait, I'm sorry I brought it up. Now isn't the time to discuss this."

"No, it's okay," she assured me. "I've given this a lot of thought. I really have. That fight between Daddy and Gabe happened thirty years ago. It's ancient history. I think it's time the truth came out. I really do. No more secrets. No more damned secrets. That's how people get hurt – by secrets. Not by the truth."

"What if Connie doesn't feel that way?"

"She does. I know it. Finish the book, Hoagy. Stay and finish. Wanda wants you to."

I moved back into the guesthouse two days later, ears ringing, ribs taped, the very model of a modern ghostwriter.

That was the same day the publisher announced I would be finishing Sonny's book. Their press release hinted that I was privy to never-before-published disclosures concerning Knight and Day's breakup. The L.A. papers played up the story big. After all, there wasn't much else new to report on the case, other than that Vic was still being held for observation. The *L.A. Times* even ran that old jacket photo of me from *Our Family Enterprise*, the one where I'm standing on the roof of my brownstone in a T-shirt and leather jacket, looking awful goddamned sure of myself.

Emil Lamp, boy detective, gave me a lift from the hospital in his unmarked police sedan, which was as spotless as he was. He gripped the wheel tightly, hands at the ten-of-two position, and observed all the traffic laws.

"I thought you were going to cooperate with me, Hoagy," he said. "I thought we had an understanding."

"We do.'"

"Then why the grandstanding? Why do I have to pick up the newspaper to find out your plans?"

"That's the publisher's doing, not mine. I was planning to tell you."

"Yeah?" he said doubtfully.

"True story," I assured him. "I gave it a lot of thought and decided I could best protect Sonny's interests by sticking around and finishing. I need a final chapter. I don't have one right now."

"I see."

"I also want to do whatever I can to help."

"Sure, sure. Tell me about these disclosures of yours they're talking about."

"They exaggerated a little. All I've got is an idea."

"Share it with me.'"

"That I can't do."

"Why not?'"

"It's a touchy matter. I have to handle it a certain way."

"What way is that?"

"The right way."

Lamp frowned. "I'm not happy about this, Hoagy."

"Look, if it ends up having anything to do with the murder, you'll be the first to know. Believe me, I want Sonny's killer brought to justice as much as anyone."

We crossed Sunset on Beverly Drive and cruised past all of those giant houses on all of those tiny lots. A city work crew was pruning the towering curbside palms from atop a five-story motorized ladder. My idea of a terrific job for someone else.

"Besides," I said, "I do have something for you. It came to me when my head started to clear."

"What is it?"

"Somebody tried to spook Sonny on his birthday. Left him a particularly ghoulish little surprise in his car."

I told Lamp about the dummy with the beanie cap and the bullet holes. Then I told him about the rest – the eight-by-ten glossy with the carving knife in it, the ripped-up tapes, the curious nonresponses of Sonny and Vic. I didn't mention that I'd once thought Sonny himself may have been behind it all.

When I was done, Lamp shook his head and said, "Boy, this is a spooky one. I'm gonna get nightmares from this case."

"Sleep with a night-light."

"Already do." Lamp grinned. "This business with the keepsakes, props, whatever from his past – this interests me. Especially since they were items that hadn't been seen for a while. Whoever was behind it is someone Mr. Day went back a ways with."

"He knew who did it."

"He did?"

"He was frightened, but he wouldn't bring you fellows in. He was protecting someone. What we don't know, I suppose, is if the same person who was trying to scare him also killed him."

"You think it might be different people?"

"I'm no expert, but it seems to me there's an entirely different personality profile between someone who sneaks around leaving sick little threats and someone who has the nerve to face a person and pull the trigger."

"You're right – you're no expert. That talks good, but so does succotash."

"Succotash?"

"It's like that old theory that people who keep attempting suicide really don't want to die. Succotash."

"Succotash. I wonder if my ex-wife has heard that one."

"I've seen plenty of repeaters make it. If they want to die, they eventually do."

I glanced over at him, wondering how it was possible that what he'd seen hadn't in any way rubbed off on him.

"But that's good info, Hoagy. I'll see if I can check it out. Thanks. I owe you one."

"How about letting Vic go to the funeral? It would mean a lot to him."

Lamp's lips puckered. "You don't think Early did it, do you?"

"No, I don't. Sonny was like a father to him."

"People kill their fathers all the time. Almost as often as they kill their mothers."

"*You* think he's guilty?"

"I really don't know, Hoagy."

"What about that theory of yours?"

"I still like it. But Early's tempting. He's in hand, and he's a fruitcake. Be awful easy to pin it on him. An ambitious, unscrupulous cop would do just that – wear him down and bully a confession out of him. Be a hero." He grinned. "Maybe even get a nice fat book contract out of it."

"You're not that kind of cop, are you, Lamp?"

"Oh, heck, no."

"But you must be pretty good. This is a big case to get assigned."

He blushed. "I get results."

We hit the circus a good three blocks down the canyon from the house. It was bigger than before. It wasn't just the press now. Now there were also curiosity seekers, gawkers, people who couldn't wait to drive by the dead man's house. People, I was reminded, make me sick.

Lamp pulled over and stopped.

"This is as far as I go," he said.

"You're not coming in?"

"Never like to bother folks when they're grieving."

"Kind of a sensitive guy, huh?"

"The job gets done."

"That's nice, Lamp."

Wanda greeted me in the entry hall with a bear hug that did my rib very little good. She cupped my face in her hands and said, "I'm so glad you're here, Hoagy."

She was very calm and composed. She wore a knit dress of black cashmere and black boots. She had a pearl necklace on, and her hair was brushed and shiny and there was a bit of makeup on her eyes. She took my hand and led me toward the living room.

From the study came the sounds of Harmon negotiating Sonny's funeral on the phone.

"We're talking about burnished mahogany here, you greedy cocksucker! Not fucking gold!"

The man was still being Sonny's agent, looking out for him even after death did them part. After forty years, I don't suppose you just shut it off.

Connie sat on the living room sofa, staring into the brook. She looked pale and shaken. She looked old. I sat down beside her and told her how sorry I was. She kept looking into the brook. I felt like an intruder, so I started away.

Softly, she said, "He told me how much you meant to him, Hoagy. He was lucky to know you."

"I was the lucky one."

Lulu was so happy to see me she whooped and moaned and tried to crawl into my shirt. The guesthouse was as I'd left it. My bags were on the bed. I unpacked and stretched out and listened to my ears ring for a while. Then I turned on the TV. One of the local stations was playing a special retrospective of Sonny's movies. I watched a few minutes of *Jerks* – one of the classic scenes, where Sonny tries to figure out the blender and gets a malted in the face. He was so young, so full of talent and life that he practically jumped off the screen. I turned off the set and went back inside the house.

I helped as much as I could over the next day and a half. I drove over to Connie's and fetched her mail and messages for her. I took care of some of the funeral arrangements. I spelled Harmon on the phone. The reporters were dismayed when they discovered I was the one screening their calls. They tried everything to get info from me – flattery, sympathy, bribery. One of them even said, "C'mon, Hoag. You're one of us. You *owe* us." But the family didn't want any statements issued. They got nothing from me.

Sonny was buried at Hillside Memorial over near the airport on a brilliant, cloudless day – a sunny day, as all of the papers would report. He joined the company of Al Jolson there, among others. The closed-coffin service was held in a chapel on the grounds. Sonny once told me it had been fifty years since he'd been in a temple. Now he was back, and everyone came to see him off.

It was a major-league Hollywood funeral. Sinatra was there. Hope. Burns. Lewis. Martin. Berle. Sammy Davis, Jr. Gabe Knight, of course. Shirley MacLaine was there. Gregory Peck. Danny Thomas. Gerald and Betty Ford. Tommy Lasorda.

And Vic Early was there, too, wearing a navy-blue suit. A police officer stood at his side. I went over to the big guy before the service.

"Hey, Hoag," he said softly. He seemed to have trouble focusing his eyes.

"How are you doing, Vic?"

"Sorry about going after you. I saw red. Couldn't help myself."

"Forget about it."

"I know you had nothing to do with it. You were good for him."

"Thanks. What's going to happen to you?"

"They've been giving me tests. The lawyer says they'll have to let me go pretty soon. Either that or charge me, and they got no grounds to do that."

"No idea what happened that night?"

"I was asleep, Hoag. He needed me, and I was asleep. I swear."

"I believe you. Where will you go?"

"I don't know. Without Sonny, I've got no place. Nobody."

"If there's anything I can do, let me know."

"Okay, Hoag. Sure. No hard feelings?"

"No hard feelings."

He smiled. "'Poon one for me, huh?"

"I'll do that."

Sinatra read a personal message from the President calling Sonny's death "a tragic loss" and Sonny "a true American, a man whose humanity, generosity, and love of his country and its people served as a beacon in the darkness." Sinatra did not break down and sob, as was reported by a *New York Post* reporter who wasn't even on the grounds, let alone in the chapel. It was Gabe Knight who cried. Gabe gave the eulogy. In a shaky voice, he described Sonny as "a man who never lost a child's wonder at the joys and pains of life." He called him "a man of vulnerability, of emotion, of greatness – a man who was, and would always be, The One." Gabe concluded by reading the final stanza of "their" song:

> *In the roaring traffic's boom*
> *In the silence of my lonely room*
> *I think of you.*
> *Night and day.*

Then he broke into tears and had to be led away by the cantor, who was Monty Hall.

The pallbearers were Gabe Knight, Harmon Wright, Sinatra, Sammy Davis, Jr., Bob Hope, and Dean Martin.

Afterward, Connie and Wanda sat shiva for Sonny at the house. Chairs were set up in the living room. There was food and coffee in the dining room. A lot of the celebrities from the funeral fought their way through the press outside the gate to come in for a brief chat with Connie and Wanda, and with each other.

Sinatra commandeered the sofa: he and his wife sat on either side of Connie to comfort her. Harmon Wright and his wife would probably have been a greater comfort, but who was going to be the one to tell Francis that?

This was some gathering. Just a few impressions:

– A gaggle of comics standing in a corner swapping Sonny Day stories. Shecky Greene saying, "One day, I was down to my last six cents, not a booking in sight, Sonny slipped a fifty in my pocket and told me something I'll never forget: 'Be yourself.'" And Jackie Mason firing back, totally deadpan: "And *still* you made a living.'"

– Sammy Davis, Jr., telling people about a premonition of death he'd gotten while flying over the Bermuda Triangle only two days before Sonny's murder. "If I'd have *knowed* it was gonna be Sonny," he said, "baby, I'd have *jumped* out."

— Milton Berle, standing alone near the coffee urn, his hand shaking badly as he raised his cup to his lips. He snatched a furtive glance around to see if anyone noticed. No one was looking at him at all.

The phone kept ringing. I took a lot of the calls in Sonny's study. That's where Gabe Knight found me. He poured himself a brandy from the decanter at the bar and raised it inquiringly. I nodded. He poured me one and brought it over to me. He seemed quite cool and collected now, a far cry from his emotional behavior at the funeral.

"I understand you're continuing with Arthur's book, my young friend," he said quietly. He looked past me out the window and sipped his brandy.

I sipped mine. "That's right."

"Admirable. He'd like that."

"I think so."

"Though possibly unwise."

"Really? Why?"

"You could get hurt."

"That's already happened," I said, fingering my still-tender nose.

"Even worse."

"Are you threatening me?"

Gabe smiled, or at least his mouth did. His eyes never joined in. "Let's say I'm trying to be helpful."

"If that's the case, then tell me why you and Sonny fought at Chasen's."

He raised an eyebrow. "So he didn't tell you?"

"He didn't get a chance. Somebody stopped him. *What* was he going to tell me?"

"Believe me, the less you know, the better off you are, young *friend*. Go home to New York. Back away from this thing."

"Or what?"

"I speak with your best interests in mind. One man is already dead. Don't jeopardize your own life. Go home."

"Not until I know the whole story. Tell me and I'll go."

Someone called Gabe's name from the living room.

"Coming!" he called pleasantly. Then he turned back to me. "I warned you, my young friend. Remember that."

Gracefully, he strode back into the group. I reached for my brandy and discovered my own hand was shaking now.

I retired to my guesthouse early. There were still fifty or so people in the main house, but the guesthouse was far enough away that their coming and going didn't bother me. I took one of the pills the doctor had given me, but I didn't need it. I passed out the second my head hit the pillow, Lulu comfortably ensconced in her usual position.

I don't know whether it was the smoke or Lulu's nosing at me that woke me. All I know is I opened my eyes sometime later to find my room on fire. The desk had been thrown open and dumped – transcripts, notes and tapes were in flames. The drapes had caught. So had the bedspread. Fire crackled all around me. Lulu was huddled at my side, trembling.

Quickly, I grabbed her under one arm, and threw a blanket over the papers burning there on the floor. As the blanket began to smolder, I dashed across it, through the smoke and flames toward the door. Tears streamed down my face. Flames licked at my skin. I collapsed on the lawn in my boxer shorts, singed and choking. One of the cops from the gate was running toward me. So were a few of the mourners.

"You okay?" asked the cop.

I nodded, gasping for air, coughing.

"Anybody else –?"

I shook my head.

He ran inside anyway, to see if he could put out the fire. But it was too late. We watched the little cottage burn. All of the mourners were out there now on the lawn, watching.

Gabe Knight was one of them. But he wasn't watching the fire. He was watching me.

The fire trucks arrived in time to keep the flames from spreading to the trees and the main house, but the guesthouse was gone. So were my clothes. They gave Lulu some oxygen. Me, too. Coughing, like laughing, is no fun with a cracked rib. Wanda, after she made sure I was okay, ran into the big house and brought me out Vic's flannel robe to wear. It smelled like Ben-Gay, but it was warm.

They were still hosing the charred wreckage down when a voice behind me said, "Smoking in bed again?"

It was Lamp, wearing a windbreaker.

"Mom know you're out this late?" I asked.

"I got a permission slip. What happened?"

"Somebody made a bonfire out of all my papers."

"Any idea who?"

I shook my head. "Everybody thinks they're a critic these days." I glanced up at him. "I suppose your little theory pans out."

"I think we can assume somebody's trying to scare you real good," he agreed calmly. "Was your door locked?"

"Yes. Not that it's ever done any good."

"Well, we'll go through this mess in the morning. Maybe we'll find something. Does this kill the book?"

"No. I made a copy of the tapes when I was in New York and sent them to the publisher. I suppose," I said, "it could have been set by anybody who was here."

"Or not."

"Or not?"

"It could also have been someone who knew the security system here, knew how to get onto the property without being spotted, and then how to hightail it out of here."

"Like who?"

"Like Vic Early. Early escaped on his way back from the funeral this afternoon, Hoagy. He's presently at large – and a prime suspect, I'm afraid. Get some sleep. I'll be by in the morning."

Lamp headed off to his car. Wanda appeared next to me.

"I guess," she said, "we'll have to find you a bed."

The last place I wanted to sleep was in Sonny's room.

Too much of him was there. The yellowed photo over the fireplace of him and his brother Mel standing in front of Pine Tree Lake with their arms around each other. The vast walk-in closet with the 500-odd pairs of new shoes in a custom-built wall rack. The bathroom, with his colognes and tonics still laid out beside the sink.

I would have preferred another room, any other room. But Wanda insisted. She said she wouldn't sleep a wink unless she knew I was right, there across the hall from her. So I gave in. I was too weary to argue.

I opened the doors to the small terrace and let some fresh air in. The breeze carried the stink of the fire on it. There were cops on the gate and the front door of the house. Harmon had driven Connie home. The caterers had cleared out. It was very quiet. I eased into Sonny's big bed and lay there on my back in the darkness with Lulu, my wheels still turning.

It couldn't be Vic. Sure, it didn't look terrific for him right now. But he couldn't have wanted Sonny dead. Or me. It was Gabe. Gabe was the one who told me to back off. Gabe was the one who threatened me. But why? To save his ambassadorship? I doubted it. So what if he had slept with his partner's wife? That was thirty years ago. Ancient history, Wanda had called it. Who could possibly care now?

Way in the back of my mind, something began to gnaw at me. Something Sonny had once said. An odd fact that didn't fit anywhere. What was it? And why was it gnawing at me?

For the second time that night, I fell into a deep sleep. And for the second time I was pulled out of it.

This time it was by the rustling of the sheets and the feel of a warm, smooth body there in the bed with me, a long, lean body over me, astride me. . . .

"Wha – "

"Ssh."

It was her famous scene, the one from *Paradise*. She was in her movie again. She was performing.

I felt her hot breath on my face, her hands on my chest. And I felt something else.

I was performing too.

Who cared if she was nuts? Who cared if this wasn't strictly, one hundred percent real. I didn't. If this was her movie, I wanted to be in it, cracked rib or not. God, did I want to be in it.

It wasn't until dawn that we collapsed, spent. Lulu padded in from the terrace and sniffed at us, jealous and disapproving. I patted the bed and she jumped and lay between us, nuzzling my hand for attention.

"I was wrong," Wanda murmured.

"About what?"

"I *would* want to be that woman the first night."

CHAPTER
TWELVE

(Tape #1 with Detective Lieutenant Emil Lamp of the L.A.P.D. Recorded by the pool of the Sonny Day estate, March 7.)

Hoag: Sure you don't mind my taping this? It'll make it easier for me to remember the details.

Lamp: (garbled)

Hoag: Could you please sit a little closer? I'm not sure how strong this mike is.

Lamp: I said, it makes me feel like I'm the one being interviewed. Lost the other recorder in the fire, huh?

Hoag: Yes. Had to buy all new clothes this morning, too. Wanda took me down to Lew Ritter, along with my police protection and about fifty assorted members of the press. I felt like a Kennedy. They followed me right up to the underwear counter. One of them even asked me whether I wear boxers or briefs.

Lamp: Which do you?

Hoag: Hey, you want to know, buy a newspaper. They . . . they practically have Vic strapped in the electric chair. Any sign of him?

Lamp: None. He's flat out disappeared. And doing himself no good either.

Hoag: Orange juice? Fresh squeezed. No chemicals.

Lamp: Thanks. Where's Miss Day?

Hoag: Real estate class. She should be back any minute.

Lamp: I'm surprised she went back to school so soon.

Hoag: Said she wanted to get things back to normal. Or what passes for it around here.

Lamp: And you? Back to work?

Hoag: My publisher is express-mailing me a copy of everything that burned. I have to rent another typewriter. Be back into it tomorrow. Your men find anything yet?

Lamp: Ashes. You must be a pretty sound sleeper.

Hoag: Very.

Lamp: I asked around at the parking garage where Mr. Day found the dummy. The attendant remembers him, of course, but not anything unusual about that day – nobody asking about the car or placing a life-size Sonny Day doll in it or anything.

Hoag: I suppose that would be too easy.

Lamp: Never hurts to ask. I don't suppose he told you where in Topanga Canyon he stopped to burn it. There might be some remains.

Hoag: Just a fire road.

Lamp: A million of those. We could look a year and not find it.

Hoag: Assuming it's there at all.

Lamp: What's that mean?

Hoag: His ex-partner told me the man was not above spinning yarns to get attention. He also said he was paranoid.

Lamp: Think he could have actually made up something that screwy?

Hoag: With one hand tied behind his back.

Lamp: Do you think he did?

Hoag: No, I don't. He was genuinely scared. But I thought you should know that it is a possibility.

Lamp: When did you speak to Mr. Knight?

Hoag: That day – Sonny's birthday. And again last night. He's extremely interested in the outcome of the book, what with the Chasen's thing and all.

Lamp: I probably shouldn't be telling you this, but the department is very interested in seeing Knight not get dragged into the investigation.

Hoag: Heavy political muscle?

Lamp: Same with the agent, Wright.

Hoag: If you're real nice to me, I'll tell you some very interesting stories about Wright someday over a beer. You do drink beer, don't you?

Lamp: I've been known to.

Hoag: Hard to believe anyone would sell it to you. How much influence does all of that muscle have on you and your investigation?

Lamp: (laughs) If you're real nice to me, I'll tell you some very interesting stories about that someday over a beer.

Hoag: That's not exactly a straight answer.

Lamp: That's not exactly a straight question.

Hoag: (silence) Ah, here's Wanda now.

Day: Hi. Hello, Lieutenant.

Lamp: Miss Day.

Day: Don't get up, please.

Hoag: What's in the box?

Day: A present.

Hoag: For me?

Day: Open it.

Hoag: Maybe later?

Day: Right now.

Hoag: Okay. *(silence)* Hey, a new pair of mukluks. Now I can really get back to work. Thank you. You're very thoughtful. Wait, what's this underneath? . . . It's a shirt. My god, it's a suede shirt.

Day: I saw it in the window of the Banana Republic on Little Santa Monica. It'll go so well with those khakis, don't you think?

Hoag: Wanda, you shouldn't have.

Day: That's not what you said last night.

Hoag: Well, thanks.

Day: I want a proper thank-you.

Hoag: Later.

Day: Promise?

Hoag: Yes.

Day: I'll hold you to it. And now I'll leave you. Bye, Lieutenant.

Lamp: Yes. Bye.

Hoag: *(silence)* I take it you don't approve.

Lamp: None of my beeswax, Hoagy.

Hoag: Then why the look?

Lamp: I don't know what you mean.

Hoag: Go ahead. Say it.

Lamp: Oh, heck, I'm just not sure I've figured you out yet.

Hoag: Nothing much to figure. Sometimes circumstance brings two people together.

Lamp: You told me . . .

Hoag: What I told you was the truth. Then.

Lamp: I see.

Hoag: So what's on your mind? Vic?

Lamp: Yes. Still think he didn't do it?

Hoag: Sonny could have been murdered by anyone who was here last night. Anyone who has an interest in keeping Knight and Day's secret from seeing print.

Lamp: Could be. But I have to tell you – I've cooled off on that theory. My job is to go by what I see. I see a guy with violent tendencies. I see a guy who was here at the time of the murder, and who knew where the murder weapon was hidden.

Hoag: That doesn't mean anything. I knew where it was, too. Half a dozen people did.

Lamp: Maybe so. But none of them escaped from police custody. None of them were fugitives when that fire was set. Early's escape suggests guilt. It gives me a focus, something concrete. My job now is to build a case against him. You were around, Hoagy. Can you think of any possible reason why Early would have wanted his boss dead?

Hoag: It's inconceivable. The man's total orientation was to protect Sonny, not to harm him. Besides, he's a guy who loses control. You saw him when he went for me. If he had killed Sonny, he wouldn't have gone into the study and gotten a gun. He'd have torn his head off. Like he did to me. Like he did to that sleaze in Vegas. You know, you ought to check that guy out. I mean, he really got creamed. You never know.

Lamp: I did. He hasn't been out of Las Vegas in the past two weeks. Strictly a local man. Good thought, though. I wanted to check out something with you, Hoagy. Seems in 1972 Early was linked with the beating of a guy at the Daisy Club. Guy almost died. The charges were later dropped. Know anything about that? Come up at all?

Hoag: You *are* good.

Lamp: Routine police work. Well?

Hoag: Sonny wanted to mention it in the book. He got some bad press over it at the time. Vic was . . . I guess you'd say upset about it coming up again. Sonny and I discussed it. He said he'd talk to Vic about it, that Vic would understand.

Lamp: I see.

Hoag: Now wait, I know how that looks. . . .

Lamp: Like a motive.

Hoag: It can't be Vic.

Lamp: Why not?

Hoag: For starters, he was with me the day Sonny found the dummy.

Lamp: Are you sure about that?

Hoag: We were together at UCLA. Then we were both here at the estate.

Lamp: Where were you?

Hoag: Working in the guesthouse.

Lamp: Where was he?

Hoag: In the main house.

Lamp: Doing what?

Hoag: How should I know?

Lamp: What if he went out?

Hoag: He'd have told me.

Lamp: What if he didn't want you to know?

Hoag: (silence) Forget it. That's not what happened.

Lamp: He could have gone out for half an hour without you or the housekeeper knowing. It's possible, isn't it?

Hoag: Vic Early didn't do it.

Lamp: How can you be so sure?

Hoag: I have a reason to believe it.

Lamp: What reason?

Hoag: Call it a hunch.

Lamp: I see. You going to share this particular hunch with me?

Hoag: I'm not ready to.

Lamp: I didn't think so. That's okay. That's fine. But understand my position. I'm not going to sit around and wait for you. I can't, simply on the strength of some *hunch* you've got. I have to go with the facts. You're speculating. Speculating can take you anywhere.

Hoag: Like where?

Lamp: Like . . . to you.

Hoag: Me?

Lamp: You. You're awfully at home here all of the sudden. You and Miss Day. Mighty nice set-up. Hugs and kisses. Expensive shirts. I checked up on you, you know. You've been kind of down on your luck lately. Broke. A drinking problem. Famous wife divorced you. . . .

Hoag: Wait, are you suggesting *I* killed Sonny?

Lamp: No, no, no. I'm *speculating*, remember? Face it, you really stand to clean up on this book now. You're already back in the limelight. Plus you've got Miss Day. I assume the house will go to her. Place must be worth, what, five million? More?

Hoag: Ten or twelve, I'd say. I was on the plane at the time Sonny died, remember?

Lamp: So maybe you didn't act alone. Maybe you've been plotting this a long time. Maybe you set Early up. Hmm. Very interesting.

Hoag: And total bullshit.

Lamp: Precisely my point.

Hoag: It is?

Lamp: Yes. See, that's what happens when you speculate. You reshape the picture, recolor it, make it look any darned way you want. That's why I go with facts.

Hoag: You're a lot sneakier than you look, Lamp.

Lamp: Just trying to prove a point.

Hoag: Pick another way next time.

Lamp: Didn't mean to upset you.

Hoag: Let me ask *you* something, Lieutenant. Is there any category under the law for what I am?

Lamp: I'm not following you.

Hoag: I'm being realistic, like you want. See, any way you color that picture, I'm somehow responsible. Even if you say it's Vic. I could have put my foot down. Told Sonny flat out no, we leave the Daisy anecdote out.

Lamp: Oh, heck, you can't blame yourself for what somebody else does. Whatever happened, Hoagy, it happened around you, not because of you. It's not your fault if Vic Early shot Sonny Day. Or if Joe Blow did. Go easier on yourself. Now, do you have any idea where Early might have gone?

Hoag: No. No family or friends that he mentioned. You could try the UCLA athletic department. He seemed to know people there.

Lamp: Okay. That's a start. Thanks for your time, Hoagy. I suggest you relax, finish your book, take care of Miss Day. Let me do my job. Okay?

Hoag: So much for your little Chasen's theory then?

Lamp: So much for my theory. That's speculation. Early is concrete. It's Early – until and unless the facts show otherwise.

(end tape)

CHAPTER
THIRTEEN

The facts did show otherwise a few days later. Three days to be exact.

I spent those days taking Lamp's advice. The tapes and transcripts arrived from New York, the IBM Selectric from a rental outfit down on Sepulveda. I set myself up in Sonny's study at his massive desk, his pictures and awards looking down at me. I was up to Knight and Day's postwar glory days now, and finding the going rough.

Sonny wasn't around anymore to look over my shoulder and growl, "Yeah, that's just how I felt, pally," or "No, that ain't me." I had a pile of tapes, some notes, some impressions, and the power to create a man out of it. I was on my own.

It felt a lot more like a novel now.

I was also having trouble concentrating. Every time I started to look through the transcripts for a specific anecdote or phrase, I instead found myself searching in vain for that something Sonny had said, that *thing* that kept nibbling away at me. I couldn't shake that. Nor the awareness of where the book was headed now, and the conversation I'd have to have with Connie about it.

I spent a lot of the time staring out the study window at the eucalyptus tree. And swimming laps. And 'pooning.

And with Wanda. I was in her movie a lot now. Background music was playing. The setting was lavishly appointed. A lot of action. Very little dialogue. No questions. No past. No other present. Just now.

Only once was there so much as a flicker of reality to us. She came into the study one morning, sat down on my lap, and ran her fingers under the shirt she'd given me.

"What will happen when you finish? Will you go back to New York and leave me?"

I pulled the snaps of her denim shirt open. "I can't even imagine leaving this room."

And we didn't. Like I said, it was only a flicker.

Occasionally, we chatted idly about going down to Spago or to a movie, but we never left the estate. There were two more cases of Dom Perignon in the cellar, and when we got hungry for food, Maria was there to cook us something. It did occur to me that this was the best life I'd led in a long time.

The only trouble was that Sonny had paid for my rebirth with his life.

I was out on the lawn 'pooning and trying to hear his voice when Lamp called. I was hitting the towel nine times out of ten again. The old eye was coming back. The voice wasn't.

Maria took the call. I picked up in the study.

"Start speculating again," Lamp announced without even a hello.

"What happened to your facts?"

"Know where Vic Early is? Know where he's been for the past four days? The Veterans Administration hospital on Sawtelle. He went straight there after he escaped. Checked himself in. They logged the time. He was there on the night of your bonfire. He's been there all along. Just took us awhile to catch up with him."

"What's he doing there?"

"That's the strange part. Maybe not so strange. He said he felt he was going to have to end up there, that there wasn't going to be much choice, and that he wanted that choice to be his own. He escaped because he wanted to walk in there on his own two feet. He's a proud guy. I kind of like him, to tell you the truth."

"So do I."

"Guess you're feeling pretty smart about this."

"Not really."

"I'm not going to say you were right and I was wrong. The facts looked a certain way, so I went with them. Now they look different. Early's not eliminated. He still could have pulled the trigger. But I have to look elsewhere."

"Back to your theory?"

"And to speculating."

"About anything in particular?"

"Yes. About who might have gotten mad at Sonny Day for telling secrets. *Real* mad."

C H A P T E R
F O U R T E E N

(Tape #2 with Harmon Wright. Recorded in his office at HWA, March 14.)

Hoag: Thank you for seeing me again.

Wright: Of course. I think all of us owe it to Artie to see his story come out. He was on his way back. That's what makes his death such a tragedy.

Hoag: You knew him a long time.

Wright: Longer than anyone. Longer than Connie or Gabe. God, he's been such a big part of my life for so many years. The phone calls. The tantrums. The crises. It's hard to get used to him not being here.

Hoag: There are a few loose ends I'd like to tie up.

Wright: Fire away.

Hoag: During our last interview, Sonny and I were discussing the events that led up to Knight and Day's breakup. According to Sonny, their feuding came to a head over *The Boy in the Gray Flannel Suit*.

Wright: Artie, he provoked that last fight.

Hoag: He did?

Wright: Absolutely. He wrote a picture that had no part for the guy in it, and then he told them this is the picture I want to do. They said fine, but put in a part for the tall guy. He said no, you make me do that and I'm walking. I told him, Arthur, they got you for three pictures, exclusive. You don't make movies for Warners, you don't make pictures for anybody. He wouldn't listen. He drew a line and he wouldn't cross over it.

Hoag: He told me Gabe was the one who drew that line, that Gabe demanded a musical.

Wright: That was only to save face. Gabe had never expressed any interest in doing a musical. Not until he got wind that Artie wanted to do a picture without him. I talked Gabe into at least reading the script for *Gray Flannel Suit*. He did, and he said it was a stupid picture – which it was – but only because Artie made it plain he didn't want him involved in it.

Hoag: Did Sonny back down and write in a part for him?

Wright: Absolutely not.

Hoag: I see. That's a little different than the version I heard.

Wright: Sonny Day wasn't perfect. You ought to know that by now.

Hoag: So what happened?

Wright: The studio took Artie's side, of course. He was the indispensable one. They gave Gabe forty-eight hours to think it over. I tried to get the two of them to talk to each other. They resisted. I said, after all you've meant to each other, you can at least have lunch. They met at Dave Chasen's. They were through as partners before the entrée came.

Hoag: You're saying they fought over this movie?

Wright: It's like I told you before – those two fought because they were seriously sick of each other.

Hoag: Connie threw Sonny a big birthday party the night before. Gabe was there.

Wright: A lovely affair. I remember it well. That was the night Gabe showed me what kind of actor he was. He gave Artie a lovely speech. He cried. He was very moving. Genuinely. Just like the other day at the funeral. The way he broke down. You think he felt any loss from Artie's death? No, sir. He loathed the man.

Hoag: Gabe told me he loved him.

Wright: He's never loved anybody in his whole life. Only himself. No surprise, him going into politics. Watch him move right up. A cabinet post. Then a candidacy.

Hoag: President Knight?

Wright: Sound crazy to you?

Hoag: Actually, no. It doesn't. Are you aware of any kind of personal conflict between Gabe and Sonny? Something that cut deeper than their professional differences?

Wright: Such as what?

Hoag: Such as an involvement between Gabe and Connie.

Wright: I don't talk about stuff like that.

Hoag: Stuff like what?

Wright: Smut. Gossip. I'm an attorney, a businessman. What people do between the sheets is none of my business. Or of the readers of Artie's book.

Hoag: I see.

Wright: Don't see. Don't see anything. Connie Morgan is one of the finest, loveliest women I've ever known. She's also a client. You lift one finger to harm her or her reputation and you'll have me for an enemy, and you won't like it.

Hoag: I wouldn't do anything that wasn't in the best interests of the family. Wanda seems to feel –

Wright: Leave Wanda out of it, too. She's had enough problems, the poor kid.

Hoag: Did Sonny mention anything to you about getting a threatening letter?

Wright: When?

Hoag: A few weeks ago.

Wright: No.

Hoag: Any idea of why someone would have sent him one?

Wright: No. No idea.

Hoag: Are you aware that he and I hit a kind of impasse shortly before his death?

Wright: I know what he told me.

Hoag: Which was?

Wright: That you stopped trusting him. That the two of you fought and you went home to New York, mad. He told me he missed you and kept wanting to call you.

Hoag: When did he tell you this?

Wright: That night. His last night.

Hoag: By phone.

Wright: No. I was there.

Hoag: You were at Sonny's house the night of the murder?

Wright: Yes. I'm here at the office very late. It wasn't unusual for me to stop by his place for a nightcap on my way home. See how he was doing.

Hoag: You don't say. I don't recall your dropping by since I've been here.

Wright: That's because I didn't want to bother you two. I know how important chemistry is between creative people.

Hoag: I see.

Wright: Artie, he wasn't doing so well that night. He was real upset about what happened between you and him.

Hoag: Did you have any other reason for stopping by?

Wright: I don't know what you mean.

Hoag: When I told you we intended to discuss your early career with Bugsy Siegel in the book, you seemed bothered. I wondered if perhaps you discussed it with him that night.

Wright: (silence) It came up.

Hoag: Did you ask him to leave it out?

Wright: Let's say I pointed out that he wouldn't exactly be giving me a shot in the arm by mentioning Benny and the old days. Especially the business about the missing money. . . .

Hoag: So that did happen?

Wright: Whether it did or didn't is immaterial.

Hoag: What's material?

Wright: My personal health and well-being. Not all of those old-timers are dead and gone. A couple I can think of are still damned powerful. And they never, ever, forgive.

Hoag: You mean after all of these years you're still afraid you'll be found floating facedown in your pool?

Wright: Don't mock me. You don't know them.

Hoag: What did Sonny say when you told him this?

Wright: He said it was very important to him that the book be honest. I understood that, but I told him I didn't think he had to drag *me* into his goddamned therapy. I thought he was being selfish and inconsiderate and I told him so.

Hoag: What did he say?

Wright: He said, "It matters to me. And if it matters to me . . ."

Hoag: "It *matters*." And what did you say?

Wright: I never bullshitted Artie. I told him he was leaving me with no choice but to send a letter to his publisher's attorney, threatening legal action if there was any mention in the book about my past or my previous associations.

Hoag: How did he react to that?

Wright: He had a drink. And then . . . he had another drink. Started getting ugly. Then started sobbing. The usual routine. I tried to put him to bed, but he yelled at me to get lost. So I went home.

Hoag: What time was that?

Wright: A little before one, I think.

Hoag: Just before he called me.

Wright: I wouldn't know about that.

Hoag: Who else was there at the house?

Wright: Vic. He went to bed while I was there.

Hoag: Wanda?

Wright: She was out.

Hoag: Do the police know you were there that night?

Wright: Do I look stupid? I tell them I was there, it'll be all over tomorrow's papers. I've worked very hard to build my reputation. That's all I need, to be linked to Artie's murder.

Hoag: Surely there's nothing incriminating about an old friend stopping by for a drink.

Wright: I've seen dozens of careers made and destroyed on nothing more than rumors. I told that Lamp nothing about it. None of his business. Artie was alive when I left. I'm telling you because we're on the same side – Artie's side. Sure, I know what you're thinking about me at this very minute – rough background, prison record, buddy of Benny Siegel. He'd have no problem pulling a trigger. Wrong. I run the largest talent agency in the world. I'm a respected business leader. I don't pull triggers. That's the truth.

Hoag: Thank you for being so honest with me.

Wright: I never lie to a client. That's the secret to my success. So listen, Hoag, now that Sonny's gone and you're carrying on, I hope you'll see things my way.

Hoag: What way is that?

Wright: That it isn't necessary to drag my yesterdays into this book. Who needs lawsuits, right? You know, you're a bright, creative person. Good looking. Make a nice impression.

Hoag: I'm a helluva guy.

Wright: You'd make a helluva producer.

Hoag: I'm a writer.

Wright: Producing *is* writing – without a typewriter. You'll love it. And I think you can be a big, big success at it. I'd like to take your career over. Handle you personally.

Hoag: This is a real honor.

Wright: Why not? I got packages all over both coasts. No reason not to cut you in on them. For Artie's sake. All I have to do is pick up the phone. Or not . . .

Hoag: Or not?

Wright: Artie ever tell you the saying they used to have about me in the old neighborhood?

Hoag: No, he didn't,

Wright: Then I'll tell you, and it's something to keep in mind if you ever want to earn another dollar in this or any other town: "Don't mess with the Heshman." Think it over, huh?

(end tape)

CHAPTER
FIFTEEN

ou know, I could actually make out better by not going ahead with this book."

"How so?" she asked, her big toe lazily caressing my calf under the sheet.

"Harmon. Gabe. They've both made it plain they'd take care of me financially – if I were to back off."

"You won't. You'll finish it, and you'll finish it in the right way."

"You were so against it before. Why are you so for it now?"

"Because I know what it means to you. I know *you*."

I smiled. "Just about."

It was past midnight and we were in Sonny's bed, where it started, where we always returned. For lighting there was the small fire I'd built in the fireplace. For refreshment there was the bottle of Dom Perignon, which was in a bucket on the floor next to Lulu, who was busy staring down the tub of beluga that sat on the bed. Caviar is an unusual taste for a dog, but not for a dog who likes mackerel. I spooned some onto a square of toast and gave it to her. She almost took a finger with it. Then I refilled the glasses and Wanda took hers and she said "skoal" and it was the wrong thing to say.

It belonged to another midnight snack. Another bed. The one at Blakes' Hotel in London, when Merilee and I were on our honeymoon. Together. Perfect. Forever. I got out of bed and went out onto the terrace. But the wave of melancholy found me out there and crashed over me just the same. It had all seemed so right that night in London. It *had* been right. It still was.

"What's wrong?" Wanda called to me from inside.

"Nothing."

"Tell me."

I came back inside and put another log on the fire. It was pine and very dry. It burned quickly.

"My memory," I said.

"What about it?"

"It's a damned good one."

She reached for a cigarette and lit it. "I guess I know what's bothering you. You're thinking about how sorry you are. Sorry you got started with me."

"No. Never."

"Then why are you shutting me out? What is it?"

"It's Merilee." I drained my glass. "It always will be Merilee."

"Oh."

"You've made me feel alive again, Wanda. For that I'm grateful. Very grateful. But I'm not over her. It's not over. You've made me realize that."

"I thought she was married to Zack – "

"She is. For now."

She shook her head. "Nice try, Hoagy. I'll make it easy for you. I'll take it from here. You've gotten your rocks off sixty-two different ways and now you're starting to ask yourself questions. Questions like: 'Am I the one who's going to straighten her out?' 'Am I the one who's finally going to make her happy?' 'Am I going to have to dump her, like all the others did?' That's *really* it, isn't it, Hoagy? See, I've been through this before. Believe me, I've been through it."

"Nice work. You managed to trash both of us without even working up a sweat."

"Fuck you."

"It's not as if this kind of thing happens to me every week. Or ever."

"It's not like I tell guys about Gabe and Mommy every week," she told me back. "Or ever."

I let her have that one.

She put out her cigarette and lit another. "I thought we were doing okay, Hoagy."

"We were. But it can't go on."

"You're going back to New York?"

"As soon as I can."

"Last time I was in New York," she said, "I saw a fender-bender between two cabs on Sixth Avenue. The drivers got in an argument right there in the middle of the street and started shoving each other. Instead of trying to break it up, all the people on the sidewalks were yelling, 'Hit him! Hit him!' I could never live in a place like that, where there's so much hate."

"You mentioned once that this place isn't real. That is. Hate is real."

"Connecticut is nice. I was happy there."

"That's right. You lived there on the farm with Connie. Did you know he was never out there? Not once. He never even saw the place."

"No, I didn't. That's amazing. What else . . . what did he tell you about me?"

"Really want to know?"

"Uh-huh."

"That he cherished you. And that when you started to withdraw, to . . ."

"To get weird."

". . . he thought God was punishing him."

"Perfect." She sighed and slumped against the pillows.

I poured the last of the champagne into her glass and had some of the beluga. Lulu still hadn't taken her eyes off it.

"This is where I belong," Wanda said. "L.A. I belong here."

"Ah."

She suddenly jumped out of bed and stood glaring down at me, her hands on her hips, her long, naked flanks tensed. "What's that mean?"

"Nothing."

"Didn't sound like *nothing*. Sounded like 'Okay, Wanda. Whatever you say, Wanda. You're the basket case, Wanda.'"

"Kind of touchy, aren't you?"

"For somebody who's getting dumped?"

"You're not getting dumped. It's . . . I just can't live in your movie anymore."

"Try *hell*!"

She whirled and stormed out of the room, slamming the door behind her.

I went after her. Lulu, a sentimentalist, went right for the caviar.

I caught up with Wanda at the top of the stairs and took her by the arm.

"Let me go!" she cried. "Let me go!" She yanked her arm free and ran down the steps and out the front door of the house, stark naked, screaming "Motherfucker!"

I let a curse of my own go. And then I followed her out there.

She was on the lawn, screaming "Motherfucker! Motherfucker!" in the general direction of the house. She was quite hysterical, and the cops guarding the place were getting quite a free show. I tried to grab her, but she took off on me. She was quick on her feet. I chased her around the reflecting pond. I chased her *through* the reflecting pond. I followed her into the orchard. And out of the orchard.

I finally intercepted her over by the log arbor. I tackled her around both legs. The two of us thudded to the grass and lay there, cold, wet, panting.

"Everything okay there?!" one of the cops yelled.

"Fine!" I yelled back, my chest heaving. "Just a disagreement!" She was sobbing now. I held her until she stopped.

"Feeling better?" I asked.

"Sorry. Didn't mean to make a scene. Not very sophisticated of me."

"I'd better check into a hotel."

"No, don't. Please stay, Hoagy. I'll . . . I'll make up another bed for you. Okay?"

"Okay. Thanks."

I got to my feet, held my hand out to her. She took it. I pulled her up.

"Still pals?" I asked.

"Still pals."

I smiled. "Ex-pals?"

She smiled back. Then she shook her head. "No, ex-lovers."

CHAPTER
SIXTEEN

(Tape #2 with Connie Morgan. Recorded in her dressing room at the Burbank Studio, March 20.)

Morgan: It's nice to see you again, Hoagy.

Hoag: Same here. Good to be back at work?

Morgan: Very. Everyone has been so kind and understanding.

Hoag: That looks like a new knitting project.

Morgan: Yes, it is. No point in . . . in finishing the old one.

Hoag: Sorry I mentioned it.

Morgan: Don't be. That's the worst thing you can do when you're grieving – avoid the subject. You have to keep it out in the open, talk about it, let your feelings flow. Otherwise . . . I'm sorry, what did you want to see me about?

Hoag: A sensitive matter. To do with Sonny's book. With . . . with the past. It's a matter he had difficulty talking about. But, I believe *was* going to talk about. . . .

Morgan: Go on.

Hoag: The last thing I want to do is cause you further pain, Connie. I want you to know that. I'm . . . I'm going to raise a subject. If you feel like talking about it, that would be great. If you don't, we'll drop it. And consider leaving it out of the book entirely. Okay?

Morgan: You're talking about the breakup, of course. About the fight.

Hoag: Yes. You mentioned to me before that your marriage to Sonny was on shaky ground for a long time before you divorced him. You mentioned that he had a number of affairs. What we didn't discuss was whether you yourself had any.

Morgan: What are you getting at?

Hoag: That you and Gabe Knight were lovers for several years. That the affair came to Sonny's attention and caused the fight. That they broke up because of you.

Morgan: This is what you want to put in the book?

Hoag: I've been asked to finish Sonny's book, and finish it as he intended to finish it. I want to do that. But not at your expense. So . . .

Morgan: You're leaving it up to me.

Hoag: Yes.

Morgan: I appreciate that, Hoagy. I really do. You, I suppose, got this from Wanda?

Hoag: She feels it should come out. No more secrets.

Morgan: A worthy sentiment. I understand it. I understand your side, too, I think. Arthur was killed before he could say this to you. But he wanted to say it, and it represented the final breakthrough of your difficult collaboration.

Hoag: Yes.

Morgan: Have you spoken to Gabe about this?

Hoag: I intend to. However, the vibes I've gotten from Gabe so far aren't exactly positive.

Morgan: (silence) He was a sweet man, you know. A bit of a rat on the surface, but nice underneath. From the beginning, on the set of *BMOC*, there was an attraction between us. A look, an awareness. But Arthur was the one who pursued me. I was Arthur's. And Gabe was married. Not that it meant anything to him. For a long time nothing happened between us. Not until we all came back from New York and Arthur took up with Jayne and moved out, and I was alone a lot. Believe me, I . . . wanted to tell you about this before, Hoagy. It's been on my mind that I wasn't completely truthful with you. It's bothered me.

Hoag: You've had other things to worry about.

Morgan: Try to understand, please. The way I was brought up – it's all been very difficult for me. Difficult to . . . to start up with Gabe. And to talk about it now, even after all of these years.

Hoag: I understand. And I repeat, you don't have to if –

Morgan: I was the lowest I'd ever been. My husband had chosen to be with someone else. He didn't want me anymore. It gave me a very low opinion of myself. Especially because I wasn't being offered parts anymore. There were younger, prettier girls around town now. I was an old hag who had nothing to offer. I was vulnerable. Gabe called me one night, suggested we have a drink and talk about our problems with Arthur. We met at a small club in the Valley and ended up pouring out our troubles to each other. You see, Arthur was making Gabe's life just as miserable as he was making mine. Gabe felt useless, untalented, unappreciated, too. We were two unhappy people, both of us groping for the nerve to break it off with him, both of us loving him. We felt better talking about it, sharing it. And soon we were also talking about those looks on the set a long time ago, and the next thing

I knew Gabe was telling me he loved me. We . . . he took me to an apartment he kept near there for his trysts, I suppose. And he made love to me. I didn't enjoy it. All I kept thinking was . . . I wish this were Arthur. But I continued to see him. And gradually over the next few months, I did begin to enjoy it. His attention. His passion. He wanted me. My husband didn't.

Hoag: I keep getting the feeling something happened that night at Sonny's birthday party. Can you tell me what it was?

Morgan: I'm not proud of it. It's the one thing I'm most ashamed of. The drinks were flowing and . . . Gabe and I got reckless. He . . . we . . . I let him corner me and convince me to run upstairs for a quick . . . a quick fuck. That's really the only proper word for it. I followed him up there, feeling wild and wanton. We went into the bedroom, Arthur's and mine, and . . . lord, we were drunk, mad. Maybe we were hoping to get caught. We ripped open a few zippers and buttons and he began to take me right there on the bed, with hundreds of people downstairs. My husband. His wife. The door was locked. We locked it. But the door to the bathroom wasn't. It connected to a sitting room on the other side. And . . . I'll never forget this. I opened my eyes at one point and looked over his shoulder and there she was. Wanda was standing there in the bathroom doorway, in her little ruffled white dress, staring. I screamed. She screamed. And then she was gone. She ran off to tell Arthur. And before we could straighten ourselves and get out of there, Arthur broke down the hall door and found us in there together.

Hoag: The other guests . . . ?

Morgan: They didn't hear us. There was an orchestra playing. Laughter and noise. Arthur grabbed Gabe by the neck. I thought he was going to kill him. After all, I was still his wife, even if he didn't want me anymore. And I was . . . so *ashamed*. I convinced him that violence wasn't the answer. Then he ordered Gabe out – out of his house, his life. Gabe said wait, we have to talk this out. Arthur relented. They chose a public place, Chasen's. Ironic, isn't it? Lovers often pick a public place to break it off. It helps to avoid a messy scene. Only, Arthur and Gabe *had* their messy scene. And that was the end of the team.

Hoag: Did you go on seeing Gabe?

Morgan: No. Arthur and I had a long, serious talk about it. You see, it destroyed Wanda. She went into a deep depression that she just wouldn't come out of. She'd had problems, but this was much worse. She had to be hospitalized this time, for several weeks. When she was

ready to come home . . . well, we decided her health was more important than anything else, so Arthur cleaned up his act, I stopped seeing
Gabe, and we maintained the semblance of a happy home for the next
several years. It helped her a little. Not much, but a little. Arthur and
I kept up appearances until he met Tracy St. Claire and lost his head
over her. That's when we split up. That's the truth, Hoagy. That's what
happened. It's sordid and awful and I'm terribly ashamed.

Hoag: That's the secret that's been hidden all these years?

Morgan: Yes. This may surprise you, but Arthur was a gentleman.
So is Gabe. Gentlemen don't discuss these sorts of matters. Heshie
knew, but he'd never betray a client's secret. No one else knew, except
Wanda of course. It wounded her deeply. She shut it out for a long,
long time. When she came home from the hospital, she acted as if it
had never happened. It wasn't until she was older that she could begin
to confront it, but then she started experimenting with drugs and had
to be hospitalized again.

Hoag: Is there still anything between you and Gabe? That attraction?

Morgan: No. It's over.

Hoag: Did Sonny tell you he was going to discuss this with me?

Morgan: Yes.

Hoag: When?

Morgan: That night. I was there. Heshie and I were both there.

Hoag: He didn't say anything to me about you being there.

Morgan: Heshie's my agent. He was being discreet.

Hoag: Does Lamp know this?

Morgan: Yes. Not about Heshie, but about me. Arthur called
me and asked me to come up. He said it was very important. He
sounded upset. Heshie was already there when I arrived. Arthur had
been drinking and was in a vile humor. You know how he was when he
got like that. He told me he intended to tell you. Then he proceeded
to taunt me. He told me I was so old it couldn't possibly trash my
reputation any for the truth to come out. He said it would probably
help it, the public finding out that once, long ago, somebody still . . .
still *wanted* me. His language was much more colorful than that. He
said he'd been waiting a long time to get even with Gabe and now he
would. He was hoping to kill Gabe's political future. Gabe would be
finished, he said. I told him flatly that I was against it, that it was horrible of him to even consider it. So did Heshie. Arthur wouldn't listen
to either one of us. So we left. We stood by our cars discussing it. We
were both upset. Heshie for me and for himself – Arthur intended to

reveal his past associations, as you know. We honestly didn't know at that point what he would do. I suppose he phoned you soon after we left.

Hoag: Do you know if Gabe was also there that night?

Morgan: Not that I know of. Arthur may have phoned him. I don't know. Vic was there. Wanda was still out.

Hoag: Who with?

Morgan: This is out of personal interest?

Hoag: Perhaps. We've become good friends. Started to talk. She's . . . she's not exactly a snap.

Morgan: I know. Wanda's delicate. I love her dearly.

Hoag: Perhaps the truth coming out will help her. She seems very decided about it being the right thing.

Morgan: Possibly.

Hoag: What do *you* think?

Morgan: I think the important story of Arthur's life is his victory over his personal demons, not this. This thing . . . this was an incident, a tragic one. But a personal one. I wanted to tell you about it. Actually, it comes as a relief to tell you. But I'm not going to tell you what to do with it, Hoagy. I think whatever you decide to do will be the right choice. If you believe it's important to the book, I'll understand. I leave it up to you. You and your good judgment.

Hoag: Thank you. *(silence)* I think.
(end tape)

CHAPTER
SEVENTEEN

Maybe Gabe followed me to the Burbank Studio from Sonny's house. Maybe Connie told him I'd be there to talk to her. Either way, he was waiting there for me in the backseat of his limousine when I got to Wanda's Alfa in the studio parking lot.

He lowered his window when he spotted me. "Now," he said, "would be a good time for a chat."

I was going to ask him if I should hop in or follow him in the Alfa when I noticed that his bodyguard was pointing a gun at me from behind the wheel.

I figured we were carpooling.

We zipped right on through Toluca Lake and into Encino. One flat, dreary strip of shops after another lined the wide boulevard, broken up occasionally by a fast-food place, a gas station, a motel. We didn't talk.

Gabe rode next to me with his hands folded in his lap. He wore a lavender polo shirt, khakis, white bucks, and sunglasses. A pink sweater was knotted around his throat. All dressed up for a game of golf, or for the murder of the first major new literary voice of the eighties.

I stared out the darkened window at the scenery and marveled at the irony. Just a few short weeks ago, I would have welcomed death, provided it came swiftly and painlessly. But now – now I didn't want to die. Not with the juices flowing again.

The bodyguard finally took a left off Ventura and we eased into a neighborhood of apartment houses left over from the Fabulous Fifties. Like a lot of buildings in Los Angeles, they hadn't aged well. Things that aren't made well seldom do. The one we pulled up at had the letter C missing from the words *Casa Esperanza* that were affixed in fancy script to its dingy white face. The tiny kidney-shaped swimming pool crowded into the front yard was cracked and discolored. The palm tree at the curb looked dead.

We pulled in and took the driveway around back, where there were carports and storage closets for maybe a dozen units. We got out and climbed the outdoor staircase toward one of them. I could hear several TVs blaring. I could still hear them after Gabe's bodyguard had unlocked a door and the three of us had gone inside and he had closed it behind us. He remained there with his arms crossed. He was bigger than Vic.

The apartment had a plastic sofa, dinette set, pole lamps, gold shag carpeting. There was a bedroom.

"I always find it useful to keep a small apartment for myself," Gabe said.

"I know," I said. "Connie told me."

He raised an eyebrow. "In case you're getting any ideas, young friend, there's no point in raising a fuss. I own the building, and I rent exclusively to old widows who can't hear too well – especially over their soap operas."

"Okay, what do you want?" I tried to keep the quaver out of my voice. I failed.

He motioned to his bodyguard, who came up behind me, pinned my arms together, and sat me down gently in a dinette chair. Then he produced a couple of lengths of clothesline. Soon my hands were bound tightly behind me with one piece, my ankles with the other.

Gabe went into the bedroom and came back holding a black leather thong, the kind they sell at the rough-trade sex shops. He approached me, stopped, and coolly looked me over. Then, he whacked me flush across the face with it. He hit me so hard the impact would have bowled me right over if the bodyguard hadn't been holding me from behind.

My cheek caught fire and one whole side of my face started to twitch all by itself. Then blood began to ooze from where the leather had struck. I could feel it trickling down my cheek.

"You didn't heed my warning, young friend," Gabe said softly. "I advised you to back off or pay the consequences. You ignored me. I'm extremely upset."

He got himself a glass of water from the tap in the kitchen and held it up to the light to see what was floating in it. Satisfied it wouldn't kill him, he took a gulp. Then another. Then he dabbed delicately at his mouth with the sleeve of the pastel sweater still tied around his throat.

"Nobody seems very afraid of old Gabriel Knight these days," he said. "I warned *him*, too. And he ignored me."

"The letter," I said. "You sent him that letter."

"After all the ugly incidents he'd been through, I was certain he'd back away from a threat. Especially an anonymous one. I misjudged him."

He motioned to his bodyguard again. I heard the door open behind me, then close. The building shook as he went downstairs to the car. Gabe put the thong down on the coffee table, sat on the sofa, and crossed his legs, minding the crease in his trousers. "What did Connie tell you?"

"The truth."

He laughed. "The truth? Young friend, I've been in show business for over forty years. If there's one thing I've learned, it's that the truth is whatever you want it to be. I repeat, what did she tell you?"

"About the two of you."

"What about us?"

"Your affair. How Wanda caught you on the bed at Sonny's birthday party. And how you and he fought over it."

A flicker of something crossed his face. "I see. And she's letting you print this in the book?"

"She's left it up to me to decide what's right."

"And?"

"I was planning to ask you how you felt about it." The ropes were digging into my skin. My fingers were going numb. "But you've given me a pretty good idea. I suppose you're going to have to kill *me*, too."

He smiled, amused. "You think I killed Arthur."

"Why else would you threaten me? Tie me up? Use your little toy on me?"

He nodded. "It does look bad for me, doesn't it?"

"One thing confuses me."

"Only one?"

"Why?" I asked.

"Why?" he repeated.

"Yes. You slept with his wife thirty years ago. So what? Nobody believes politicians are perfect anymore. I can't imagine this would affect you."

Gabe scratched his jaw thoughtfully. "There's more at stake here than you seem to realize, young friend. I have an *image* to protect. I'm a clean-cut, small-town boy. That small town takes a lot of its pride from being my hometown. I have children there from my first marriage. Grandchildren. Think of the effect this would have on them. And think of Connie. She's a very proper, very old-fashioned Southern belle. Times have changed. She and I haven't. The public doesn't want us to. We are simply not the sort of people who do that sort of thing – and get caught doing it by a ten-year-old girl whose subsequent psychological problems have been well documented. That's why it matters."

"You can't possibly believe it's a matter of life and death. It's still image. It's not real."

"Oh, it most certainly is. Pick up the newspaper, young friend. Look at who's running the whole country. Don't tell me there's a difference. There's *no* bloody difference anymore." He got to his feet and began to pace, his hands clasped behind him. "I certainly wish I could figure out what to do with you. I could smack you around all day. I could offer you money. But I'll not talk you out of printing this story about Connie and myself. I can tell that about you. You're a moralist, a lapsed moralist who has found himself a cause again. Not much of one, but certainly more than you've seen in some time. You won't be put off course easily, will you?"

"If at all."

"Plus, I understand you and Wanda . . ."

"What about us?"

"Don't get uppity. I have a right to ask. I'm her godfather, you know. That makes it even more difficult for me. I'd hate to hurt her."

"For your information, she's *for* the truth coming out."

"Is she? That's interesting."

He paced around some more. Then, abruptly, he went to the door, opened it, and stepped outside. The building shook again as the bodyguard came back upstairs.

To untie me.

Gabe stood there watching us, his lips pursed.

"You're letting me go?" I rubbed my wrists, surprised.

"You're right," he said. "It was thirty years ago. No one will care. Besides, I can't go through with this. The plain truth is, I'm just not a violent man."

They led me down to the limo and drove me back to the studio. Gabe sat next to me, but he was very far away. He seemed lost in his memories. He barely reacted when we reached Wanda's car and I got out. Just waved a couple of fingers at me. Then they drove off.

My cheek was throbbing. I checked it out in the Alfa's rearview mirror. It was split open and looked like rare tenderloin. Blood still oozed out. By the time I finished this project I was going to look like an aging middleweight. One who had led with his face.

I tried to come up with some answers while I drove home, but I didn't get much past the questions. Questions like: Why did Gabe suddenly back off and let me go? What had changed his mind? *Was* he Sonny's killer? What was I going to put in the book?

I didn't have to wonder for long. While Gabe and I were busy having our little chat, Connie was busy making it easy for me. Sort of.

Wanda was the one who answered the phone. I had just walked in, and she had just asked me what the hell had happened to my cheek when it rang. She picked it up and said hello and listened. Then her eyes widened. She didn't say anything more. She just put the receiver down tenderly, like it was an egg, and walked away.

I called after her but got no response. I picked up the receiver.

"That you, Hoagy?" It was Lamp. He sounded a little shaky. Behind him, I could hear voices and phones and typewriters.

"It is."

"It's Connie Morgan. She telephoned me from her studio. Said she had something to tell me. By the time I got over there, I found her dead in her dressing room. Overdose of sleeping pills. There was a letter in her hand. A letter for me in which she confessed that she's the one who blew her husband away. Seems he was going to tell you about this secret affair she had going with Gabe Knight in the old days. You know, for the book. She went up there that night to talk him out of it. She said they quarreled and that a lot of repressed anger and jealousy came out of her. And so she went and got his gun. Instead of saying good-night out on the front lawn, she shot him. Wiped the gun clean and drove on home. She set the fire, too. To scare you off, get you out of there. Really something, huh, Hoagy? You there? Say something."

I cleared my throat. No words came out.

"Her letter says you interviewed her this morning and you'd pretty much figured the whole thing out about her and Gabe. That meant the secret was going to come out anyway, even though Sonny Day was dead. She couldn't do anything to stop it. And she couldn't live with her guilt. Her grief. So she took her own life, too. Can you imagine? *Connie Morgan* a *murderer*. What next, huh? What next?"

"I really don't know."

"That notion of yours you were working on, Hoagy. Was this it?"

"Kind of."

"Well, I'll send a couple of men over to keep the press from chewing your fence down over there. They'll be back. You can count on it."

"Okay. Thanks."

"You'll be wanting to see to Miss Day now."

I found Wanda by the swimming pool, staring into the water, not blinking. I said her name. She didn't hear me. She didn't know I was there. I remembered something Sonny once said about her: She was such a fragile little child he was afraid she'd crack if he squeezed her too tight.

She'd cracked.

I phoned her doctor. He arrived within fifteen minutes, a rumpled, weary little man with wire-rimmed glasses. He gave her a shot and we carried her upstairs to bed. He told me not to be too concerned, that she was probably just in shock. The shot would keep her out until the morning, when he'd be back. Then he put something on my cheek that hurt like hell and bandaged it. The wound took a long time to heal. I still have the scar.

The phone started ringing. It was the same old gang. Newspapers. TV. The *Enquirer*. The *Star*. The gossip columnists. I finally left it off the hook.

I put some Garner on and poured myself a Jack Daniel's. Then I sat down at Sonny's desk and looked out at the little eucalyptus tree.

It was over. The story had ended. And what a satisfying ending it was for everyone. Lamp had his murderer. The press had a juicy crime of passion and a suicide. The public a chance to see some idols smashed. My publisher had a book that would sell even more copies. Everyone was satisfied.

Everyone except me. Now I felt like I was somehow responsible for *two* deaths. I also had this funny feeling just like I used to get when a scene I'd written didn't work. Oh, it would seem solid enough on the surface. But I'd have this feeling, this sense that somehow something was off. I'd turn the scene over again and again, searching for the flaw. Eventually, if I looked hard enough from every possible angle, I'd find it. This was just like that.

Something here was off.

There was still Gabe. Something was still gnawing at me about him, the something Sonny had once said that I couldn't seem to find anywhere. And then there was his behavior. The flicker that had crossed his face when I told him I knew the truth about him and Connie. The abrupt turnaround he'd made. Why had he let me go? Why was it suddenly okay with him for me to reveal the true story about Knight and Day's breakup?

Simple explanation: I didn't have the true story. I thought I did, but I didn't. The flicker that crossed Gabe's face, that was him

registering an emotion – relief. Relief that the secret was going to stay
a secret.

So what was it?

I poured myself another drink and started searching through the
transcripts one more time. Sonny had told me something about Gabe.
Something that mattered. I had to find it. I read slowly and carefully.
I read every word Sonny had said to me in our sessions, hearing his
voice again, his inflection, his pride, his hurt.

It got dark out. Lulu padded in, hopped up on the sofa, and went to
sleep. I kept at it, line by line. I pored over everything, even the sections
that weren't about Gabe. The Gates Avenue stuff. The Catskills.

Whatever it was, I couldn't find it. Nothing.

It was late now, and I was bleary eyed. I looked in on Wanda.
She was fast asleep in Sonny's bed. She looked like a little girl asleep
there, secure and innocent. I went back downstairs and into the
kitchen. Maria had left me a salad before she turned in. I had some of it,
standing there in the kitchen, and washed it down with a bottle of beer.
I returned to the study with a second beer and tucked a shot of Jack
Daniel's into it. Then I sat back down at the desk.

Whatever it was Sonny had said to me, he'd said it off the tape.
When we weren't working. When we were eating. Or exercising. Or . . .
or what? What else had we done? Nothing. Where else had we gone?
Nowhere. Just Vegas. *"A lotta shtick under the bridge."* Vegas . . .

And then it hit me. Hard. What he had said about Gabe, and
why it had been gnawing at me. Because it did matter. It mattered,
all right. It explained everything. It explained the way Gabe had
acted. It explained why Connie had been in such a hurry to confess.
And to take her life.

Now I knew the secret. Now I really knew why Sonny Day
had died.

CHAPTER
EIGHTEEN

(Tape #1 with Wanda Day. Recorded in Sonny Day's study, March 21.)

Day: God, you look like Daddy sitting there behind the desk.

Hoag: Are you sure it's okay for you to be up?

Day: I'm fine.

Hoag: Maybe you should rest some more. The doctor will be –

Day: I'm okay. Just needed a little time to . . . deal with it.

Hoag: You sure?

Day: Positive.

Hoag: Sit for a second then. I want to talk. Here, beside me . . . That's good.

Day: I was thinking about driving down to Baja for a few days, to get away from this and clear my head. Want to?

Hoag: Sounds great. But first . . .

Day: Yes?

Hoag: There's something I've been meaning to ask you. It's personal.

Day: There's no such thing as personal between us.

Hoag: Okay. Now that Connie's confessed, now that she's . . . now that it's out in the open . . . will you tell me about it? Could you tell me what happened that night?

Day: What night?

Hoag: The night of Sonny's birthday party. Connie told me you found her and Gabe on the bed together.

Day: Oh.

Hoag: Would you mind talking about it?

Day: Is it important?

Hoag: I think so.

Day: Okay. Yes. I did find them. *(silence)* Everybody there got real sloshed that night. Everybody but me, of course. I was what, ten? But I saw what was going on between Mommy and Gabe. I saw the two of them making eyes at each other and whispering. And I saw them sneak upstairs. I followed them.

Hoag: How come?

Day: Because I knew they were going to do something nasty up there.

Hoag: And?

Day: They went down the hall into Mommy and Daddy's room. They were giggling. They shut the door. I heard them lock it. But I fooled them. I went around to the sitting room. And I went into the bathroom. I was very quiet. I tiptoed in . . . and I slowly slid the bathroom door open. They hadn't even bothered to turn off the light. Her evening gown was up around her neck and he was on top of her. His tuxedo pants were down around his ankles. Her . . . her legs were wrapped around him and she was moaning. And her face was all twisted and her lipstick smeared. They were fucking their brains out, Hoagy. Right there in the bedroom, with my father and everybody downstairs. And then . . . and then she *saw* me. She screamed and threw him off her. And I screamed. And I ran downstairs and found Daddy and I said, "Come quickly, *Mommy*." And he said, "Mommy what?" And I grabbed his hand and dragged him up there and he found them. He said he was going to kill Gabe. Gabe said, "Let's talk this out like gentlemen." And they did, the next day at Chasen's.

Hoag: I understand it really shook you.

Day: I freaked out totally. Mommy was always the sane one. When I realized she was out of control, too, just as crazy as him . . . I had to go into the hospital for a while.

Hoag: *(silence)* There's something else I wanted to ask you. Something that's been bugging me.

Day: Okay.

Hoag: It's about Lulu.

Day: Lulu?

Hoag: Yes. Remember the night the guesthouse burned down?

Day: Of course.

Hoag: Well, something very odd happened that night. See, it was the flames and the smoke that woke me up.

Day: What's so odd about that?

Hoag: That it wasn't Lulu who woke me. That she didn't bark at Connie when Connie came in and set my papers on fire. I still can't figure out why she didn't bark.

Day: She *knew* Mommy.

Hoag: She knew Sonny, too. Saw him every, day. But she barked at him the night he came into my room drunk. She didn't bark at *you* that night. When you came to me in Sonny's bedroom. Remember?

Day: I'll never forget.

Hoag: I suppose that's because she'd slept with you before. When

I was in Vegas. In the hospital. But Connie . . . Connie she didn't know that well.

Day: That is a little odd. But what do you expect – she is *your* dog.

Hoag: Very, funny. I suppose there's an explanation for the other things, too.

Day: Other things?

Hoag: Yes. Like how you were so dead set against Sonny's doing this book at first. Then, after his death, you suddenly wanted me to finish it.

Day: Because I love you. I told you.

Hoag: That's one way of looking at it.

Day: There's another?

Hoag: Yes. That you wanted to steer me in a certain direction. After all, you *are* the one who fed me the story about Connie and Gabe. You *are* the one who assured me she'd want to have the truth come out. You've been steering me all along, haven't you?

Day: Yes. To the truth. Because of *us*, Hoagy. What are you . . . why are you saying all of this?

Hoag: Because there are just too damned many odd little things, Wanda. Things that don't add up. At first, I couldn't put them together to mean anything. But then last night . . .

Day: What happened last night?

Hoag: I finally remembered something Sonny told me once about Gabe. It seemed a minor thing at the time, really. It wasn't on the tapes. It wasn't even going to end up in the damned book. That's pretty amazing, if you think about it. I mean, if you think about how hard I worked to get at the truth. And about how it's actually the key to the whole thing.

Day: Hoagy, you're not making sense.

Hoag: The night Sonny and I spent in Vegas, he got me a hooker as a present. She was waiting there in my bed for me. A beautiful blonde.

Day: Stop trying to make me jealous.

Hoag: Naturally, I didn't do anything. I couldn't then. So I woke him up and told him I didn't want her. He didn't quite grasp what I was saying, since he didn't know then about my condition. He thought I wanted someone else, someone different. He mentioned that lots of guys have . . . unusual tastes. Gabe, for instance, *"Gabe used to go for little girls."* That's what he said. Gabe liked little girls.

Day: So?

Hoag: So I didn't recognize that at the time for what it was – a major slip of the tongue. It was late. He was tired. Otherwise he wouldn't have said it. See, Gabe's weakness for little girls is kind of important. Especially when you consider how deeply, how so deeply he resented the way Sonny got the applause and the glory. And how Sonny rubbed it in. And when you consider how Sonny's own lovely little girl started to act kind of strangely. Withdraw. Grow more and more depressed. Display coldness toward her father. Pretty classic symptoms, wouldn't you say?

Day: Of what?

Hoag: I've figured it out, Wanda.

Day: Figured what out?

Hoag: Stop it, damn it! Stop the movie. That wasn't Connie up there on the bed with Gabe during the birthday party. You made that up, and Connie went along with it, as did Gabe. The truth is it was *you* up there with him. *She* was the one who tiptoed in from the bathroom. She found you and Gabe together. That's why Gabe and Sonny fought in Chasen's. That's why they split up. That's the secret everybody has been hiding all these years. There was never anything between Gabe and Connie. It was Gabe and *you*, and that night he finally got caught at it. He made a birthday toast – "To Sonny Day, the man who gave me everything." I'll say he did. Then they sang a duet – "their" song. Then Gabe went upstairs and molested his partner's little girl. Just like he had been doing for years. That's why Gabe and Sonny fought. That's why you were hospitalized. And that's why the real reason for their breakup has always stayed a secret. Sonny loved you. He couldn't reveal it – it would destroy you. And Gabe would be ruined if it ever came out that he was a child rapist. So they made a pact of silence. Which Sonny had decided to break. Maybe. You stuck that photo on my pillow with the knife. You ripped up my tapes. You were hoping I'd get the message. Split. You were hoping *he'd* get the message. You sent him the death threat. It's been you all along. Sonny was no stranger to your little tricks. He knew it was you. That's why he never wanted to bring in the police. You didn't go to Baja for his birthday. You were in town. You left him the dummy, the one you stole from his office years ago. That time you genuinely frightened him. He panicked. Fell off the wagon. Drove me away. It worked just like you hoped it would. What you hadn't counted on was that he'd decide to tell me the truth – to save you.

Day: Save me?

Hoag: He cherished you more than anyone in the world, Wanda.

He'd do anything to protect you. He told me that night on the phone that things had gotten out of hand, that the truth had to be told. He said the demons wouldn't go away. To him, you were crying out for help. He was afraid for you. He wanted to help you. He decided the truth was the only way you'd get that help. You hadn't figured on that. You hadn't figured he'd beg me to come back, and that I would. You heard him talking to me in New York on the phone that night. You got the gun. You shot him. You got back in bed. You were there. Connie said you were out on a date – to cover for you. She knew you did it. Gabe knew it, too. He warned me I was getting in over my head. He tried to scare me off by making me think *he* did it. He even told me he sent Sonny the death threat. Gabe's behavior yesterday puzzled me completely. First he was menacing. Then he was a lamb. That's because I'd been fooled. He knew his secret was safe. What he didn't know is that Connie had done herself in. Left a confession behind. Why did she do it? Was she afraid you'd tell the real story? Because we were lovers? Is that it? *(silence)* Wanda?

Day: It wasn't rape.

Hoag: It wasn't what?

Day: I mean . . . at first it was. It started after we moved back from Connecticut, I was seven. He'd pick me up after school in his car. Everybody always thought he was playing golf. Or he'd come into my room when he and Victoria were visiting. He'd put his finger inside me and unzip his pants and force my face down into him. Make me suck him off. He told me if I said a word to anybody, they'd send me away to an insane asylum for life. And . . . and you're right. He did it to get back at Daddy. Daddy drove him to it. It was his doing. If he hadn't been so mean to him, so cruel, so rotten, Gabe wouldn't have done it. Sonny Day fucked him. He fucked Sonny Day back. The best way he knew how.

Hoag: That's why you and Sonny always battled, isn't it?

Day: I hated him. At first, I hated Gabe, too. But after a while I didn't. I was lonely. I looked forward to his attention. Our secret. I made him happy. I pleased him. And he was nice to me. He brushed my hair. He called me his little angel. I-I loved him. He was my hero. The hero of my movie. My white knight – he was even named for it. Only, I loved him the wrong way. Or that's what they said. They said a little girl isn't supposed to love a grown man that way. They said I was sick. So they locked me up. But it didn't stop me. When they let me out, I still saw him. Until I moved to France and started acting. But I never stopped loving him. He was the only man who really cared about me. No one else ever has. Not Daddy. Not my husbands. Not anyone.

Hoag: What about me?

Day: I love you, Hoagy.

Hoag: Then why did you set my room on fire?

Day: I-I wasn't trying to kill you. I did it so you'd have to move into the big house with me. At least, part of me did. Oh, god, Hoagy. I'm freaking out again. I can't tell what's real . . . you were my new white knight. In my movie. Part of me wanted you that night, in Daddy's bed. Only part of me was afraid for you, too. Afraid I'd hurt you. That part of me set the fire. . . . Shit, I can't tell what's real anymore. *Shit!* Daddy . . . Daddy, he wouldn't listen to me. He didn't love me. He wouldn't keep my secret anymore. He was going to tell everyone about it. That was wrong. My secret. You don't do that. Not my secret. So I stopped him. And I went to bed and pretended I'd been asleep. And no one knew. Except Mommy. And Heshie. And Gabe. They knew. But they keep my secret. They always keep my secret. So it's okay. See, it's okay. *(silence)* Do you love me, Hoagy? Like I love you? *(silence)* Hoagy?

Hoag: What we had together, Wanda . . . I have to know. Was it *real*? Or were you just performing?

Day: I love you. And you love me. I'm glad you know now. About my secret. I really am. It came between us. Nothing will now. Let's go to Baja, Hoagy. Right now. Mommy's funeral won't be for days. We can swim naked and grill fish and drink tequila –

Hoag: It sounds fabulous . . .

Day: Great. I'll get some things together. Be down in a minute.

Hoag: . . . only, I think I'd better call Lieutenant Lamp first.

Day: Lieutenant Lamp? Why?

Hoag: Wanda, you're a sick woman. You know it. You said so yourself. He'll make sure you get help. You need help.

Day: Do you love me? If you love me, you'll keep my secret.

Hoag: I can't.

Day: W-Why not? I don't understand. You . . . you *bastard*! You don't give a shit about me, do you?

Hoag: I *do* love you, Wanda. *Understand* that. But I also cared about Sonny. I cared deeply. You killed him. You're also to blame for your mother's death. For this you have to be punished. I won't protect you.

Day: I don't believe this.

Hoag: I don't believe in much myself. But I do believe this.

I'm calling Lamp.

    Day: He won't believe it. I'll deny it.

    Hoag: He'll believe it all right. I've taped this entire conversation –

    Day: You *bastard*! *Motherfucker!* Give me that tape!

    Hoag: No! Ouch! Let go! *Stop that!*

    Day: Give it to me! Give it to me or –

    Hoag: Or *what*?! You'll kill *me*, too? Then who? Gabe? Harmon? It's over, Wanda. It's all over. Fade-out. The end.

    (end tape)

C H A P T E R
N I N E T E E N

Only it wasn't over yet. Not for her it wasn't.

She still had an escape scene in mind. As soon as I turned off the tape recorder, she dashed out of the study and up the stairs. A minute later she reappeared wearing a halter top, gym shorts, and sneakers, and carrying a nylon overnight bag and her car keys.

I met her at the bottom of the steps.

"Where are you going, Wanda?" I placed my hands on her shoulders.

"Baja," she replied coolly. "You can still come. The offer stands."

"Wanda, I can't let you leave."

"If you try to stop me, it means you don't love me. I don't believe that, Hoagy. I believe in our love. Coming?"

I shook my head.

"Then good-bye, Hoagy."

She kissed me lightly on the mouth, then slipped past me and out the front door.

"Wanda, I *mean* it!" I called after her.

She was running now, running for her Alfa, which sat in the big circular driveway with its top down. She jumped in and started the engine.

I had no car. There was no way I could stop her. No way at all. Until I glanced over to the lawn and spotted the javelin I'd been 'pooning with the other day.

She started for the gate. I started for the spear. As the gate began to open, I took my running start and I fired. My form and extension were excellent, the arch and distance magnificent. So was my aim. The javelin speared her windshield dead center, shattering the glass on impact. The tires screeched and then the little Alfa careened off the driveway and into an orange tree.

She flung open her door and started to scramble out, but there was nowhere for her to run to. The cops from the gate were already dashing toward her to see if she was okay.

She slumped back down into her seat, defeated.

Lulu was sitting on the front porch, clearly impressed. I'd told her many times before about my 'pooning prowess, but she'd never actually seen it for herself.

"Everybody," I explained, "ought to be good at something."

Then I went inside to call Lamp.

It was a small, dark bar on Santa Monica Boulevard over near the freeway. Not far from where we'd just seen Connie Morgan buried. Lulu sat next to me in a booth toward the back, munching on a pretzel. Her flight carrier was in the trunk of Lamp's car, along with my bags. Lamp sat across from us, helping me drink a pitcher of draft. Lamp didn't look sixteen anymore. The Day family had aged him.

There would be a trial. Being a witness, I'd have to come back for it. But I was free to go for now. Lamp had the tape I'd made of our final conversation. He had the truth. The press didn't. He'd been ordered not to tell them. Wanda's secret was going to remain Wanda's secret. At least it was for now. Harmon had seen to that – with a few phone calls. *"Don't mess with the Heshman."*

Yes, Wanda killed Sonny. Yes, Connie knew about it. That was why she confessed, why she took her own life. That much was public. But no one knew the real reason why. All they knew was that Wanda had been mentally disturbed, and that Connie had done what she did to protect her daughter from further pain. No one could condemn a mother for that. Especially America's favorite mother.

"It's a strange thing sometimes, Hoagy," Lamp said quietly.

"What is?"

"Justice. I mean, it will be served. A person committed a crime, and she'll pay for it. Justice will be served. But, then again, it won't be served at all."

"Nothing you can do to him, huh?"

He shook his head. "Orders."

I filled his glass. "Give me a couple of months. I'll take care of him. I'll ruin him. You can count on it."

Lamp brightened. "You're putting it in your book?"

"Absolutely. People have always wondered why Knight and Day broke up. Now I can tell them. True story."

"What about your publisher? Aren't they afraid of a lawsuit?"

"Harmon's trying to lean on them. But if there's one thing I know, it's that you can't lean on people who smell money."

We touched glasses. Lamp was grinning now.

A couple of Mexican gardeners in T-shirts, jeans, and straw cowboy hats came in out of the bright sunlight, sat down at the bar, and ordered Coors.

"By the way, Hoagy . . ." He reached into his suit pocket and yanked out a dog-eared paperback of *Our Family Enterprise* and inched it across the table at me. "Would you mind autographing it for me?"

"It'd be a pleasure, Lamp."

I took out a pen and thought for a second. Then I wrote on the inside flap: "*To Lieutenant Emil Lamp. Don't ever change.*" Then I signed it and pushed it back to him.

He read it and blushed. "Aw, heck. Thanks, Hoagy. Thanks a lot. About . . . about Miss Day. I'm sorry. Seemed like a nice lady."

"She was. Also a crazy lady. But thanks." I took a deep breath, let it out slowly. "We got time for another pitcher?"

"Why not?"

"You sure you're over the legal drinking age?"

He winked at me. "They're willing to serve me here as long as I don't have more than two."

So I got us another one and we drained it while it was still cold.

They'd just mowed the lawn in front of the Veterans Administration hospital. It smelled fresh and green outside. Inside, the building was modern and clean. I can't say it was cheerful.

It took me awhile to find him. I had to go through the nurse on the desk downstairs, and another one on the third floor. He shared a sunny ward with a dozen or so other Vietnam vets. Several of them were asleep. Three were playing cards. A couple more were listening to Sony Walkmans. Vic was sitting up in bed. There was a *Sports Illustrated* in his hands, only he wasn't reading it. His eyes were glazed over. A dribble of saliva was coming out of the corner of his mouth. He was in la-la land. Tranked out. I waved a hand in front of his face. He didn't blink.

I wrote my name, address, and phone number on the back of a card and left it on his nightstand, in case he wanted to get hold of me. In case he ever could. Then I patted him on the shoulder and went back downstairs to Lamp's car.

It was finally spring in New York. The yushies were out in Riverside Park, jogging, bicycling, pushing their babies in their strollers. A few old beatniks were digging up the soil of the community flower garden. Two teenaged boys with pale faces and punk haircuts were tossing a baseball back and forth.

Lulu and I took the path down to the Hudson Boat Basin. I sat down on a scarred bench that faced the river and looked out at the haze over New Jersey. Lulu curled up and went to sleep with her head on my foot.

I thought about Sonny, and what he'd meant to me and how much I missed him. I thought about Wanda. The smell of her. Being inside of her. Alive again. I thought about Merilee. Maybe I'd send her a copy of the book when it came out. I'd like to think she'd want one.

The sun fell behind the Jersey Palisades and the lights came on in the park. Time to go back to the typewriter. I stood up. Lulu roused and shook herself and steered me back to our apartment.

The Man Who
Lived By Night

the second
Stewart Hoag & Lulu Mystery

For Helen Tucker Handler –
Miss New Jersey, 1919,
or thereabouts

I'm the shadow man
A stranger in my own strange land
I'm the shadow man. Here I am.

The sun here, it never shines
There are no directions upon the signs
Always on the outside
Always looking in
I'm the shadow man.

from the song by Tristam Scarr

"I am whoever they want me to be. If they want me to be a
shit-kicking rock 'n' roll rebel, I am one. If they want me to
be a drugged-out, decadent bleedin' millionaire, or a war
protester, or a stud, or a poet, or a god, I am one. I am
whoever they want. I am no one."

from an interview with Tristam Scarr
in *Playboy* magazine, May, 1973

CHAPTER
ONE

Tris Scarr lied to me from the beginning. He promised me his limousine would meet my plane at Heathrow to drive me out to Gadpole, his place in Surrey. There was no limo. There was no message for me. There was no phone listing in Surrey for a Scarr, T. I was on my own. And I was not surprised. That was Tris Scarr for you. It wasn't for no reason that an entire generation of rock 'n' roll fans, myself included, knew the lead singer of Us simply as T. S.

I phoned Blakes to see if they had a room, and they did. A taxi took me there. It was the evening rush hour, and raining hard. That didn't stop Lulu, my basset hound, from insisting on a whiff. I rolled down my window. She planted her back paws firmly in my groin, stuck her large black nose out into the wet, fumy air, and snuffled happily. This was her first trip to London. She'd been looking forward to it.

Blakes is a small, quiet hotel on a small, quiet street in South Kensington. I've always liked the place, even though it has gotten chic lately. Merilee and I spent our honeymoon there. I liked it even more when I found out Mr. Tristam Scarr had an account there. I got a cozy room on the top floor in the back. There was a terrace. After I hung up my trench coat and Borsalino, I ordered smoked salmon sandwiches and a pot of tea from room service. Then I phoned the barman. I was working my way through the single malts that year. We decided he'd send up an aged Glenmorangie.

Next I phoned Jay Weintraub, T. S.'s lawyer in New York, and told him we had a problem.

"So he forgot to send a car," Jay soothed. "Not such a big – "

"If it was a priority he would have remembered."

"It is. Look, Hoagy, this is T. S. He's a unique, complex individual. He's been about the most famous rock personality in the world for over twenty years. You got to make allowances for people like that."

"You know what you get when you make allowances for people like that, Jay?"

"What?"

"A book that no one can be proud of."

"I don't see that happening with a writer of your caliber involved."

I let him have that one.

"Give him a chance, Hoagy. Be patient. T. S. has a hard time trusting people, with everything he's been through. They told me, I mean, you got a rep for being able to handle the tough ones."

"If they're genuinely serious about going through with it."

"He is. I know he is. He's ready to take the step. Bombshells he's got. Between you and me, I think he misses the limelight. And the money doesn't hurt."

The publisher was putting up $1.95 million for Tris Scarr's life story. I was getting a sliver of the pie, plus expenses, to help him tell it.

"I'll call Gadpole," offered Jay. "See if I can straighten this out. He'll get in touch with you. Hang out. It . . . it may not be *right* away."

"When, Jay?"

"Soon."

"When, Jay?"

"I don't know, okay? Just chill out. Please?"

I split the salmon sandwiches with Lulu. She had water with hers. I washed down mine with the tea and a short glass of Glenmorangie. It wasn't the worst scotch I'd ever tasted. Possibly, it was even better than the Glenlivet.

I drew myself a bubble bath. Next to clotted cream, baths are the best part of being in England. The tubs are actually long enough to lie down in. I've never understood the point of short American tubs, other than to drown small, loud children in. I poured myself another Glenmorangie, climbed in, and oozed down, down, down into it.

I didn't mind hanging out. Merilee, my ex-wife, happened to be arriving in a couple of days to play Tracy Lord in a revival of *The Philadelphia Story* at the Haymarket. Anthony Andrews of *Brideshead Revisited* was starring opposite her as C. K. Dexter Haven. There had been a rumor in Liz Smith's column before I left that Merilee and her new husband, that fabulously hot young playwright Zack something, weren't getting along. He was not making the trip with her.

I lay there in the tub, sipping my single malt and wondering. Wondering if she'd be happy to see me. Wondering what, if anything, would happen between us now that I sort of had my juices back. *Merilee.* We had fallen for each other in that fine, first flush of our own successes. She was Merilee Nash, Joe Papp's newest, loveliest darling. I was Stewart Hoag, that tall, dashing author of that fabulously successful first novel, *Our Family Enterprise* – the man who the *New York Times* had called "the first major new literary voice of the eighties." God, we were cute. And she stayed cute. Won a Tony for the

Mamet play. An Oscar for the Woody Allen movie. Time put her on its cover. Me, I dried up. No juices – of any kind. No second novel. No marriage. I crashed. But that was behind me now. These days I was as happy as a man whose best days are behind him can be. I was even, at long last, working on a second novel. But it was coming in drips, not waves. Possibly, I'd have to finish living it before I could finish writing it. Possibly, I'd even have to grow up a little. In the meantime, I got by as a ghost. I'm ideally suited to my second, somewhat less dignified career as a ghostwriter – partly because celebrity memoirs are more fiction than anything else, partly because as a former luminary I have something in common with my subjects that the lunch-pail ghosts don't. What was it Norma said in *Sunset Boulevard*? "Great stars have great pride." Yeah. That pretty much covers it.

Of course, I have encountered one small occupational hazard. A ghost is a seeker of celebrity secrets, past and present. As it happens, there's often someone around who doesn't want those secrets dug up. I carry a pen, not a gun. Trouble is not my business. But my business can be trouble.

I ate dinner in the hotel, just in case T. S. called. I wore my navy blue Ferre suit with a starched white shirt, silver cuff links, maroon-and-white polka-dot bow tie and calf-leather braces. I looked like a million bucks. The hush when Lulu and I descended into the plush basement dining room was perceptible.

Chris Reeve was dining there with a stunning blonde. In town to make *Superman Eleven*, no doubt. He and Merilee did a play in Williamstown one summer, and I had learned that his only off-camera superpower was dullness. I ducked into the tiny bar only to be cornered by a Pittsburgh steel heir who assured me we'd chucked spears against each other on an Ivy League playing field a couple of decades before. I didn't remember him, but these days I find I don't remember much. The novel came up. He'd loved it. I bought him a drink. Or, T. S. did.

I got a corner table, where I tucked away duck liver pâté, lamb chops and a bottle of Côtes du Rhône. Lulu had a little grilled red snapper. I finished off with a pear tart, coffee and Calvados. Lulu had a little more snapper. No call came from T. S. We took a turn through the tidy, orderly streets of South Ken. The rain had let up. It was misty and gloomy out now. I like gloomy. Gloomy is deep. Gloomy is profound. Clear skies are for other people. Clear skies are for volleyball players and arbitrageurs and screenwriters. Lulu was getting into London. She sniffed gleefully at every bush and tree and lamppost, and got muddy paws and ears for her trouble. We went to bed late. Still no call.

The next morning I headed for Jermyn Street. At Floris I bought my cologne and talc. At Turnbull and Asser I bought a new shawl-collared target-dot silk robe. Merilee had stolen my old one. I always did have trouble holding onto my clothes, since she looked so much better in them than I did. The young, rakish T & A clerk, whose name was Nigel, also sold me some white shirts, after he gave up trying to sell me those gaudy striped ones. From there I strolled over to Savile Row. At Strickland's, Mr. Tricker fitted me for a sixteen-ounce gray cheviot wool suit, once he got done sniffing at my Ferre. While I was there I ordered a new pair of cordovan brogans from Maxwell's. There was still no call when I got back to the hotel. I spent the afternoon out on my terrace in the fog with Lulu, a blanket, a pot of tea, the Glenmorangie and *Six Decades*, a collection of Irwin Shaw short stories which I reread every couple of years to remind myself what good writing is. No call. I went to see the new Ayckbourn play. Still no call.

It woke me in the middle of the night.

"It seems there was a mix-up." The voice was soft and well educated. There was no trace of the famous Liverpudlian accent. Jay had warned me T. S. didn't actually talk the way people thought. That was put on. "I thought you were arriving next week, you see."

I said absolutely nothing. Just listened to him breathe. It sounded like the receiver was stuck halfway down his throat.

"A mix-up, you see," he repeated, a bit uneasily now.

I still said nothing.

Neither did he. Until, after a very long silence, he finally said, "I'm sorry."

"I'll be on the morning train to Guildford. Have someone meet me there."

"Yes. Right. Of course."

"Isn't there something else you wanted to say?"

"Such as?"

"Such as that there was no mix-up. That you purposely forgot so you could test my boiling point, and that you won't do it again."

He chuckled. It was the mad, malevolent chuckle of the Jolly Buganeer from *Skullbuggery*, the Us pirate-theme album that sold eight or nine million copies in the early seventies, and was made into that vomitous Ken Russell movie.

"It wouldn't do to push me, mate," he snarled. Now he sounded like the tough teddy who punched his way out of Liverpool-total transformation. "I push back, and bloody hard."

"Fine. Push someone else back. I quit."

I hung up on him. Then I waited for him to call back. Stars always do when I hang up on them. They aren't used to being treated that way. It challenges them. They like it.

I let it ring three times before I answered it. I listened to more heavy breathing. And then, finally:

"I won't do it again."

"Thank you. Good night, Tristam."

"Good night, Hogarth."

I turned over and went back to sleep. Our collaboration had begun.

A claret-colored Rolls-Royce Silver Cloud met me at the Guildford train station. The uniformed chauffeur was in his forties, beefy, red-faced and moustached. I helped him load my bags in the trunk, then Lulu and I sank into the back seat. There was a bar back there. Also a television, a refrigerator, a lot of dark wood and dove gray leather, and a glass divider, which was shut. The ride wasn't bad, if you're into total comfort.

The outskirts of Guildford were dotted with ugly new housing and shopping developments. That's one thing the British do even worse than we do. But soon there was little more than beechwoods and heathland and crumbling stone fences. And peaceful storybook villages. Shere. Gomshall. Wotton. The ramparts of a ruined Norman castle stood guard at the top of a hill outside of Dorking. At Bletchingley, we turned into a narrow, hedge-lined road, and the chauffeur opened the divider.

"That'll be Place Farm on your right, sir," he intoned, as we cruised past a stone castle so colossal even Donald Trump would be content to retire there. "Anne of Cleves lived here. Henry the Eighth gave it to her when they divorced in the year 1540."

"Just think what she'd have gotten if Marvin Mitchelson had been around then."

"Sir?"

"Nothing."

In another mile or so the hedged road ended at a wrought-iron gate. Here, two guards in business suits were on duty. One of them opened the trunk of the Rolls and began to paw through my bags. The other asked me to please get out of the car.

"We walking the rest of the way?" I asked.

"Routine security, sir," he replied. "Nothing personal."

The accent was American. So was the suit. Sears – the Arnie Palmer collection. He patted me down for hidden weapons, then said I could get back in. The other guard slammed the trunk shut. The gates swung slowly open. And into the realm – the secure realm – of Tristam Scarr we drove.

The road was crushed gravel and lined with beeches. It took us past meadows, past woods, past terraced gardens, past a lake. Then it cut through a clustering of little stone buildings – houses for staff and security people, stables, garages, a chapel. Almost a village unto itself. It was hard to imagine driving for so long without ever leaving your own property. Hard to imagine, but nice. A covered bridge took us over a stream and then there was Gadpole. It was an eighteenth-century brick manor house, three stories high with a glassed dome at its center. I doubt there were more than sixty rooms.

"Rock pays," I said.

"It does indeed, sir," agreed the chauffeur. "Handsomely."

Two more guards were on the front door. There were fourteen of them altogether, I was to learn. All of them retired FBI agents.

The housekeeper wore a sweater and pleated skirt of matching bottle green cashmere and knobby brown oxfords. She was in her sixties, plump, pink-cheeked and silver-haired. She smiled and fluttered a hand at me as I got out.

"Yes, yes, Mister Hoag," she called out cheerily. "Please do come in. He'll not be awake for hours, but he's asked me to make you comfortable. I am Pamela."

"It's Hoagy," I said as we went inside. "And this is Lulu."

"Why hello, Miss Lulu."

Lulu promptly rolled over on the polished marble floor of the entrance hall, four paws up, to be petted. She has a knack for buttering up anyone who might be in a position to slip her tasty morsels.

Delighted, Pamela knelt with a refined grunt and patted Lulu's belly. To Lulu she said, "What a sweet little thing you are." To me she said, "My, her breath is rather . . ."

"She has funny eating habits," I informed her. "As I'm sure you'll find out."

Gadpole wasn't an understated house. The entrance hall was two stories high and encrusted with ornate molding. A curving marble staircase wide enough to accommodate a Range Rover led up to the second floor. A tall doorway framed by columns and an angular pediment opened into the immense living room, where there was plenty more wedding-cake plasterwork, and a ceiling painted with nymphs and swans. The furniture was lacquered Louis XV. The tables were gilted with leaf patterns, the chairs intricately carved and upholstered in red silk. It was all exceedingly rococo and, seemingly, genuine. On the walls were a lot of formal portraits of a lot of dead English people. On the floor were richly colored Persian rugs. It wasn't at all the sort of place I'd expected from a man who once dropped his black leather pants in front of eighteen thousand screaming fans at Madison Square Garden and dared the police to arrest him. (They did.) It was more the kind of place I imagined Truman Capote would have lived in if he'd been born a peer. And who's to say he wasn't.

Lulu sneezed. She was shivering. So was her master.

The house was as warm and snug as a meat locker.

"I've had the west wing guest suite made up per your instructions," said Pamela. "I do hope you'll be comfortable."

"If there's heat there we'll be fine."

She chuckled. "You American visitors are always cold."

"And Mr. Scarr?"

She frowned, bit her lower lip fretfully. "I'm afraid Mr. Scarr feels very little."

The west wing guest suite was on the second floor, and so far down the long, carpeted hallway that it was in a different century. This one. The sitting room was masculine and clubby, right down to the hunting scene prints on the walls and the nicely worn leather sofa and armchairs grouped around the fireplace, which was, mercifully, lit. The typewriter I'd asked for was set up on a massive walnut desk in front of the tall windows that overlooked Gadpole's maze. Clearly, whoever had positioned it there had never tried to write a second novel. Pamela opened a wardrobe cupboard to reveal a television, videocassette recorder, stereo system and small refrigerator. There were bookcases full of interesting-looking books and a sideboard full of interesting-looking bottles.

In the bedroom there was a huge four-poster bed and another wardrobe, this one for clothes. Someone had already brought up my bags.

"I'll be in the kitchen if you want breakfast," said Pamela.

"Thank you. Lulu will lead me to it."

Actually, Lulu had claimed the leather chair closest to the fire and showed no signs of ever wanting to move. Possibly she preferred this to our dingy little fifth-floor walk-up on West Ninety-Third Street. Possibly she wasn't the only one.

"Your rooms will be made up daily," Pamela went on gaily. "Anything you need cleaned or laundered please leave by the door, and I'll have it taken care of. I do hope you'll be happy here, Hoagy."

"I think I can manage for the next twenty or thirty years."

There was a Macallan single malt on the sideboard that was almost as old as I am. It was certainly a lot smoother. As I sampled it I unpacked the Fair Isle sweater vest I'd had knitted for Lulu when she had bronchitis one winter. I didn't want her developing breathing problems again. She snores when she has them. I know this because she likes to sleep on my head. She wriggled gratefully into it. I put her bowls down in the bathroom. Also the cases of the only canned food she'll eat – Nine Lives mackerel for cats and very strange dogs. Then I hung up my clothes and decided to explore.

There wasn't much else in the west wing besides closed doors. The east wing was closed off entirely. The stairs up to the third floor and the dome terminated at a small landing, where there was a set of heavy double doors. Closed. Here sat another guard, reading a copy of *USA Today*. He looked up at me. He didn't smile.

"Mr. Scarr's room?" I asked, glancing at the doors.

"And recording studio. And kitchen. The works. He's got it all over Hef. You'll be Hoag."

I nodded.

"He's asleep now. Or doesn't want to be bothered. Later."

Downstairs I found a library, a formal dining room, a paneled billiards room and a grand ballroom that dwarfed the living room. A Knicks game could go unnoticed in there. Lulu was the one who found the kitchen, where Pamela was rinsing berries in the sink and humming. It was a modern kitchen, and not small. There were three refrigerators and a commercial-size hooded range.

"Have you eaten?"

"No, ma'am."

"Then pour yourself some coffee and sit," she commanded, indicating a cluttered country pine table. "He'll not be stirring for hours and hours. He only lives by night, you see."

"Like Count Dracula?"

"You've seen him then?"

"We've never met."

But I knew him. Just about everyone in America had since 1964, when he first appeared on *The Ed Sullivan Show*, his scowling, pockmarked face thrust brazenly forward at the camera, nostrils flared with impudence, voice a raspy primal scream. That night he sang Us's hit version of the Little Richard song, "Great Gosh Almighty." There would be so many more hits through the years – "Come On Over, Baby," "More for Me," "This Must Be Love," "New Age," "Miss Eloise," "We're Double Trouble," "For Johnny Baughan." Sure I knew him. He was T. S., full of talent and anger and himself. Strutting. Preening. Pointing at the audience. Condemning it. Alongside him there on the Sullivan stage stood Rory Law, his blond hair an uncombed mop, his snaggled teeth working on his lower lip as he fired off the brutal guitar chops that gave Us its distinctive sound. T. S. and Rory. Boyhood friends. Co-founders of Us. Popularly known as Double Trouble. Behind them, Puppy Johnson attacked the drums, sweating, grinning. Puppy Johnson, the man who, by way of Monroe, Louisiana, became Britain's first black rock star. The man who the British press labeled "the wild man of Borneo" for his drumming style and his lifestyle. Thumping away next to him on bass was Derek Gregg, the tall handsome one with the choirboy face and the angelic voice.

They were nasty and rude. They were rebels. Together, the four of them rode the second wave that washed ashore in America after the Beatles hit. That was the one that brought the Rolling Stones, the Who, the Animals. Us would last as long as anyone. They would outlast rhythm and blues, rockabilly, acid rock, reggae, heavy metal and disco. Their sound was their own, and no one did anything better. But that wasn't the only reason they got as much attention as they did. They were the bad boys. They took too many drugs, threw too many punches, used up too many women. They fought with the world and with each other. Always, it seemed, there was feuding and controversy. Violence. Scandal. Death. Only a year after that first Sullivan appearance Puppy Johnson was jailed in Little Rock, Arkansas for the statutory rape of a fifteen-year-old white girl. The group was banished from America. Two years later Puppy was dead from a drug overdose. The band went on. Triumphed. Broke up. Reformed. Triumphed again until that ghastly night in Atlanta's Omni auditorium, summer of '76, when Rory Law was gunned down on stage by a former disciple of Charles Manson. T. S. went on alone from there. Tried performing solo after the release of his album *Shadow Man*. But when someone threw a lit firecracker up on stage one night, and it exploded next to him, he walked off and never came back. He bought Gadpole and went into seclusion. After John Lennon's assassination he hired a full-time force of security guards to protect him. He seldom came out now. In fact, he had not been seen in public in over ten years.

Sure I knew him. Long ago, Tris Scarr had been my idol – the one after Mantle and before Mailer. Tris Scarr had provided the soundtrack for my coming of age.

Only, I didn't know him. No one did. He was, as Jay Weintraub had said, a complex man, a man of different faces, of contradictions, of anger. A man whose personal turmoil *was* rock 'n' roll. He had gleefully cultivated high-class friends and sophisticated tastes, yet at the same time blasted those who had money and privilege. He had partied and drugged and wrecked hotel rooms, yet was considered a sensitive poet and a serious intellectual. His stormy love life had consumed some of the most famous beauties of the past three decades, most notably Tulip, the London supermodel – The Mod Bod – whom he eventually married. He was T. S. He had seen it all and done it all – to himself and to others. He was a man who had stories to tell, and he'd agreed to tell them. The feuds. The women. The drugs. It all.

"Bacon and eggs do, Mr. Hoag?" asked Pamela.

"Always have. And it's Hoagy. Please."

"As in Carmichael?"

"As in the cheese steak."

She frowned. "I see." She went into the pantry and returned with eggs and a slab of bacon. "How do you like your eggs, Hoagy?"

"The same way I like everything else," I replied, stirring my coffee. "Soft-boiled."

CHAPTER
TWO

It was my fault we got lost in the maze.

Lulu hadn't wanted to go in there. She was having too much fun barking at the herd of deer nibbling on the grass at the edge of the woods. She even made a few of them bound off in terror. It was the happiest I'd seen her since she treed a baby squirrel in Riverside Park. But I insisted, and I'm bigger. Grudgingly, she waddled along next to me through the carefully pruned geometric corridors of ten-foot-high box hedges. First right, then left. Then left, then right. I had never been in a maze before. I liked it in there, and the notion we wouldn't be able to find our way out never occurred to me – I assumed Lulu would know how to, being a dog. I assumed wrong. To give her credit, she tried. But all she found was one dead end after another. Ultimately, all paths led to the gazebo in the maze's center, where there was a cast iron table and chairs and a metal strongbox. On the box was printed the words OPEN ME. I did. Inside it was a flare gun and a note: FIRE ME. Twenty minutes later the chauffeur arrived.

"I'm quite embarrassed," I said, apologetically.

"Don't be, sir. Happens to all of our guests."

"Even when they have a dog with them?"

"That is a new one, actually"

The chauffeur cheated. He had a map. We came out on the other side, where T. S.'s car collection was stored in converted stables. He liked Alfas. He owned two – a '31 1750 Zagato Grand Sport and a '59 Giulietta Sprint Coupe Racer. He liked Ferraris. He had a mouth-watering red '59 Pininfarina and a '67 275 GTB four-cam. He liked nice cars, period. There was a '52 Aston Martin Lagonda cabriolet, a '55 Mercedes 300SL gullwing, a '39 Packard Dutch Darrin convertible, a '64 Studebaker Gran Turismo Hawk, a '72 Maserati Ghibli spyder, a '52 Bentley R-Type Continental, a '56 T-Bird, a '57 Corvette. There were others. He even had a Delorean.

"Nice collection," I observed to the chauffeur, who had gone back to rubbing the Silver Cloud with a chamois. "If you like this sort of thing."

"Mr. Scarr does, sir," he replied pleasantly. "He does indeed."

I stuck out my hand. "It's Hoagy.

His hand was meaty and strong. "Jack, sir. Pleased to meet you."

"Been with him long?"

"A number of years. Yessir. Relatively quiet, this. Not like before. The girls used to paint lipstick kisses all over his car. Throw themselves in its path in the hope of meeting him. Plenty of goings on."

"You must have quite a few stories. I'd like to hear them sometime for his book."

"I'm only a chauffeur, sir. You flatter me."

"It won't hurt a bit – scout's honor."

He shrugged his heavy shoulders noncommitally. And said, "May I be so bold as to offer you a suggestion, sir?"

"Fire away."

He stepped toward me until his face was very close to mine. His breath smelled of beer and pickled onions and either very strong cheese or very old socks. "Don't look into the past."

"That's my job – looking into the past."

"Then I wouldn't look too closely"

There was a hint of menace in his voice now. At my heels, Lulu growled softly.

"Any particular reason?" I asked.

"I'll put it this way. You look like a bright young gent . . ."

"Not so young."

"It wouldn't be bright."

A threat, no question.

I nodded. "Duly noted. Up this road get me back?"

"Yessir."

"By the way – how does the Delorean run?"

"It doesn't."

It was dusk by the time we reached the house. After I fed Lulu I phoned the Haymarket. Merilee had arrived, but was presently in rehearsal. I left word where she could reach me. Then I popped open a bottle of lager and watched part eight of a sixteen-part series on BBC 1 called *Giant Worms of the Sea*. Whoever thinks British television has it all over American TV has never actually watched any. Then Pamela phoned to say dinner would be served in fifteen minutes. I asked if we were dressing. We were not.

The only light in the dining room came from the silver candelabra at the center of the huge dining table. Only one place was set. Mine. There was grilled rabbit and silver serving dishes of fried potatoes and buttered brussels sprouts waiting for me. A bucket held a chilled Sancerre. I dived in. It was delicious. It was also a tiny bit creepy eating there alone in the cold, dark dining hall, surrounded by more portraits of more dead English peopIe, the only sound that of my teeth tearing into the bunny wabbit. I knew there had to be cooks and maids around, but Pamela administered them so discreetly they were never in evidence. I was grateful when she finally came in to ask if everything was all right.

"Excellent," I assured her. "Most flavorful rabbit I've ever tasted."

"You've Jack to thank for its freshness. He's our gamekeeper. It's his hobby – pheasant, quail, hare. A fine shot, he is. Care for dessert?"

"No, thanks."

"Coffee then?"

"If it's no bother," I said. "Wouldn't it be easier if I ate in the kitchen?"

That tickled her. She laughed. "Formality makes you Americans so uncomfortable. Yes, yes, of course. You may eat where you wish. Was the time all right?"

"When do *you* eat?"

She reddened slightly in the flickering candlelight, heightening her lovely complexion. "Seven."

"Seven it is then."

She started back to the kitchen for my coffee, stopped. "I intended to ask you – have you a favorite food?"

"Only licorice ice cream."

"I'm so sorry."

"Not as sorry as I am."

The guard at the royal bedchamber door was a different one, but he didn't smile at me either. Just nodded and knocked. A voice answered from inside. I went in.

"Hiya, Hogarth," Tris Scarr said dully, as he shuffled slowly toward me in backless slippers, his posture stooped. "Come in. I was just eating m'breakfast."

Someone once described Tris Scarr as the only man alive who could look angry by the mere physical act of breathing. It was his nostrils – the way they flared. But he didn't look angry now. He looked weary and weak and sallow. His eyes were heavy-lidded and pouched, his pitted, unshaven face gaunt. He wore a loosely belted green paisley dressing gown. Below it, his bare legs were skinny and pale. Blue veins protruded from the tops of his feet above his slippers. He was smaller than I expected he'd be – five feet eight tops, and he couldn't have weighed more than 130. His hairless chest was positively concave. He still wore his black hair long and scraggly, only now it was streaked with gray. I hadn't, I realized, seen a photograph of him in several years – there hadn't been any photographs since he'd moved to Gadpole. In some ways, he still looked like that same rude, naughty boy of the swingin' sixties. In other ways he looked much older than forty-five. It was as if his body was in the process of skipping middle age entirely.

He stuck out his hand. It was delicate and unsteady, the fingers yellowed from chain-smoking unfiltered Gauloises. I shook it. He had less grip than my grandmother, who is 90.

The room was immense and round and several stories high, what with the glass dome over it. In the middle was a sunken island of low sofas arranged around a big square coffee table crowded with sketch pads, note pads, books, packages of Gauloises, ashtrays, bottles of pills, more bottles of pills, a wine bucket with a half-empty bottle of sauterne in it, and a half-eaten jar of baby food that had a spoon stuck in it. Strained liver. Goes great with sauterne. Especially for breakfast. There was a bedroom through a half-open door, and a small, modern kitchen. His soundproofed recording studio was on the other side of a glass partition. In there was an old upright piano, an organ, guitars, and a full drum kit. Beyond it was a booth with tape machines in it.

There were lamps, and they were on, but silk scarves were draped over the shades. No music was playing. T. S. never listened to music at any time during our collaboration. The only sound came from the grandfather clock next to the door.

I sat down in one of the sofas. He coughed – a phlegmy cough – lit a cigarette with a disposable lighter, poured himself some sauterne and didn't offer me any. Then he sat down across the table from me and stared at me. And kept staring at me. He wasn't what you'd call warm. He wasn't what you'd call *there*.

Finally, he cleared his throat and said, "You don't use a tape recorder."

"I will. I thought we'd want to get acquainted first."

He absently flicked the ash from his cigarette. It landed next to him on the sofa. There were, I noticed, dozens of burn marks there in the upholstery. "Acquainted?"

"Acquainted."

"If you wish." He yawned and sipped his wine. "Have you

questions then?"

I glanced over at his studio. "I didn't know you were still recording."

He shrugged. "Personal things. Different things."

"Will you be releasing any of it?"

"Through with all of that. Don't care if people hear it."

"You sound like J. D. Salinger."

He brightened, though not a lot. "The American writer. Yes. I've read he's written dozens of books but he won't let anyone read them until he dies. I admire that."

"Why?"

"Because people are bloody fools."

I didn't fight him on that one. "You're through performing, too?"

Another cigarette ash landed on the sofa. This one began to smolder. "Rockers don't grow up. We just grow old, y'know? I've had it with that. No more pretending I'm still T. S. I want to write, paint, be m'self. Rock 'n' roll music comes from being young, from being angry." He looked around at his dome. "Not from this."

"What do you want from this book? Understanding? Appreciation? Respect?"

"Bugger that. I don't care what anyone thinks of me anymore. I'm looking to close the door and be done with it. Walk off into the sunset like John Fucking Wayne."

"He once called you a sick limey fairy."

"Then I must have been doing something right, wasn't I? I wasn't there to give 'em a cup of tea and tuck 'em into bed, mate. I was there to shake 'em up. Turn up the heat. Rock 'n' roll, it's their last chance, isn't it?"

"Whose?"

"The teenies, before they go off to be everything they don't want to be. Just like their mums and dads before 'em."

"Is that your philosophy of rock music?"

"There is no philosophy. Just the music. That's all there is. See, I . . ." He trailed off.

"Go on," I urged him. "Please."

"I didn't want . . . I *don't* want to end up like Elvis."

"Fat and dead?"

"Before that."

"Fat and semi-alive?"

"I met him once. When we played at Las Vegas in . . . perhaps it was the '69 tour. Or was it '71? Can't remember. A blur, it is. We went to see his midnight show at one of those hotel-casinos. It was . . ." He shuddered, horrified by the memory. "Pathetic. There he was with his fat face, bursting out of his white sequined trousers. Couldn't sing for shit. But his fans, they were screaming for him like he was still the king and they were still hot and nasty little teenies. They weren't, you see. They were old and fat themselves. Housewives. Lorry drivers in green leisure suits." He shuddered again. "Afterward, we met him in his suite."

"How was he?"

"Zonked. Totally zonked. Didn't know who we were. Didn't know who he was. It shook me. I went back to my room and wrote a song about it."

"*Shoot the Old Hound Dog*. I remember it."

"Elvis, he was *my* idol."

The cigarette ash continued to smolder on the sofa next to him.

"How do you see yourself now?"

"See myself?"

"Are you a hero? A victim? A survivor?"

He shrugged. "I'm T. S. I'm here. This is now. Tomorrow . . ."

"Tomorrow?"

"Tomorrow there'll be another now." He cocked his head and cupped an ear with one hand, as if he'd heard the sound of distant drumbeats. I'd heard nothing. "That's lovely, isn't it? 'Another now.'" Pleased, he reached for a pen and scribbled it down on a pad. Then he tossed the pad back on the table. "Sorry. If I don't get them on paper these days, I forget them."

"You aren't alone," I assured him. "Any regrets?"

"Only that I'm not nineteen."

"Why nineteen?"

"It was good then. It was the best. Oscar Wilde, he once said that living well is the best revenge. Well, Oscar Wilde never got up on a stage and played rock 'n' roll music. It was good then. All of it. Me, Rory, the mates, the music. I . . . m'body is failing me now, Hogarth. Plumbing's ruined all the way down the line. Can't eat. Can't shit. Can't even take a bleedin' piss. Have to sit in a bleedin' diaper half the time. Take stomach pills, heart pills. I'm *old*, mate. Old before m'time. We all are – those of us who are left. A lot of the mates are already gone. Rory. Puppy. Brian. Bonzo. Moon. Hendrix. I probably haven't much time left m'self . . . Nineteen. It was good then. Playin' all night for 'em in the little clubs. Playin' for the love of it.

Pullin' chicks. Feelin' good. No hassles. No Lord Harry . . ." His features darkened.

"Lord Harry?"

"Smack. Heroin."

"It was rumored you were an addict. I never knew for sure."

"Two years of supercharged heaven, followed by the price. Still paying that. Anything hard would kill me now." He had a spoonful of the strained liver and shook his head. "It's all different now. Used to be you'd park your bum on a stool and they'd turn on the machine and you'd have a recording by morning. Now it takes months and months. Now it's Moogs and sixteen bleedin' channels. Sound paintings, they call 'em. It's not about *music*. And touring, Christ, it's not about music either. It's about laser light shows, and private jets and personal bleedin' masseuses, and videos on the MTV. Do you watch that MTV over there?"

"No, I have goldfish."

"Rock's big business now, mate. That's the total opposite of what it's supposed to be about."

"You helped make it that way."

"I know that. Sick about it, too."

"You could always give the money back," I suggested, grinning.

Briefly, his famous nostrils flared. Then he relaxed and let out a short, harsh laugh. "Not *that* sick."

"If you want to walk away then why don't you just do it? Why bother to write this book?"

He scratched at his stubbly chin, thought that over. "Because I need to say some things before I go. Because I'm tired of Pete Townshend telling everyone he's so bloody deep. Because . . . because I want to show them, all of them, what's really inside Tristam Scarr."

"I thought you didn't care what people thought of you anymore."

"I don't. I care what *I* think, see?"

"Yes, I believe I do. But before we go any further I have to tell you that your couch is on fire."

Very slowly, he turned and looked at the cushion next to him, which was most definitely in flames. His expression, or rather lack of it, didn't change. He just kept looking at the flames, until he calmly reached over with his bare hand and patted them out, seemingly oblivious to whatever in the way of heat or pain this might involve. Then he turned and focused on me once again.

"I need a couple of assurances from you," I said.

He narrowed his eyes at me. "Assurances?"

"Working on a memoir, a good one, can be very demanding. Not to mention tortuous."

"I want a good one." He said this to me like he was a spoiled kid picking out a bicycle. "I want the best one."

"Fine. Then I'm going to push the hell out of you. That's my job. I'm asking you to have faith in me. If I'm not satisfied, I have a reason for it. I don't want image from you. I don't want *People* magazine. I want *you*. I want to know what you were feeling and dreaming. I want to know what color the wallpaper was. It's going to be hard and draining and time-consuming. I'm going to be a pain in the ass at times. Jay said you're committed to seeing this through. I want to hear that from you, because if there's the slightest chance you're going to get tired of this after a few days then I'd just as soon not get started at all."

He frowned, puzzled. "Jay?"

"Jay Weintraub."

"Ah, the lawyer. Yes. How do you know him?"

"He hired me."

"I see. Well . . . Yes, you have that assurance, Hogarth. I'm yours. I'm not going anywhere, except to hell."

"The other assurance I need is that you'll be totally honest with me. You have to tell me the truth."

"The *truth*." He turned the word over aloud several times, as if it were a strange, metaphysical concept. "That will be the interesting part. So much of it has been lies through the years. Hasn't been, strictly speaking, *real*, y'know?"

"No, not exactly, but I'm still on New York time – give me a while to catch up. What do you mean by 'real'?"

"Real as in Derek, the teeny dreamboat – "

"Your bass player."

"– used to bugger muscular boys."

"Oh?"

"Real as in who he actually wanted to turd-burgle was Rory."

"He did?"

"Only Rory was fucking m'Tulip."

"He was?"

"Who I was actually married to for two bleedin' years before anyone was allowed to know about it. The truth . . ." He shook his head. "The truth never entered into it at all. Christ, *Puppy* . . ." He trailed off, reached for a cigarette and lit it from the stub of the first.

Myself, I managed not to salivate on my trousers. Tris Scarr had just dished up enough dirt for three best sellers, and he wasn't even warm yet. I cleared my throat, and said "Puppy?"

"He was killed, mate."

"An accidental overdose. I remember."

"That was no accident. He was done in. Don't you see?"

"No, I'm afraid I don't."

"Done in," he repeated, emphatically.

"You're suggesting that someone *murdered* Puppy Johnson?"

"I'm not suggestin' it. I'm sayin' it."

"But who?"

"Never found out. Never will now." He took a sip of his wine and narrowed his eyes at me again. "Need any more assurances, Hogarth?"

I smiled. "We're going to do just fine, Tristam. In fact, we're going to write ourselves one helluva book."

"The best. I want the best."

"And you shall have it."

"I'm accustomed to working from midnight to dawn. Can't seem to change. You mind?"

"Not at all. I can type during the day. Take care of the other interviews."

He frowned, confused. "Other interviews? I thought this was *my* book."

"It is, but other sources will spark your remembrances. Also provide us with some objectivity. Don't worry – I'll sift everything through your voice."

He nodded. "I see."

"Who might be of help?"

He took a long time answering that one. "There's Derek . . ."

"What's he up to these days?"

"He's being a toff in Bedford Square with his guns."

"Guns?"

"Antiques. He collects them."

"How about Tulip?"

He didn't answer me.

"Or your ex-manager?"

"Marco's running a disco these days. Tulip . . . she's running around on ceilings. Bonkers, she is. Found the Lord. Pastries, as well." He swiped at his nose with the back of his hand. "There aren't a lot of good feelings, mate. I reckon some of that's my fault. What I mean is, they may not want to talk."

"Leave that part to me," I told him. "I'll need a car. Either you can loan me one or I'll rent one and send Jay the bill. Up to you."

"I'm to pay for it?"

"Part of the deal."

"I see. In the contract, is it?"

"I can go down and get my copy if you – "

"No, no. Not necessary, Hogarth. I believe you. Just didn't know, you see. Feel free to take any of the cars."

"Thank you."

"The utility cars, of course. Not the show cars. The show cars are mine. Jack will give you the keys. He's the – "

"Chauffeur. We've met."

"Capable bloke. Was our roadie for a time. Anything else?"

"I'd like to be able to listen to your old records. Didn't bring mine."

"All of them?"

"If you have them."

"Oh, I have 'em," he assured me, getting slowly to his feet. Our talk seemed to have drained him. He shuffled over to a wall of bookcases, came back with a boxed set of Us record albums called *Completely Us*. "Collector's item. All electronically reprocessed. Getting three hundred pounds for it."

"I'll take good care of it." I took it from him. Together, we started for the door. "You know, I saw you play Shea Stadium on your second American tour, in '65." I could still see him jumping around on the Shea stage that night. Now he was out of breath from crossing the room.

He grinned crookedly at me. "Yes, I thought you looked familiar – you were the one in the front row wearing blue jeans, right?"

"I meant . . . I mean, you were great. You guys were a great band."

"We were the best, mate." His nostrils flared. "And Michael Jagger can kiss m'bloody arse."

"Tomorrow, I'll bring my tape recorder."

"I'll be here, Hogarth. Dead or alive."

Lulu was asleep in her chair before the fire. The message I was hoping for was waiting there on my desk, courtesy of Pamela, who'd also turned down my bed. Possibly I would have to take her back to

New York with me.

I sat at the desk and made notes of my initial conversation with Tris Scarr. He was reserved and elusive and in charge. Which approach should I take with him? Buddy? Bully? Shrink? Which would work on him? Which would bring him to life on the page? Too soon to tell.

After I'd put on my new silk dressing gown and poured myself a Macallan I pulled out the very first Us album, *Great Gosh Almighty – It's Us!* For the cover, the four of them had formed a human pyramid in Hyde Park, wearing matching gold blazers without lapels, skinny black neckties and goofy faces. They were just boys – gawky, pimply boys. On the back cover was that very same human pyramid shot from behind. Har har. And some copy: "*Their names are Tris, Rory, Derek and Albert (though his mates call him Puppy). All London is talking about these four swinging young lads from up Liverpool way who play to the Mersey beat but their own way. They're mod. They're now. They're gear. They're Us!*"

I put the album on the stereo, and listened to the title cut. I've finally reached a point where I can hear rock from my youth and not be preoccupied by its evocations of school dances on gymnasium floors and sweaty, unsure fumblings in overheated cars. It's just music now, and this was fresh, joyous music, bursting with energy and exuberance. Tris's voice was a ballsy wail, Rory's chords sharp and scorching. Derek's bass was tight and steady underneath, Puppy drove them, his drum shots crisp as breadsticks. They were pure and full of juice, their sound uncompromised by the drugs and the years. They were good. It had been good then, he'd said.

I poured myself another scotch and turned the music down. Then I stretched out on the bed and called her. My heart began to pound when she said hello. It always does.

"So how's Anthony Andrews?" I asked.

"Just a total dreamboat," she replied in that very proper, very dizzy teenage-girl's voice that is hers and hers alone. "Also desperately in love."

"With . . . ?"

"Anthony Andrews. Hoagy, darling?"

"Yes, Merilee?"

"Hello."

"Hello yourself."

Lulu heard her voice over the phone. She always can. Don't ask me how. She came charging in from the living room, considered her chances of making it up onto the big four-poster bed, ruled them out, and barked. She has a mighty big bark for someone with no legs. I shushed her and hoisted her up. She dug in next to me and gazed expectantly at the phone.

"Actually, it's going unbelievably well so far," Merilee said. "Which is just as well – we open next week. You'll come, won't you? To the opening."

"Love to."

"Good. I'll make sure there's tickets for you two at the box office."

"I have to tell you that Lulu's not much of a Philip Barry fan – she thinks he's strictly yesterday."

"She feel that way about her mommy, too?"

"Hardly. She speaks of you often, and in glowing terms. I'll see if I can get the night off. We'll have supper afterward. Or is there a party?"

"For you, I'll skip it," she said. "Unless, of course, you want to go."

"Let's not," I suggested.

"Let's not," she agreed. "So how's T. S.?"

"Not all there. Actually, I've never met anyone before who so aptly fits the phrase 'shell of a human being.' With the possible exception of myself, of course."

I waited for her to contradict me. She didn't. "I used to have his picture on my wall when I was at Miss Porter's," she said. "His jeans were so tight you could see the outline of his dinkus."

"I always figured you were more of a Derek Gregg type."

"Never, darling. *Everybody* liked him."

"Especially the boys," I advised, confidentially.

She gasped. "No, really?!"

"From the horse's mouth."

"Ooh, tell me more."

"Remember when Puppy Johnson died?"

"OD'd on liquor and pills, didn't he?"

"T. S. says he was murdered."

"I don't know about that one, Hoagy," she said skeptically. "There's always weirdness attached to major rock deaths. Some people believe that Jim Morrison is still alive somewhere, and that Brian Jones was actually murdered by the CIA. When I was shooting that thing in Tennessee with Sissy we went to Graceland one weekend. Some of Elvis's fans there think he's off living in a parallel universe. It's all a lot of baked beans, isn't it?"

"Most likely. I've missed your quaint little expressions."

"Besides, it was over twenty years ago," she pointed out.

"That may be true, but his chauffeur did threaten me tonight."

"Hoagy, you're not getting into the middle of something ugly and scary again, are you?"

"I certainly hope not."

"I worry about you sometimes."

"You do?" I asked, pleased at this. "Why?"

"You don't know when it's time to walk away."

"I'll take that as a compliment,"

"I gave it as a constructive criticism."

"Oh."

She cleared her throat. "Is there a novel?"

"I think so. There's something."

"That's wonderful, darling! I'm so glad."

"You might not be so glad when you hear what it's about."

"Why, what's it . . . Oh no, you're not doing something tacky and Nora Ephronish are you?"

"That'll be for the *Times* to decide."

She sighed. "Kind of funny, the two of us being here at the same time, isn't it?"

"Yeah. Funny."

"I always think of London as our city."

"I stayed at Blakes."

"You romantic fool."

"You got that half right."

"Which half?"

"Where are you staying?"

"A darling little mews house on Cromwell Road. I'm subletting from a British actress who's doing a movie in New York." She sighed again. "I don't know what it is about this city. I mean, it's most definitely not romantic. It's damp and gray and it smells of exhaust fumes and simply awful cologne.."

"Merilee?"

"Yes, darling?"

"How's Zack?"

She hesitated. "Zack's home having some problems. We have that to talk about, too."

We were silent a minute.

"Darling?" This she said softly.

"Yes, Merilee?"

"It can never be like before, can it?"

"It can be better."

"Good night, darling."

"Sleep tight, Merilee."

I hung up. Lulu was watching me. "Just forget it," I snapped. "There's no chance. None. It'll never happen."

She whimpered. I told her to shut up. Then I took a bubble bath.

CHAPTER THREE

(Tape #1 with Tristam Scarr.   Recorded in his chamber Nov. 19. Wears navy blue sweat suit, Air Jordan basketball sneakers, clean shave. Appears more clear-eyed than first meeting, though uneasy.)

Hoag: Ready?

Scarr: Ready, steady, go, mate.

Hoag: From the beginning, if we may.

Scarr: The beginning. Very well. I was born one evening in . . . '56, it was. Supposed to be doing m'studies in m'room. Wasn't. See, Rory's brother, Bob, who was stationed in Bremen, had told us about this station you could get on the wireless called Radio Luxembourg. They played rock 'n' roll music, which the BBC didn't back then. A fabulous moment, mate. Door closed. Turning the dial. Searching. Seeking. Hearing nothing but static. And then, very faintly . . . *it.*

Hoag: It?

Scarr: "Heartbreak Hotel." Elvis. It was nasty and hot. It was me. I freaked. From that moment on, I knew what I wanted to be, y'know?

Hoag: Yes, I do. I had a similar experience the first time I picked up *Mad* magazine. I like that anecdote. It's private, and has feeling. But can we go back to the *very* beginning?

Scarr: Wee laddie days? *(pause)* Very well. I was an only child. Born April 10, 1944.

Hoag: In?

Scarr: Rubble. Officially, it was called London. The war was still on then, of course. Mum was a nurse. Dad was a bombardier in the RAF. Dropped bombs. Poof. Martin and Meta. Named me Tristam after his grandfather. I think they met at a service dance. Neither of them was very young at the time. Or happy. They're both dead now. Bought 'em a house in Brighton to retire at. It was the only place they ever lived at was their own. He was a short geezer. Hairs sticking out of his nose and ears. Sold things door to door, or tried to. Eight-in-one kitchen implements. Miracle bloody cleaners. M'dad was accustomed to having doors slammed in his face all day long. He never complained. Just kept dreaming. He always believed the big pot of gold was just down the road.

Hoag: He wasn't wrong – he was only off by one generation.

Scarr: You got that right. Mum, she became a practical nurse. Strong woman. Very good posture. Liked everything clean, especially her little Tristam. Wore his proper school uniform, he did. Starched white shirt. Black blazer. Gray short pants. Tie. Gap. My very first act of rebellion was to be dirty . . . She saw to old ladies who were dying, and was always telling Dad about it at the table. "She's got blood in her stool again, Martin. Blood in her stool. . . ."

Hoag: You were raised in . . . ?

Scarr: A bunch of nothing London suburbs. Acton, then Ealing, then Twickenham, Teddington, Kingston . . . We were always moving.

Hoag: Wait. Time out. I thought you grew up in Liverpool.

Scarr: No. Never.

Hoag: But everything I've ever read about you said –

Scarr: All made up. They made up a lot.

Hoag: You mean the record company?

Scarr: And our manager, Marco Bartucci – the man who made us Us. Liverpool was hot. Kids from greater London weren't. So they gave us fake biographies. Christ, they said Puppy's dad was a merchant seaman from Dingle, the Liverpool docks. He was actually in jail in Louisiana for killing a man.

Hoag: And your Liverpool accent?

Scarr: The scouse was put on, like a costume. Show business.

Hoag: It certainly is. You were saying you moved around a lot.

Scarr: Mum would ask the neighborhood shopkeepers to put it on the slate. Then, when they'd get touchy about money, we'd move on to another furnished flat somewhere. "Someday, Tristam," m'dad would say, "I want you to be a *professional* man. A man in a proper chalk-striped suit and bowler who rides the train into the City every morning with the *Times* under his arm. Yessir."

Hoag: Did you want that?

Scarr: Not if he did, mate.

Hoag: You didn't get along?

Scarr: It wasn't as if we ever had a go at one another. He never had goes with anybody. Over anything. Too weak. Too afraid. He just quietly took it up the bumhole. I hated that about him. It was as if he was spending his whole life getting ready to die. Only thing he succeeded at.

Hoag: What kind of boy were you?

Scarr: You mean was I a jolly little pink-cheeked laddie? The apple of Martin and Meta's eye?

Hoag: Something like that.

Scarr: It wasn't like that.

Hoag: Didn't think it was.

Scarr: I was sickly. Asthma. Pneumonia. Tonsils. Always had breathing problems. Still do. I was home in bed a lot, swallowing bad-tasting medicines, Mum nursing me like one of her old ladies. Didn't have many mates, between that and moving to the different schools. I remember I did a lot of jigsaw puzzles. Picadilly Circus. The Grand Canyon. Diamond Fucking Head. And I spun these fairy tales in m'head – that I was a pirate king or an Indian fighter. Someone brave and strong, with mates . . . Mostly, I remember silence. The wallpaper was blue.

Hoag: You know, I've never met a celebrity who had a happy childhood.

Scarr: Nobody has a happy childhood. We just happen to get asked about ours, is all.

Hoag: Did you do well in school?

Scarr: Not very. Missed too much. Wasn't very bright either. *(laughs)* I showed no evidence of any talent of any kind as a boy. Except for m'ears. I can wiggle them. Very few people can.

Hoag: You can wiggle? I can, too. All of the Hoag men can. Let's see . . . *(silence)* Pretty decent. But can you wiggle one ear at a time?

Scarr: Impossible. No one can.

Hoag: I can.

Scarr: Balls. *(silence)* You're not really doing it.

Hoag: I am, too.

Scarr: Yes, well, as I said – I was not a good student. Somehow, I did manage to pass m'eleven-plus exams and move on up. We were living in Teddington then, I was sent to Hampton Grammar. Some pretty posh people sent their teenies there. A good crowd for young Tristam to meet on his road to becoming a professional man. Only, I fell in with the wrong crowd.

Hoag: By the wrong crowd you mean Rory?

Scarr: I do, mate.

Hoag: Can you remember the first time you two met?

Scarr: *(laughs)* It was in '56. I was twelve. I knew of him, of course, because he got himself in so many scrapes. A blond bloke, with a big chest and unusually short legs. Self-conscious about that, he was. To the day he died he was sensitive about his height. He was a cockney, a hard nut – quick with his mouth and his fists. The other boys were afraid of him. He was already a bit of a ted. Wore these heavy black shoes and smoked ciggies and didn't show up for classes. One day he comes up to me in the corridor and takes m'fountain pen out of m'shirt pocket and doesn't give it back. I says, "Let's have m'pen." He says, "Piss off." I says, "*You* piss off." He says, "You're a skinny little cunt, aren't you." I says, "It's m'mum's pen – she'll have m'hide if I lose it." He says, "Then she's a cunt as well." The other lads are listening by now. I'm sort of on the spot, I am. If I let him keep the pen then I've got no bloody social standing from that day forward. So we had a proper punch-up.

Hoag: Who won?

Scarr: He did. Bloodied m'nose. Tore m'shirt.

Hoag: But he gave you the pen back.

Scarr: No, he kept the pen. But he did decide I was a mate. Next morning he says to me, "I'm gonna smoke me a fag in class today." I says, "Go on." He says, "Watch me." And he did it – lit up a bleeding Woodbine right there in the middle of class. Teacher couldn't fucking believe it. Got himself royally caned for that, Rory did. But he just didn't care. They couldn't teach him anything and they couldn't hurt him. He figured as how he was smarter than all of them.

Hoag: Was he?

Scarr: Rory? He was just bloody contrary's what he was. Different. Crazy. Still, I reckoned as how he was onto something.

Hoag: What was it?

Scarr: Being alive. *(pause)* His dad was a big, tough bloke. Had his own roofing business. He and Rory fought all the time. "Mr. Law" he called his dad, with a sneer. Quick with the belt, the old bugger was – especially after a few pints. Rory's older brother, Bob, usually got it, only he was away in the RAF at that time, so Mr. Law went after Rory.

Hoag: You and Rory became friends.

Scarr: Mates, right off. There was this, I don't know, righteous energy between us. We sparked off of each other. Did things together we'd not dream of doing on our own.

Hoag: Such as?

Scarr: Such as . . . Christ, what didn't we do? Started trash fires inside of stores. Threw rocks at nuns and cripples. Ran in front of cars in the street to make 'em hit the brakes. One time we grabbed a neighbor's cat and stuck a firecracker up its arse and lit it to see what would happen.

Hoag: And what happened?

Scarr: (laughs) They may have nine lives but they only got but one arsehole.

Hoag: That's absolutely disgusting.

Scarr: Isn't it? I'd never been happier. Even started getting a bit of a rep in the neighborhood for being a scruff. M'dad decided to have it out with me about it. Says to me, very serious, "You're being a bad boy, Tristam. Your schoolwork is inadequate. Your behavior and language are unacceptable. You'll never be a proper gentleman at this rate, just a lout. I want you to stop seeing this Rory Law."

Hoag: And what did you say?

Scarr: "Make me."

Hoag: And what did he say?

Scarr: Not a thing. I won. *(pause)* Show me that ear thing of yours again, would you, Hogarth?

(end tape)

(Tape #2 with Tristam Scarr. Recorded in his chamber Nov. 20. Appears subdued. Wears only a tweed overcoat, long johns. Hair is in a ponytail.)

Hoag: You look tired tonight, Tristam.

Scarr: I was practicing. Haven't been to bed yet.

Hoag: Taking up a new instrument?

Scarr: No, it's that ear thing of yours. I don't get it, mate. What's the trick?

Hoag: There's no trick. Either your ears can move independently of each other or they can't.

Scarr: Show it to me again. *(silence)* Bloody hell!

Hoag: Let's talk about when you heard Elvis sing "Heartbreak Hotel" on the radio that first time. You wanted to sound like him, look like him, *be* him . . . ?

Scarr: Me and Rory both. We were ripe for it, y'know? Something new. Something that our parents and teachers wouldn't approve of. Something that was ours. Rock 'n' roll music, it simply didn't exist here in '56. We had Tommy Steele and Johnny Gentle and vanilla pop like that. But we had no one like Elvis. No records. No radio. Nothing. Just the American movies.

Hoag: What movies?

Scarr: We were just knocked out by *The Wild One* with Marlon Brando. The motorcycles. The black leather jackets. The way the adults were so freaked out by him. The *attitude*. It was like he was saying, "Fuck all of you," y'know? I'll never forget this one conversation. Somebody says to him "What are you rebelling against?" And Brando, he says, "Whattaya got?" *(laughs)* Whattaya fucking got! We couldn't get over that. James Dean in *Rebel Without a Cause*. That was another movie we freaked for. And *Blackboard Jungle,* with all of these wonderfully scruff students who hated Glenn Ford's bleedin' guts. The theme song to that was "Rock Around the Clock," sung by Bill Haley and the Comets. Me and Rory we ate those movies up. Saw 'em over and over again. America, it seemed like some kind of paradise to us over here then. It was Technicolor. We were black and white. It was Marilyn Monroe. We were Dame May Whitty. You blokes over there had your own bleedin' cars to take your dolly birds for rides in. Our parents couldn't afford cars here, mate. America, it was the land of the free.

Hoag: Wait, wait: "What's that I see/From across the sea?/The land of the free/More for me/Over there, the sky/It don't ever get gray/Ain't no one to tell ya/What not to say/More for me."

Scarr: You were a regular bleedin' little rocker, weren't you? Wouldn't know it to look at you now.

Hoag: Good breeding prevails in the end.

Scarr: Don't wager on it, Hogarth. Where was I? . . . Ah yes, once we got into Radio Luxembourg, we got turned on to a lot of the American rock 'n' roll music – Jerry Lee Lewis, Eddie Cochran, Buddy Holly, Ricky Nelson. Blew our minds. All of it. It was definitely where we wanted to be.

Hoag: What about skiffle? Wasn't that an important influence on early groups like Us?

Scarr: Skiffle was a craze, and it *was* ours – kind of a cross between washboard folk and trad jazz. Got started by the song "Rock Island Line" by Lonnie Donegan, who played in Chris Barber's jazz band. A skiffle band had two guitars, a banjo, washboard and upright bass. Three chords. Four/four beat. Very basic like, y'know? But it was *there*. We could hear Elvis and Bill Haley in it. And we could *do* it. All we needed was a 78 of "Hock Island Line," which cost six shillings, and a guitar. And we didn't necessarily have to play it that well. Guitar was entirely different back then. Wasn't the top-gun lead thing it became after Clapton and Page came along. Back then it was more of a rhythm instrument, like a ukelele. The saxophone was the lead instrument. Ricky Nelson had a guitarist who could bend a note, James Burton. And Cliff Richard, who I reckon you could call the first genuine British rock 'n roll star, he had a fellow called Hank Marvin who could play.

Hoag: You and Rory decided you wanted to play.

Scarr: Rory, he got his mum to give him one for Christmas. I sent away for mine, a Spanish acoustic with wire strings that made m'fingers bleed. Came with an instruction book, *Guitar Made Easy*, by this geezer with glasses called Johnny Baughan.

Hoag: You wrote a song about him, too.

Scarr: Yes. "For Johnny Baughan." He was m'first and only music teacher. The book was mostly about how to play folk songs, but it did have these diagrams in the back showing where to put the fingers to make this or that chord. So we got our guitars, Rory and me, and we set about learning 'em. After school. Instead of school. At m'flat, since nobody was around during the day, and we had a phonograph. We smoked Woodies and played the 78 of "Rock Island Line" over and over and tried to imitate how it sounded. It could be done, y'see. So could the look, the Elvis look. The look was perhaps even more important. Creased duck's-arse hair with sidies – that's sideburns, to you. Drainies . . .

Hoag: Drainies?

Scarr: Drainpipes, which is what your jeans looked like since they were so bleeding tight. Only way to get 'em that tight was to wear 'em in the bath with you, the water as hot as you could stand it. M'dad figured as how I was daft. Looked in on me once in there and said "Mrs. Scarr, your son Tristam is taking a bath with his new trousers on, he is. Moaning, he is."

Hoag: Moaning?

Scarr: Bath was also where I learned to sing. The echo, y'know. At first I tried to imitate Elvis. Then it was Little Richard.

Hoag: Why him?

Scarr: My voice wasn't deep enough to do a really proper Elvis.

Hoag: That sandpapery quality your voice has – was that how you sounded from the start?

Scarr: Christ, no. That took years of Woodbines and whiskey and screaming into shitty microphones.

Hoag: What did you sound like back then, in the tub?

Scarr: Like any other lad, I expect. Bad. Actually, I've never had a great voice, mate. Or even a good one. It's *effective*.

Hoag: Aren't you being a little modest?

Scarr: I'm being honest, like you asked. I mean, Rod Stewart isn't Placido Fucking Domingo either, y'know?

Hoag: How did you end up being the singer?

Scarr: Rory didn't like doing it. Thought it was too feminine.

Hoag: You were telling me about the look.

Scarr: Right. Pointy black shoes – winkle-pickers we called 'em. Black leather jacket. Pink shirt and socks.

Hoag: Sounds like a swell outfit.

Scarr: Oh, we were bleedin' swells, all right, with our Spanish acoustics, spots on our faces, twelve, thirteen years old. Double trouble, we were.

Hoag: What did Martin and Meta think of all of this?

Scarr: They'd always figured as how I'd never amount to anything, and this here was proof of it.

Hoag: What about the others at school? What did they think of you?

Scarr: That we were teds. The surprise was the dollies. For the first time, they started taking notice of us two scruffs at the chip shops. Partly because they knew Mum and Dad wouldn't want 'em to. Partly because our trousers were so bloody tight. *(laughs)*

Hoag: You mentioned Little Richard. He was an important influence?

Scarr: I told you about Rory's brother Bob being away in Bremen. When he finished his conscript and came home we were telling him how much we loved Elvis and Bill Haley, and he said if that's the case then it's time you hear the *real* thing. He said Bill Haley didn't invent "Shake, Rattle and Roll" – Joe Turner did. And he pulled out a bleedin' trunk full of records he'd bought over there by black performers we'd never heard of – Little Richard, Chuck Berry, Fats Domino, James Brown, Elmore James, Jimmy Reed, Muddy Waters – on labels like Chess of Chicago, and Sun of Memphis. Rhythm and blues, Hogarth. A lot of the rock 'n' roll music we'd been into was nothing more than a cleaned-up white version of R and B, which was much nastier than Elvis. We freaked out over it, of course. Wore out Bob's records. Went into London looking for more in the jazz shops on Charing Cross Road. Found some used ones – Otis Spann, Bo Diddley, T-Bone Walker . . .

Hoag: Was anyone else listening to R and B here?

Scarr: Mate, nobody here had ever *heard* of it. Except for a handful of us. There were a few other blokes at school playing skiffle, forming groups. It was when Rory and me were fourteen that we decided it was time to start a group of our own.

(end tape)

(Tape #3 with Tristam Scarr. Recorded in his chamber Nov. 21. Wears flannel shirt and faded denim overalls. Seems especially anxious to talk.)

Scarr: There's something I neglected to mention before. About myself. You should know about it.

Hoag: Yes?

Scarr: I can raise one of m'eyebrows. *(silence)* See?

Hoag: How about the other eyebrow?

Scarr: Other eyebrow?

Hoag: Can you raise it, too? On its own, I mean.

Scarr: No, that one doesn't move. *(pause)* Are you saying you can raise *either* eyebrow? *(silence)* Bloody hell!

Hoag: You decided to form a rock 'n' roll band. How come?

Scarr: To meet dolly birds.

Hoag: That was the only reason?

Scarr: That was plenty. First thing we did, right off, was work on a name. Had to have a name, didn't we?

Hoag: You know, I keep finding myself surprised when you and Rory sound like a couple of kids. But you *were* kids.

Scarr: That we were. We talked it over real serious like. Came up with a number of possibilities – The Desperados, The Rebels, The Rattlers, The Rock Men, The Rough Boys. That's what we settled on – The Rough Boys. Sounded, I don't know . . .

Hoag: Rough?

Scarr: That's it. Now that we had a name we had to have some proper electric guitars. Our acoustics just wouldn't do, not for rock 'n' rolling. We begged our mums and dads for the money to buy 'em, but they said no – Rory was about to get thrown out of Hampton, and I wasn't doing much better. To them, rock 'n' roll music was partly to blame. It *was* all we did.

Hoag: So where did you get the money?

Scarr: *(pause)* From the cash drawer of a fish-and-chips shop.

Hoag: You're kidding.

Scarr: This old geezer, Murray, ran this little neighborhood shop near my flat. A trusting sort, he was – used to turn his back to the money drawer when he was working the fryer. The *open* money drawer. It wasn't as if we planned it. We were just in there ordering chips one day, talking things over, and we saw this money sitting right there, and bam, that electricity I told you of passed between us. The geezer never knew what hit him.

Hoag: I don't suppose you paid him back when you hit it big?

Scarr: Make a nice story, wouldn't it? With interest, and perhaps a blanket to keep him snug in his old age? Fact is, it wasn't so much as a consideration. Fuck the bugger. Never claimed I was an angel. Don't try to make me out one. We took the money straight to Bell Music in Ewell Road, Surrey. They had gorgeous equipment there. It was a trip just to hold it. Made me feel like Chuck Berry. We had just enough for a pair of hollow-body Hoffman Senators and two old secondhand Vox fifteen-watt amps. Took 'em home, plugged 'em in, ran our fingers over the strings, and it was incredible. The sound reverberated. It was *alive*.

Hoag: Did you and Rory have any sense of your individual talents this early on?

Scarr: Hmm . . . good question.

Hoag: I try.

Scarr: Rory had a knack. He would toy with a progression of chords, and have it come out sounding like something. He could *invent*. Me, I was the one ready to stick m'bleedin' neck out. Comes time for the vocalizing, for showing some personality, a lot of the blokes faded to the back of the stage with their guitars. Not me. I wanted the mike. I wanted people paying attention to me, thinking I was special.

Hoag: You still say you were doing all of this just to meet girls?

Scarr: Don't get deep on me, Hogarth . . . Of course, I also had poetry inside me, though I didn't know that yet. There were plenty of unknown R and B songs around for us to play. Didn't need to write our own for years.

Hoag: You mentioned there were other guys at school forming groups.

Scarr: Scruffs and misfits, all of 'em. Jim McCarty and Paul Samwell-Smith were at Hampton. They ended up forming the Yardbirds with Chris Dreja, Keith Relf, and Top Topham. Then Top left and Eric Clapton took his place. I got to know Eric and Keith a couple of years later when we were at Kingston Art College together.

Hoag: I never knew you went to college.

Scarr: Not college – *art* college. Every bleedin' rocker in the U.K.

went to art college, Hogarth, except for Michael Jagger, who went to the London bleedin' School of Economics. Lennon went to one. Keith Richard, Townshend, Ray Davies of the Kinks, Eric, Pagey, Ron Wood, John Mayall . . . Know the old saying about how whores turn to religion when they get old? Rockers turn to painting. Art college is why. Art college and acid. *(laughs)* It was where they stuck us if we were dim and contrary and weren't in prison yet. I reckon they thought we'd be pacified by playin' with the finger paints. It was all a goof. Plenty of free time. Plenty of dollies in black stockings going through their artistic phase, if you know what that means. The only one who actually took it serious was Townshend, who to this day thinks he's not so much a rocker as a bleedin' concept artist, whatever the fuck that is . . . Where were we? . . . Yes, there were a few other blokes at Hampton playing. And we needed one to play bass – Derek. Rory and I both knew him, though not well. He sang in the choir. Was very popular. Good-looking. Nice clothes and manners. The sort that even the loveliest dolly birds wanted to stroke on the head. Christ, the *teachers* loved him. He had a few bob – dad was a dentist. Underneath, though, Derek was really a scruff, very into the Everly Brothers and Duane Eddy. Got a girl preggers when he was fourteen.

Hoag: Is that so? What happened?

Scarr: She had the baby, I believe. Of course, it was all hushed up good and proper when we hit it big. You'll have to ask Derek about it. I'm sure he'll recall – it isn't as if he's come in through the front door much since then, has he?

Hoag: He had a guitar?

Scarr: A Watkins Rapier. When we told him we wanted to have him in the Rough Boys to play bass and sing harmony with me, he said, "No problem." That's what he said to just about everything through the years – "No problem." An agreeable bloke. Any group that stays together has to have one or two like him, with all the madness around . . . We took his Rapier to Bell Music and had it restrung as a bass. Derek kicked in for a microphone for us to sing into. *(laughs)* You know how on stage he always came over and sang his harmony into my mike, standing there face to face with me?

Hoag: One of your trademarks. Sure.

Scarr: That came about because one mike was all we could afford that day at Bell Music.

Hoag: How did you three sound?

Scarr: Awful. Derek didn't know how to play the bass. But

he picked it up soon enough. And he had that sweet, high-pitched voice that sounded good against mine, especially as mine got rougher. What we needed then, of course, was a drummer, and that got to be something of a hassle – very few blokes knew how to play the drums, and those who did didn't know how to play rock 'n' roll. Derek found us our first one, Andy Clarke, who played them in the school band. The four of us sounded bloody awful together. After a while, we finally figured out it was Andy, so out he went. And we were back to having no drummer. Then Rory got the boot from Hampton, which meant he had to work for Mr. Law in the roofing business.

Hoag: He didn't get along with his dad.

Scarr: Or with heights. Also meant we had to practice nights now, only that's when everybody's mums and dads were home. So we had no place to play. That was the first time we broke up. First of many.

Hoag: What you needed was a drummer whose parents both worked nights.

Scarr: Did better than that, actually. One day on the job Rory met this bricklayer called Jackie Horner who said he'd played drums in a trad jazz band and had a hankering to try rock 'n' roll. Couple of years older than us, he was. Had an uncle who ran a lorry repair garage, and he said we could use the garage to practice in at night. A fucking dream, this was. Could play as loud as we wanted, as late as we wanted. Even nick a tow van for gigs, once we started getting 'em . . . Christ, haven't thought about those nights in the garage in a long time. It was so wonderfully scruff there. Freezing cold, smelling of oil. We'd play half the night, eating chips, drinking beer, smoking Woodies. Whatever dolly Derek was seeing would come by for a listen and bring her dolly friends. Was a big thing for 'em, hanging around late at night in this unheated garage with greasy rock 'n' rollers. Naughty, y'know? They were our first groupies. Wonder where they are now . . . What was that one's name . . . Molly? Yes. She and I'd get it on in the back of a lorry with a blanket around us. She wanted to be a beautician, as I remember. Can't remember her face.

Hoag: How did you guys sound?

Scarr: Like a band now. Jackie's drumming pulled the different pieces together, gave Derek's bass a proper beat to hold onto. This was terrific progress for us. Meant they could dance to us now.

Hoag: What was your repertoire?

Scarr: Our "repertoire"? *(laughs)* The basics – "Blue Suede Shoes," "Jailhouse Rock," "That'll Be the Day," "Maybelline" . . .

Hoag: Tell me about your first gig.

Scarr: This dolly who was hot for Derek convinced her rich dad to have the Rough Boys play at her graduation party. Rory and me, we didn't even know how much to charge. Jackie thought ten pounds was fair, so that was our price – in advance, so we could buy our outfits. We all wore black trousers, white shirts and red ties. It wasn't until we pulled up in our town van at this posh house, and saw all of these posh kids going in, that it hit us that we'd never played in front of an audience before. At least not an audience of more than four appreciative dollies. Must have been fifty laddies and dollies, and some mums and dads as well. Staring right at us.

Hoag: At Woodstock you played in front of half a million.

Scarr: We froze – all of us except for Jackie. Hands shook so bad we couldn't set up our gear. Jackie had to calm us down, light us a Woodie. A solid soul he was. On our first number, "Maybelline," m'voice cracked. But after I worked up a proper sweat I was fine. We were fine. They danced. They clapped. Had a grand old time. So did we. Christ, it was a gas up there, being the life of the party. *The life* – that was the best part of it for me, I think . . . From there we started playing youth club dances, church halls, picnics, here and there.

Hoag: Looking back, did you have any idea where this was going to lead you?

Scarr: None, other than to get us laid – and in punch-ups.

Hoag: Punch-ups?

Scarr: The dollies would give us the eye. I'd have 'em up on stage. Give 'em a big kiss, tell 'em their boyfriends were ugly. The boyfriends didn't much fancy that. More often than not they'd be waiting for us out in the parking lot. A rocker had to be able to give it back in the early days. Rory and me and Jackie gave it back good. Derek always hid in the van – afraid for his face he was. It actually didn't occur to us then that the Rough Boys might be a ticket for us, Hogarth. We thought about today. Having a laugh. Having it off. We didn't think much about tomorrow. Didn't seem to be any point in that. Wasn't as if any of our lot were going anywhere, were we?

Hoag: When did your thinking change?

Scarr: Not long after that. I remember the date distinctly – October of '62. That's when the Beatles released "Love Me Do." Things just exploded here after that. If you happened to be in a group like ours, you started thinking maybe it'll happen to us, too. Maybe we'll be the next ones. Why not, y'know? Within two years we were big. Very big. A bloody shame that Jackie couldn't be part of it. He was the one who had to go when Puppy joined the group. Marco's doing. Bloody shame, what with Jackie being so important to us early on.

Hoag: I suppose every famous band has its Pete Best, the poor slob who missed the boat. Whatever happened to him?

Scarr: He's Jack, mate. M'chauffeur.

(end tape)

CHAPTER
FOUR

I'd been living at Gadpole a week before I realized someone else was living there, too. Like I said, the place wasn't small.

I had dressed early for Merilee's opening and was shooting pool in the panelled billiard room and snatching occasional glances at myself in the bevelled mirror behind the bar. Hard not to peek. There's only a very select handful who can appear totally at home in a tux: Fred Astaire. Cary Grant. Marlene Dietrich. Me.

"So you'll be the writer then?" asked a female voice, most English.

I turned to find a willowy black-haired girl there in the doorway. She was unusually tall and wore a sullen expression and no makeup. She didn't need makeup. Her hair was lustrous and abundant, her eyes an arresting cornflower blue, her lips fat and pouty. Her arms and legs were very long, her hands and feet man-sized. She wore a wool buffalo plaid shirt untucked over black tights and pink ballet slippers. She was very sexy, if you like them tall and sullen and certainly not yet twenty.

"That's right," I replied, going back to work on the table. I had a nice light touch that evening. "It's Hoagy."

"I'm called Violet. Pammy told me you were here. Don't you just love her?"

She seemed particularly young with her mouth open and words coming out, or maybe I was just getting to be particularly old. "Yes, I do. You're a friend of T. S.?"

"Kind of."

"Been modeling long?"

"A few months. I was just in Paris." She frowned. "How did you know I model?"

"I'm clairvoyant."

She giggled. "Is that like being gay?"

"Better. You don't have to take it up the . . . I'm sorry. I'm *very* sorry. I must be spending too much time with T. S."

"Oh, you don't have to worry about me. I've done everything." She leaned against the bar and lit a cigarette, very blasé. "And then some."

"Been around, have you?"

"Kind of."

Chances were she had been. Women who hang around with rock stars have to be game for anything, such as sex with four guys at once, or having an array of objects rammed into various personal orifices, or sitting naked in tubs full of hot fudge, or all of the above. Writers, we don't have female followers like that. Ours tend to be short, nervous copy editors named Charlotte or Rhonda who mostly want to talk about Pynchon and Coover.

"Ooh. I love your dog!"

Lulu was watching us disapprovingly from under the bar.

"She loves to be loved."

Violet smiled at me. She liked me looking at her, and I was looking at her.

"I was expecting someone old and crawly with a beard, actually," she informed me. "You're cute for a writer."

"It's true. I was voted cutest American writer of the year in '83. Joyce Carol Oates came in second."

She frowned. Modern American literature didn't seem to be one of her strengths. A point in her favor. "Would you be going into London?" she asked.

"No, I always dress like this for a quiet evening at home."

"Can I come? It's so bloody boring out here."

"I'd be happy to give you a lift in, but I do have plans."

"Oh. Forget it then – I thought we could go dancing."

I checked my grandfather's Rolex. "I'd best be off," I said, racking my cue.

"Where are you living, anyhow?"

"Second floor, west wing, guest suite. End of the – "

"Ooh, the leather room?"

"The very one."

"I'm directly down the hall in the blue room," she said. "I love leather. Especially black leather."

"Then I'm sure you and T. S. have a lot in common."

"Oh, we do."

Jack offered me my choice of the two, count 'em two, utility vehicles. These were kept apart from T. S.'s show cars in a small garage adjacent to Jack's office and rooms.

One was a dinged-up '79 Peugeot 504 diesel station wagon. The other was a gleaming twenty-year-old Austin Mini Cooper. I went for the mini.

"By the way," I said, taking the keys from him, "I should be very cross with you."

"Me, sir?"

"You didn't tell me the other day you're Jackie Horner, original drummer of the Rough Boys."

His red face got redder. "That was a long time ago, sir." He scruffed at the ground with his foot. "Boyhood stuff"

"Still, I really *am* going to interview you now."

"About?"

"Your recollections. Your feelings about what it's like to have gotten so close to it, but . . ."

"Missed it?" he demanded indignantly, puffing his chest out. "Didn't miss it. Not at all. I'm right here. Got m'health, a few bob in the bank – that's more than a lot of 'em can say, believe me."

"You're not bitter?"

He let out a short, humorless laugh. "Doesn't pay to be bitter."

"So why the words of warning the other day?"

"I have my reasons."

"What are they?"

"You're familiar with our right-hand drive?" he asked, changing the subject.

"I am."

Lulu and I climbed into the mini. It had a burled walnut dash, a small fridge and a monster stereo system. The seats were upholstered in mink. Lulu settled into hers, immensely pleased.

I rolled down my window. "Say, this isn't exactly factory issue, is it?"

"Customized by a chap in London who does Rolls work for the Arab sheiks. A little something extra under the bonnet, as well. You'll go left at the main road. In five miles you'll reach the A-Twenty-three. Follow that in."

"Thank you, Jackie."

"It's Jack, sir. Please."

"My mistake. How about that interview? I can work around your schedule."

He smiled, reached in, and straightened my bow tie for me. It didn't need straightening. "Have a good trip, sir."

The mini kicked right over. I eased her slowly down the gravel drive toward the front gate, checking out the right-hand drive and Jack in the rear view mirror. He was watching me, hands on his hips. What was he hiding?

I found an ice-cold bottle of Dom Perignon in the little fridge, along with a chilled pewter mug. I helped myself. There was no current stuff among the tapes – only sixties soul music. No complaints here. I put on some Aretha Franklin very loud. The guards opened the front gate wide, and we were on our way.

Lady Soul was hot. The mini was hotter. I found the highway and worked my way happily through the city-bound traffic and the champagne. Lulu rode sitting up so she could take in the foreign sights out of her window and, occasionally, snuffle at them.

We reached London in time to do some vital reconnaisance for later in the evening. Then I drove us over to the West End and ditched the mini around the corner from the theater. The Haymarket is a fine old stage – intimate, well-maintained, steeped in theatrical history and tradition. There used to be a few theaters like it left on Broadway, only they tore them down a couple of years ago to make way for a hotel complex that belongs next to an airport. In Atlanta.

Merilee had reserved a pair on the aisle. I let Lulu have the aisle seat so she could see better. She whimpered softly when the lights came up on Merilee. She wasn't the only one. Merilee looked gorgeous that night, her waist-length golden hair and white dress aglow under the stage lights. Not that my ex-wife is conventionally beautiful. Her nose and chin are patrician to the point of mannish, and her forehead is much too high. Plus, she's not exactly delicately proportioned. Her shoulders are broad and sloped, her back muscular, her legs big and powerful. She was, I realized, significantly taller than Anthony Andrews. She had to wear flat shoes and slouch into her hip to stay eye to eye with him.

They played it bright and peppy, like Barry is meant to be played. Her Tracy was steely control on the outside, a dithery, vulnerable mess on the inside. It's hard to not think of Hepburn in the part – Barry did write it for her. But that night, on the Haymarket stage, Merilee made the role of Tracy Lord her own.

When it was over, Lulu and I worked our way through the opening night mob backstage to tell her. She was in her dressing room, surrounded by admirers and backers, laughing, giddy. I watched her from across the room until she spotted me. Her smile dropped. Her green eyes widened. We stared at each other for what seemed like hours. Then I smiled, and she smiled. And the other people in the room and the years and the bad times melted away.

"How was I?" she asked, accepting the dozen long-stemmed roses I'd brought her.

"It wasn't the worst thing you've ever done."

"Thank you, darling."

"And you've never looked lovelier, but I suppose you already know that."

"A gal only knows it if her guy says so."

"Am I your guy?"

"Could be. I forgot how nice you look in a tux."

"Careful, my head turns easily."

She dabbed at my upper lip with her finger. "You shaved off your mustache."

"Like it?"

"It reminds me of how you looked when we met."

"I'll take that as a yes."

"I gave it as a yes."

Slowly, each of us became aware of this moaning sound originating from floor level. Lulu, ears back and tail thumping, was desperately trying to scale Mount Merilee.

"Oh, Lulu, sweetness! No, you'll tear my costume!"

Merilee bent over and held Lulu down with her hands. These Lulu nuzzled and licked, all the while circling Merilee in a frenzy.

"You'd best take her out, darling," Merilee said. "I'll change."

"Not too much," I cautioned.

She laughed. It was one of our corny old jokes from back when we were falling madly in love, and I'd meet her backstage every evening.

She emerged a half hour later dressed in a Laura Biagiotti skirt and sweater of mocha brown cashmere, a blouse of white silk and Tanino Crisci boots. There was a trench coat over her arm and a first-class Worth & Worth Statler fedora on her head. The Statler had been mine, until she convinced me it was too small for me.

She liked the mini. Lulu liked sitting in her lap.

We went to the Hungry Horse, which is on Fulham Road in what was a hip South Ken neighborhood twenty years ago. Now there seemed to be a lot of places there offering American cheeseburgers and televised NFL football games. Certainly, this was not my idea of hip, but then neither is Pee-wee Herman.

They serve old-fashioned English food at the Hungry Horse. The dining room is a few steps down, and small, and you go in the back way through the kitchen. The tables are set against little settees. I let Merilee have the settee. I sat across from her, or I should say them. Lulu went right for her lap again. She had not paid me the slightest attention since we'd met up with Merilee.

"I've missed her," said Merilee, scratching Lulu's ears.

"I see it's mutual," I noted drily.

"She reminds me of us. The good part."

"You like to be reminded?"

"From time to time." Merilee flushed slightly, looked away. "When I'm feeling as if something is missing from my life. When I'm feeling . . . ordinary."

"That's one thing you'll never be."

We ordered blood-rare roast beef, Yorkshire pudding and a bottle of Medoc. And two martinis, very dry.

"Nothing to start with?" asked the waiter.

"Just extra olives in our martinis," I replied.

He frowned. "How many would you like?"

"Bring the jar," Merilee said. "Please."

For Merilee Nash he'd gladly have tangoed with a sheep. He returned a moment later with our martinis, very dry, an ornate bowl brimming with cocktail olives, and an autograph book, which he held before her shyly. She signed it.

I held my glass up. "To a successful run."

"To *then*." She clicked my glass with hers. "The good part."

We drank.

"How are the parents?" she asked, dunking an olive in her drink and devouring it.

I come from one of those families where no one speaks to each other. Merilee they loved. "Alive, last I heard. Yours?"

Merilee comes from one of those families where everyone speaks to each other. Me they never liked. "Well."

I dunked an olive in my drink. I was about to swallow it when I saw her gazing at it longingly. She'd always insisted mine tasted better than hers. I let her have it. Then I had one of my own. "And Zack?"

She looked down into her drink. "Zack is having serious problems with his second play."

It had been several years now since Zack had made his Broadway splash. He was overdue. "What's it about?"

"Us, apparently. Him and me. It's caused him to withdraw from me. And to get churlish." She sipped her martini. "Also to drink too much."

"Say, this sounds mighty familiar."

She smiled ruefully. "Doesn't it?"

"It's so unlike you. Truly. I mean, you're such a perfect person except for this one teeny little flaw of yours."

She stiffened. "Flaw? What flaw?"

"I hate to be the one to break it to you, Merilee, but you have terrible taste in husbands."

She covered my hand with hers and looked dreamily into my eyes. "You noticed."

We tore into our food when it came. Merilee eats like a sophomore nose tackle and never gains an ounce. It drives her friends crazy. Her women friends.

"So is it over?" I asked. "You and Zack?"

"It's acrid."

"Acrid?"

"Tell me about T. S.," she said, gently but firmly steering us elsewhere. I let her do so.

"Haven't figured him out yet. He's moody. Self-centered. Cooperative, but evasive when he wants to be. A tough nut, no question."

She helped herself to some of my roast beef. "And the novel? What's it about?"

I cleared my throat. "The last couple of years."

"I see," she said, the weather on her side of the table getting noticeably chillier. "And I'll play a featured role in it?"

"I'm trying to deal with what happened."

"From your point of view."

"It's my book."

"That's right, it is," she agreed, sharply. "I'm going to write a book myself. I'll call it *I Keep Marrying Men Who Blame Me For Their Problems*."

"Not true, Merilee."

"Not fair! I do the best I can! Why do I deserve this?"

"Look, I don't blame you. But I do have to write about us. That's how I work things out. The thing that drove us apart was I *couldn't* write."

"All of which makes it okay – even if I get trashed in print."

"You won't get trashed."

"But I will get undressed!"

"If you insist. Shall I blindfold the waiter?"

"Not funny," she snapped, glaring at me.

Lulu shifted restlessly in Merilee's lap and looked from Merilee to me, then from me to Merilee.

"It appears," I said, "as if this isn't going to work out very well. I suppose it was unrealistic to expect it would." I looked around for our waiter.

"No," she said, placing her knife and fork down on her plate. "Wait, Hoagy. Let's not do this, okay? Let's not talk about the past, the future, any of it. Can't we just enjoy now? Enjoy each other?"

I got lost in her green eyes for a second. "We can sure try."

"Good. But first I have something very serious to ask you."

"Yes, Merilee?"

"What are we having for dessert?"

We had a positively immoral concoction of cake topped with whipped fresh cream, and finished it off with coffee and port.

Then we walked, Merilee's hand on my arm, her gait as long and loping as my own. Lulu ambled happily a few feet ahead of us, so busy showing us off to the passersby that she didn't notice we were being followed. Nor did Merilee. I wasn't absolutely sure myself – I'm not exactly what you'd call an expert on trench-coat surveillance – but I swore I sensed somebody walking a careful half block or so behind us, staying stride for stride with us, measuring us.

"Hoagy, are we one of those awful couples who can't get along together but can't get along apart either?"

That one caught me flat-footed – pleasantly so. I hadn't known we were anything to her anymore, except dead.

"We've never not gotten along in London," I pointed out.

"That's right," she exclaimed, squeezing my arm. "Get me drunk?"

"With pleasure."

She thought we'd be pulling in at the Anglesea, a fine old pub on Selwood Terrace with rough wooden floors and Ruddle's on tap. We'd had fun there on our honeymoon. But I steered us past it to a fairly undistinguished looking family pub on Old Brompton Road.

It was crowded and smoky in there, and it smelled of beer and fried fish. The working-class clientele gave us the eye as we worked our way through them toward the bar – me for the tux, Merilee for being Merilee. I ordered pints of heavy Guinness draft for us and a piece of finnan haddie for Lulu. The meaty Hungry Horse menu hadn't much appealed to her. When our mugs were set before us we clinked them and drank deeply. Merilee then swiped delicately at the creamy foam on her upper lip and made a little noise akin to a discreet hiccough. Among her many gifts she happens to possess the world's most elegant belch.

The barman treated us to our second round in exchange for an autograph, which Merilee happily signed. As she handed the prized napkin back to him, she pointed to a sign prominently displayed over the bar.

"Tell me," she said, "why is tonight called Poultry Night?"

The barman flushed with embarrassment. "Well, miss, it's because . . . uh . . ."

"Because?" she pressed.

"Every woman . . . she gets a free . . ."

Merilee yelped.

". . . goose."

"Splendid custom," I declared, raising my mug to the quick-fingered drinkers behind us, as well as glancing about for a familiar face, or a shifty-eyed face, or for anyone who looked like he didn't want me to spot him. No one.

Three pale, knobby-knuckled workmen at the end of the bar bought us our third round. We returned the favor. Then I decided it was time to test those tapping feet.

"Shall we?" I asked, indicating the two square feet of vacant floor beside the jukebox.

"I thought you'd never ask, darling."

I made my song selection and gathered her in my arms. A little shudder went through her when Ray Charles's version of "Georgia on My Mind" came on. It was our song – the one we danced to over and over again that first night, at a Polish seaman's club on First Avenue and Ninth Street, where we drank up peppery vodka and each other, and then went home and didn't leave the bed for six weeks.

She was gazing at me now, her eyes brimming. "How did you know they had it?"

"Easy – I checked out every jukebox within a ten-block radius."

"You romantic fool."

"You got that half right."

"Which half?"

"Ssh."

We swayed slowly, cheek to cheek. She smelled of Crabtree and Evelyn avocado oil soap. Her smell. Also her secret – she won't tell anyone she bathes in it for fear a beauty magazine will reveal it and she'll end up smelling like every other woman in America.

When it was over Nat Cole sang us "Don't Get Around Much

Anymore." Joe Williams did "In the Evening," Mel Torme "Blue and Sentimental." It was an uncommon juke.

"I don't mean to be indelicate, darling," Merilee murmured in my ear, "but are you rising to the occasion these days?"

"Try me."

She sighed. "I have."

"Try me again."

"I'm not so sure."

"Then why did you bring it up? So to speak."

Her green eyes twinkled. "A gal just likes to know these things."

We pulled up at her place on Cromwell Road a little after three. It was hidden from the road. To get there we turned in at a driveway, then passed under an archway, jogged around and found ourselves in a wonderfully private little cobbled mews of precious dolls' houses. Hers was a cheery blue number with flowers growing in the window boxes. If she had mice they were doubtless singing ones.

Our tail followed us in, then backed out onto Cromwell Road when he saw we were staying. He was in a taxicab now. Picked us up the second we left the pub.

We sat there not talking for a while with the engine running and Lulu asleep in her lap.

I broke the silence. "Going to invite us in?"

She didn't answer me right away. When she did she said, "No, I'm not."

"Okay."

"That's it? You're not going to argue with me? Paw me? Pant?"

"Too old."

She took a deep breath and let it out slowly. "It isn't simple, darling. There's Zack . . ."

"I know."

"There's also the fact that you and I failed once before, and there's no reason to believe we'll do any differently now. I don't want to live through the same pain all over again. I'm too old, too."

"I don't come with a warranty," I said. "I'm not a Hyundai Excel."

"And I'm not Donna Reed."

"Neither was Donna Reed."

"Good night, darling."

"Sleep tight, Merilee."

She woke Lulu up, kissed her on top of the head and got out. I watched her go inside of her house. So did Lulu, who scratched at the window and whimpered. I told her to shut up.

The taxi was still there, double-parked on Cromwell Road about a hundred feet from the driveway, lights on, engine running. Waiting. There were two people inside of it. One was the driver. I couldn't tell if the person in back was a man or a woman. Didn't know what he or she wanted. Sure as hell didn't feel like finding out just now, either.

I floored it. Took the first right turn on two wheels, then took a left, then a right. I kept checking the rearview mirror but I really didn't need to. I'd lost the taxi in two blocks. No way it could stay with the souped-up mini. By the time I reached the A-23 I was the only one on the road. Just me and the fog.

It was the eleventh consecutive gloomy day since I'd arrived in England, and it suited me just fine.

A click woke me.

It was the sound of the door to my suite being closed. From the inside. The floor creaked in the sitting room. Someone was moving around in there in the darkness. Lulu growled softly from her perch atop my head. I muzzled her.

A match was struck. I could see its wavering yellow glow through the open bedroom door. And hear a shuffling sound – the papers on my desk were being examined. The match went out. More footsteps in the darkness. Closer. Lulu tensed. Another match was struck. The things on my dressing table were being pored over now – the contents of my wallet, my money clip.

I turned on my bedside lamp. "Can I help?"

Violet stood at my dressing table. She wore a black Chicago Bears T-shirt and absolutely nothing else. Her breasts strained against the T-shirt.

"A match," she said, with admirable calm. She showed me the unlit cigarette that was between her fingers. In her other hand was a book of matches. "I was looking for a match, you see. Couldn't find one anywhere. Very sorry if I woke you."

"That's okay. Only, you didn't find those matches in here. I don't smoke."

"They were over by the fireplace."

"And you're not," I pointed out.

"I wasn't stealing!"

"I didn't say you were. Want to tell me what you were doing in my things?"

She lit her cigarette, came over to the bed and sat down on the edge of it. Lulu sniffed disagreeably at her, jumped down and waddled into the sitting room.

"I don't think she likes me," Violet said, watching her go.

"Nothing personal. She just gets possessive."

"I couldn't sleep, y'know? And I was a bit curious about you."

I smiled. "Okay."

"May I have a drink?"

"Help yourself."

"You?"

"Had plenty tonight, thanks."

I watched her pad into the sitting room in her nondecent T-shirt. I watched her come back, too, stirring a whiskey and soda with her index finger, which she sucked on when she was finished using it. She sat back down on the bed and took a sip of her drink. She took another sip. Then she leaned back on her elbows, crossed her bare, impossibly long legs and admired her naked foot. It was a lovely foot, slender and high-arched. She began to swing it up and down, up and . . .

"What would you like to know about me?" I asked.

"Whether you like me," she replied, looking me straight in the eye.

"You're right out of my moistest fantasies. Such as they are."

She tasted the whiskey on her lips with the tip of her tongue. "I could get in there with you."

"Are you always this shy?"

"Tris wouldn't mind y'know. Really."

"I'm married," I said. "Somewhat."

"Oh." She shrugged. "We wouldn't have to do anything, actually, except sleep. It's so much nicer sleeping with someone else, isn't it?"

She wasn't wrong. Or difficult or demanding. Or Merilee. Always, it came back to Merilee.

"Thanks, anyway. Why don't you sleep with Tris? He should be turning in soon – it's nearly dawn."

Her eyes widened. "There's a naughty name for that, isn't there?"

"Statutory rape?"

"Incest, silly. You did know he's m'daddy, didn't you?"

CHAPTER
FIVE

(Tape #4 with Tristam Scarr. Recorded in his chamber Nov. 24. Wears same clothes as three days before. Does not appear to have bathed, shaved or slept since then. Room is considerably darker than before. Has turned off several lamps. Wears dark glasses.)

Hoag: I met your daughter, Violet. She's lovely

Scarr: Careful of her, mate.

Hoag: Oh?

Scarr: She likes to nick things. What they call a . . . a . . .

Hoag: Thief?

Scarr: Kleptomaniac. Don't doubt she's a nymphomaniac as well. And an overall maniac. Just like her jolly old mum.

Hoag: Who is . . . ?

Scarr: Tulip.

Hoag: Ah. The floral motif should have been a giveaway.

Scarr: They haven't gotten along, she and Tu, since Tu found his holiness. Tries to impose her beliefs on the girl. And raises bloody hell over her things being mussed with. So I let Vi crash here, if she's into it.

Hoag: She seems very mature for her age.

Scarr: She's fifteen, if that's what you're wondering. Why, did you climb into her nickers? It's cool with me if you did. I can't exactly tell her not to do the things I did, can I? It'd be bleedin' bullshit. *(pause)* Did you?

Hoag: I've spoken with Jack a couple of times. I wouldn't exactly say he's hostile, but, well, he *is* hostile.

Scarr: He's fucking jealous is all.

Hoag: I wondered if it was something else. Something he didn't want coming out.

Scarr: Such as?

Hoag: I was hoping you'd tell me.

Scarr: I'm not tracking, Hogarth.

Hoag: The man's dead set against talking to me.

Scarr: So leave him be.

Hoag: Can't. He's too valuable a source.

Scarr: I see. I'll have a word with him then.

Hoag: Thank you. I'm interested in what the music scene was like here in '62, when the Rough Boys were first getting gigs.

Scarr: Uh-huh. There was a small R and B thing happening in and around London. Like a cult thing, really. *(pause)* Did you fuck her? It's okay, mate. I mean it.

Hoag: It didn't come up.

Scarr: *(silence, then laughs)* There's a good one. Bloody good.

Hoag: Now can we . . . ?

Scarr: Right. We talked about how Lonnie Donegan, of skiffle fame, had played in Chris Barber's jazz band back in the fifties. So had Alexis Korner and Cyril Davies, until they split to form Blues Incorporated, which I reckon you could call Britain's very first blues band. Charlie Watts of the Stones-to-be was on drums. Jack Bruce of Cream-to-be played bass. Blues Incorporated tried playing the trad jazz clubs around London, only the serious jazz fans – the bleedin' intellects – thought they were too scruff. So they started up their own club in a basement under a teashop in Ealing – the Ealing Club. Those of us who were into R and B took to hanging out there when we weren't playing a gig. Me and Rory, Michael Jagger, Keith, Brian, John Mayall, Long John Baldry . . . We were all mates then, before there was competition and egos and the like. We'd rap about music and gigs, and anybody could have a blow up on stage. Got up there m'self one night, roaring drunk I was, and sang "Ooh-ee Baby," the Albert King song, with Blues Incorporated. Cyril backed me up on harp. Played it like a monster. Right then I decided to learn harp m'self. *(yawns)* All of which meant the Rough Boys started sounding bluesier. We added "Please, Please, Please," a James Brown song, and "Spoonful," the Howlin' Wolf song, which Cream did years later. After Blues Incorporated split up, Cyril formed a new band, the All Stars, and they got a gig at the Island. That's Eel Pie Island, which was an old twenties dance hall out on this island in the middle of the Thames at Twickenham. Cyril put in the word for us and got us a gig there as well. There was a small blues circuit then – the Railway Hotel in Harrow, St. Mary's Parish Hall in Richmond, Studio Fifty-One in London. We played all of 'em. Met people. Talked ourselves up. Only, we kept playin' the weddings and church dances as well, which was a mistake. Couldn't get known for anything that way. I thought we should be a blues band. The Beatles were already rockin', y'know? Rory and the others, they still liked playing "Blue Suede Shoes." While we were busy arguing over it, Decca went and signed up the Stones to a recording contract. Pissed me off. *(yawns)* They were playin' at Crawdaddy then. Turnin' it into a big R and B club. We followed 'em in there after they signed with Decca. We were always followin' 'em. Played the Marquee after 'em as well. Only now – now the knock against us was we was too much like the bleedin' Stones. We sounded different, but the people makin' decisions, the record people, they went by categories. Rory fought the categories. He believed in the power of the music. *(yawns)* I . . .

Hoag: You didn't?

Scarr: Hmm? . . . Sorry . . . I was more a realist, I reckon.

Hoag: Realist?

Scarr: To me all we lacked was a proper gimmick. Or management. It's all a hustle, isn't it? You've got to get noticed, is all . . . I think I've had it for tonight, mate.

Hoag: You do look somewhat beat. I meant to tell you, Tristam – somebody was following me in London last night.

Scarr: Know that feeling. So well. Seems real, doesn't it? It's the acid . . . So real . . .

Hoag: This *was* real.

Scarr: Mmm-mmmmm . . .

Hoag: Any idea why someone would be following me? *(silence)* Tristam? *(silence)* Hello?

(end tape)

(Tape #1 with Jack Horner recorded in his office Nov. 25. There is a cluttered desk, portable heater, girlie calendar, gun rack. Contents: Browning 20-gauge over-under, Remington 1100 automatic, pre-'64 Winchester bolt action sporting rifle. Door leads into parlor of his apartment. Spartanly furnished.)

Horner: I'd like to apologize about before, sir. Didn't mean to appear rude.

Hoag: Are you still opposed to looking into the past?

Horner: I am. But I understand you have a job to do. Mr. Scarr, he made it clear to me.

Hoag: What did you mean before when you told me, "It wouldn't be bright"?

Horner: Just talk, sir.

Hoag: I thought you might have been referring to Puppy's death.

Horner: Puppy's death?

Hoag: T. S. seems to think it was no accident.

Horner: (*silence*) I was road manager when it happened. I knew what went on.

Hoag: And?

Horner: Pup, for all of his wildness, he knew his limits. He wouldn't have taken that much speed on his own. Someone slipped him a monster dose without him knowing it. Replaced the pills he was taking with stronger ones. At least, that's what I always figured.

Hoag: Any idea who?

Horner: Had to be one of us, didn't it?

Hoag: Did it?

Horner: It's not like they were on the road when it happened. They were recording, or trying to, at Rory's country place in the Cotswolds. I was helping with the equipment. The band was there, Tulip, Marco, a couple of ladies . . .

Hoag: You're saying you think someone in or close to the band murdered Puppy Johnson?

Horner: Who else could it have been?

Hoag: Did you tell this to the police at the time?

Horner: Yessir, I did. And there was a thorough investigation – all quite hush-hush, so the papers wouldn't get hold of it. But the pills were never found. No case was made against anyone. So it was ruled an accident.

Hoag: (*pause*) T. S. seems to feel you're pretty bitter about being dropped from the band. That you hated Puppy.

Horner: I told you before, I'm not a bitter man. And I don't appreciate you suggesting –

Hoag: What were your responsibilities as roadie?

Horner: I did what needed to be done.

Hoag: Did you buy Puppy's dope for him?

Horner: From time to time – when they were on the road. At home they were all on their own. I wasn't any drug dealer. I don't know where that speed came from and that's the truth. One minute they were playing in Rory's studio. Next minute Pup was dead. That's all I know.

Hoag: T. S. and I were talking last night about the club days, before the Rough Boys caught on.

Horner: That was wartime, that.

Hoag: Between the different bands?

Horner: Between T S and Rory. That was their way, when they were young. Arguing was how they talked. Punching was how they argued. Hot-tempered, both of 'em. Sometimes they'd go at it right there on stage. Derek and I would just look at each other and roll our eyes . . . Rory, he got in a proper punch-up with Mr. Law over his work habits as a roofer, or lack of 'em. He and T. S. took a room together, near the garage where we played. Bloody awful place it was – two bare mattresses on the floor, a single suitcase between the two of 'em, cigarette butts and beer bottles everywhere. The lights and heat were coin-operated, which meant it was always freezing and dark in there. And they were always sick. Never ate. I'd go over and they'd be wrapped in blankets on the floor in the dark, coughing, Rory strumming away on his guitar. Even slept with the thing. The Rough Boys weren't earning more than a few bob a week for the four of us. Some nights there'd only be five, six people listening to us in the clubs. I still laid bricks. Derek was a clerk at a men's clothing store. Those two, they lived the music twenty-four hours a day. They wanted to be rock 'n' roll stars, or die trying . . . The thing you should bear in mind, Mr. Hoag, is it was always T. S. and Rory's band. Derek and I were just along for the ride. Until . . . until it was just Derek along for the ride.

Hoag: Can we talk about that?

Horner: (pause) I suppose it goes all the way back to when we attended the Negro Blues Festival, autumn of '63 at Fairfield Hall in Croydon. Giorgio Gomelsky, who managed Crawdaddy, pulled it together. Giorgio managed the Stones until they left him for Andrew Loog Oldham. This blues festival, it was a showcase of American blues greats – Muddy Waters, Otis Spann and the one and only Mad Dog Johnson. Mad Dog was a giant, enormously fat old geezer from Louisiana. Six feet six. Weighed twenty stone easily. And admitted to being seventy years old. They called him Mad Dog for two reasons. One was he could make the mouth harp sound just exactly like a dog growling. Two was that he was stark, staring mad. This we didn't know yet. All we knew was he was the real thing. T. S., he got it into his head we should somehow hook up with him. Rory wasn't mad about the idea, but he had to admit that the Rough Boys needed a push. We approached Mad Dog backstage after his performance, where we found him with his "niece," Mabel, who was perhaps twenty and traveled with him. T. S. told him how much we dug him, and how we played the blues ourselves and would love to play with him sometime. Mad Dog just mumbled something, and then T. S. tried to shake his hand. In response, Mad Dog swatted T. S. away with the back of his hand, sent him flying against the wall. And went after him, cursing and spitting. He'd have killed T. S. if we all hadn't pried him off. Turned out he didn't like to shake hands. Turned out he drank twenty-four hours a day, ranted and raved and was violent. Carried a loaded gun as well. Still, T. S. was not to be denied. After he came to he asked this Mabel to get Mad Dog to Crawdaddy the next night. She did, and he got up there with us, this ancient black giant who didn't even know where he was half the time. It was a wild gig – him drinking whiskey from the bottle, yelling out lyrics that made no sense, doing these strange things with his harp, like flickering his Adam's apple with his fingers as he played it. But it got us noticed. Which was what T. S. was after, I think. Right off a bloke came up and said we ought to let him manage us.

Hoag: This would be Marco Bartucci?

Horner: No. Marco came later. This was a geezer named Eli Gushen, who said he was a cinema hall manager, and assured us he could get the Rough Boys, featuring Mad Dog Johnson, a gig in a package tour. Those were a big deal back then. They'd put one headliner together with an assortment of musical acts – some on the way up, some on the way down, some on the way nowhere – and they'd tour the cinema halls performing one-night stands. Eli got us a spot in a two-week tour of the north, opening for Jerry Lee Lewis. Twenty pounds a week for us all. So we hit the road. Spent our days in a motor coach, our nights in mining town railway hotels, living on eggs and chips, washing out our socks in the sink, all of us in one room except for Mad Dog and Mabel. "This is it, lads," T. S. kept saying. "We've made it." Christ, we were practically cleaning up after the elephants – Jerry Lee would not even say hello to us – but T. S., he was in heaven. And he worshiped Mad Dog. Pestered him constantly for stories about the old days. Nicked his expressions, like "Lord have mercy" and "Hoo, Lord." And that quality to his voice that he became so famous for, that rough quality, it came from imitating Mad Dog . . . He was a bit of business, was Mad Dog. There was always this ungodly whooping and hollering coming from his room. One night he shot out his hotel room window and got all of us thrown out.

Hoag: How did you go over musically?

Horner: Piss poor. At least at Crawdaddy and the other clubs around London there were a few blues followers. Not in the north. Saturday nights there they wanted to drink up a lot of ale and hear "Rock Around the Clock." We got booed for playing the blues. T. S.

and Rory got into quite a row over it. The tour was basically a disaster. A rip-off as well. Eli was holding our money, see, saying we'd get it after the tour. Only we didn't – he claimed it had all gone to cover our expenses. Turned out he was a kind of pimp who got young groups like us to fill out the bill for nothing. We got our money though. Rory and me took him out back of the bus and beat the shit out of him and emptied his wallet for him. He was only worth seven pounds, so we took his coat and his shoes and sold those. T. S. thought we should give the money to Mad Dog. His work visa was up and he had no passage home to America. So we did. Not that T. S. was entirely without reasons of his own. See, he was having it off with Mabel and wanted to give her the go.

Hoag: Tired of her?

Horner: Not exactly. *(laughs)* Mad Dog wasn't the only member of the family who packed a gun, sir.

(end tape)

(Tape #1 with Derek Gregg recorded in parlor of his Georgian town house in Bedford Square, Nov. 26. Room dominated by cherry wood gun case featuring museum-grade collection of American muzzle loaders, including 1775 Maryland Committee of Safety musket with brass wrist escutcheon, A. Waters and Son 1842 smoothbore percussion musket, 1847 Sappers & Miners musketoon. Former Us bassist looks remarkably like he did twenty years before. Sandy hair still cut in moppet style. Few if any lines on face or neck. No suggestion of paunch under black silk shirt. Jeans and boots are also black. Companion is a muscular swarthy young man in matching attire. Gregg asks him to leave us. He does so, sulkily.)

Hoag: It's very nice of you to give me this time.

Gregg: No problem. Anything for Mr. Cigar.

Hoag: Lovely muskets. Do they work?

Gregg: Of course. No point in having them if they don't. I belong to a black powder shooting club. We frolic about the fields and streams exactly as they did a century ago. It's great fun. Sometimes we even wear underwear.

Hoag: I'd think ammunition would be hard to come by.

Gregg: I have it made.

Hoag: That you do. Own any contemporary arms?

Gregg: No, I don't bother to collect garbage. You like to spar, don't you?

Hoag: Not particularly.

Gregg: You're good at it.

Hoag: Everyone ought to be good at something. I've been hearing about the old days, when the band was starting up.

Gregg: The scruff days. And they were scruffs, Rory and Mr. Cigar. Their idea of a gas was to nick two air guns from a sports shop, go out to the junkyard, and let fly at the rats.

Hoag: Hit any?

Gregg: They did indeed. Right good shots they were. Brought their kills to school with them, so all of us could see.

Hoag: How tasteful of them. I understand you had a bit of a reputation yourself. Something about a pregnancy.

Gregg: Christ, he's not putting that in, is he? The girl, her parents adopted the baby. The boy still thinks his mum's his sister. "Boy." There's a laugh – he's thirty. I'm a grandpa, believe it? I've always sent the family a little money. Quietly. And I'd prefer it stay quiet, for the family's sake. You can understand, can't you?

Hoag: Yes, I can. However, that kind of decision isn't mine to make. If you want something left out I suggest you take it up with Tris. It's his book. Speaking of which, I have something rather delicate to ask, if you don't mind.

Gregg: I don't mind. I feel quite comfortable with you. It must be your eyes.

Hoag: What about them?

Gregg: They're sad. I don't trust happy people. They lie.

Hoag: Especially to themselves.

Gregg: You're very perceptive.

Hoag: I'm a helluva guy. Tris . . . he says you loved Rory. Is that true?

Gregg: *(pause)* Members of a band develop a closeness outsiders can't totally appreciate. We eat, sleep, bathe, and fuck in front of each other. We communicate with each other in our own language – the music. There's a bond. And there's love. I'm not ashamed to admit I loved Rory Law. He never fully returned it, but that never changed how I felt. Mr. Cigar threw it in my face when he learned of it. He could be cruel if he had something on someone.

Hoag: Did you and Rory ever . . . ?

Gregg: Have it off? Once, back in the crazy days. Chateau Marmont Hotel in Hollywood, '68 maybe, during one of those stoned-out after-concert orgy shows – the band and eight or ten groupies in a variety of configurations. Sexual experimentation was a vital part of the scene back then. Part of the adventure. Rory and me, we found ourselves together that night, and he looked at me and I looked at him and . . . he enjoyed it. He did. Though later he denied that, which hurt me. Is my gayness to be a part of this book?

Hoag: How would you feel about it?

Gregg: I'd absolutely love it. It'll be a gas, won't it?

Hoag: It'll open some eyes. How did it feel to be gay and yet be a sex symbol to millions of teenage girls?

Gregg: It was merely one part of a much larger illusion. We were never who the record company said we were. They made us up, like they did the old-time Hollywood movie stars. Christ, a lot of people still didn't know until he died of AIDS that Rock Hudson was gay. His studio had even married him off . . . Of course, early on, I was not a practicing homosexual. It simply wasn't done – at least, not among the working class. *(laughs)* I had my share of birds, and plenty of laughs. For a while. It just wasn't me, y'know? It was . . . it became very hard for me later on, traveling with Rory, wanting to make him happy, and seeing him destroy himself on drugs and stupid, greedy women. No woman ever made Rory happy, from when we were lads until the day he died.

Hoag: And Tris?

Gregg: Mr. Cigar never thought of women as people. Just things to fuck and forget.

Hoag: I very much want to understand him, but he's eluding me so far.

Gregg: He's the Shadow Man. You can't get inside of him. No one can. If you remember one thing you'll understand him as well as it's possible to: He was a bloke who was willing to do whatever it took to become a rock 'n' roll star. And that's a lot. And not all of it is pleasant. Rory, all he wanted out of life was to play his music and party. He cared nothing for the money or the business. He had his faults, of course. He was defiant, irresponsible, childish. But he was *right there*. Not Tris. He held back. He watched, calculated. Tris could chat up people who might do him good. He could sell himself. Rory couldn't. Tristam Scarr is an actor. He always has been an actor. I remember that first time he got up and sang at the Ealing Club for Alexis and Cyril –

Hoag: He was drunk. He told me about it.

Gregg: He was stone-cold sober. He *pretended* he was drunk so they would think he was some wild headstrong lad crazy with love for the music. He's shrewd. Always seems to know what the right move is, and never has trouble making it. He's not a nice man. It doesn't matter to him how he gets something. Just that he gets it. As we got more successful, he starting asking this and that about the business end. Too late though. We had already been royally fucked over by Marco, who financed his other businesses with our profits and then told us we were broke. We had to pay Marco off with the rights to all of our early songs in order to get clear of our management agreement with him. He robbed us. They all robbed us . . . You've a job, Mr. Hoag. The only man who may have understood Mr. Cigar is dead. I doubt any woman knew him at all, except possibly for Tulip. I remember when they started going around together. She was the supermodel – beautiful, glamorous, socially connected. You couldn't pick up a mag without seeing her face on it. And she was still around after a few weeks, which was unheard of for Tris. When I asked him about her he said, "I don't feel like throwin' her out in the mornin'." That was all he had to say about the woman he married. Deep down, you see, the only person he's ever really loved is himself. I'll never forget the first time we played "I'm Walkin'," the Fats Domino song, at Crawdaddy. Mr. Cigar, he starts acting it out up there on stage – that was the night he invented The Strut, you see – and the girls, they start screaming over it, loving it. Excited him so much he got a raging hard-on right there on stage. He told me afterward he thought he was going to fire away right in his bleeding trousers . . . Rory, he lived for today. Tris, he lived for tomorrow. And now it is tomorrow, and there he is, all alone in the tower of his castle. Hasn't a mate in the world, y'know. Not one. Not that I'm being critical – I can afford to do anything I want, thanks to him. Did I mention I'm opening a conceptual art gallery next month at Beauchamp Place? I'll be featuring the work of Jeffrey, who you've just met. He's so very talented . . . I always admired Mr. Cigar, to be honest. I mean, it takes a terrific pair of balls to simply not care if everyone you know thinks you're an absolute shit. Like the business about dropping Jackie. When Marco approached us about taking Puppy into the group, Tris was the one who said yes. Didn't hesitate. He had to talk Rory into it. Had to talk Rory into pretending we were from the 'Pool, as well.

Hoag: How did you meet up with Marco?

Gregg: The Rough Boys basically broke up as a group after Mad Dog returned to America. Nothing formal. We just stopped playing together. Double Trouble went back to their vomitous little room and to hanging about the clubs. They jammed for a bit at Club 51 with Jeff Beck, only Jeff and Tris didn't get along. Then Tris called me at the men's shop one day and asked me to meet him and Rory at Crawdaddy that night and to say nothing to Jackie about it. They were there with two men. One was about forty, and shaped more like a teapot than any person I've ever met. Marco Bartucci was also the first person I'd seen wearing muttonchop sideburns – still has them, I think. He was sweating profusely. Kept wiping his face and neck with a Western-style bandana.

Hoag: What was his background?

Gregg: He was raised in Glasgow of an Italian family. Said he'd worked for Larry Parnes in the fifties. Parnes was the promoter who brought along Tommy Steele and Johnny Gentle and Dickie Pride. I think Marco was some form of errand boy for him, though he claimed to have signed the Beatles for their very first road gig, opening for Johnny Gentle – before they were famous, of course. Lately, he'd been scouting talent in America, which is another way of saying he was waiting for something, or someone, to come along.

Hoag: And the man he was with?

Gregg: The other man was an American black in his early twenties. He had on a dark green suit of some shiny material, ruffled shirt and sunglasses, even though we were indoors and it was night. He wore grease in his hair to keep it straight. Chewed gum and kept tapping his fingers on the table. He was very wound up. Marco introduced him as Mad Dog Johnson's nephew, Albert, who went by the nickname Puppy and who played the drums. I said, "Pleased to meet you." He said, "Likewise." He spoke very softly, almost in a whisper. Marco had brought him over from America with the idea of making him into a rock 'n' roll star. See, there hadn't been a black rock star yet in Britain. Marco saw this as an opportunity.

Hoag: Smart.

Gregg: You'll never hear me call Marco stupid. What he had in mind was to put Puppy together with a young British R & B group. We came to mind because we'd toured with Mad Dog. I turned to Mr. Cigar and said, "What about Jackie?" And he replied, "Jackie's out." *(pause)* I was the one who told him. He wished us luck.

Hoag: Was Jackie upset?

Gregg: Why should he have been? He had no inkling of what was about to happen. Neither did I. Christ, I'll never forget the first time

I heard Puppy play. A positively thrilling moment, it was. Puppy, he took the drums into an entirely new dimension. Made them into a lead instrument almost. Nobody played drums like Puppy did.

Hoag: Tris believes he was murdered.

Gregg: (laughs) That old business? He never gives up. It was foretold, or so he believes. He also happens to believe in flying saucers, gypsy curses, and voodoo.

Hoag: Foretold?

Gregg: The night before Puppy died some freaky witch who Rory used to drop acid with warned us that great tragedy was about to strike us. She saw it in her tarot cards or some such shit. Mr. Cigar, he took her warning seriously. Asked her if it was going to be some kind of accident – like getting bashed by a lorry – and she said no, it would be no accident. She said there was great hostility in the air. Christ, she was just some cow who painted her fingernails black. I can't believe he's still going on about that.

Hoag: You don't think Puppy was murdered.

Gregg: I know he wasn't. I was there. He took too much speed and drank too much champagne. That's what happened. Nothing more to it than that. Don't listen to Mr. Cigar.

Hoag: Jack agrees with him.

Gregg: Jack is loyal. And dim.

Hoag: He believes Puppy was done in by someone in the band, or close to it.

Gregg: That is just utterly absurd. Believe me, Mr. Hoag, Puppy's death was an accident. None of us killed him. It's absurd to even consider the idea. Puppy was our mate. Furthermore, he was our ace. He put money in our pockets. Why on earth would any of us have wanted him dead?

(end tape)

(Tape #1 with Marco Bartucci recorded in his office at Jumbo's Disco Nov. 26. Is casually dressed – wears an inferiority complex in place of a necktie. Does look like a human teapot, with muttonchops. Is uneasy, hostile.)

Bartucci: What does T. S. want of me?

Hoag: Information. To fill out his recollections.

Bartucci: I see. So now he's asking me to help him sell books. Why should I? What have I to gain from it? Not that I'm a self-centered person.

Hoag: No, of course not. I think your interests will be served by talking to me. It's an opportunity for you to tell your side.

Bartucci: You want *my* side? Very well, here it is: whatever T S. says about business I deny. Lies. All lies.

Hoag: Are you warm?

Bartucci: No, why?

Hoag: You're perspiring.

Bartucci: I always do. Means nothing.

Hoag: I understand you and the band came to a rather ugly parting over money.

Bartucci: I gave those boys everything, and for that, this terrible, unjustified smear continues to follow me about. As an example, the gentleman I've started this club with, my backers, they're Middle Eastern gentlemen, and they know very little about the past and Tris Scarr's groundless accusations. Now they're going to read about me and wonder.

Hoag: That shouldn't present a problem to you. The club seems to be doing quite well.

Bartucci: Thank you. I try.

Hoag: Unless . . .

Bartucci: Unless what?

Hoag: Unless you're stealing from them, too.

Bartucci: (silence) I'm afraid I don't like you, Mr. Hoag.

Hoag: It's a problem I run into fairly often.

Bartucci: T. S. hasn't changed. He's still the same rude, nasty boy who slurped his food and called anyone a cunt if they looked at him sideways. I can't stop him from saying what he wants. I never could tell him anything. He had total contempt for me. All rock musicians have contempt for their managers. They can't stand people who are responsible, but at the same time they expect someone to be responsible for them. And when things don't go exactly as promised, they scream bloody murder. A misunderstanding – that's all we had. I didn't steal from them – I *invested*. I made some mistakes. I'll admit to that. But if it hadn't been for me he'd still be hanging around Crawdaddy, playing for beer and smokes money. I made Us. He'll deny that, but it's a fact. They were a blues band going nowhere. Nobody wanted them. They needed direction. I gave it to them.

Hoag: Can you tell me about Puppy?

Bartucci: The boy never knew his real father, who was in jail for life. Mad Dog lived with the mother off and on, and helped to raise him. So he took Mad Dog's family name, and called him his uncle. He was a big, strong, muscular boy. He'd been a paratrooper in the army. Loved jumping out of airplanes. I remember once when he was very stoned in Stockholm he jumped out of a third-floor hotel window for fun. Broke both of his ankles. "The rush, man," he said, as we waited for the ambulance to arrive. "The rush." After the army, he got work on what they called the chitlin circuit, drumming for Little Richard, Ike Turner, the Isley Brothers. The first time I saw him he was playing at the Apollo Theater in Harlem behind some absolutely nothing soul singers. He was an unusually athletic drummer. Put on a show as well. He'd twirl a drumstick up in the air while he played, as if it were a baton. Or he'd spin 360 degrees around on his stool without missing a beat. Or he'd flick his tongue at the girls. I was taken by him. I went backstage and introduced myself. He was an up, good-humored boy. He mentioned that his Uncle Mad Dog was over here in Britain at the time being a famous American Negro blues artist. He was thinking about coming over here himself, just to see what it was like. I told him I was moving back soon, and that if he ever did come to look me up. And he did. He was finding it very strange being here. There were Jamaicans and Bahamians here at that time, but there were very few American blacks like Puppy. It was because of Puppy that Hendrix came over, you know. The two of them had played together in Harlem when they were very young. Puppy paved the way for Jimi, and for others. He was a revolutionary – not that he thought of himself that way. God no.

Hoag: What did you tell him when he showed up?

Bartucci: That I'd do what I could. Nothing came to me until I happened to bump into T. S. and Rory one evening soon after that at Crawdaddy. I knew them casually, to say hello.

Hoag: What were they like?

Bartucci: Talented. Cocky. Hungry. I happened to mention I knew someone they'd enjoy meeting, since they'd worked with Mad Dog. So the four of us got together for drinks, and the boys went crazy over him. He was, after all, their own age, yet he'd actually played with people like Little Richard, who was one of T S.'s idols. They wanted to hear all about his experiences, all about Chicago and Memphis. Puppy was flattered. Also a bit overwhelmed. In America, white people knew very little then about blues performers like Son House and Leadbelly. The boys knew all of their songs. They talked to Puppy for hours. And then they heard him play.

Hoag: They were impressed.

Bartucci: Ginger Baker and Keith Moon were the very best of the young drummers around town then, Mr. Hoag. Puppy was so much better than them there was simply no comparison. T S. and Rory watched him play, I swear, with their jaws down to here. They were dying to play with him, of course. I suggested that if they were serious that they think young and fresh as opposed to bluesy. And think about Liverpool. The 'Pool was *the* place then. The Mersey sound was *the* sound. So they got together with Derek and the four of them started playing together. And they cooked, right off. Toe-tapping music. Can't-sit-still music. It was Puppy. He made the difference. When they had it together I took them to Liverpool with a new name. We talked about promoting Puppy as Mad Dog's nephew, but the boys had already been down that blues road and failed at it, so we decided not to mention Mad Dog. When EMI signed them up, their people made out Puppy was the son of a Yank seaman who settled in the 'Pool after the war. They wanted the other boys to be from there as well, and to have scouse accents. Rory hated that part so much he elected to be the silent one.

Hoag: I always wondered why he let Tristam do all of the talking. I'm interested in your thoughts on Puppy's death.

Bartucci: What about it?

Hoag: Do you think he was murdered?

Bartucci: (silence) I never did believe his death was an accident.

Hoag: You didn't?

Bartucci: Because of Puppy's drug bust, Us was banned from appearing in America, where the major money was and still is. Without tour support, their record sales there slumped considerably. The ban wounded Puppy deeply. He offered to quit the group, let the others go on without him. They wouldn't hear of it, of course. They were fiercely loyal. Puppy was very, very down those last few weeks. That wasn't like him – ordinarily he was Mr. Up, Mr. Good Times. The parties, the drugs, the girls – they were always his doing. He was the instigator. That was why Tulip never cared for him. She thought he was a bad influence on T. S., who she was trying to turn into a gent. Puppy, he was a man of uncontrollable appetites, of major highs – and major lows. When a man like that gets down . . . It was no accident, his death. Puppy took his own life. Suicide. That's what I've always believed. Sad, really. Such a talent. So young.

(end tape)

CHAPTER
SIX

That was the day my new suit was ready at Strickland's, so I stopped off after I finished with Marco and tried it on. It seemed to fit. So did Marco's explanation of Puppy's death. Suicide. It made a lot of sense to me in this case. It certainly made more sense than Tris and Jack's murder plot. Like Derek had said: Why on earth would any of them have wanted Puppy dead? No reason, at least none that was apparent.

A ghost is brought in partly to keep a celebrity from making a consummate asshole out of himself. To that end, I decided I'd play down the murder theory in Tris's memoir – allude to it but not dwell on it. If I did, Tris would come off as paranoid and drugged-out. The critics would go after him. The book clubs would steer clear of him. Besides, there was plenty else for us to concentrate on, like Derek's gayness and his love for Rory. Definite bombshells. There would, I hoped, be more.

Illusion. No one was who they'd seemed to be. That was the *Us* story. What was Tris Scarr's story? I didn't know that yet. He was still peeling away like an onion – layer by layer, and with great difficulty. I was also getting the sinking feeling he was holding out on me, not letting me in on something about himself that was important. I had no idea what it was, or why I had this feeling.

He was the Shadow Man. What glimpses I'd gotten of him outside of his chamber had been few, and creepy. They were always at night, when he prowled the estate like a burnt-out lost soul. Once, I woke up to see him outside my window in the floodlit field behind the house, dressed in soccer shorts and cleats, intently kicking a soccer ball to an invisible goalie. Another night I saw – and heard – him careening through the maze like a human pinball on a Norton Commando 750cc motorcycle, bounding off hedges, splattering gravel. And once, while I was reading late at night by my sitting room fire, I heard the hall doorknob turn, then stop. When I went out in the hall, there was no one there. Only the smell of Gauloises.

He was the Shadow Man. How did the song go? "Don't come over to my side/You won't like what you see." What had he seen? I had to know. It was time to start beating on him. And to talk to Tulip. If only she would return my goddamned calls.

Lulu and I strolled along Savile Row, both of us blinking from the glare. It was the very first sunny afternoon since we'd arrived, and the city seemed completely different. Shiny. Bright. The air was fresh and tangy. The Christmas shoppers were smiling. It wasn't my London.

I got a haircut at Truefitt's in Bond Street from a tall, vaguely Indian-looking guy named Christopher. From there we headed over to the Saville Club on Brook Street. It's a stylishly run-down establishment that has a reciprocal arrangement with the Coffee House, where I sometimes go for lunch in New York. I had a lager and some ham sandwiches at the bar. Lulu had kippers. Then we started back to where we'd left the car. I was still watching for a tail – had been all day as I went from interview to interview. I was not being followed. I was quite sure of it.

It was when we were passing a corner newsstand that I spotted Merilee's picture – a publicity still from her show – and the screaming afternoon tabloid headline: "MERILEE SHE ROLLS ALONG!" I bought the paper and stood there and read it:

Actress Merilee Nash, here to appear in the sold-out West End revival of *The Philadelphia Story* opposite Anthony Andrews, seems to find London just 'love-erly.'

The Oscar-winning American star has flown playwright-husband Zachary Byrd's coop and is snuggling with a tall, unidentified associate of our own Tristam Scarr.

Merilee and friend enjoyed a cozy opening night celebration at the Hungry Horse on Fulham Road, followed by a crawl through neighborhood pubs and a lengthy tête-átête outside her rented mews house on Crowell Road in an Austin Mini Cooper registered to the rock star.

Calls to T. S.'s home in Surrey, Gadpole, were in vain. "No comment," said a spokesman for the legendary rocker, who is reputed to be penning his memoirs for an American publisher. Several calls were placed to husband Byrd in New York. Byrd, Pulitzer Prize-winning author of the play *Labor Day*, was not available.

So that explained our tail that night. A member of the ever-vigilant British tabloid press had been shadowing Merilee. Part of me was relieved. Clearly, I wasn't in the middle of anything ugly or scary as it had first appeared. Part of me was wounded – the pride part. It's amazing how fast you can go from being a star to being a "tall, unidentified associate." Easiest thing in the world. All you have to do is nothing.

I tossed the paper in the trash.

I'd parked the mini on the corner where Clifford Street runs into Saville Row. I'd just started to unlock the car door when it happened. Actually, I didn't hear the first shot. What I heard, and saw, was the window exploding next to me. I wasn't quick to react. Just stared like an idiot at the shattered window, wondering how it could have happened. It wasn't until I heard the boom of a second shot and saw it blow out the back window beside my left elbow that I grabbed Lulu and hit the pavement. A tire popped a few inches from my head. The air hissed out. I could feel it on my ear. Someone was screaming now – a woman across the street. Then tires screeched and someone – whoever it was – sped away. Gone.

Slowly, I got to my feet. My hands were cut up from diving into broken glass, but otherwise I was okay.

Lulu wasn't.

If there's a sadder-faced creature in this world than a basset hound with a broken foreleg, I've yet to see it.

Merilee had made up a special bed for her in the mews house out of a crate and cushions, and placed it before the fireplace, which had a blaze going in it. There Lulu lay, bandaged, drugged, mournful. The gunshot had made a clean break. The vet had set it and kept her overnight at the pet hospital for observation. I had spent it tossing and shivering on the short love seat in Merilee's living room, wondering what I'd gotten myself into and eavesdropping as she assured Zack on her bedside phone that the tabloid story was a gross exaggeration and that she and I meant absolutely nothing to each other.

That wasn't what her green eyes had said when she bandaged up my hands in her tiny bathroom.

She was padding around in the kitchen now in old jeans, a

Viyella shirt, and ragg socks, assembling Lulu's favorite meal – her mommy's tuna casserole. The kitchen was bright and high tech and the biggest room in the miniature house. The adjoining living room was barely big enough for the love seat and two companion armchairs, all of them of Fifties Moderne mustard-colored vinyl. I was busy in there entertaining Farley Root, a gawky, apologetic police investigator in his mid-thirties, with uncombed red hair, buckteeth, and an Adam's apple the size of a musk-melon. He wore a nile green three-piece polyester suit and had, possibly, the worst case of razor burn on his neck I'd ever seen. He looked like he shaved with a John Deere. He was perched on the love seat, sipping tea and trying hard to act cool even though the famous Merilee Nash was right there in the kitchen. He was also trying hard not to claw at his raw, itchy neck. He was failing at both.

Merilee came in with the teapot. "A warm-up, Inspector?"

He gulped some air. "Thank you, miss. Please. And I'm not actually an – "

"So what's this about, Inspector?" I asked. "More questions?"

A uniformed constable at the scene had already asked me the routine questions. He'd gotten the routine answers. I'd told him I had no idea why anyone had shot at me. The streets, we'd agreed, weren't safe anywhere anymore.

"Yessir," replied Root, pulling out a small notepad. "Sorry to bother you, Mr. Hoag. Just a few other matters I was interesting in pursuing. And, please, I'm not actually an – "

"No problem. And make it Hoagy."

"As in Carmichael?"

"As in the cheese steak."

He frowned. "Very well, Hoagy." He shifted on the love seat, gulped some more air. "It has come to our attention since you were questioned yesterday that you . . . you and Miss Nash, I mean . . . are perhaps in the midst of what could be called a domestic situation of a somewhat . . . uh . . ."

"Do you mean those awful tabloid stories?" Merilee asked, from the kitchen.

"I do, miss," he replied, relieved. "I don't mean to pry into your personal lives, but the press reports were followed by a shooting incident. One could draw the conclusion that – "

"My husband is in New York, if that's what you're wondering," she said. "Hoagy and I were once married, and we remain friends. That's all there is to the story. He's here now because of what happened to Lulu."

Lulu stirred in her bed at the sound of her name. Almost.

"Makes perfect sense, miss," said Root. "I-I do appreciate your candor, and being so understanding of my situation. I'm . . . allow me to assure you I've no interest in bothering you or invading your – "

"We understand," I assured him.

"Thank you, Hoagy," he said. "If I may take a bit more of your time . . . There was also this matter of the mini's owner. You say you're presently in the employ of . . ."

"Tristam Scarr. I'm helping him do his memoirs."

"You're a writer?"

I tugged at my ear. "Yes, I am."

"Any connection there, do you think?"

"My being a writer?"

He swallowed. "Do you think the shooting might have had to do with the work you're doing for Mr. Scarr?"

"I don't see how. It's just a collection of anecdotes about the old days, his views on his life. As I said yesterday, Inspector, I really can't think of anyone in London who would want me dead."

"I understand. And I'm not actually an – "

"But I will call you if I think of anything."

"Thank you, sir. Appreciate that. And I'll ring you if we turn up anything, though I can't say I'm optimistic."

"Not getting anywhere?"

"No one who witnessed the attack seems able to identify precisely from where the shots originated, or to give us any description of who fired them. I'm afraid we don't even know so much as what kind of weapon was used." Root glanced at his notepad. "You mentioned you believe it was not a handgun."

"It sounded more like shotgun to me. It boomed."

"As does a large caliber handgun, such as a three-fifty-seven Magnum," Root pointed out.

"Could have been one of those," I conceded. "I would have thought you'd find a bullet, no?"

He shook his head. "The two that shattered the mini windows passed directly through the passenger-side windows as well. The one that clipped your hound here glanced off of the front tire and then passed underneath. As you had parked at an intersection, all three then proceeded on down Savile Row. They did not break any storefront glass. They do not appear to have glanced off any nearby buildings. We've found no glance marks. We're still searching, of course. However, it's a long street. And if the bullets happened to lodge in a pile of rubbish or in the side of a passing lorry, well, they may never be found."

"No spent cartridges anywhere?"

"No, sir. Whoever shot at you was neat and careful. Fired from their car, most likely. Gone before anyone really took notice of them."

"I don't imagine it was buckshot," I said. "Even if he'd had it on full choke there'd still be some pellet marks in the side of the car. From hitting Lulu, I mean."

Root nodded. "We're examining it. Nothing so far."

"I don't suppose anyone mentioned seeing a puff of smoke."

"Smoke? No. Why?"

"Just wondered."

Root tucked his notepad away in his coat pocket. "Yes, well, sorry to have troubled you."

"No trouble at all."

He struggled to his feet and lurched into the kitchen with his teacup. "Thank you so much for the tea, Miss Nash. It's been an honor to meet you. I've admired your work in films for many years."

"Why, thank you, Inspector," she said brightly.

He cleared his throat. "Actually, I'm not an – "

"You know, Inspector, I have an idea you might benefit from," I told him, as I steered him toward the front door. "Personally, I mean."

"Sir?"

"Talc." I fingered my neck. "Clear that rash right up. Floris makes one with a very light scent, number eighty-nine."

Root craned his neck uncomfortably. "Rather ugly business this. Can't seem to shake it. Number eighty-nine? Just may give it a go."

"Do you use an electric razor?"

"I do."

"They're murder."

"That they are. Good-bye, then."

"Good-bye, Inspector."

I knelt at Lulu's bed and scratched her ears. She treated me to her most profoundly pained look. A definite ten on the hankie meter.

"If you're trying to make me feel guilty," I told her, "you can stop now."

For that I got a whimper. A very weak whimper.

The casserole was bubbling away now in the kitchen. Merilee makes her tuna casserole with sautéed shallots and mushrooms, a touch of sherry, and a thick topping of melted Gruyère. She tasted it, frowned, and added a touch more sherry. I sipped the Laphroaig I'd gone out for. It was strong and smoky. Possibly too smoky for me. I told Merilee I'd be taking Lulu back to Gadpole with me after she'd eaten.

"I can carry her," I said. "And she'll be fine on the train."

Merilee turned off the heat under the casserole and uncovered it. Lulu prefers it served tepid. "I think she should stay here, darling. At least for the weekend."

"What for?"

"She's comfy here. She's close to the hospital. And I don't think she's safe with you."

"Merilee, she'll be fine. There's no need to worry."

"That, Mr. Hoagy, is a load of baked beans. You were very nearly murdered. Both of you. Why didn't you tell that policeman what's really going on?"

"Because I don't *know* what's really going on." I poured myself another Laphroaig and Merilee some more of her cooking sherry. Of course, she cooks only with Tio Pepe. She won't put in food what she won't also drink. "Clearly, I am on to something – something that somebody wants to keep buried in the past. Maybe it's Puppy's death. Maybe it's something else. I don't know. I have to find out."

"And until you do you're putting her in danger."

"She'll be fine," I repeated.

Merilee sipped her sherry, unconvinced. "Why shoot at you? Why not T. S.?"

"I suppose because he's so well protected. It would also draw a lot of press attention. And speculation. This serves as a nice, quiet warning: Whoever did it is probably hoping T. S. will get scared and forget about the book."

"Will he?"

"I doubt it. My guess is that as long as T. S. personally feels secure he won't be bothered one bit."

Merilee put her hand against the casserole dish. It was no longer hot. She carried it over to Lulu's bed and presented her with the whole damned thing. None for his Hoagyness. "Here you are, sweetness," she cooed, patting her. "Now you eat this *awww* up so you can get *stwong* again."

Lulu pawed feebly at the dish with her good foreleg. Then she wriggled herself forward in her bed a bit and stuck her head in the dish. Chomping noises followed.

"This is truly low, Merilee. This is beneath you."

She frowned. "I really don't know what you mean, darling. I'm just giving her a little TLC."

"We agreed that I'd keep her. You got the apartment, the Jaguar – "

"And I'm not contesting it. But she's wounded, and my maternal instinct is taking over. I can't help it."

"You're trying to take her away from me."

"I'm not."

"She's my dog."

"She's our dog."

"She's *my* dog!"

A low moan emerged from Lulu's bed. She'd stopped eating and was watching us, genuinely distressed. It's true what they say – divorce is always hardest on the little ones.

"Merilee, I don't want to get into some kind of ugly, protracted custody battle with you."

"I don't want that either."

"Good. So I'll make this very simple: If she stays, I stay. We're a package deal. You take one, you get both."

Merilee raised an eyebrow, the same one she raised when Mel Gibson made his play for her in that sweaty tropics melodrama they did together. Her only flop. On screen, that is. "Now who's getting low?"

I went to her and took her in my arms. She didn't resist. "I got a stiff neck sleeping on the love seat last night."

"It *is* short."

"Your bed isn't."

She sighed. "Hoagy . . ."

"Yes, Merilee?"

She pulled away, went to the closet, and came back with her red Converse Chuck Taylor high-tops and her mink. "Let's walk."

Kensington Gardens was where we went. It was a Saturday afternoon and there were people there – pipe-puffing dog walkers, loners with their shoulders hunched and their hands in their pockets, young couples with baby strollers. It wasn't like being in Central Park. No trash. No graffiti. No dead rats lying in the walkway. No teenage roller skaters with boom-boxes. Also, no one carrying shotguns.

This I could be fairly sure of. I was looking. Getting shot at will do that to you.

We walked in silence alongside the Serpentine, enjoying the quiet, until we came upon a young father teaching his little boy how to ride a bicycle. The boy was chubby and apple-cheeked, and wore a tweed cap.

"Oh, darling," exclaimed Merilee, squeezing my arm. "I want one of those."

I coughed. "A midget human life-form?"

"No, one of those caps."

"Oh. Somewhat oversized, I assume."

"Yes. Would you . . . ?"

"Would I what, Merilee?"

"Would you buy it for yourself and then give it to me?"

I took her to Bates, a tiny, cluttered old hat shop on Jermyn Street. The proprietor's cat from much earlier in the century still stood guard there from inside a glass case – properly stuffed, of course. It wouldn't be long before the clerk who fitted me would be joining Puss in there himself, I reckoned. I got a charcoal gray herring-bone tweed that would have gone nicely with my new suit, and presented it to Merilee when we got outside on the sidewalk. She tried it on right away, admired her reflection in the store window from one angle, then another. Then she burst into tears.

I held her until they stopped. Then I gave her my linen handkerchief and asked, "What is all this?"

She dabbed at her face with the handkerchief. "All this," she replied, sniffling, "is that I'm still in love with you. I didn't sleep a wink all night. I couldn't. All I could do was think about how much I want you back."

I'd been waiting three years to hear Merilee say those words. Now that she had I found myself feeling just a little dubious. "I see," I said quietly.

She eyed me. "Well, don't jump up and down," she said drily.

"I won't."

"What's wrong? Are you thinking it's just because of Lulu?"

"You're the one who said your M-instinct has been aroused."

"It's not all that's been aroused."

"Actually, I was thinking about Tracy."

"What's Tracy got to do with it?"

"Merilee, you do happen to be playing a woman who does happen to fall back in love with her ex-husband."

She mulled this over, as we stood there on Jermyn Street. "There is that," she conceded. "I *am* an actress, and therefore a nut. This whole situation is rather . . ."

"Neat?"

"And it's bothering you."

I shrugged. "My professional nutsiness drove us apart. I suppose it's entirely appropriate if yours brings us back together. I guess I can handle it. Just promise me one thing."

"Name it."

"Don't ever do *Macbeth*. Not even if Papp begs."

She laughed girlishly. "Papp doesn't beg."

We kissed. It started soft and sweet, but didn't stay that way for very long.

She pulled away, gasping. "Darling, we're being indiscreet."

"So?" I gasped back.

"Not fair to Zack."

I caught my breath, looked around. People on the street were indeed watching us. "You're absolutely right. Let's go somewhere nice and quiet, and get discreetly naked."

We didn't stray far from the feathers the rest of the weekend. Lulu seemed cheered by our reconciliation. She even started to hop around the house a bit, which meant now I *had* seen something sadder than a basset hound with a broken foreleg – a basset hound with a broken foreleg trying to walk. Not that she's particularly gutsy. This was strictly a ploy for sympathy. And smoked salmon.

Merilee and I had one ground rule. We would talk only about London. No talking about afterward allowed. But there was no ordinance against thinking about it, and that's what I did as we cuddled there in the middle of the night, all cozy and warm under our down comforter and tray of salmon sandwiches and cocoa. I let myself think about Zack out and me back in. Back in the eight art deco rooms overlooking the park. Back in the sweet life – acclaimed, promising, madly in love. Maybe you can't go back, but you can always try. Hmm. Maybe here was the ending for novel number two. A *happy* ending.

I let myself think about us. Sure I did.

Monday morning the dampness and gray skies were back. Merilee showed me to the door wearing my old silk target dot dressing gown. It definitely looked better on her than it did on me, especially with nothing on underneath it. I undid the sash, opened it wide and probed its contents, purely for the sake of scientific analysis. She pressed against me and let me feel her warmth and her strength. Then she stood on her toes and put her mouth to my ear.

"Come back, darling," she whispered.

"I don't think you need to worry about that."

I scratched Lulu's neck and told her to stay off the paw. She didn't argue with me. She was going to stay there with Merilee for the time being. It did make sense not to move her. Besides, I'd be back as often as I could manage. I'd have to bring Lulu's vest. Also my new target dot dressing gown, so Merilee and I could lounge about the mews house in our his-and-his robes.

It was Jack's day off. Pamela met me at the Guildford station in the Silver Cloud. She was outfitted in a mannish black pants suit, white shirt, and black necktie, all of this topped off by a black chauffeur's cap. I rode up front with her, and immediately regretted it. She drove like a demon.

"You'll be pleased to learn," she announced, rounding a corner with a screech of rubber, "that I've finished typing up the transcripts of your tapes with Mr. Scarr."

"Excellent." Among her myriad other talents, Pamela typed a hundred and twenty words per minute, and none of them were Etaoin Shrdlu. "Pamela, I think we should talk seriously about your coming back to New York with me when I'm done here."

"My Lord, Hoagy," she exclaimed, blushing. "It's been years since I've received such an indecent proposition from such a young gentleman."

"Not so young. And not so indecent. My ex-wife and I – what I mean is, we may be looking for someone."

"So you two *are* together again."

"Why, yes. How did you –?"

"It was I who spoke with the gossip sheet when they rang up. They'd traced the number off of the mini. I told them nothing, of course."

"I appreciate your discretion."

"I've plenty of practice, believe me. I spoke to the police as well."

"So did I."

Pamela sped through the traffic with the lunatic zeal of a Canarsie-born cabbie. At one intersection a truck driver had to hit his brakes hard to keep from plowing into us. He shook his fist at her.

She clucked at him and said "I've never been to New York."

"You'll do just fine."

"I was so sorry to learn of Miss Lulu's misfortune. Is she better?"

"Actually, she's getting seriously spoiled."

"Do give her my best."

She made the trip to Gadpole in half the time it took Jack. We had passed through the main gate and were cruising through the cluster of staff houses and service buildings when I heard the sharp crack of pistol fire. Then silence. Then more pistol fire. I shuddered, remembering just how close those shots had come the other day.

"Jack executing some of the help?" I asked.

"Getting in some target practice, I expect."

"I'll get out here, if I may."

"You may."

Behind some gardener's sheds, two targets were set into a twenty-foot-high mound of earth. Jack stood fifty feet away, firing off bull's-eyes with a twenty-two-caliber target pistol. So did another shooter, who was tall and lean and dressed in matching camouflage safari jacket, fatigue trousers, and baseball cap. It wasn't until I got up closer behind them that I realized the other crack shot was that precocious little multimaniac herself, Lady Vi.

They didn't notice me there until they stopped to reload, and I said "You're rather good, Violet."

She treated me to a devilish grin and pointed her gun at me. "Bang bang."

Jack snatched it from her. "Never, ever point a weapon at someone, Vi! I've told you!"

"It's empty!" she protested.

"No matter whether it is or it isn't," he lectured sternly. "You could be mistaken. And *most* sorry."

Just to satisfy himself, Jack pointed the empty gun at one of the targets and pulled the trigger.

It wasn't empty.

He stood there staring at the hole he'd made in the target. Then he looked down at the gun in his hand and, slowly, up at me, horrified.

"Yet another bull's-eye," I observed with a brave smile and jelly knees. Clearly, I'd have to steer wide of guns for a while. Also cracks in sidewalks, black cats, and precocious, long-limbed teenagers.

This one was tickled thoroughly pink. "Just having a bitty goof," she exclaimed with a merry laugh as she grabbed her empty gun back from a still-stunned Jack. "Can't a girl have a goof?"

"I don't see why not," I replied graciously. Jack and I watched her reload the target pistol. "And how is she with a sporting rifle?" I asked him.

"Even better," he replied softly.

"But not as good as Jackie," she pointed out. "No one's as good as Jackie."

"Taught her m'self," he said. "Since she was a little thing." He stuck a hand out to me. "Allow me to welcome you back, sir." Happy to see you're all of a piece. How's the pup?"

"Not very happy," I replied, shaking his hand.

"Poor little bugger," he said.

"Sorry about the mini," I said. "Quite a car."

"Indeed, sir. I'll have her towed back here soon as they're done with her. Get her put back together good as new. You're welcome to the Peugeot, in the meantime." Jack swiped at his nose with the back of his hand. "Terrible business, this. I know Mr. Scarr is most upset."

"Yes, I should think he would be," I said quietly.

Jack's eyes narrowed. We stood there staring at each other.

Violet broke in, offering me her gun, barrel down. "Care to shoot a round?"

"Thank you, no," I replied. "Javelin is more my style."

"Javelin?" she asked, frowning. Evidently she wasn't too up on track and field, which was probably just as well. Who knew what havoc she could wreak with a discus.

"It's a spear," I explained. "Long. With a point at the tip."

"Ooh, sounds fun."

"Somehow," I said, "I had a feeling you'd think so."

It was time to get out my mukluks. I always wear them when I'm at the typewriter. I wore them when I was writing the novel, and I don't dare change now. There's no telling where inspiration comes from. Who's to say it isn't footwear?

I put on *It's Us Again* good and loud to get myself in the mood. The album was recorded after the group's first American tour. "More for Me" was its big hit. I set out the tape transcripts and notes, sat at the desk and put a sheet of paper in the typewriter. Almost at once I was aware that something was missing – Lulu always sleeps under the desk when I work, with her head on my foot. I got up, pulled a heavy tome from the bookcase, and tried resting that on my foot. It wasn't warm and I couldn't feel it swallow, but the weight was right. Much better. Don't ever tell Lulu that she was replaced by Anthony Trollope.

I like to set the tone of a memoir with an introductory chapter that takes place in the present. This lets the reader know right off what the celebrity's attitude is toward the life and career he or she is about to look back on. It gives everybody a handle, including me. Unfortunately, I couldn't do this with T. S. I didn't have the handle yet. In a perfect world, I would have waited until I did before I started writing. It's not a perfect world. Publishers have deadlines.

So I started with Tris's account of his childhood. I covered his early memories of his parents and Rory and getting hooked on Brando, Elvis, and the music. I took it up through the formation of the Rough Boys and those nights spent jamming in the lorry garage. I gave him a tough, uncompromising voice peppered with coarse language and the hint of a sneer. It was the voice that came through on the tapes. It was his voice.

I just wished I knew what he wasn't telling me about himself. I was starting to take it personally.

Dinner was a roast chicken, in the kitchen with Pamela. I asked her a bunch of questions about how many invisible people it took to maintain Gadpole (thirty-three) and what all of them did. Eventually, I cleverly managed to bring the conversation around to Jack.

On Friday afternoon, when someone had decided to use me, the mini, and Lulu for target practice, Jack Horner had been out, she said. Running errands in Guildford.

And Miss Violet? The irrepressible Lady Vi had been posing for a British *Vogue* layout the entire day. In London.

I turned in early, but I didn't get to sleep. For one thing, there was too much to think about. Had it been Jack who'd shot at me? He *had* been flatly opposed to my poking around in the past. Violet? Clearly, she was less than stable. Maybe she hadn't coped too well with my rejecting her. True, I'd heard a car speed away from the shooting scene, and she wasn't yet old enough to drive. But she wasn't old enough to do a lot of the things she no doubt did. Operating a vehicle without a license was probably the least of her sins. And then there were the others. Derek. Marco. Even T. S. himself, not that he got out much. Who was it? What was I in the middle of? How was I going to find out?

The other reason I couldn't get to sleep was Lulu. I was used to her sleeping on my head. I tried putting a pillow over my face but it just wasn't the same. Didn't smell like mackerel.

So I watched the videocassette of *This is the Beginning of the End* that I'd borrowed from T. S. This was the infamous Stanley Kubrick black-and-white documentary chronicling the Us '76 American tour. Their last tour. They were older now, Double Trouble were. They'd had the breakups and the crack-ups, and it showed. T. S. and Rory were no longer two wild kids. This was business now, and they were two polished pros giving their audience what it wanted. Kubrick captured that – just how much backstage preparation and role-playing and outright deception went into creating the onstage illusion of spontaneous good times. And Kubrick got more than that, more than he or anyone bargained for. His cameras were there that hot, humid night in Atlanta. There as T. S. and Rory were on the Omni stage in their torn sleeveless T-shirts, and spandex pants, faces and chests gleaming with sweat. T. S., clutching a hand mike, is strutting around the stage, taunting the screaming audience as he snarls out their encore, "We're Double Trouble." Rory, grinning his snaggletoothed grin, is straining for a note on his Stratocaster. He finds it. Leaps in the air with joy. The crowd is on its feet now, pressing towards them. And then suddenly there is a flash of light and Rory's face contorts even more. Straining for another note, isn't he? All part of the show, isn't it?

No, it's not. Blood is streaming from Rory's mouth and nose now. He is crumpling. Falling onto the stage floor. The camera is jostled, and for a moment we're looking at someone's booted feet. There are screams. Screams that change abruptly from adulation to horror. Derek shoves forward, points into the crowd, and yells. He can't be heard over the mounting shrieks.

The camera finds the shooter there in the third row, brandishing his gun, eyes crazed, spittle bubbling from his lips. There he is – Larry Lloyd Little, witness for the prosecution in the Manson trial. Fringe family member. Pimp. Out of jail after three years. Flashbulbs explode. He's babbling something. Original sin, he is saying. Or so the press later reported. Original sin. And he won't drop the gun. And the police are firing on him now, and he's hit. He goes down, terrified fans scrambling to get out of his way as he falls. And we hear a voice now in the erupting chaos, a voice from the stage crying "Help him! Can't somebody please help him!" It's a voice we've never heard before. It's the real voice of T. S. He's dropped his fake scouse accent. The act is forgotten as he kneels over his dying partner. Rory lies there on his back. His eyes are open. Derek is there. So is Jack, and Corky Carroll, the tour drummer. Then the ambulance arrives and the paramedics put him on a stretcher and take him away. T. S. is now alone there on stage. Rory's blood is on his hands. He's looking around, bewildered, lost. Derek comes over, tries to comfort him. "Why?" T. S. keeps saying. "Why?"

I hadn't seen the movie in a long time. It seemed even more powerful to me now, for a lot of reasons.

I was still awake at three a.m. when I heard a door open and close down the hall. Violet's door. I slipped my trench coat on over my nightshirt, quietly opened my own door, and stuck my head out into the dimly lit hallway. No one. Just the sound of footsteps – reaching the stairs, going down the stairs. I followed, stepping lightly. It was so silent in the great house I could hear the mice scratching around in the walls. I started down the curved staircase. The footsteps were on the marble floor now, heading toward the kitchen. A late-night snack?

There was no one in the kitchen. Just the hum of the refrigerators. The pantry door, however, was open an inch. Pamela always kept it closed. No one was in there, but the door to the herb garden was unbolted. I stepped outside into the cold. No palace guard seemed to be stationed here, and it was dark – a blind spot in the security floodlights. I heard the gate to the vegetable garden squeak, and the soft crunch of gravel under feet. I pursued through the gardens until I came to a stone fence about four feet high. This I climbed over.

I was in a small meadow behind the garages. Ahead of me, in the darkness I could just make out Violet striding briskly toward them. She went inside a back door to the utility garage, which connected to Jack's apartment.

His lights were on. I found a window that had a nice view of his parlor. Jack was sitting in a lounge chair in front of the fireplace, which had an electric space heater inserted in it. Violet stood before him with her head bowed like a penitent child. He was gesturing sharply at her, and she was apologizing. I couldn't hear the words through the window. Until he raised his voice:

"You know what happens to bad girls, don't you?"

"I *said* I was sorry, Jackie! I *did*!"

He grabbed her roughly by the arms, pulled her across his lap and yanked her sweatpants down, exposing her round, firm, altogether perfect young bottom. This he spanked with his meaty hand. Hard. She yelped. She yelped each time he smacked her, which was either six or seven times. She began to sob. Then Jack said something to her. Whatever it was, it made her giggle. Then she sat up and put her arms around his neck and kissed him, and he carried her into the bedroom.

CHAPTER
SEVEN

(Tape #5 with Tristam Scarr. Recorded in his chamber Nov. 29. Wears bathrobe and slippers. Is very agitated.)

Scarr: They still have no idea who shot at you?

Hoag: None. Do you?

Scarr: Me? Why should I have any idea?

Hoag: Well, there's your little theory about Puppy's death to consider.

Scarr: (pause) So he *was* murdered. I'm right. Have been all along. And whoever it is is afraid I'll say something, aren't they?

Hoag: I want you to know I don't scare easily, Tristam. I scare *very* easily.

Scarr: You'll be quitting then.

Hoag: That's up to you.

Scarr: Me?

Hoag: Oh, for Christ's sake – let's stop jerking each other's chains, shall we?

Scarr: Giving me something of an attitude, aren't you, mate?

Hoag: I don't think so. I've gotten shot at. *Me*, not you. I have a right to know why, and you're not telling me.

Scarr: I've told you everything I –

Hoag: Who killed Puppy?

Scarr: I already told you! I don't know!

Hoag: Bullshit.

Scarr: Don't push me, mate! When T. S. says he doesn't know, he means it.

Hoag: More bulishit.

Scarr: What is it you want? A punch-up?

Hoag: What I want is the truth.

Scarr: I repeat: I do not know who killed Puppy

Hoag: Okay. Fine. Duly noted. I don't know if I believe you or not, but I suppose that's my own problem.

Scarr: Why won't you believe me?

Hoag: I'll tell you why – because I don't know you. We may have spent some hours together talking, but I still don't know you. And until I do there's no such thing as trust.

Scarr: (silence) You're trying to relate me to your terms. They don't apply. I'm not anyone else. I'm T. S.

Hoag: And who is T. S.?

Scarr: He's . . . I'm . . . someone who's monstrously, royally, fucked up. And always have been. Okay?

Hoag: How?

Scarr: Christ! *(long silence followed by sounds of heavy breathing)* Ever since I was a lad, alone in m'room, I've felt . . . *(sounds of heavy breathing, sniffling) apart.* Isolated. I-I was often sick, as I told you . . . But . . . But . . .

Hoag: Yes? Go on.

Scarr: What I didn't tell you was . . . There was this thing inside m'head. This terror. It would last for days, weeks. Total fucking freak-out. I couldn't eat or sleep. I'd get headaches. So bad I couldn't keep m'eyes open. I'd just sit there in the dark, alone. I-I still get them. Had one last week. A bad one.

Hoag: You did seem a little out of it.

Scarr: I thought money and fame would make it all go away. That's what drove me to make it in music. I was wrong. None of it has ever gone away. That's the biggest disappointment of my life . . . All the drugs, they just made it worse. Acid very nearly destroyed me. Made me so bleedin' paranoid I-I couldn't believe in anyone, especially if they wanted something of me – and everyone wanted something of me . . . I've never been one to take things as they come, see the good in them. I'm totally preoccupied by the bad. The truth is I never enjoyed any of my success. I'm not capable of it. And that has made me want to lash out at people, destroy what I was building.

Hoag: Did you ever get professional help?

Scarr: My unconscious is the heart and soul of my creativity. I could never let someone fuck with it. I've always been looking for answers on my own. It's taken me a long fucking time to realize there just aren't any.

Hoag: Did Rory know this about you?

Scarr: He didn't understand it, but he knew of it, from when we were lads. M'glums, he called it. Rory, he was the only one who could sometimes pull me out of it. He was my mate. My only true mate. When I lost him, I just freaked out. Most people thought I retired because I was afraid of being shot myself. That was only a part of it. It was losing Rory. I still feel his . . . his *loss (sounds of weeping, then silence)* Christ . . . Haven't had a good bleedin' cry in don't know how long. Sorry about all of this, Hogarth.

Hoag: Congratulations, Tristam.

Scarr: For?

Hoag: For breaking through – from the public you to the private you. This has been far and away our most important night's work. I'd say it calls for a drink, my friend.

Scarr: This goes in the book?

Hoag: It does.

Scarr: I don't know if I –

Hoag: Trust me.

Scarr: *(pause)* Sancerre do?

Hoag: Always has.

Scarr: You haven't a glass, Hogarth.

Hoag: Another cause for celebration – you finally noticed.

(end tape)

(Tape #6 with Tristam Scarr. Recorded in his chamber Nov. 30. Still wears robe and slippers.)

Scarr: I've read the pages you sent up. I like it so far. Very much.

Hoag: I'm glad.

Scarr: You don't think there's too much soul-searching about the laddie days?

Hoag: It's dynamite.

Scarr: If you say so.

Hoag: Good man. I'd like to hear about Liverpool.

Scarr: It was gray and depressed and nowhere – unless you happened to be a rocker. The Mersey sound had taken over the charts. Brian Epstein's doing, actually. Aside from the Beatles, he'd brought along Gerry and the Pacemakers, who had two number ones, "How Do You Do It?" and "I Like It." Then Billy J. Kramer did "Do You Want to Know a Secret?," a Lennon-McCartney song, and that went to the top as well. There was The Searchers, Cilla Black . . . The 'Pool's where it was at. London wasn't, at least not for us.

Hoag: How long did you live up there?

Scarr: A week.

Hoag: Wait, I thought you –

Scarr: Moved up there? No. We got it together around home.

Found ourselves a new name. Most people thought Us had to do with racial harmony or like that. Actually, it came from sitting around one night with a list of twenty-five names and liking that one the best. Marco staked us to some better equipment. Fender Strato for Rory, Fender Precision Bass for Derek. Vox AC thirty amps. We started out by playing a lot of the songs we'd been playing, only more up-tempo. That was Puppy's influence. He was totally up. Had what I call The Energy, y'know? And he was so bleedin' good we figured we'd give him a couple of drum solos. No band had done that before. When we had it together we took the train up and checked into a cheap hotel. Marco knew Ray McFall, who owned the Cavern, which the Beatles had made famous. Got us a gig there. A dingy jazz cellar in the city center, it was, walls dripping with sweat. Record company executives in suits were queued up to get in the door, hoping lightning would strike the same place twice. What did they know about the music? They knew shit . . . We'd been at it for years, y'know? When it finally did happen for us, it happened *bam* – EMI offered us a contract on the spot. They'd signed the Beatles. When they got wind we weren't actually locals they figured as how we should say we were, as did Marco. He handled the contracts. Gave each of us an allowance. We were bleedin' louts about the business end. Signed whatever the fat little cunt put in front of us. Fucked us royally, he did . . . We cut our first single at the EMI Studios in London. George Martin, the Beatles' producer, was our producer as well. Very polite. Also very much the big boss man. Told us "Great Gosh Almighty" would be our first single, with "Shake, Rattle and Roll" as the B-side. Told us Puppy's drum solos didn't fit. Told me to leave m'harp in m'pocket. The entire thing was over in four hours. Then the hype started. Marco gave us Beatles haircuts and gold blazers and new identities. Derek was the Face, Rory the Serious Musician, Puppy the Joker. I was the Talker. I was always to put on the scouse accent. Got to be second nature, after a while. What took getting used to was the things they started planting about us in *Rave* and *Fabulous,* the teeny fan mags, like who our favorite film stars were and what we ate for breakfast. I mean, they never even asked us. Then they put us in a cinema hall package tour, opening for the Everly Brothers in Northampton, Leicester, Nottingham . . . That's when it started to pop for us. It was the girls, mostly. It was how they responded to Puppy.

Hoag: How did they respond?

Scarr: They screamed. Tried to climb up on the stage. Rushed the stage door afterward, wanting to meet him, touch him. I mean, the man was doing some very sexy, outrageous things up there. Inflaming 'em. He was *black*, mate. The boyfriends, they tore up their seats. Threw rocks and bottles at the coach as we pulled away. Rioted, practically. Marco, he milked it, started alerting the police and newspapers in each town before we arrived. That got us the "Fear Jungle-Boy Riot" headlines. Turned us into a sensation. The police had to form a human chain in front of the stage every night. And "Great Gosh Almighty" went to number three on the charts.

Hoag: How did Puppy react to all of this?

Scarr: He was a performer. He loved the attention, particularly from white girls.

Hoag: How did you and Rory feel about this – that this is what it took to put you over the top?

Scarr: This was our shot, mate. We didn't care how we got it. The important thing was what we did with it once we had it. Plenty of groups came and went with their one hit, their one gimmick. Staying hot, that was something else. Had to keep the hits coming, one after another. Only a handful of groups managed that – the Beatles, Stones, the Who, and Us.

Hoag: What did it take?

Scarr: No great mystery there. To stay on top, a group had to grow musically. Had to care about the music, not just the trappings. Fight for the music, which meant you telling the record company what to do, rather than them telling you. Rory and me, we wrote our first song together in the motor coach between Sheffield and Leeds. I put some lyrics down. He strummed some chords. We hummed a melody, and soon we had something – "Come on Over, Baby." We recorded it soon as the tour ended. Now that Puppy was a celebrity, George Martin let us include a drum solo. And I played m'harp. "Come on Over, Baby" shot to number one. That got us a spot on *Ready, Steady, Go*, the top telly program. And it got us released in North America.

Hoag: You mentioned the Beatles, Stones, The Who. You go back a lot of years together. Your readers will be interested in your thoughts on them.

Scarr: The music?

Hoag: The people.

Scarr: I don't know about that, Hogarth . . .

Hoag: Let's try a word association. I give you a name, you tell me what pops into your mind. *(pause)* Lennon . . . *(silence)* Jagger . . . *(silence)*

Scarr: Look, I'd rather not do this. I don't wish to write about my mates in this book. I really don't.

Hoag: Derek said you have no mates.

Scarr: Did he? I could get a hundred of them here in thirty minutes. All I have to do is ring them up.

Hoag: So why don't you?

Scarr: *(silence)* Perhaps I will one day soon. Perhaps I will.

Hoag: I'll be looking forward to it.

(end tape)

(Tape #2 with Derek Gregg. Recorded at his new art gallery, The Big Bang Theory, Nov. 30. Workmen are still in process of unfinishing it – walls and ceiling are being stripped to bare brick and exposed pipes. And left that way.)

Hoag: Interesting decor.

Gregg: Perfectly dreadful, isn't it? Whatever's in, I always say.

Hoag: I'd like to talk about what was "in" here in '64, when you first hit it big.

Gregg: They called it Swingin' London, luv. We were a part of it. But it was bigger than us. It was a wave of new talent that was shaking up just *everything*. Actors like Michael Caine and Terence Stamp. Fashion designers like Mary Quant, with the miniskirt. David Bailey, the photographer, was changing the meaning of glamour, and models like Tulip were changing the meaning of beautiful. She asked about you, by the way. I said you were okay. She'll see you.

Hoag: That's terrific. Thanks. Are you two close?

Gregg: We all remain close – we went through a revolution together. Suddenly, it was hip to be a commoner, to be loutish, untutored, real. Suddenly, we were the celebrities. The photographers followed us day and night. The more the older generation put us down, the more the young ones wanted to be just like us. We rolled around in it, we did. Shit, we were twenty-two. We dressed flash and behaved flash. Drank and partied all night at the Ad Lib Club and Bag O' Nails. Each of us had three or four different flats where we crashed with three or four different girls. Even me. Treated them all the same – "Hang out, doll. Maybe I'll be back." Mr. Cigar, he emerged as this major spokesman on public issues. "Who'd you be voting for in the upcoming election?" they'd ask him. "Donald Duck," he'd reply, and it would be on the front page the next day. I remember he said to me one night that if he stuck two lit Woodbines up his nostrils, every teeny in Great Britain would start smoking his cigarettes like that . . . We had *power*. That's what it was. It was a trip. I miss it.

Hoag: After "Come On Over, Baby" was released in the U.S., you –

Gregg: We went on over, yes, and it was a big disappointment. Here at home we had a number one song. There, we were merely another new British group. There were no screaming girls when we landed. No press conference. Nothing. Mr. Cigar wanted to fire Marco on the spot, he was so pissed off. We stayed at an overheated salesman's hotel on Thirty-Fourth Street, the New Yorker. We did not get booked on *The Ed Sullivan Show* or play Carnegie Hall. We were on the radio with some guy called Murray the K, and our gig was at a discotheque in Times Square called The Cheetah. But we did go over well there. Met recording people. Also met the Warhol crowd, and fell in with them. Went down to that utterly bizarre place of his, The Factory, where we got turned on to marijuana. Mr. Cigar started his thing with Edie Sedgewick then. I personally had my first gay experience with someone I met there. Through Puppy we met Jimi Hendrix, who was playing at a basement dive in Greenwich Village. He blew us away with his music. He and Rory were both guitar freaks – spent hours together in the guitar shops on West Forty-Eighth Street. New York was a happening place. But once we left there, Christ, it was like being back in the northern provinces. In Philadelphia we lip-synched "Come On Over, Baby" on the *American Bandstand* program, and also appeared on a chat show called *The Mike Douglas Show*. The host had been a big band singer, so he thought it would be a gas to put on a Beatles wig and join us. Rory simply handed the fellow his Strato and walked off. God, he hated that shit . . . From there we hit the road in a rented motor coach, with Jack at the wheel. Marco had booked us on a tour of the South, playing auditoriums and fairgrounds in places like Birmingham and Jackson where the civil rights thing was really quite volatile. The idea was that Puppy's antics would set off the same fireworks they had back home in the north.

Hoag: Did they?

Gregg: Too much so. After our first couple of appearances our gigs were canceled in a lot of cities down the road. Too risky, they called us. That got us some national attention, made Pup a cause célèbre. When we arrived in Los Angeles we even got invited – dig this – to a dinner party at Sammy Davis Jr.'s home. It was a show of racial support for Pup by the liberal show-biz crowd, or some such thing. Blew us away – all of these famous Hollywood stars like Sidney Poitier, Gregory Peck, and Natalie Wood showed up there to support us. Mr. Cigar freaked out over meeting Natalie Wood, with her having been in *Rebel Without a Cause*. He asked her all about James Dean. Then he took her home and fucked her. And told *everyone* . . . Tris was really taken by America. He particularly took to the glamour and unsavoriness of L.A. – Grauman's Chinese Theater, Disneyland, Marilyn Monroe's grave. He ended up living in Malibu for a few years when we got into tax trouble. I chose the Italian Riviera. To each his own . . . Do they know yet who shot at you?

Hoag: Planning to confess?

Gregg: (laughs) You have a wonderful sense of humor. That bothers me about Jeffrey He's so solemn. So *dumb*.

Hoag: On the face of it, it couldn't have been you. You're strictly a black powder man.

Gregg: And?

Hoag: Three shots were fired at me in the space of no more than ten seconds. Can't do that with a muzzle loader – it takes too long to reload. You've got your powder, your wadding, your ball. Then you've got to push all of that down with your ramrod. No way it was done with a muzzle loader. At least, not a *standard* muzzle loader.

Gregg: Meaning?

Hoag: If I remember correctly, they made a few single-barrel muzzle loading *repeaters* with superimposed loading. Mostly experimental. Very hard to find now. Museums have them, a few wealthy collectors. Do you own one?

Gregg: (silence) No, I own two – an 1828 Jenning/Reuben T. Ellis Repeating Flintlock four-shot and an 1863 Lindsay Repeating Percussion Rifle-Musket.

Hoag: Make quite a puff of smoke, don't they?

Gregg: They do. What of it?

Hoag: Then again, you *could* have done the job simply by using three different standard muzzle loaders, all of them loaded and at hand . . . Couldn't you?

Gregg: You don't actually believe *I'm* the one who shot at you, do you?

Hoag: You did seem pretty upset about Tris mentioning your child in the book.

Gregg: Oh, that. We had a phone conversation, Mr. Cigar and I. He promised me you'd be cool – not name any names. So long as the boy's identity is protected, I have no problem. I'm not angry. Besides, firing long arms in the street isn't exactly my style. I prefer a quieter, more civilized approach.

Hoag: Poison?

Gregg: *(laughs)* No. I'm really an old-fashioned sort of bloke at heart, Mr. Hoag. I hire lawyers. Quite dear ones.

(end tape)

(Tape #2 with Marco Bartucci. Recorded in his office at Jumbo's Disco Nov. 30. Hasn't licked his stubborn perspiration problem.)

Bartucci: Our second tour of the States was an entirely different story from the first. *More for Me* was the number one selling album there. At the very same time, their movie, *Rough Boys*, was the summer's hottest release, and it in turn had a hit soundtrack of its own. Ever see it, Mr. Hoag?

Hoag: Eight times in one weekend.

Bartucci: The kids screamed for them now like they had for the Beatles. They sold out Shea Stadium. Played the *Sullivan Show.* Three sold-out shows at the Hollywood Bowl. A monster tour I put together, not that I'm trying to pat myself on the back.

Hoag: Of course not.

Bartucci: In Chicago, I took them to Chess Studios, where they recorded some of their favorite R and B songs backed up by old-time Chicago bluesmen. *Chess Moves* it was called.

Hoag: How come it was never released in the U.S.?

Bartucci: The record company thought it would compete with the live album of the *More for Me* tour. The boys enjoyed the Chess sessions. They enjoyed the tour. Marco took care of everything for them. After the show, Jack filled their rooms with liquor and pot and fifteen or more game young ladies – innocent fun compared with what went on later, with the heroin, the sexual perversity, the wanton destruction of hotel property. Back then, they were merely fun-loving, horny boys. Touring was a tremendous release for them. Here at home there was great pressure on them to go into the studio and make more hits. There were also the domestic pressures. T. S. and Tulip had married. Secretly – EMI and I felt it was best that way. Here was this impudent stud, this bad-boy idol of millions. He just oughtn't be married to the famous daughter of a prominent barrister, especially one who took him to the ballet and taught him to eat with a knife and fork. It wasn't his image. It wasn't *him*. The second he got away from Tulip on tour, he rebelled with both hands. This made Rory happy. He preferred the old T. S. The old clubs, too. In the giant arenas, with all of the kids screaming, Rory said he was starting to feel like a performing monkey. One night, to prove a point, he stopped hitting the strings entirely. The kids were making so much noise they didn't even notice. *(laughs)* That tour was a gas. Until they lowered the boom on poor Puppy, of course.

Hoag: What happened exactly?

Bartucci: We should have stayed out of the South. But we'd gotten so much press there before . . . When we'd arrive in a city, the police and hotel management would get tipped off by me with regard to what type of party scene the boys might get themselves into – and how we certainly would appreciate it if this stayed quiet. They always cooperated. After all, the boys generated a lot of local revenue. I always carried a suitcase full of cash, as well. Never had a problem, until we got to Little Rock, Arkansas, where we encountered a particular police official who was not at all into the idea of some black musician getting white girls stoned and then balling them. This fellow was *not* going to look the other way, no matter how much money I offered him. Far from it – he wanted to make a statement. And he bloody well did. His men broke down the door to Puppy's hotel room at two a.m. and found him there in bed with a naked fifteen-year-old white girl, and in possession of hashish and amphetamines. And he was in some very, very deep shit, the poor boy. Statutory rape, they called it. The drug possession charge was no small matter either. The record company, Capitol, sent down a big-time New York attorney at once. I told the other boys to take off, but they refused. They were loyal, those three, I'll grant them that. The lawyer bargained and arm-twisted and somehow kept Puppy out of jail. He pleaded guilty to possession and to unlawful trafficking with a minor, or some such thing, in exchange for which he was fined ten thousand dollars and placed on probation for three years. We were elated – until Washington decided to get in on it. Your government was most displeased to discover Puppy was actually one of yours – it meant they couldn't make a point of kicking him out of the country. So they kicked the rest of us out. Revoked our work visas, and made it very clear that Us was no longer welcome in America, at least not if Puppy Johnson was in the band. So we came home. Toured the Continent. *Chess Moves* sold well here. And then that bloody psychedelic thing happened.

Hoag: They started dropping acid.

Bartucci: The Beatles, they flourished from LSD – gave the world *Sergeant Pepper*. Everyone else produced the worst kind of self-indulgent crap imaginable. The Stones, under the influence of acid, did *Their Satanic Majesties Request*, unquestionably their worst album. And Us, oh my, they got so very weird, those boys. Withdrew to their country retreats and blasted off into their own little worlds. T. S. went into what I call his T. S. Eliot stage. Started writing unbelievably wretched stream-of-consciousness lyrics. Poetry, they called it. Rory, he got obsessed with Irish folk ballads from olden times. Derek started collecting Victorian pornographic art, as well as slender blond boys. Puppy just got into being rather glazed. Surly as well. The product of all of this, when they finally went back into the studio, was *Rock of Ages*, which they called a musical exploration of their once and future selves.

Hoag: "Mystical vipers/Windscreen wipers/Across the twisting purple corridors/Inside our minds."

Bartucci: I called it crap. Christ, they expressed themselves musically as druids! Chanted! And their music of tomorrow – it was *noise*. Two entire cuts were *noise*. There wasn't one marketable single on it. Plus they took some very nasty shots at the royal family. The EMI people loathed it, fought with them every step of the way. *Rock of Ages* was a critical and commercial failure, here and abroad. Their first failure. But you couldn't tell the boys this accurately reflected its quality. Oh no. Their heads were too large. They actually blamed EMI for its failure – creative interference, they called it. So T. S. brought in Tulip's father to examine all of their contracts and financial affairs. He told them they should form their own label, which naturally appealed to their grandiose delusions. He also told them I was stealing from them. I wasn't, as I've made clear to you, but the more drugs they took, the more they believed him. T. S. still blames me for the tax troubles he got into – and I wasn't even around by then. They called me the vilest names, after all I did for them. Left me with no choice but to hire a solicitor of my own. We reached a settlement. Parted company. They went on to do some of their most successful work. But the truth is they were never happy again. Look what happened to them – heroin, divorce, death. There were no good times after that, Mr. Hoag. It gives me no pleasure to say so. I bear them no grudge. The hard feelings, those went away years ago . . . Anything else I can tell you? I'm rather busy.

Hoag: Just one thing: Where did you go after our interview on Friday?

Bartucci: Why do you ask?

Hoag: I was wondering if you happened to be around, say, Savile Row.

Bartucci: I was right here. Working.

Hoag: Can anyone here vouch for you?

Bartucci: Vouch for me?

Hoag: Yes. Do you mind if I ask some of them?

Bartucci: I most certainly do mind. Where I go and what I do is none of your or Tristam Scarr's damned business. And you can tell that cheap, phony bastard I said so!

Hoag: Sure there still isn't just the tiniest grudge?

Bartucci: I think you should leave, Mr. Hoag.

Hoag: I'll do that. Again, thank you for your time and your –

Bartucci: Get the fuck out of my – !

(end tape)

(Tape #1 with Tulip recorded in her Chelsea flat Dec. 1. Located on King's Road directly over a shop specializing in metal-studded collars and handcuffs. Parlor is messy. The Mod Bod weighs possibly fifty pounds more than in her heyday. Face is fleshy, blotchy. Hair uncombed and greasy. Wears large silver cross on chain around her neck. Holds Bible in her lap.)

Hoag: I've met your daughter Violet. Lovely girl.

Tulip: She's no longer mine. I've lost her. He's won.

Hoag: Do you mean Tris? *(silence)* So what are you doing with yourself these days?

Tulip: Do you mean now that I'm the Mod Blob?

Hoag: I mean now that you're not nineteen, and London doesn't swing like a pendulum do.

Tulip: I've a small family income. And I'm very active in my church.

Hoag: According to Tris it's not one of the more established faiths.

Tulip: It's so like him to condemn what he doesn't understand.

Hoag: Could we talk about when you first met him?

Tulip: I was thin, rich and beautiful. A spoiled little bitch as well. Anything I'd ever wanted I'd gotten. Us were the hot new group, very gear. I was at the Ad Lib one night with David Bailey and a few others. And so were the two of them, Tris and Rory. I'd heard what people were saying about them, that they chewed up pretty little girls and spit them out. Perhaps that attracted me. I don't know. I do know I thought it couldn't possibly happen to me. Not Tulip. It was Rory I got involved with first, actually. He was the sweetest, baddest little boy. Had this way of cocking his head to one side when he talked to me, as if he knew he was bad and couldn't help himself. And he *couldn't*. Rory was the first man I ever fell for, and I fell hard . . . And it all turned out to be true, what people had said. He *was* mean. He lied to me, slept around on me. S-So I started sleeping with Tris, to get back at him. Only I fell even harder for Tris. Sounds awful, doesn't it? I was an awful, drugged-out bitch. I was a slut.

Hoag: You were his wife.

Tulip: Yes, I was. And by the time that became public I was sleeping with Rory once again, God help me, and poor Derek was wishing *he* was. Madness, all of it. A loss of self-control brought on by abandoning the Lord and his teachings.

Hoag: What was it like being secretly married?

Tulip: I despised it. Ours was a proper marriage – for a while, at least – but the newspapers made me out to be some kind of rock 'n' roll tramp. And I had to take it. He had his bloody image to maintain.

Hoag: Derek thinks you're the only person who ever really got to know Tris.

Tulip: (pause) Tris was . . . is . . . a vulnerable person. Shy, actually. Whatever came out of him, whether it was meanness or genius, came from this well of insecurity. As a result, I could never hate him, even when I wanted to. He never did learn how to feel comfortable with people. They in turn never wanted to understand him. When I met him he was twenty-two. The music he made, the life he led – it was all totally new. What he came to resent, I think, was that everyone wanted him to stay the same angry boy making the same angry music. They wouldn't allow him to grow as an artist or as a person. He was, for example, very excited and fulfilled by *Rock of Ages*. Until people totally rejected it . . . Our life together was a fairy tale. We were lovely, special little children who could buy all the toys and candy we wanted, and there were no adults around to slap our hands and tell us no. They bought these lovely *Alice in Wonderland* cottages in the Cotswolds, and filled them with toys and animals. Tris had an elephant, a giraffe, an entire zoo of his own, just like Dr. Dolittle, until he decided one night it was cruel and set them free. The village was not pleased . . . London wasn't fun anymore. Fans would hassle us. Jack would drive us in sometimes for a night out, but mostly we stayed in the country. We all had cooks, and there were always lovely people around. George and Patti Harrison, Eric, Keith, Brian, Woody. All the mates. Lots of girls. Lots of jams. Lots of magic mushrooms, mescaline, THC . . .

Hoag: What kind of relationship did you have with Puppy?

Tulip: Puppy thought I was some kind of evil witch, bad for Tris and Rory's heads, bad for the band. He was forever mean to me. And then after the ban he was just mean to everyone. Puppy didn't care for the country life. He only came out when they got together to play. Usually he'd crash at Rory's, where all of the equipment was.

Hoag: Like the weekend he died?

Tulip: Yes. Like the weekend he died.

Hoag: Can you tell me about that?

Tulip: It was after *Rock of Ages* flopped. Tris and Rory were taking it very hard. They felt personally betrayed by the fans and the critics. Puppy blamed himself for them not being able to give it American tour support. The weekend he died they'd gotten together at Rory's to talk about their next album. They were not getting far. I think their faith in each other had been shaken. It was frightening, the amount of pressure that was put on them by Marco, by EMI, by the good new groups – Cream, Traffic, Procol Harem. There was no laughter in Rory's house that weekend. No joy. I remember this girl he was seeing then, she picked right up on that.

Hoag: The tarot card woman?

Tulip: Yes. That's right.

Hoag: Do you remember her name?

Tulip: (pause) No. She was just some girl. Rory didn't see her for long. He didn't see anyone for long . . . They were in the music room, trying out some things, drinking some champagne, talking. Marco had just left to go back to London.

Hoag: What was Marco doing there?

Tulip: Hassling them, mostly. Jack and I were out in the kitchen with a few other girls and friends. They didn't like for us to be in there with them when they were in the early stages. I remember there was an argument. Rory said something like, "Fuck this flower-power shit!" Then there was this terrible crash. Derek came rushing out, terribly pale, and said "Jackie, Pup has passed out and we can't bring him to." We all went in and found him collapsed amidst his drums. Jack tried to revive him while the rest of us looked for whatever it was he'd taken.

Hoag: You didn't find anything.

Tulip: No. The pills weren't to be found. By the time the ambulance arrived, he was gone. The Lord had taken him from us.

Hoag: Do you think someone acted as His agent?

Tulip: Agent?

Hoag: Tris thinks Puppy was murdered by one of you.

Tulip: We were all to blame.

Hoag: You were?

Tulip: He died for our sins. That's why the Lord took him. To punish us. To *warn* us. But we didn't heed His message. We were too blind. So things got worse. More drugs, more pain, more death . . . Us wasn't the same after Puppy died. They used studio drummers from then on, none with his talent or flair. The focus shifted more to Tris and Rory. *We're Double Trouble*, the album they turned out after Puppy's death, was shit-kicking, wired rock 'n' roll. They'd put away the hollow-body blues. The acid as well. From then on it was coke, smack, speed, all of the above. We three became serious smack freaks. I was getting it on with both of them then, God help me.

Hoag: How did they handle that? Didn't they fight over you?

Tulip: Never. Deep down, they always meant more to each other than any woman could.

Hoag: Even you?

Tulip: Especially me . . . Their new sound clicked. They bounced back bigger than ever, and started acting like genuine bad-ass stars. Pissing people off. Getting shit-faced and disorderly in public. Seeing what they could get away with – just like two bad little boys. And when they toured, forget it. I tried going with them on their return tour to America in '68. It was male macho madness. They trashed their hotel rooms with fire hoses. Threw the furniture in the street. One night in Detroit Rory got in a brawl with the hotel manager because they wanted to put him on the second floor. I said to him "So what?" He said "It's no bleedin' *fun* to dangle a groupie out of a second- story window." In Kansas City, I came in one morning and found Tris in *our* bed with two girls and someone's pet monkey. I split. I couldn't take it. The following year, when they went over to tour promote *Skullbuggery*, Rory asked me to go with them. I didn't want to but he begged me. So I traveled as Tris's wife on the tour, while I was actually living with Rory. It was sick, sick, sick . . . My friends were always asking me which of them was better in bed. I always said it was like comparing coke with smack – they were both obscenely great and it was impossible to say which would kill you faster. At least Rory didn't beat me.

Hoag: Tris beat you?

Tulip: Tris was often violent when he was on smack. Broke my nose once. *Skullbuggery* stayed at number one for something like five months. Then they put out *Nasty, Nasty,* and it was nearly as big. That's when they had to cool out somewhere for tax reasons.

Hoag: Tris moved to L.A.

Tulip: And Rory and Derek to Italy. I stayed here and tried to get myself somewhat back together. Got off drugs. Went to Italy and got off Rory. Then I flew to L.A. to see Tris. He was living in a rented mansion in Malibu, and much, much closer to the edge. Shooting up. Drinking too much tequila. Hanging out with problem children like Moon, and Dennis Wilson of the Beach Boys. Dennis he'd gotten to be friendly with after the '68 tour, when Dennis was living on Sunset. Both of those two are dead now. The night before I got there the police caught Tris going a hundred and fifty miles per hour on Pacific Coast Highway in his Porsche – with a suspended license. I had to bail him out of jail. He'd changed for the worse. He was so absolutely full of anger. Hate.

Hoag: Do you know why?

Tulip: You'd have to ask him. He wouldn't open up to me. That's why I left him – that and the smack. It wasn't until Jack and Derek moved out there and got hold of him that he started getting himself together again. When he did, I took him back. Had Violet. Then we split again, for good . . . All of it's such a blur now. I can't even remember most of the faces. I have my photo album, of course, but I haven't been able to look at that for years now. Freaks me out too much. I took a lot of the pictures myself, actually.

Hoag: I'd love to see it.

Tulip: I actually fancied I'd be a photographer one day. David Bailey said I was quite good. I never followed through, though. Never followed through on anything, except falling apart. If I hadn't found the Lord, I'd be dead just like Rory. Poor, poor Rory . . .

Hoag: I really would love to see it.

Tulip: Hmm? Oh, it's somewhere . . . I had to put it away when I found Violet pawing through it. Pawing through my past. I'll dig it up for you. Come back tomorrow

    Hoag: Thank you. I will.

    Tulip: All I ever did was model. Not that that's anything. You're just a slab of beef.

    Hoag: How do you feel about Violet following in your footsteps?

    Tulip: It's her life.

    Hoag: And T. S.?

    Tulip: What about him?

    Hoag: How do you feel about him?

    Tulip: I don't feel anything about him anymore.

    (end tape)

CHAPTER
EIGHT

Lulu was getting soft.

Too much of Merilee's cooking and too little physical activity had dulled her razor-sharp huntress instincts. She was slow to react when I let myself into the mews house. In fact, she didn't react at all.

I knelt and scratched her ears. She sniffed at my fingers with the cool reserve she usually shows roach exterminators and federal census takers. I hadn't visited her on her bed of pain for two whole days. I was getting the treatment for it.

"This has gone far enough," I told her firmly. "I've already apologized numerous times for what happened. And you *know* I can't be here with you all the time."

I reached down to hoist her out of her bed. She resisted me, grunting unappreciatively. I'm bigger. I lifted her up and held her. Usually, she likes to nestle into me and put her head on my shoulder like a dance partner. Not now. Now she squirmed in my arms, and wanted to be put down. I obliged her.

"Okay, be a martyr," I said, as I headed for the phone. "See what it gets you."

Tris was still asleep and not taking any calls. I told Pamela I'd be late for work the next evening because I wanted to look through Tulip's photo album. She said she'd pass the news on to Mr. Scarr. She also said she'd quite enjoyed transcribing our last couple of tapes.

"I really do hear him now, Hoagy."

"Glad you think so," I said, pleased she'd noticed a difference. I *was* getting him now. If only I was getting closer to figuring out who'd shot at me, too. Then I'd be making real progress.

I had just enough time to soak in a hot tub with a Laphroaig – it *wasn't* too smoky for me – before it was time to watch part ten of *Giant Worms of the Sea*. I was very into this series now I wasn't sure why. Two possibilities came to mind. Either it was an acquired taste or I'd been in England too long.

When the show was over, I put my new suit on over a black cashmere turtleneck and spooned out a can of mackerel for Lulu. She glowered at it like it was Alpo beef chunks. Still, I said good-bye fondly, hoping she'd feel guilty over the way she'd been treating me. I'm sure she didn't.

The mini was still out of service, so I was using the Peugeot diesel wagon. It went from zero to sixty in a day and a half, and had no fridge, but driving it made me nostalgic. I'd had a diesel just like it the year I lived in the Perigord Valley, subsisting on goose liver pâté and chilled Monbazillac while I struggled with the first draft of *Our Family Enterprise*. Ah, youth.

I parked near the theater and waited for Merilee at the performer's entrance like a stage-door Johnny, flowers and all. A dapper older gent was also waiting there for a cast member, though I think it likely the fluffy blond object of his affections was named Steve.

She came out wearing her long, treasured Perry Ellis tweed suit – she'd wept when he died. A high-throated white silk blouse, alligator belt and shoes went with it. Her eyes got soft when I handed her the flowers.

Fans at the curb pushed autograph books at her. Flashbulbs popped. It was, possibly, indiscreet for the two of us to be seen together like this. But we'd decided it would be tawdry if we behaved like we had something to hide. We had never been tawdry, and didn't intend to start now

"How's T. S. ?" she asked, as I steered her toward the car.

"I'm actually starting to respect him a little," I replied. "Not that he's a very nice guy – guys who make a commitment to being the best seldom are. He knows he hurt people. But he was willing to pay that price. You don't meet many people anymore who care that much about their art. *And* have talent."

She squeezed my arm. "Ever think you'd find yourself identifying with a rock star?"

"Who's identifying with a rock star?"

"Sorry, darling. I must have misunderstood."

Merilee had something on her mind. She sat with her back stiff as we rode to the restaurant, and kept wringing her hands in her lap. I kept up a line of polite chatter and waited her out. I waited a long time. She held it in all the way to the Grange, which is a very fine eating place on King Street in Covent Garden. She held it in through the martinis, complete with extra olives. She held it in while we destroyed their beef Wellington and two of their most amusing bottles of Haut-Médoc. It was only after the table had been cleared and the coffee poured that she spilled it:

"Zack wants to come over."

I tugged at my ear. "For how long?"

"A-A few days. He said he feels like we're drifting apart. He wants to –"

"Have it out?"

"No. I don't think so."

"Any idea when he's planning to come?"

She swallowed and examined her coffee cup. "Tomorrow afternoon."

I pushed my coffee away and called for a Calvados. Then I took a deep breath and let it out slowly.

"Sometimes," she offered, "things aren't as neat as one would like."

"Things are never that neat."

"Zack is my husband, darling. While he's in London he expects me to be his wife."

"And what do you expect?"

"I expect nothing anymore," she replied bitterly. "I feel like a cigarette."

"You don't smoke. You've never smoked."

"You're right. I'm being actressy. Sorry." She swept her hair back. "I'm going to be a good wife to him while he's here. I'm going to be the best damned wife I know how to be, even though I am being torn apart at the seams. And I'm very, very sorry about this. For you and for me. I've been so happy the past few – "

"Don't. Don't be sorry. I'll take my things with me in the morning. Call me when you can, okay?"

She looked at me quizzically. "You're being awfully damned understanding."

"You were once very understanding."

Her glance flickered south of my equator. "I tried to be."

I drained my Calvados. "Good thing I've got the station wagon. I can put Lulu right in the back, bed and all."

Merilee cleared her throat uncomfortably. "I still think she should stay with me."

"Merilee, she's my dog – even if she doesn't happen to be speaking to me right now."

"She's *our* dog."

"She's *my* dog. I told you before – we're a package. If I go, she goes with me."

"I know, I know. Only, I still think she's safer with me."

"No."

"You may still be in danger."

"No!"

"You could stop by anytime and visit her. Keep the key."

"Merilee, you're asking me to give her up."

"Just temporarily." She put her hand over mine. "I need her, darling. Don't you see? If she's there, you're there. Holding on to her is the only way I'll make it through this. Please, darling. Please?"

It's a good thing Merilee Nash doesn't have a diabolical nature. I'd assassinate a head of state for her, if she asked me like that. "And what about afterward?"

"We agreed we wouldn't talk about afterward."

"To hell with what we agreed, Merilee."

"Very well. What do you want?"

"I think that's pretty obvious."

"Try making it a little more obvious, if you don't mind."

"I don't mind. What happens at the end of *The Philadelphia Story*?"

"The curtain comes down."

"Before that."

Merilee flushed. "I-I get married to my first husband again."

"Suggest anything to you?"

She sighed. "Happy endings are for plays, darling. And very, very old ones at that."

"I kind of like happy endings."

"I always thought you preferred the tragic, deep kind."

"Not when I'm in the cast."

Her forehead creased. It does that when she's trying not to cry. "God, you look good in black, Mr. Hoagy."

"You look good in everything, but I suppose you already know that."

"A gal only knows it if her guy says so."

"Am I your guy?"

"I wish I knew, darling," she said softly. "I'm so sorry."

"Don't be." I cupped her chin in my palm and got lost in her green eyes for a second. "You're still mine for one more night."

And was she ever.

London's vacant-stare district that season was King's Road, Chelsea. Zonked, translucent punks shuffled along the sidewalk in black leather, their hair dyed a spectrum of repulsive colors. The wandering victims. They looked like they had framed eight-by-ten glossies of Sid Vicious hanging over their beds of nails.

I still didn't know whether punk was a posture or a statement. More important, I didn't care. I had enough problems of my own. I'd just said good-bye to Merilee and to Lulu, and I didn't know when I'd see either one of them again. The Irish oatmeal Merilee had made me eat before I left still sat in my stomach like a bucket of ready-mixed joint compound. My head ached.

I left the Peugeot at the curb outside of Tulip's building. I was about to buzz her flat when I noticed the street door had been jimmied open with a pry bar. The frame was smashed and splintered, the door ajar. I looked around. No one on the street seemed to be paying any attention to the ruined door, or to me, or to anything. I went in.

Tulip's flat was on the second floor in the front, and her hall door matched the one downstairs. Splintered and open. I hesitated there at the top of the stairs. This looked like a job for somebody else. Somebody with guts and a pit bull.

I listened at her door, mouth dry. My heart started to pound. Silence. I knocked and called out her name. More silence. I took a deep breath. Then I pushed open the door and went in.

The closet in her entry hall had been ransacked. Its contents – scarves, shoulder bags, an old fringe buckskin jacket, an even older clear plastic rain slicker adorned with psychedelic flowers – were scattered on the floor.

I called out her name.

There had been a television and a cheap stereo sitting in a wall unit in the dingy parlor. They were gone now. Their outline remained in the dust there on the bare shelves. Lots of dust. I couldn't imagine what it looked like under her bed. I hoped I wouldn't have to find out.

I called out her name.

Dresser drawers had been yanked open in the bedroom. Underwear, socks, T-shirts were strewn everywhere. The jewelry box on her dressing table had been emptied and overturned. The bedroom closet had been tossed.

Dresses were heaped on the floor, shoe boxes dumped open upon them.

I called out her name.

The medicine chest over the bathroom sink had been pawed through. Open pill bottles were scattered in the sink, their contents dissolving in brightly colored smears under the dripping tap.

I called out her name.

Then I turned and banged into her.

Tulip was standing right there behind me in the doorway to the kitchen, her still-beautiful eyes open very wide, her face pale. She was pointing in the general direction of the parlor, and she was trying to say something to me but there was this unfortunate matter of the boning knife that someone had plunged into her stomach. All she could get out was a gurgling noise as she staggered toward me. I started to reach for her but not before she pitched forward into me. She was not a feather. We both went down, she directly on top of me – and if you think that doesn't still give me nightmares, guess again. I pushed her off of me and over onto her back as gently as I could. But there was no need for me to be gentle. She was dead now

Whoever did it to her had been thorough. He'd taken the silver cross from around her neck, too.

The British press handled the murder of Tulip, the once-famous Mod Bod, as a kind of sad postscript to the sixties and Swinging London. Her old glamour shots were pulled out and splashed over the front pages, along with the recollections of those who'd been there. Or claimed to have been there. A revolution, Derek had called it. The staid newspapers indulged in sober discussion of the early burnout and death that had overtaken so many of the youthful Carnaby Street luminaries – Brian, Puppy, Hendrix, Moon. The tabloids went straight for the low road, with gleeful stories about her weight, and how it had ballooned. Stories about how she'd taken to spending her time at a storefront halfway-house mission called the Church of Life. Stories about how she'd lived, and died, in total squalor.

I was there. It wasn't squalor. But it didn't swing, either.

Jay Weintraub released a brief statement to the press on Tristam Scarr's behalf: "Tulip was the only woman I have ever loved. She was the mother of my only child. Although we spent our lives apart in recent years, our feelings for each other never changed. I will always love her, and miss her terribly."

It was the only comment on her murder that T. S. made, and he didn't make it. He was in no shape to do so. Her death had so severely jolted him that a doctor was keeping him sedated.

The statement came from me. All a part of the service. Just don't ask me to do thank-you notes or windows. I get a little crabby.

Our editor phoned from New York to make sure I was on top of this sizzling new development. I assured him I was, right down to the bloodstains all over my trenchcoat. *Rolling Stone*, he disclosed, would pay dearly for my exclusive first-person account. It would, he suggested, give the book "monster topspin." I said it was a great idea. I lied. I had no intention of exploiting Tulip's death. But editors feel better about themselves and you if they think you agree with their suggestions. Especially editors who use words like "topspin."

By all the press accounts, Tulip had walked in on a burglary taking place in her flat, and had gotten killed for it. Whatever she owned of value had been taken. The ransacking of the drugs in her medicine chest suggested that her murderer was an addict.

The police, however, had a problem with this theory. I learned about it from Farley Root, that same apologetic buck-toothed, redheaded investigator in that same nile green suit. He made the trip out to Gadpole two mornings later, joined by a strapping uniformed officer who didn't speak. The three of us sat around the kitchen table. Pamela put on tea.

"Nice to see you again, Inspector," I said.

"It's kind of you to say so, Mr. Hoag."

"Hoagy," I said.

"Hoagy. Right. And while we're at it, I'm not actually an – "

"Your neck looks much better. Try that talc?"

Root reddened, glanced self-consciously over at the uniformed officer, who was working hard at not smirking. "I did," he replied. "Floris number eighty-nine. Very soothing, as you suggested. Thank you."

"My pleasure."

Pamela served us our tea as well as some hot scones. Then she returned to the laundry room, where she was in the process of removing the bloodstains from my trench coat. Don't ask me how. I never press the masters for their secrets.

"Turn up any of those bullets yet?" I asked Root.

He bit into a scone, driving his long front teeth into it like a gopher. "No sir, we haven't," he replied, gnawing. "But that brings me to my business – Miss Tulip's murder. It does seem rather straightforward on the surface. She returns home, discovers someone there in the act, and there we have it. Unfortunate timing. Break-ins are rather common in that district. Several have taken place in recent weeks, though none with so grievous an outcome."

I sipped my tea and waited him out.

"I can find only one flaw in this reasoning," Root said.

"Which is . . . ?"

"You, sir."

"Me?"

"Yessir. I don't wish to jump to erroneous conclusions, but this is the second bit of ugly business you've been party to in the past several days. I was inclined to classify the first incident as random street violence, and you as the victim of a bit of bad luck. But I'm afraid with this second incident . . . Well, you can see my point, can't you?"

I tugged at my ear. "Yes, I believe I can."

"Glad to hear that," Root said, pleased. "Now then, Hoagy can you account for how you've found yourself at the scene of two violent attacks recently?"

"No, I can't."

Root stared at me, visibly disappointed by my answer. "I see," he said at last. "You told the officers at the murder scene you had an appointment with Miss Tulip. What exactly was your business?"

"As I told you before, I'm helping Tris Scarr do his memoirs."

Root asked me for the name of the publisher. I gave him topspin's name. Then he told me to continue.

"Tulip played a big part in his life," I said. "I'd met with her in reference to that. And I was supposed to meet with her again."

"How did she seem to you?"

"Seem?"

"Her state of mind."

"About as messed up as the rest of us. Maybe a little more."

Root nodded. "Any idea what sort of people she knew?"

"Not really. She did tell me she was involved with her church."

Root glanced through his notepad. "Yes. Fellow who operates it, called Father Bob, used to deal drugs. Been to jail for it, actually. There's also some question as to the validity of his divinity school training."

"Think he might be involved in it somehow?"

"No, I think you are, Hoagy," Root said evenly.

He watched me for a reaction from across the table, bony, freckled hands folded in front of him, eyes impassive. Bashful he wasn't, not when he felt he was being shut out.

I cleared my throat. "I appreciate your candor, Inspector."

"I place great stock in candor. And I'm *not* actually an – "

"And I do understand how you feel. I wish I had an explanation for what's been happening to me. Around me. But I don't. I'm sorry."

"As am I."

"I will make a deal with you, though."

Root glanced over at his uniformed colleague, then back at me. "A deal?"

"Yes. If I do come up with something, I'll share it with you – if you'll share something with me now."

"I don't make deals such as those, sir," Root said firmly.

"Too bad."

He swallowed, craned his neck. "Share what with you?"

"Have you inventoried the contents of Tulip's apartment?"

Root turned to the other officer, who nodded.

"Could I get a copy of the inventory?" I asked.

Root frowned. "For what reason?"

"Let's put it this way – I need it."

He thought it over carefully. "Very well. You shall have it," he said, draining his tea.

Pamela appeared instantly from the laundry room. "More tea, Inspector?"

"No thank you, madam," he replied. "And I'm *not* an – "

"Another scone, perhaps?" she said.

"Thank you. No. But I would appreciate a word with Mr. Scarr, if that's possible."

She shook her head. "I'm afraid it isn't. Mr. Scarr wasn't strong to begin with, and the loss of Tulip has quite simply devastated him. The doctor insisted he not be disturbed."

"Of course. Terribly sorry. Didn't mean to seem insensitive." Root lurched to his feet. "We'll be going then."

I showed them out, past the guards on the front door, and the surveillance cameras and the floodlights.

"Certainly believes in security, doesn't he?" observed Root, as he climbed into his unmarked Austin Metro.

"He believes in feeling safe," I said. "Can't say I blame him."

Root rolled down his window, stuck his head out, "One more question, Hoagy."

"Yes?"

"What is a cheese steak?"

"A hero sandwich – thin strips of steak topped with sauteed onions, mushrooms, and melted cheese."

"Good Lord, sounds wonderful."

"If you want a good one you have to go to Philadelphia. The Liberty Bell is there. It's not the worst place there is."

"Can't say I'll be getting to Philadelphia soon."

"Neither will W. C. Fields."

Tris looked different to me. Partly it was his hair. Pamela, that woman of many talents, had trimmed it for him. But mostly, I realized, I'd Just never seen him in the daylight before. He looked even more cadaverous and ghoulish than he did in his dimly lit royal chamber. Flesh-toned he was not.

He and I rode together in the back seat of the Silver Cloud to Tulip's funeral, which was at her church in London. He wore a chalk-striped navy blue suit, white shirt, dark striped tie, ankle boots, and the look of a lost, bewildered little boy Jack and Violet were up front, Jack behind the wheel with his jaw set grimly. Violet had on a black dress. Her luxuriant black hair was tied tightly back, and she was sniffling. For the first time since I'd met her, she looked her age.

Four bodyguards rode in the car ahead of us.

"I intended to thank you, Hogarth," Tris said softly.

"For what?"

"The statement you wrote. It was very sensitive. I couldn't have said it so well myself."

"Sure you could have. You just needed a little time to recover."

He dragged deeply on a Gauloise, let the smoke out of his famous flaring nostrils. "Thank you. I mean it."

"Forget it. We ear-wigglers have to stick together."

"That we do." He gazed out the window. "It's true, Hogarth."

"What's true?"

"What Derek said – I have no mates. Not true ones. Not anymore. I-I don't make 'em easily, and when I do, I make 'em for life. I make 'em for forever . . . It's not as if she's gone. Or Rory's gone. They're in here." He tapped his head with his finger. "They're still in here."

"I understand."

"Do you, mate?"

"Sure. I'm the same way."

He smiled at me. I smiled back. Inwardly, I sighed. It was happening – he and I were getting emotionally involved. It was only natural. I'd gotten him to open up, share his secrets, his dreams, his hurts with me. That didn't happen without feelings happening, too. From both directions. I didn't know to do it any other way. How did the lunch-pail ghosts do it? I wondered. No, I didn't. I didn't ever want to know that.

Tris punched the leather seat between us hard with his fist. "Damn them!"

"Damn who?"

"The fates. I mean, why Tulip? Why *her*?"

I glanced over at him. Quietly I said, "It wasn't the fates, Tristam."

He narrowed his pouched eyes at me. Then he reached for a button on the door panel next to him, and said, "Excuse us for a moment, people." The glass divider to the front seat slid shut. Jack and Violet couldn't hear us now. "What are you talking about, Hogarth? What is this?"

"It's trouble."

"What sort of trouble?"

"That break-in wasn't what it appeared to be. The use of the pry bar, the theft of the valuables, the ransacking of the medicine chest – all that was just done to cover up what really happened."

"Which was?"

"Which was that somebody Tulip knew dropped by to visit her, and kill her, and take something. Something that was very valuable to them, but not to anybody else."

"Such as what?"

"Her photo album. I saw the police inventory of the apartment contents this morning. No photo album. It's gone."

He put out his cigarette and lit another. "Right . . . Pammy said you'd phoned, and were planning to go see this album of Tu's." He scratched his head. "Can't seem to recall anything about it though."

"She took pictures."

He let out a short laugh. "That I recall. Always in m'face with her bleedin' Nikon camera, she was."

"And she kept them. Pictures of you guys on tour, on stage, at home. Pictures of London, pictures of Paris, New York, L.A., everywhere."

An odd look flickered across his face, like he'd just taken a pan of ice water down his pants. It was gone in an instant.

"There must have been a photo in the album that I couldn't be allowed to see," I went on. "A photo that would have told me who killed Puppy, and who shot at me. But it's gone now, and so is she. She must have been able to tie it all together. That's why she had to die. Now we'll never – " I stopped myself short. "Unless . . ."

"Unless what, Hogarth?"

"Nothing. Just a thought."

"You've told the police all of this?"

"No. Not yet."

"Why not? It seems to me they – "

"It's part of the past. Your past. That's not their area. It's mine."

He grinned at me crookedly. "And you're still bleedin' mad about your dog getting shot."

"And I'm still bleedin' mad about my dog getting shot."

At least she used to be my dog. I wasn't so sure anymore. I was still waiting to hear from Merilee. And trying not to think about her and Zack.

Tris put his hand on my arm. "Who is it, Hogarth? Who's doing these things?"

"I don't know yet."

I had ideas though. Plenty. I'd asked Pamela if she'd told anybody besides Tris that I'd be checking out Tulip's album. She had. She'd told Jack – the very same Jack who, once again, was away from Gadpole running errands when a certain violent shooting incident was taking place. There was no question that Jack looked mighty fine for it. After all, he had the biggest personal ax to grind against Puppy. He had shown the most resistance to talking about the past with me. He was good with a shotgun. And there was his relationship with Violet to consider. Maybe she was somehow involved in it with him. She did like to shoot. And to steal. Yeah, Jack looked mighty fine. But he wasn't the only one. The others could have known I was going to look at Tulip's album. Tulip could have mentioned it to them herself. Told Derek. Told Marco. It could have been one of them. It could have been any of them.

Yeah, I had ideas. Too many.

The Church of Life was housed in a shabby storefront down the street from Tulip's flat. Boisterous reporters, photographers, and TV cameramen were crowded onto the sidewalk and into the street out front, waiting anxiously for this rare public glimpse of the great T. S. He put on a pair of cool-cat wraparound shades when we pulled up. Then he tensed and took a deep breath. Jack jumped out first and opened his door for him.

They barraged him with questions the instant we stepped out of the Rolls. T. S. answered none of them. He had already made his one statement. His phalanx of guards somehow cleared a path through the crowd and we headed inside, T. S. with his arm protectively around Violet, who was about six inches taller than he in her heels.

Inside, the Church of Life looked a lot like a Bowery soup kitchen. There were long, scarred tables with benches on either side, a coffee urn, a bulletin board, the pungent smell of commercial disinfectant. Derek Gregg and Marco Bartucci, the human teapot, sat across from each other at one of the tables. No one else had come to see the Mod Bod off. Her parents were dead. The press were kept out.

At the far end of the room was a pulpit, where Father Bob presided. Father Bob had eaten fried eggs for breakfast that morning. Some of the yolk was still in his beard, which was black and bushy. He wore wire-rimmed glasses, a paint-splattered gray sweatshirt with the sleeves cut crudely off at the elbows, and rumpled black corduroy trousers. Thick black hair sprouted on his arms and up from under the neck of his sweatshirt, nearly meeting his beard.

The urn holding Tulip's ashes was on the table next to him.

The funeral service was short and casual. Just a few comments from Father Bob on how we all touch each other in life and in death. Then he presented Vi with the urn, and kissed her on the forehead.

T. S. exchanged a few words and a hug with Derek – and, after a hesitation, one with Marco, who was weeping openly. Then he headed back out to the car. Jack also hugged Derek. But the former Rough Boys drummer steered carefully around Marco. Marco noticed. I noticed. Marco noticed I noticed.

"Awful business, Mr. Hoag," Marco said, coming over to me. "Awful."

"Indeed," I said. "Had you see her recently? Spoken to her?"

Marco frowned. "Why, no. Why do you ask?"

"Just wondered if the two of your were close."

"One needn't be in regular touch to be close. She was the loveliest of them all, Mr. Hoag. She was so lovely she could break your heart-without even trying." Marco ducked his head and swiped at his nose. Then he waddled out.

I watched him go, wondering just how long he had carried the torch for Tulip, and if he had ever tried doing anything about it, the poor, greasy little crook.

Tris was slouched in the back seat of the Silver Cloud, staring out the window. He stayed that way as we worked our way out of London.

Then he sat up abruptly, opened the portable bar, and poured himself a brandy. His hands shook so badly he dribbled most of it onto the carpet. I grabbed the decanter from him and filled his glass. He took it all down in one gulp, then fell back against the seat, a hint of color in his cheeks now.

"All dead," he said hoarsely. "All dead."

I poured a brandy for myself.

"I'm the only one left, Hogarth. I'm next. Don't you see? I go next."

"You're right. You do."

He glared at me. "That's bloody reassuring of you, mate," he snarled.

"We all go next, Tristam. We're all headed in the same direction. No getting around it. Just do me one favor."

"What's that, Hogarth?"

"Hang out for a little while longer – I'm not done with you yet."

He let out a short harsh laugh and held out his empty glass.

I filled it for him. We killed the brandy together. By the time we rolled into Gadpole we were singing the refrain of "More for Me" together. He sounded a lot better on the album. I sounded great.

CHAPTER
NINE

(Tape #7 with Tristam Scarr recorded in his chamber Dec. 7.)

Hoag: Tulip mentioned that something was bothering you when you lived in Los Angeles.

Scarr: What did she say about it?

Hoag: That you were restless, angry self-destructive. And that when she tried to get you to open up to her you –

Scarr: Beat the living shit out of her one night. Broke her nose and a couple of her front teeth. Next morning I didn't even remember it happening. That's how bombed I was getting, Hogarth. She kept getting real on me. Hassling me about Lord Harry. Hassling me about trashing m'life. All for m'own good, of course, but no one could tell me nothing then. She left me after that night. Went back to London. We got back together again when I got straight. She was eight months preggers at the time. Hadn't told me about that. A bit of a shock. We stayed together for another year or so, until it was over for good . . . To answer your question, a lot was bothering me in L.A. I was thirty years old and I was still acting sixteen. The whole T. S. bit was stale. I was tired of the music, the image, the road, Rory. I wanted to grow up. But I didn't know *how.*

Hoag: Who does? We're all faking it.

Scarr: I realize that now, but I didn't then. I just knew I didn't want to be T. S. anymore, and didn't know who I wanted to be instead. So I got angry. I got high. I copped out – blamed the fans for locking me into that image. Blamed the record company. Blamed Rory. Blamed everybody but m'self.

Hoag: You were still on top, weren't you?

Scarr: Yes, but our time was passing. The sixties were over. New bands with new sounds were coming along – Electric Light Orchestra, Genesis, Yes, Bowie, Roxy Music. We weren't on the cutting edge anymore. None of us were, really. Christ, McCartney was scoring a bleedin' James Bond movie. I thought Rory was holding me back. Rory thought I was holding him back. We stopped communicating. Started saying things about each other in the papers we didn't mean. And sometimes didn't even say, actually – you know how they are. He called me a manipulative swine. I called him a cockney lout. We were hurting inside, both of us. But we couldn't deal with it maturely, like brothers. So we split up. He went off to Italy. Did his solo album, *Bad Boy*.

Hoag: How did you feel when it became a hit?

Scarr: I was happy for him. Don't you see, Hogarth? There was no rivalry between us. The press made out that there was, so they could sell their papers. But there wasn't. Each of us needed to grow a bit. To do that, we needed to be apart. I needed to be *me*. The problem was that *me* was shards of broken glass.

Hoag: How much did the drugs have to do with that?

Scarr: (*pause*) I did a lot of 'em, and had a lot of good times doing 'em. Acid opened up my mind. I've no regrets about taking it, or smoking what I smoked. Coke and Lord Harry are another matter. They can take you over, especially if your life happens to be fucked up at that particular time. I got plain strung out on Lord Harry in L.A. And then it became the problem.

Hoag: Tulip said you were running with a pretty wild set of mates – Keith Moon, Dennis Wilson . . .

Scarr: Dennis who?

Hoag: Dennis Wilson of the Beach Boys.

Scarr: (*pause*) Oh, him. Yes, I recall him now. But we were never mates. She is . . . was mistaken about that. Just a bloke I got bombed with a few times. I was bombed all of the time, you see. I didn't want to be conscious. Things looked too much like shit when I was. So I basically tried to obliterate m'self on Lord Harry and women who'd let me do astonishingly cruel things to them. There were a number of them after Tulip left me, mostly would-be actresses who looked magnificent in bikinis, and out of them as well. I used them. They used me. Got their pictures in the paper when I was getting thrown out of Gazzarri's or Ciro's for being an abusive swine. Moon lived down the beach from me. Lennon was around for a bit as well. I believe Yoko had thrown him out. We three used to go out and raise decadent, drugged-out hell together.

Hoag: Were you doing anything musically – growing as you wanted to?

Scarr: I did a few country blues things in the studio with Phil Spector that I rather liked. Ry Cooder played guitar. I played m'harp. Whoever was around sat in – Bonnie Raitt, Stevie Stills, Lennon, Moon. Like a party, it was. But I had to be put in the hospital before

I could get an album together, which I regretted. Only the one single, "Lucy Goosey," ever got released.

Hoag: Why were you hospitalized?

Scarr: Ulcers, the bleedin' sort. M'body was telling me to slow down, or I'd crash. Derek and Jack came out and took charge of me. Got me out of L.A. to the desert somewhere. Rented me a house with a pool and a full-time doctor. Saved m'life.

Hoag: You kicked?

Scarr: I did. Started eating proper. Swimming twice a day. Took nothing stronger than a glass of wine. And they got me talking to Rory again on the telephone. He'd cleaned up his own act as well. Was a sort of bleedin' jet-setter now – summers on the Riviera, winters skiing in Gstaad. Even had a live-in steady, a teenage Italian actress named Monica, who didn't shave under her arms . . . Christ, it was fantastic talking to Rory again. He was my *brother*, y'know? I think that was one of my biggest problems in L.A., my being away from Rory. We rang each other every night. Talked and talked about what had been going on between us. And when I was fit enough, I went and stayed with him at his place on the Riviera. We both broke down and cried like babies when I got out of the taxi . . . We wanted to play together again. We were ready. But only if it could be like it used to be, before the star-tripping and the bullshit.

Hoag: This is how the Johnny Thunder thing came about.

Scarr: That's right. It started as a sort of goof, y'know? The idea of being sixteen again, going back to the Sun Records rockabilly sound of Elvis and Buddy Holly. Playing old equipment – a hollow-body Rickenbacker, a stand-up bass. Our musical roots, really. The more we talked about it, the more we kept saying why not? So we got together with Derek and the drummer we'd been using, Corky Carroll, and found a fantastic sax player, Johnny Almond. We five formed Johnny Thunder and the Lightnings. We did everything as if it was still '57. We dressed in plaid jackets, bow ties, and drainies. Greased back our hair. Jack found us a vintage motor coach and we toured the provinces in it, playing only small clubs, drinking scotch and Coke, s moking Woodies. No drugs. No Us songs. We pretended Us didn't even exist. Some people dismissed it all as a bleedin' stunt, but it was a gas for us. We even recorded the album live in the studio. *(laughs)* Never occurred to us it would be a smash.

Hoag: Its success set off the fifties nostalgia craze. You were also credited with making a statement – that rock music is theater.

Scarr: The most important thing it did was help us deal with the madness of the past few years. Rory and I began to turn those feelings into songs as we rode in the motor coach, like we had in the early days. That's where we wrote *New Age*.

Hoag: "Now is the time to turn the page/To stop looking back/To put away the rage/No more lonely nights/We're living in the new age." Were you?

Scarr: In a manner of speaking, yes. Tulip and I were back together, and happy. Musically, Rory and I were excited again. Excited by the new dance music sounds, like reggae and disco. Excited by the new technology in the studio. We couldn't wait to get in there. In many ways, *New Age* was our most satisfying album. It was an *up* album. We were up. Didn't last long, of course.

Hoag: What happened with Tulip?

Scarr: Violet happened. Tu just got incredibly protective after she had her. Wanted an entirely different life from the one we were leading, away from musicians and dirtiness. She put it to me just as the band was getting ready to tour America in support of *New Age*: Give it up, she said. Give it up or lose us. It wasn't a choice I wished to make, but she left me no alternative. She wouldn't budge. I-I simply couldn't give up the music. It was my life. So I lost her. Lost them. Greatest sacrifice I ever had to make for my music, but I made it. Never did live with anyone again. Couldn't. Tu got stranger and stranger after that. Discovered Himself. Got involved with that Reverend Bob and his pathetic little church.

Hoag: He used to deal drugs, the police found out.

Scarr: You don't say. Do they suspect him of killing her?

Hoag: I don't believe so.

Scarr: Have you heard anything from that Root person?

Hoag: No. It's my move now.

Scarr: Have you chosen it yet?

Hoag: I think so.

Scarr: *(pause)* I keep wondering if she suffered.

Hoag: It wasn't a pretty way to die, but I don't suppose there is one. I understand Jack buried her urn in the center of the maze.

Scarr: Yes. Violet planted tulip bulbs as a marker.

Hoag: That's nice . . . Let's talk about that last tour. I got a chance to watch the Kubrick movie.

Scarr: I never have, m'self. For obvious reasons.

Hoag: How did that come about?

Scarr: He approached us. Why not, we said – the more the merrier. Christ, it was already a monster production. Our own bleedin' plane. Truckloads of sound and lighting equipment. Wasn't long before we were all saying how sorry we were we'd given up on Johnny Thunder. Especially after Rory slipped.

Hoag: Slipped?

Scarr: He'd asked his Italian actress, Monica, to come with him. Instead of which she dumped him for Roman Polanski, who immediately put her in some movie he was making. Rory never did understand that people use each other, that people using each other is the entire basis of most human relationships.

Hoag: Including you and Tulip?

Scarr: I said *most*, mate. Rory didn't take it well. Got back into a bad-ass-rocker-on-the-road thing. Did coke and teenage girls by the ton. Snorted and performed. Snorted and fucked. Snorted and crashed. Snorted and started all over again. Never ate. I didn't know how he could do it. It would have broken me. And it broke him, actually. He collapsed backstage after the Denver show and had to be put in hospital. We put out a statement saying the thin air had gotten to him.

Hoag: What were you doing while Rory was being a bad-ass rocker?

Scarr: (laughs) The truth? I wasn't a lad anymore. If I didn't follow a strict physical regimen I couldn't keep my wind up while I boogied around on those football arena stages. I had to jog two miles every morning. Get my rest. And as for the girls, I wasn't that interested in 'em anymore. They bored me. Had no minds of their own. No style. They were just shapely, empty receptacles, waiting to be filled. The fact is, Tulip had spoiled me for other women. She knew what she wanted. She had taste. Ideas. There'll never be another like her.

Hoag: Can we talk about the night Rory died?

Scarr: (pause) We were wrapping up "We're Double Trouble," our encore number, just as we had been every night on the tour. I noticed this flash down in front, but when I saw Rory fall, with blood coming from his nose, I thought it was the coke – he's bleeding from all of the snorting, I thought. Collapsing again, like in Denver. I was the last to know, you see. It wasn't until I saw that bugger waving the gun and heard Derek screaming that I got it. And then . . . then all I kept thinking was it's happening like with Puppy all over again. Only it *mustn't*. We mustn't lose Rory. "Why can't someone help him?" I kept wondering. "Why can't anyone help him?"

Hoag: You dropped your scouse accent up there.

Scarr: So I've been told. I have no recollection of that. I must have been in shock. When it finally hit me, when it sunk in that Rory was dead, I kept thinking – this will sound dreadful – I kept thinking it was a blessing. Rory died playing his guitar on a stage. He died the way he was meant to die. He was never meant to grow old, to become an aging wreck like I am. In so many ways he's better off . . .

Hoag: There are certain people, like Jim Morrison, whom you can't picture with gray hair. Rory is definitely one of them.

Scarr: Yes. Because he was the spirit of rock 'n' roll. Forever young. More wine, Hogarth?

Hoag: No thanks. I'm driving into town tonight.

Scarr: Business or pleasure?

Hoag: Neither.

Scarr: Ah, you've heard from Merilee then.

Hoag: Not exactly.

Scarr: *(pause)* Don't do anything you'll be sorry for, mate.

Hoag: Sound advice. You'll forgive me if I don't take it.

Scarr: Mates always forgive. If it works out between the two of you, I'd very much like to meet her. Bring her to the party, why don't you?

Hoag: Party?

Scarr: I'm giving a blowout a week from Saturday.

Hoag: Well, well. What's the occasion, Christmas?

Scarr: Who needs an occasion to say hello to a few hundred old mates?

(end tape)

CHAPTER
TEN

ack was in his office cleaning his Browning when I went out to fetch the Peugeot, his meaty bricklayer's hands caressing the shotgun lovingly. A half-empty mug of stout sat next to his elbow on the desk. I watched him there from the garage for a second before he noticed me and nodded. I nodded back, and decided it was time to drop my hook in the water.

"Vi have other plans tonight?" I asked him casually from the office doorway.

Jack tried very hard to not register a reaction. He almost succeeded. "Miss Violet? I wouldn't know, sir." He kept rubbing his gun.

"Wouldn't you?"

"What are you suggesting?"

"You two are close, aren't you?" I patted myself on the flank. "Very close . . . ?"

I wanted a reaction. I got a reaction. First Jack put the shotgun down, which was nice. Then he got up, whirled, and cuffed me across the face with the back of his hand. My cheek went instantly numb. With his other hand, he grabbed me by the throat and slammed me against the wall and held me there, his purple face close to mine. His breath hadn't improved.

"Don't stick your nose in other people's business."

"Sticking my nose in other people's business *is* my business," I got out, hoarsely

"Maybe you ought to change your business."

"Can't. Too old."

"You won't get much older if you don't back off. Got it?"

"I believe so. Yes."

He let me go. It wasn't until I felt the jolt of my heels that I realized he'd been holding me an inch or two off of the ground. He sat back down and finished his beer in one gulp. I stood there rubbing my neck. It felt like it had been squeezed in a bench vise. My cheek was burning where he'd hit me.

"Kind of touchy, aren't you, Jack?" I suggested gently.

He squinted up at me, like he'd gotten soap in his eyes. Then he dropped his head in his burly arms and began to weep. "She's m-making me *crazy*, Mr. Hoag," he sobbed. "Never in my life have I felt this way about any woman. I-I can't sleep. Can't eat. She's in my mind constantly. The smell of her is in my nostrils. She's so alive, so fresh . . . Christ, I-I'm going to *explode*!"

I took a seat and waited him out. When he was done crying, he wiped his eyes with the back of his hand and blew his nose into the gun rag he'd been using. It left an oily smear across his cheek. Then he held his hand out to me. I wish I could say I didn't flinch.

"I want to apologize for going after you, Mr. Hoag. Lost my head for a second. Sorry."

We shook. I said, "So what's the problem – is she going out on you?"

"She's *playing* with me. She won't get serious. I keep asking her to – "

"She's very young, Jack."

"Got a problem with that?" His voice was nasty again.

"Absolutely not. I'm in no way judging you – I just mean she may not be ready to get serious."

"I see." He nodded. "What should I do?"

"Who am I, Dr. Ruth?"

"Who is Dr. Ruth?"

"Give her time, Jack."

"I can't. This is it for me, Mr. Hoag. She's the one. We could have a life together here, she and I. A good life."

"Give her time," I repeated.

He lowered his eyes. "Did she . . . has she made a play for you?"

I cleared my throat. "A play for me?"

"She said she was in your room one night."

"Oh, that. Just acting frisky, I suppose. Besides, I'm involved with someone else. Somewhat. You don't have to worry about me, Jack."

"God bless you for that, Mr. Hoag."

"God has very little to do with it."

I patted him on the shoulder and left him there with his shotgun and his pain. He had about as much chance of settling down with Lady Vi as I had of being named chairman of the Federal Reserve. I think he knew it, too. But it didn't change how he felt. She was the one. That was all he knew.

Maybe I knew a little about what that was like.

The lights were on in the mews house. There was movement

behind the shades. Zack was there. It had to be Zack. She would be at the theater now, onstage.

I sat there in the Peugeot, watching the shadow on the shades and thinking about Jackie Horner. Thinking about how he was feeling. Thinking about how I was feeling. Rotten things, feelings. Much better off without them.

Zack left a little before eleven. He's tall and lanky like I am, except he carries his shoulders stiffly, as if he's still wearing the hanger in his coat. The coat was a loden cloth. There was an Irish tweed hat on his head. He made sure the door was firmly shut before he headed out, hands buried deep in his pockets. He walked unsteadily. He was potted.

It would be easy, really. Just start up the Peugeot. Put her in gear. Pick up some speed. Run the pretentious asshole over. No one would ever know. It would be easy.

But no, that wasn't the crime I'd come here to commit.

I waited until he'd turned the corner before I got out and headed for her front door, fingering my key. I could hear a faint whooping noise from inside as I put the key in the lock. The whooping got downright loud when I made it inside and shut the door behind me. It was Lulu – tail thumping, ears flapping, she was hobbling toward me across the living room floor.

"Oh, I see," I said coolly. "So now you're happy to see me."

Not as happy as I was to see her. I picked her up and held her. She whooped some more and licked my nose and tried to crawl inside my trench coat. I stroked her and said some soothing, intimate things I won't bother to repeat here. Then I tried to put her down, only she wouldn't let me. So we investigated together.

This part wasn't so pleasant. His clothes were there in the bedroom. Brooks Brothers all the way. His toiletries were there in the bathroom. Ice-Blue Aqua Velva. Whew – no wonder Lulu was happy to see me. There were dishes in the kitchen sink they'd eaten from, glasses they drunk from. I'd hoped all of it would tell me something, like how the two of them were getting along, and where I stood. Maybe a real detective could read all of that from the evidence. I sure couldn't. I put Lulu down in her bed. She started to protest until I picked her and the bed up together and started for the front door. I opened it to find myself face to face with a real detective.

"Good evening, Hoagy," Farley Root said. He wore a belted black nylon raincoat and a scuffed black leather cap, and was jiggling one bony knee nervously.

"Good evening. Inspector," I said. "Merilee isn't here. She's at the theater."

"It's you I wished to speak with, if I may. And I'm not actually an – "

"No problem," I said, ushering him inside. "Just in the process of doing a little friendly dognapping. But how did you know I'd – ?"

"I followed you here."

"All the way from Gadpole?"

"No, we've a team system. I picked you up not far from here."

I'd had no idea I was being followed. That tabloid reporter must have been clumsy. Clearly, Root and his men were not.

I put Lulu and her bed back down before the fireplace. She snuffled at me, confused by this change of plans. "Why follow me?" I asked Root.

"I like to know where everyone is. A fetish of mine. Hope you don't mind."

"As fetishes go it's not too terrible," I assured him. "Have a seat."

He took off his hat and coat and lunged for the love seat. He wore a plaid jacket and checked slacks. It was not an improvement over the green suit. "What happened to your cheek?" he asked.

"What, this old thing?" I fingered it gently. It had gotten red and tender. "It's nothing – just ran into a big hand. Whiskey?"

"Love one. Bit chilly out."

I poured two Laphroaigs and handed him one. He gripped the glass so tightly I thought he'd break it. I sat in the chair opposite him.

"Wondered if you'd ever received that inventory report," he said, swallowing the scotch over his giant Adam's apple.

"I did."

"And . . . ?"

I sipped the Laphroaig. No, it *was* too smoky for me. "And thank you."

He frowned, ran his gopher teeth over his lower lip. "You did say we would share information."

"I know."

He waited for me to offer him some. When I didn't, he narrowed his eyes at me coolly. "For your information, we've turned something up in regards to the Savile Row business. A lead slug. Twenty-gauge. A bus mechanic found it rattling about in the fuel filter of a bus he was servicing. There's a hole in the body of the bus where it entered. We checked its route sheets. It would have been in the approximate vicinity of Savile Row on that date and that approximate time. We can't be absolutely certain that it's from the attack upon you but . . ."

"We can assume it is."

"Yes."

I tugged at my ear. "Slugs, if I remember correctly, are used primarily in hunting preserves."

"That's right. As a safety precaution against accidents. A rifle bullet may carry as far as a mile across open ground, presenting a danger to hunters and game alike. Lead slugs have a far shorter range – two hundred yards perhaps. Fired from a shotgun."

"Any idea what kind fired this one?"

"Not possible. Slug's too chewed up."

"Too bad."

Still, I knew something now. I knew that Derek, a confirmed black powder man, hadn't shot me. That didn't necessarily mean he hadn't killed Puppy or Tulip. But he hadn't fired those shots on Savile Row.

Root drained his scotch. "My lord, this is excellent whiskey."

"You don't find it too smoky?"

"Not at all."

"Like some more?"

"Yes, but I'd best not. Work to be done."

That was his cue to get up and leave, but he just lingered there on the loveseat, watching me and sucking on his teeth, which didn't make a pretty sound.

"Okay," I finally said. "I do have something for you."

"Ah, good," he said, pleased. He took out his notepad and pen.

I suggested he check something out, something that couldn't be checked out without the kind of authorization he had and I didn't: the Church of Life.

"What about it?" Root inquired, making a careful note.

"Who bankrolls it – pays the rent, the upkeep, Father Bob's salary."

"What will that tell us?"

"Possibly nothing," I conceded. "Possibly a lot."

Possibly a whole lot, if what I was thinking turned out to be true.

"Very well," said Root. "I'll keep you informed." He put away his notebook and pen, got to his feet, and put on his coat, glancing over at Lulu, who was watching him from her bed. "You were having me on before about the dognapping, weren't you, Hoagy?"

"No, I wasn't, Inspector."

He started to say something, stopped. Started again. Stopped again. Then he went out into the damp night.

It may not be easy to compete with an ex-wife who happens to be perfect, but I did my best: when we returned to Gadpole, I took Lulu directly to the kitchen, where Pamela clucked over her and then cooked her up a spectacular platter of kippers and eggs. After she'd wolfed that down I carried her up to our rooms and positioned her before the fire on her leather chair. From there she gazed dreamily at the flames for about thirty seconds before her eyes drooped shut, her tail thumped once, and she was out.

I took a bubble bath myself. A light rain was tapping against the window now. After I toweled off I moved Lulu to the bed and got in with Irwin Shaw. She hobbled around me, then ensconced herself in her favorite position with a soft grunt of satisfaction.

The bedside phone rang the second I opened my book.

Merilee didn't say hello. "I assume you have her," was all she said, with a distinct lack of warmth.

"I do. And she's fine."

"This is a disgrace, Hoagy. An absolute disgrace. How could you?"

"I needed her, Merilee."

"You could have phoned. We could have worked something out. You didn't have to sneak in here like a thieving son of a sea cook."

"I really have missed your quaint little expressions."

"Explain yourself."

"I didn't want to be a bother."

"Try again. Martyrdom is not your style."

"You're right. Okay. I didn't ask you because I knew you'd say no and I'd give in to you, because I love you. Okay?"

She sorted her way through that one quietly for a moment. "Well . . . I suppose there's a kernel of honesty in there somewhere. Which is more than I can say for someone else I know. Or should I say used to know"

"Meaning?"

"The marriage is quite dead. We drove the stake through it over dinner."

My heart rate definitely picked up. "What happened?"

She sighed. "Nothing happened. I'm simply fed up with him blaming me for his problems, and with me blaming me. Not that I'm totally blameless, but at least I work at it. I try. He won't. He'd much rather look for excuses and villains. He can look elsewhere from now on. He's flying back to New York tomorrow. He's agreed to move out of the apartment immediately."

"Where is he now?"

"He checked into a hotel for tonight."

"Not Blakes, I hope."

"It hurts, darling. Something awful."

"I won't be a total hypocrite and say I'm sorry it didn't work out for you two. But I am sorry you're suffering."

"I came home from dinner in tears. All I wanted to do was hold my poor wounded sweetness."

"I needed her too. Sorry. Bad timing."

"When can I have her back?"

"Depends on the terms."

She was silent a moment. "I'm considering a package deal."

"Well, well. I guess this means I'm going to have to buy you a Christmas present."

"It most certainly does. Hoagy, darling?"

"Yes, Merilee?"

"Can we . . . can we make it work this time?"

"Of course we can. We're gifted, remember? We can do anything."

I hung up and settled back in the pillows with a contented sigh. Then I patted Lulu and reached for my book. Before I could open it I heard a rustling out in the hallway.

Lady Vi was going out early for her spanking.

When I heard her door shut I followed her to the top of the stairs and listened after her, just to make sure she wasn't scampering down to the kitchen for some warm milk and coming right back up. Silence. She'd gone outside by way of the pantry door. Good. Now was my chance.

I'd learned that she kept the door to the blue room locked when she wasn't in it. I'd also learned that Pamela kept copies of all of the room keys in a drawer in the kitchen. I had liberated the blue room key while Pamela was busy fixing Lulu's kippers. It was a big old-fashioned skeleton key. The lock was the kind you peep through. I let myself in.

The blue room wasn't exactly your typical room. For one thing, it wasn't blue – Violet bad covered the walls and ceiling with roll upon roll of aluminum foil. A nice decor statement if you want to feel like a Perdue oven stuffer-roaster. For another thing, there was very little in the way of furniture. A mattress placed directly on the floor minus box spring and frame. A dancer's bar bolted to one wall. A dressing table with a three-way mirror on it. There was nothing else. I headed for the dressing table.

She kept her loot in the bottom drawer. Here I found various wallets she'd stolen – one belonged to some Lord who owned a record company, another to the lawyer, Jay Weintraub, complete with credit cards and photos of his racehorses and two ugly kids. Violet had a thing for gold. Gold cigarette lighters, rings, bracelets, and coke spoons were heaped in the drawer. There was also a particularly lovely eighteen-carat gold Waterman fountain pen that I considered pocketing and returning to its rightful owner – me. But I thought better of it. I didn't want her to know I'd been in here.

Underneath all of this, I found what I was looking for – snapshots. Tulip's snapshots. The ones Violet had made off with that time Tulip caught her messing around in her photo album.

The odds were not great that the photo that Tulip's killer had come for hadn't been in the album, that it had been right here. It was a long shot. But those are the ones to play – that's where the big payoffs are.

There was a snapshot of Tris and Rory sitting at a nightclub table with Brian Jones and Keith Richard – drinking, smoking, all of them looking incredibly young and arrogant. On the back Tulip had scrawled "Ad Lib Club, Oct. '65." There was one marked "Bournemouth, Aug. '66." Tris and Rory were on the beach, shirtless, comically flexing their puny biceps at the camera. Another, dated July '67, was of Tris, Rory and Derek feeding the bears in Copenhagen's Tivoli Gardens. And then there was another that . . .

There was another that was *it* – the photo I'd been looking for. The photo Tulip's killer had been looking for. The one that pulled it all together. Yes, it all fit now. Horrifyingly. So horrifyingly that I almost couldn't believe what I was looking at. But there it was, plain as can be. The truth.

The trick was going to be proving it.

C H A P T E R
E L E V E N

I 'll give T. S. this – when he went social there was nothing small or shabby about it.

Delivery vans came and went for days before his party, crammed with cases of liquor, produce, meats, cheeses – enough to stock the QE2. Pamela directed the traffic, signed the slips, barked out orders, bartered. The last thing to arrive was a two-story-high spruce Christmas tree that rolled up to the front door on its own truck bed. It took a half dozen workmen to get it inside the mammoth grand ballroom and hoist it up. Tris's bodyguards were the ones who decorated it, twisting around on top of extension ladders as freely as their balance and their shoulder holsters allowed.

Everyone came. Bingo was there with his wife Barbara Bach. So were the McCartneys, Paul and Linda. Paul had gotten so cherubic he'd have made a fine Santa Claus. George Harrison, meanwhile, was starting to resemble Christopher Lee, the cadaverous British horror movie star. Keith Richard came with Patti Hansen, speaking of horror movies. Roger Daltrey came with short hair. Rod Stewart and Kelly Emberg were there. So were Steve and Eugenia Winwood, John McEnroe and Tatum O'Neal, Eric Clapton, Jimmy Page, Ron Wood, Stevie Nicks, David Bowie, Michael Caine, Joan Collins, Pelé. Mick Jagger and Jerry Hall were not there. Andy and Fergie were. The press were kept out.

It was all quite civilized. The women wore shimmering gowns, the men raffish dinner clothes. The rough boys and girls had grown up. At least they had on the surface. Greeting them at the door were their host and hostess, T. S. and Violet. Tris was unusually charming and animated. He'd obviously had some chemical help. Vi was in a flirty, mischievous mood, which didn't bode well for Jack's evening. Neither did her outfit. She had on a black leather miniskirt, black boots, and a black leather vest. The vest was unbuttoned, and there was not a thing under it, unless you count the snake tattoo decal on her stomach. T. S., in contrast, was all in white – white suit, white shirt, white tie, white shoes.

I stuck with my basic tux. I never mess with a good thing.

"You don't do this sort of thing badly," I told T. S., when there was a brief lull in the arrivals.

"Thank you, Hogarth," he replied brightly. "Feels good to party again. Too much quiet is bad for a rocker's soul."

"You were right – all you had to do was pick up the phone."

He grinned at me, his eyes beady. Speed? Very likely. "Indeed," he said, "Indeed."

A stage had been set up in the colossal ballroom next to the big tree. On it a piano, organ, guitars and drums waited to he played. On long tables there were hams, turkeys, roasts, salads, puddings waiting to be devoured. I noticed a small shadow under the table where the bowl of jumbo shrimp was. Lulu was guarding it. Anytime someone approached it she would growl softly at them from under the table. The guest would frown, look around warily and then move on. No one had dared to touch the shrimp yet.

Jack was behind the bar in a red vest and green-and-red bow tie, dispensing punch and champagne, and keeping a protective eye on his feral young lady love.

Derek Gregg arrived with his companion, Jeffrey, both of them in maroon velvet dinner jackets. Jeffrey headed off to get them punch, leaving the former Us bassist alone with me for a moment.

"Quite a little coming-out party," Derek observed drily. "And such a cozy room."

"Something of a departure for him, it would seem."

"That's your influence," Derek said.

"My influence?"

"Yes. You've helped pull Mr. Cigar out of his shell. He's no longer afraid to show himself to people. You really ought to think about psychiatry, Mr. Hoag. As a career, I mean. You do amazing work." Derek shot a glance across the room. "Oh, dear, my Jeffrey's getting jealous. Will you excuse me?"

Marco Bartucci, the human teapot, came with two Middle Eastern gentlemen in dark blue suits, neither of whom he bothered to introduce me to. "Surprised to see me here, Mr. Hoag?" he asked, shaking my hand wetly.

"A little."

"It's as I told you – we are all mates now. Life goes on."

"For some of us."

Marco mopped his forehead with a handkerchief. "Yes. The lucky ones."

"Meaning the ones who don't get caught?"

He narrowed his eyes at me. "I'm afraid I still don't much care for you, Mr. Hoag."

"Give me time. I'm an acquired taste, like raw oysters."

"Raw oysters make me quite ill. Slimy things."

"Funny, I should think you'd take right to them."

He bristled and stormed off. I really was going to have to work harder on my party chatter.

The guests provided the entertainment. Nothing formal. Just impromptu sessions among friends. Winwood, Clapton, Derek Gregg and Ringo fooled around up there for a while with "Louie, Louie," capping it off with an inspired rendition of Winwood's old Spencer Davis hit, "Gimme Some Lovin'." McCartney straggled up there after Derek relinquished the bass. Then George Harrison was up there, too, chopping off some guitar chords. I peered closely at the stage and counted heads twice. No mistake – the three surviving members of the Beatles were performing "Twist and Shout" in Tristam Scarr's ballroom.

I don't usually like big parties, but this one wasn't terrible.

Merilee drove out in a borrowed car with a friend. They got there late, since they'd both been on stage that night. Merilee wore a new strapless black dress and her pearls. Her hair was piled atop her head in a Victorian-style bun, accentuating the strong beauty of her neck and bare shoulders. The friend was done up head to toe just like a twenties flappers. She didn't look even a bit silly.

"Hoagy darling, this is my friend Diana," Merilee said. "She's doing that Sondheim musical, and it turns out we have the same leg waxer and hate the same people."

Diana's hand was strong and cold, her smile radiant. I smiled back and said absolutely nothing, which I'd learned was the best way to avoid making a fool of myself whenever Merilee introduced me to an actress I'd had an adolescent crush on. It was hard to believe it had been more than twenty years since Diana Rigg played Emma Peel on *The Avengers*. She looked the same. I lie. She looked better.

I got them champagne from Jack, who was so distracted he didn't even notice me – Vi was on the dance floor hanging all over Steve Stevens, Billy Idol's guitarist. Poor Jack. I turned away, ran smack into Chris Reeve. Poor me. I had to listen, at length, to how he'd been puzzling over Superman's motivation in a scene they'd filmed that day.

"Superman has no motivation," I finally broke in. "He's a comic book character."

He weighed this a second. Then he thanked me profusely and charged off, nodding excitedly to himself.

Maybe I *was* getting better at party chatter.

"Show me the maze, darling," Merilee begged me when I returned.

Diana had wandered off. I found something useful to do with her champagne. "Don't you want to meet T. S. first?"

"Later."

"We'll get lost," I warned.

"We'll take Lulu – the vet said she should be exercising."

"Don't be mean."

"Who's being mean?"

I found Merilee's mink and my trench, and dragged Lulu away from the shrimp bowl, limping and protesting mightily. It was cold and crisp outside. Lulu trailed way behind us as we crossed the lawn, grousing vocally I had to urge her on with promises of unlimited shrimp, crab legs, lobster bisque. Floodlights ringed the maze entrance. I pulled up there.

"You're sure you want to go through with this?"

"Absolutely," Merilee replied.

We headed in, her hand on my arm, Lulu limping along behind. After two turns we'd all been swallowed up by it.

"Have you bought my present yet, darling?"

"Yes, I have."

"Goody. Can I have it tonight?"

"It's not Christmas yet."

I thought I heard a rustling sound in the hedge next to us.

"But this is a Christmas party," she argued. "Kind of"

It *was* a rustling sound. We were not alone. Someone was in the maze with us. Lulu heard it, too. She growled softly, moved up closer behind us. Merilee seemed not to have noticed. I took her hand, in case we needed to make a dash for it.

"Then tell me what you got me," she pressed.

"No."

"Please?"

"Merilee, I've never known anyone as kidlike about Christmas as you are." I glanced over at her. "You get anything for me yet?"

"We adults don't discuss such things," she replied, sticking her tongue out at me.

I heard it again. Louder. Next to us. This time Lulu charged, teeth bared, growling ferociously. It was a bunny wabbit. She chased it down the gravel path, limping not one bit, until it disappeared under the hedge. She barked a couple of times for good measure, then strutted back toward us, immensely pleased with herself. As soon as she got within ten feet of us she put the limp back on.

"Why, that little faker," marveled Merilee.

"I think she's been around the theater world too much," I observed.

"This is nice in here, isn't it? Let's buy a country place when we get back and plant one just like it."

"Consider it planted."

We continued strolling. As far as I was concerned we were seriously lost now

"Are we playing, darling? At getting back together, I mean."

"I'm not playing, Merilee."

She looked over at me and sighed. "You'll have to wear black all of the time."

"I'll even wear black pajamas to bed at night."

"You will not."

She stopped and grabbed me. We kissed. Then she said "Have you ever kissed anyone in a maze before?"

"I've never done anything in a maze before."

"A night for firsts."

I kissed her again. "And seconds."

We got a little cold waiting for one of the guards to come fetch us after I fired the flare gun from the strongbox, but we found plenty to keep ourselves occupied.

We went back in the house by way of the kitchen, so Merilee could meet Pamela. Amazingly, Pamela seemed unperturbed by the army of chefs, carvers and dishwashers running around her in high gear. The phone call I'd been waiting for came while the three of us stood there chatting. Pamela and Merilee continued to converse gaily as I stretched the phone chord into the pantry and swung the door shut behind me.

"Evening, Hoagy," Root said. "Sorry to disturb you in the midst of your seasonal celebrating."

There was a hint of excitement in his voice. "Quite all right, Inspector," I assured him.

"Actually, I'm – "

"What's up?"

"It's about that matter you suggested I look into. I've been able to learn the chief source of funding for the Church of Life. Traced it through the bank deposits. I take my hat off to you, sir. Some kind of hunch you had."

"So who is it?"

"Came to the church to talk to the reverend about it personally. I'm still here. He's dead, you see. Murdered. Another boning knife. This morning, by the looks of him. There wasn't much here of value, but what there was is gone. Same story as Tulip's. Place is quite thoroughly – "

"Who the hell is it?" I broke in. "Who financed him?"

Root told me. Before he could ask me what it all added up to I quickly thanked him and hung up. Then I returned to the ballroom.

Violet was all over Jimmy Page now on the dance floor. This was not going unnoticed by Jack over by the punch bowl. I cut in. Delighted, she entwined her arms around my neck and we began to make our way around the dance floor, she gleefully rubbing her pelvis and her unencumbered breasts against me.

"You're sort of nice to dance with, y'know?" she said. "Our parts fit together just *so*."

"You're not so bad yourself."

For this I got her playful pink tongue in one of my ears, followed by an urgently whispered catalog of the various things she really felt like doing to me.

Jack wasn't missing any of this either.

"I think you're making Jack jealous," I said. She glanced over at him, then treated me to her tongue again. Other ear. "That all I'm doing?"

"You don't give up easily. I like that in a woman."

"Is that her?" she asked, indicating Merilee, who was deep in conversation across the room with Michael and Shakira Caine – and, fortunately, missing this.

"Yes, it is."

"She's very pretty"

"So are you."

"You really think so?" she asked, pleased.

"However, you're also a bad girl. You told Jack you slept with me that night you came to my room, didn't you?"

"No," she replied.

"Didn't you?" I repeated.

She pouted. "He jumped to conclusions."

"And you didn't bother to correct him."

"Why should I? He's the one who's crazy possessive. I mean, he's just crazy." She tossed her head petulantly. "So what if I let him think it? It's for his own bloody good. I mean, he's got to learn how to let up on a girl a little, y'know?"

"May I give you a little advice? It won't hurt a bit."

She shrugged. "Sure."

"Blow him off. Find yourself another playmate."

"Why should I?"

"I happen to know he's not very good at games.

I left her standing there on the dance floor with a confused pout, and went for some punch. Jack ladled it out for me, his eyes avoiding mine. His hands shook with jealous rage. I took the glass from him and stood there next to him, sipping from it.

"It was you who took those shots at me, wasn't it, Jack?"

His eyes stayed on the crowd. He said nothing.

"Don't bother to deny it," I said. "I know you did it."

He looked at me now. "How do you know?"

"Because I know what really happened now. I know who did the killings, and why, and that it wasn't you."

"H-How do you – ?"

"Do me a favor, Jack?"

"Sir?"

"I'm going upstairs for a moment. Then out to the service garage."

"The garage?"

"Yes. I want you to tell someone that I've gone out there. I want you to tell that person I'm taking all of the notes and tapes I've made for Mr. Scarr's book to Inspector Root in London right away. That I think I've come upon something vital to do with the murders. I'll be taking the Peugeot, by the way."

"But why are you telling – ?"

"Then I want you to phone Root at the Church of Life and tell him to get over here at once. I'll be in the garage, okay? Make sure you tell him that. Will you do this for me?"

"Yessir. Of course." Jack swallowed. "I'm . . . I'm truly sorry about what happened, Hoagy. I wasn't aiming at you, y'know."

"I know you weren't. If you had been you'd have hit me."

"She told me that you and her . . . that you two . . . I just wanted to scare you off. Get you out of here. That's all. I swear it. I followed you into London that day. Parked down the block from where you parked. Waited for you to come back. I-I've lost m'head. Plain lost it. I'm sorry. I'm so sorry."

I gave him a reassuring pat on the shoulder. "Not totally your fault. She sort of drove you to it. I won't hold it against you. But I should warn you that Lulu has been known to carry a grudge for years."

I drained my punch, which was a little too sweet, and handed Jack my empty glass. Then I told him who I wanted him to give my message to.

CHAPTER
TWELVE

(Tape #8 with Tristam Scarr recorded in front seat of Peugeot station wagon, parked in Gadpole service garage, Dec. 16.)

Scarr: (voice indistinct) Where are you off to, Hogarth? Party's just getting exciting. Pagey's got Vi's vest off. She really has got a magnificent pair of –

Hoag: Some business to take care of in town.

Scarr: (voice indistinct) Right now?

Hoag: Writers work twenty-four hours a day, Tristam. Even when we're asleep our worst nightmares are supplying us with fresh material.

Scarr: (voice indistinct) And here I've gone and opened a bottle of champers for us. What a waste.

Hoag: Would that be Dom Perignon?

Scarr: (voice indistinct) I'm afraid so.

Hoag: Well . . . maybe you ought to hop in. It *is* awfully cold out there.

Scarr: (laughs) Indeed. *(Sound of car door opening, slamming shut. Voice much clearer now)* Nothing quite like the bubbly, is there?

Hoag: Nope. *(silence)* Ahh . . . It's particularly good at killing the taste of that punch. Here you go . . .

Scarr: I'd better hold off for a bit, actually. I'm afraid I'll pass out on my guests if I have any more. You go ahead.

Hoag: Don't mind if I do.

Scarr: Funny. I don't believe I've ever been in this car before.

Hoag: It's quite slow. But it gets there.

Scarr: And where is it going?

Hoag: You covered your tracks well, my friend.

Scarr: My tracks?

Hoag: Of course, getting shot at did throw me off for a while. I made the mistake of thinking that it was part of the big picture. It wasn't. It was just Violet messing with Jack's head. Funny thing is it was also Violet who helped me figure it all out. Your little girl really fouled things up for you, Tristam. It was she who stole the one piece of evidence that could give you away – the photograph. Tulip didn't have it. It wasn't in her album. I have it now. And as soon as I get into

London, the police will have it. All of it. *(pause)* You know, it was Derek who had the keenest insight into you. He told me you are, at heart, an actor. I didn't realize just how gifted, how convincing an actor you are. Our entire collaboration has been one extended performance. All along, you've given me precisely what you thought I needed. I needed a bombshell, you gave me a bombshell – you told me someone had murdered Puppy. After I discussed it with the others I dismissed it as paranoid nonsense. But it wasn't that at all, was it? It was a shrewd ploy to push any suspicion off of yourself. Who would ever think *you* killed Puppy, especially if you were the one who brought the whole thing up in the first place? I needed intimate personal revelations, you gave me intimate personal revelations. Our breakthrough about your troubled childhood – a performance.

Scarr: You'd have quit that day if I hadn't given you that. You'd been shot at.

Hoag: Why didn't you just let me quit? You should have.

Scarr: I need a great book. You're the person who can give me one.

Hoag: Besides, you'd gotten away with all of this for so many years you figured you'd never get caught, didn't you? . . . *Rock of Ages* was the album that meant the most to *you*. It was the most you. And it was your first failure. You couldn't accept that. You couldn't accept that the critics hated it, that your fans hated it. Your swollen, drugged-out ego couldn't allow for that. So you blamed Puppy. It was *his* fault. It was because of *him* you couldn't tour-support it in America. That ate away at you. *Puppy* ate away at you. He got the attention, the acclaim, the stardom. Him, not you. Who the hell was he, anyway? Some black drummer. It drove you mad. "More for Me" – that's your personal anthem. More for me, me, me. That's been your anthem all along, hasn't it? *(silence)* Hasn't it?

Scarr: Go ahead and tell it.

Hoag: It was you who turned Puppy on to the supercharged speed at Rory's house that day. You couldn't risk buying it through Jack, so you got it from a scuzzy London drug dealer you knew, named Bob. Known lately as Father Bob. No one could find the pills at the time because you pocketed them. What did Puppy think, that you were taking some, too?

Scarr: Pup didn't care one way or the other. He'd have swallowed drain cleaner if he thought it would give him a rush.

Hoag: Things went along just great for you after that. With Puppy gone, you and Rory just got bigger and bigger. Became superstars.

Millionaires. Idols. But there was always that one nagging problem between you, wasn't there? *Tulip*. Rory kept taking her away from you. Your oldest and best mate kept taking your woman away from you. She told me that no woman could mean as much to you two as you did to each other. She was wrong. Sharing her made you *crazy*. That's what was tormenting you when you lived out in Los Angeles. That's why you shot smack. Why you drank so much. You loved her. She was the only woman you ever loved. You couldn't stand having to share her with him. Having to share *everything* with him. The stage. The spotlight. The money. It was always the *two* of you. Rory and T. S. Double Trouble. *Us*, instead of *me*. But you couldn't kill *him*. Not like Puppy. So you split up. Only that wasn't so hot either. His solo album did great. You couldn't even finish one. You needed him. That was really hard for you to swallow. It put you in the hospital. But you did swallow it. You reunited, complete with hugs and kisses. Toured as Johnny Thunder and the Lightnings – mates, like the old days. No hoopla. No drugs. You could hold your feelings in check. Besides, you and Tulip were together again. Things were going good between you. Until she had the baby, and made you choose between her and your career. Poor Tulip. No way she could win that one. And then you and Rory went on your big '76 tour, and it all started coming back to the surface again, didn't it? The hate. The resentment. Especially when his coking got so heavy you had to start canceling shows. You freaked. Called up an L.A. acquaintance of yours from back in '68, when you hung out for a while there with Dennis Wilson. You reacted a little strangely when I referred to him one day while we were working. You went out of your way to insist you and Wilson had never been friends, it seemed odd to me at the time. But you had a very good reason. Because Dennis Wilson of the Beach Boys had a houseguest off and on in '68, a struggling musician named Charles Manson. Manson and his family stayed with Wilson. One of those family members was Larry Lloyd Little. The two of you got to know each other at Wilson's in October of '68. That's the date on the back of the picture Tulip took of you and Larry having a merry chat together. That's the photo you were looking for.

    Scarr: You've got it back there with the other things, have you?
    Hoag: Of course.
    Scarr: May I? *(rustling sounds)* Oh, yes. That's it, all right. You didn't make a copy, did you?
    Hoag: No.

Scarr: You wouldn't be lying?

Hoag: You're not thinking clearly, Tristam. If I was going to lie I'd say I *did* make a copy so you wouldn't be able to kill me yet. You'd have to track it down first. *(pause)* You are going to kill me, aren't you?

Scarr: Yes, I am. And your point is well taken. Do go on with the story. I'm fascinated.

Hoag: When the Manson family came to trial, Larry Lloyd Little became a witness for the prosecution. He got out in a few years. He was out in '76, when you decided Rory had to die. You convinced him to do it for you, and in a most dramatic fashion. How did you manage that? Did you tell him Rory was some kind of force of evil?

Scarr: (laughs) Nothing quite so complicated, Hogarth. Larry was a pimp. I paid him five thousand dollars.

Hoag: Figuring the police would gun him down on the spot.

Scarr: If they hadn't, I would have. I had a gun with me on stage, in case I needed it.

Hoag: You made Rory into a rock 'n' roll martyr. Kept him forever young. That's how you justify to yourself what you did. The truth is that he was your oldest and best mate and you had him murdered. But you've twisted the truth to suit you. You've twisted everything to suit you. That's what this memoir is all about – putting your lies down on paper so as to make them into truth . . . You had the limelight all to yourself now Rory was gone. Why did you give it up? Retreat here? And why are you choosing to come back now?

Scarr: What I told you before was true – I'd had it with the T. S. persona. I wanted to grow. I couldn't as long as Rory was around for me to fall back on.

Hoag: When you end a friendship, you really end it, don't you?

Scarr: It was necessary. As were the past few years I've spent alone here. I've been able to study, learn new instruments, experiment with new sounds . . .

Hoag: Everything was going fine until the day Pamela gave you my message about going to see Tulip's photo album. And something clicked. You'd forgotten about the one thing that could actually link you to Rory's murder. You'd forgotten about that photograph. And so had she. She hadn't looked in the album for years. She told me she couldn't. And she obviously didn't remember about you and Larry knowing each other.

Scarr: Her brain was quite thoroughly scrambled.

Hoag: Yes. It was all a blur, she said. Of course, there was always the chance she would remember. Enter your pal Father Bob. You'd been paying him off to keep quiet ever since he sold you the speed that killed Puppy. You even made his dreams come true. You set him up as a resident neighborhood guru. Financed his church, paid him a salary – it beat killing him. And it came in real handy when Tulip started getting into God in a serious way. You steered her right to him, just in case she did remember about Larry and felt like confiding in somebody evangelical. It was easy for you to manipulate her behavior. All you had to do was condemn him and she'd make a beeline right for him. He kept an eye on her for you. It turned out not to be necessary. Tulip never did remember about you and Larry Lloyd Little. Not until you came to see her and demanded that picture. Then she knew. And you had to kill her. You made it look like a break-in to confuse the police.

Scarr: (silence) I never wanted to kill her. But I had to – she said she would tell the police about me. She loathed me, you see, because Violet had left her for me. She blamed me for ruining Violet. *(pause)* I had to kill her.

Hoag: You played dumb when I mentioned her photo album on the way to the funeral. You said you had no recollection of it – just another facet of your fine overall performance. Except for one little slip. When I said she had photos from all over the place, including *Los Angeles*, there was a flicker in your eyes. You were wondering if somehow I knew. I didn't. But for an instant, you wondered. And you let it show.

Scarr: My guard was down. I was mourning the mother of my child.

Hoag: Whom you'd killed. And you didn't stop there. Things were in danger of unraveling now. The police knew that Father Bob had been a drug dealer. He was a loose end. He could talk. With Tulip dead there was no reason to keep him alive, so you killed him, too, and made it look like another break-in. Neat and tidy. *(pause)* I'm curious about the others. Derek, Marco, Jack . . . have they ever known?

Scarr: No. Never.

Hoag: They weren't aware you knew Larry Lloyd Little?

Scarr: They weren't around when I was mates with Dennis. I was on holiday after our tour. Just me and Tulip.

Hoag: But Jack was so opposed to my looking into the past. Why?

Scarr: He has a good life here with me. He was afraid you'd upset the present order.

Hoag: He was right.

Scarr: Yes.

Hoag: I thought I understood you, Tristam. Clearly, I didn't. I don't. Help me understand you.

Scarr: What for? You aren't going to finish our book.

Hoag: Indulge me – for friendship's sake.

Scarr: I don't expect you *can* understand me. Not by applying your morality to me.

Hoag: It doesn't apply to you?

Scarr: T. S. is not everyone else.

Hoag: You honestly think you're above the rules that we, as semicivilized people, set upon ourselves?

Scarr: Anyone who succeeds as I have – to the very top – has ignored those rules. They've lied, cheated, stolen . . .

Hoag: You've killed four people, Tristam. You're about to make it five. No one has a right to do that.

Scarr: You disappoint me, Hogarth. Being that you respect greatness, I thought you would appreciate what I've accomplished. I thought you would understand.

Hoag: (pause) "Whatever it takes . . ." That's what Derek said you were willing to do. I guess you've just gone –

Scarr: Farther than the others dare to go. Precisely. It's fear that brings the little people up short. They'd do just as I have if they had the balls. But they haven't, the poor sods. They're afraid they'll get caught. They're weak. I'm not. I've the balls to take what I want. *(pause)* And now, at long last, it's my time. A new image, thanks to the work you and I have done. New start. New sound. *Mine.* A double album, I think. A video. A return tour. The body isn't what it was, but otherwise I'm better than ever. Richer. Fuller.

Hoag: How do you live with yourself, Tristam?

Scarr: Whatever I've done has been necessary. It had to be done, or I wouldn't have done it.

Hoag: How nice. How very, very . . .

Scarr: (silence) You were saying?

Hoag: I was . . . I was just thinking how *comforting* it must be to be a psychopath . . . Kind of the ultimate form of self-indulgence, wouldn't you say?

Scarr: I've enjoyed our talks. I'll miss them.

Hoag: (silence) Yeah, I . . . Care for the last of the champers?

Scarr: You go right ahead.

Hoag: (silence) Must have had more to drink than I . . . Feeling kinda . . .

Scarr: Yes?

Hoag: Was getting fond of you, Tristam.

Scarr: Likewise.

Hoag: You were one of my idols. Haven't many left. Come to think of it, haven't any . . .

Scarr: Sorry if I disappointed you.

Hoag: How you going to do it?

Scarr: It will look like suicide.

Hoag: Why am I . . . ?

Scarr: Your failed writing career, I expect.

Hoag: Oh, that . . . Guess I'd buy it.

Scarr: And the police will as well.

Hoag: You know what I was thinking, Tristam? If everyone in the world was . . . was like you . . . the world would go to hell.

Scarr: Welcome to hell. Scarr's the name. Shall I take that empty bottle from you, Hogarth? *(silence)* Hogarth? *(Silence, followed by sound of car engine starting, then idling. Papers rustle. Car door opens, closes. Faintly, the sound of garage door sliding shut. Then the sound of engine idling.)*

(end tape)

CHAPTER
THIRTEEN

ou could have been killed," fumed Merilee as she knelt there beside me, her brow creased with concern, her eyes big and shiny.

"I wasn't," I assured her, though I wasn't a hundred percent sure of it myself.

I was sitting on the gravel in front of the garage with my head throbbing. I was seriously groggy. Pamela kept waving spirits of ammonia under my nose and I kept waving them away. Lulu was watching me from beside Merilee, a low moan coming from her throat. From the main house came the sounds of music and laughter and voices. The party was still going strong.

"Up we go now, Hoagy," ordered Pamela, placing her hands under my arms and hoisting me none too gently to my feet. "We've got to keep you up and about or you'll be of no use to anyone.

She held onto one arm. Merilee took the other. The two of them began to walk me around the driveway on my rubbery legs.

"What if he'd had a gun?" demanded Merilee. "What if he'd just shot you instead of . . . of . . . ?

"I'd be dead," I replied. "The point is, I'm not. And I got him to show his hand. It's all on tape."

Root came out of the garage. He was shaking his head. It was Root who'd found me in the front seat of the Peugeot, out cold, about a half hour after T. S. had served me the drugged champagne and shut me in the garage with the car's engine running. It was Root who'd dragged me out into the fresh, cold air. He'd fetched the others at my request, after I started to come to.

"I don't see any tape recorder, Hoagy," Root said.

"I hid it under the driver's seat," I told him.

He nodded and went back in the garage. "Got it," he called, returning with the recorder. "Car is empty otherwise. He took your papers, tapes, all of it."

That was no problem. I'd made copies of everything, including the photograph. T. S. had bought my story that he was holding onto the only copy. It hadn't occurred to him I'd want him to kill me then and there – or to go ahead and try.

"Hoagy, darling?"

"Yes, Merilee?"

"Why *aren't* you dead?"

"Quite," agreed Pamela. "You should have died in there from the carbon monoxide."

"Oh, that. The Peugeot's a diesel. Can't kill someone from carbon monoxide poisoning by locking them in a garage with a diesel."

"Why not?" asked Root, frowning.

"Diesel engines don't produce carbon monoxide," I replied. "Or hardly any – not like gas engines do. The combustion systems are totally different. Diesel exhaust may be billowy and stinky, but it's also nontoxic. Not many people know that. I figured he didn't."

"How do *you* know it?" Merilee wondered.

"A French mechanic once told me."

"What if you'd misunderstood him?"

"I speak perfect French."

"I know, but – "

"You're saying you set yourself up?" Root asked, sucking on his gopher teeth.

I nodded, which I immediately regretted. It made something rattle inside my head. "He had to get me out of the way and he couldn't afford another murder, especially right here at his own home. That would keep things unraveling. So I gave him the perfect opportunity to stage a suicide. He put something in the champagne to knock me out. He didn't drink any of it himself, of course."

"Wouldn't the drug have shown up in your system?" asked Merilee. "I mean, if there'd been an autopsy?"

"Not necessarily, Miss Nash," said Root. "You'd be amazed at how many disappear quickly, and without a trace. Naturally, he took the bottle with him." Root turned to me. "He thinks you're dead."

"He thinks I'm dead."

"You really are a stupid ninny," said Merilee.

I took her hand and squeezed it. "Why, Merilee, that's one of the nicest things you've ever, ever . . ." My knees buckled.

"I think," said Pamela, grabbing me, "we'd best get some strong coffee into the lad."

Together, they walked me into Jack's apartment. I slumped into his lounge chair. Lulu vaulted into my lap, all pretense of gimpiness gone, and licked my nose. I really was going to have to wean her off of fish. Root lurched into the bedroom and closed the door behind him.

He wanted to listen to the tape in private for some reason. Merilee sat across from me, wringing her hands. Pamela came in from the kitchen and pressed a steaming cup of instant coffee in my hand. I gulped from it. It didn't clear my head much, but it did burn my tongue.

"How do you feel, Hoagy?" Pamela demanded.

"I've felt worse, though I can't remember when offhand. And you?"

"Me?" Pamela asked.

"It must be a bit disturbing to find out you've been managing the country estate of a murderer."

"Believe me, it is not the first time."

I stared at her a second. "Pamela, I think I'm going to have to do your memoirs next."

"I'm afraid there won't be nearly enough spice."

"We'll make some up. That's where the fun comes in." Foolishly, I gulped some more coffee. "Not that this isn't my idea of fun."

The bedroom door opened. Root stood there in the doorway, his face ashen.

"All there?" I asked him.

"Dreadful stuff," he said quietly.

"Not a pretty story," I agreed.

"Dreadful stuff. All of those years . . . All of those lives . . ."

"What are you going to do, Inspector?" Merilee asked him.

"Do?" Root swallowed. "I-I'm going to go up there and arrest Tristam Scarr for the murder of four people."

"Don't forget the attempted murder of a fifth," I said. "I'll be happy to testify."

Root belted his trench coat, squared his shoulders, and started for the door. Abruptly, he stopped. "What am I doing? What *am* I doing? That's not some sewer rat up there. That's *T. S.*"

"A sewer rat," I added.

Root ran both of his hands through his messy carrot-colored hair. "But there are members of the royal family up there."

"They've gone," Pamela pointed out. "Another engagement."

Root pursed his lips, shot a glance at the phone. "Still. I'd best ring up headquarters first."

"Why, Inspector?" I asked.

"That's just it, you see. I'm *not* an – "

"You shouldn't be intimidated by people just because they're famous."

"I'm not," he insisted, reddening.

"Look at Merilee over there," I said. "She's as famous as anybody, and she's just plain folks."

Merilee stiffened. "*Just plain folks?*"

Root mulled it over, wavering. "I suppose you're onto something there . . ." He glanced at the phone again. Then he took a deep breath. "Well, then," he announced firmly, "I'm off." He started once more for the door. This time he opened it.

"Mind if I come with you?" I asked.

He pressed his gopher teeth into his lower lip. "Want to be in on the kill?"

"I want to see the look on his face."

We all went with him.

A major musical event was happening in the Gadpole ballroom. T. S. was performing up on the stage. It was the first time he'd been on any kind of stage in over ten years, and he was giving the performance of his life – wailing, shrieking, strutting, sweating. He had come out, all right. This was his new beginning. Fittingly, he'd chosen the very first Us hit, "Great Gosh Almighty." An all-star band was up there behind him – Jimmy Page on guitar, McCartney on bass, Charlie Watts on drums – but it was T. S. everyone was responding to. The dancing had stopped. The eating and drinking and talking had stopped. Each and every guest stood there clapping to the beat, cheering Tristam Scarr's return performance on until he finally brought the song home to a thundering finish, his hand-mike held up high as a triumphant salute.

And then they roared. It was a roar of approval. Of acclaim. Of love. He stood there, eyes agleam, and soaked it up. It was all for him. No one else. *Him.*

He had made it, at last.

He was so caught up in the moment that it took him awhile before he spotted me standing there before him with Root by my side. When he did his eyes widened. His face got very white. And then Tristam Scarr's body betrayed him.

It gave out.

Jack was the first to reach him when he toppled forward. Root got there right after him. Somebody started screaming. They couldn't bring him to. Root tried cardiopulmonary resuscitation on him. Pamela phoned for an ambulance. It was no use. T. S. was gone by the time it got there.

C H A P T E R
F O U R T E E N

The story came out in waves in the press.

First, of course, came the shocking news that one of English rock music's most legendary bad boys had dropped dead in front of a couple hundred of the entertainment world's biggest celebrities. Then came the news that a police investigator, one Farley Root, had happened to be on the scene at the time. Then came the rest of it. Why Root was there. The confession tape he'd obtained. What had really happened to Puppy Johnson, to Rory Law, to Tulip, to Father Bob, and to me. Almost. A few days later came the results of the autopsy: Tristam Scarr had died of a heart attack brought on in part by a heavy dose of speed he'd taken shortly before his death – no doubt to get up for his performance. Evidence of advanced heart disease was also present. The drug and the strain of being onstage again had apparently been too much for him.

So had a certain unpleasant surprise.

I decided to stick around Gadpole until he was buried. I spent most of my time in my rooms trying to finish the job I'd come to do. But I couldn't seem to concentrate. Mostly, I just lay there on the leather sofa with a single malt whiskey in my hand, staring gloomily at the fire, Lulu dozing beside me in her chair. It was quiet up there, which suited me fine. I was not in a talky mood.

Our editor did call from New York to find out how much I had and how soon I'd have it – sooner being more commercially advantageous than later, of course.

"I really want that confession," he told me.

"You'll have it," I told him. "Does this qualify as topspin?"

"This" he replied happily, "is *heat*."

"Heat is better?"

"Listen, Hoag, did he really . . . are you sure he did all of that shit?"

"Quite sure."

"I can't figure it. A guy who has money, fame – has it all, you know?"

"Not quite. He didn't have it all to himself."

"Help us out, Hoag. Work with the lawyer, Weintraub. Otherwise he's liable to hold up the pub date for months. We're still talking about an authorized memoir here."

"I'm not writing an apology for what T. S. did."

"And we're not publishing one," he assured me. "Everybody here's been asking me . . . I mean, you spent all of that time with him. What was he like?"

I thought that one over. "Very bright. Very talented. Very unhappy. He was the Shadow Man. He lived by night. I had gotten to be sort of fond of him, actually."

"How do you feel about him now – knowing what he did?"

"I don't feel anything about him anymore."

I hung up and stretched back out on the sofa, thinking my answer sounded familiar to me. After awhile I realized it was the last thing Tulip had said to me before he killed her. I guess T. S. had that effect on anyone who got close to him. Call it a form of self-preservation.

A small private funeral was held in the Gadpole chapel. Marco and Derek drove out from London for it. Jay Weintraub flew in from New York. A limo waited to take him right back to the airport. Pamela and Violet and Jack were there. I was there. A local cleric performed the service. The estate guards and a team of police reinforcements kept the press and T. S.'s fans from scaling the walls.

Afterward, Tristam Scarr was buried next to Tulip's urn in the center of the maze. Violet insisted on that. She stared, stone-faced, at the coffin as it was lowered. She did not cry for the man who had murdered her mother.

I left Gadpole the next day – clothes, papers and Merilee's Christmas gift all packed up. Before I left, Pamela informed me that Violet was inheriting everything that had belonged to her father, making her one of the richest teenagers in Great Britain. Pamela was being appointed her legal guardian, and for the time being would remain there at Gadpole with her.

"I'm sorry to hear that, Pamela," I said, as we stood there in the kitchen, saying good-bye. "Not that you've been named her guardian, but that you won't be coming back to the States with us."

She smiled, knelt and petted Lulu fondly. "One never knows. I just might come knocking on your door one of these days."

"And we just might let you in."

At that moment Violet came padding through in her ballet slippers, eating an apple and looking very bored.

"Bye, Vi," I said.

She nodded and kept on walking.

"Hoagy is *leaving*, Violet," Pamela pointed out.

She nodded again and kept on going out the door. We looked after her.

Pamela shook her head. "She's really not a bad girl, you know. The poor dear just needs some normalcy in her life. It's not something she's gotten very much of."

Something told me Pamela would see that she got plenty of it.

I found Jack in his garage apartment, packing his bags.

"Pam has asked me to stay and help her look after things," he told me, "But I think it best I move on."

"What about you and Violet?"

Jack squared his jaw grimly. "She's an heiress now, Mr. Hoag. She'll be a great lady one day. She doesn't need the likes of me around."

"Where are you heading?"

"I don't know, sir."

I stuck out my hand. "If you find yourself in New York, look me up. I'll get you drunk. No charge."

He shook it. "That's damned kind of you, considering."

"Let's just say I've been there."

"Mr. Hoag?"

"Yes, Jack?"

He looked down at his feet. "Will I get over her?"

I managed a reassuring smile and said "You'd be surprised."

"Yes," he said gravely. "I would be."

Root happened by to take some final statements. I bummed a lift into London off of him.

"Terribly sorry about the way the newspapers made this affair appear Hoagy," Root said, as we eased down the long driveway in his Austin, my stuff stowed in the trunk.

"How did they make it look?" I asked.

Lulu sat in my lap, longingly watching Gadpole recede through the window. She'd liked it there.

"As if I . . . well, you and I know it was *you* who made the important breakthroughs in this case."

"I wouldn't say that, Inspector."

"Actually, I'm not an – " Root stopped himself, glanced over at me with a pleased, buck-toothed grin, then turned back to the road before us, still grinning.

"Don't tell me you made it," I said.

"I did."

"Well, well. Congratulations, Inspector. I knew it was just a matter of time."

"Thank you, sir. For everything."

The guards opened the gate and let us through. I waved good-bye. They didn't wave back. When we hit the main road I decided it was time to give Root the name of my tailor.

I had my introductory chapter now, the one that sets the tone of the memoir. It wasn't exactly the tone I'd been expecting earlier on, but you seldom get what you expect in my business.

I wrote it over the next few mornings at the mews house while Merilee slept. I worked at the dining table, with a fire crackling in the fireplace and Lulu asleep under my chair, her head on my mukluk. I wrote it in my own voice. I had to. The reader had to know what had transpired since I'd begun my collaboration with Tristam Scarr. Had to bear in mind that the story they were about to read was his own version of his life, and of history, and that there was another version. I covered that version in a final chapter that was also written in my voice. In it I detailed the murders, past and present, his attempt on my life, his confession, and his own death onstage at his coming-out party.

I didn't think it made for dull reading, but that's just my opinion. You'll have to make up your own mind.

The day that I put it in the mail to New York happened to be the same day Merilee finished her run in *The Philadelphia Story*. It also happened to be Christmas Eve. We celebrated all of these things with Lulu at the Hungry Horse. The waiter remembered us. He didn't have to be told to bring us a bowl of olives to go with our martinis.

Merilee seemed drained and a little down. She usually does when the curtain has just fallen on a role for the last time. That was something I understood. I felt pretty much the same way that night.

"Glad to be finished, darling?" She mustered a weary smile as we clinked our glasses.

"It was a hard one. I lost a little of myself this time. I guess that's what happens when you lose an idol. That and you get bitter. I don't want to get bitter. I don't want to become someone who just sits there waiting for the bad to surface in other people. And in myself." I drained my martini. "I keep thinking I really don't want to do this kind of work again."

"Go back to work on your novel. That's what you need to do."

"I intend to." I caught the waiter's eye and ordered us another round. "I miss New York. Tomorrow too soon to head back?"

She cleared her throat, looked away uneasily. "Something rather sudden has come up, actually. My agent called. I've . . . I'm taking this film role."

I tugged at my ear. "Film role?"

"They're already in production. In Tunisia," she said, the words tumbling out quickly. "See, they wanted Meryl, and they thought they had her, only her deal fell through at the last minute and, well, it's quite a plum for me, even if I'm not exactly their first choice. It's a Graham Greene thing. Pinter adapted it. Jimmy Woods is the male lead, and the director is – "

"Feel like some company?"

She examined the tablecloth for a full minute, her lips pursed. Then she shook her head.

The waiter came with our drinks and asked if we were ready to order. Somehow the thought of rare meat wasn't quite as appealing as it had been five minutes before. I waved him away.

"I-I need to be on my own for awhile, darling," she began. "The past few weeks – they've been wonderful. Special. But something just isn't right with me. I've gone from you to Zack, then from Zack right back to you again. I keep messing things up. I need to be on my own for awhile. Figure things out. No messes. I . . . I'll be home in a few months, okay?"

"Okay," I said, knowing she wasn't coming home, at least not to me she wasn't. What had happened between us over the past few weeks was finished. It had been London. It had been Tracy. It had been . . . hell, who knew what it had been. Whatever, it was done. For now.

"I'm so sorry, darling. Really, I am."

Her green eyes were brimming now. I got lost in them.

"Don't be sorry" I said. "We had a terrific time. We'll have other terrific times. And we'll have them soon. You're mine. You always will be mine. I'm quite sure of that." I drained my drink, glanced at Lulu in Merilee's lap. "I'm afraid it's going to be tough on you-know-who, though."

"On me, too," she said, stroking you-know-who's ears. "You don't have to wait for me."

"I know I don't. But I will."

"So understanding," she said, covering my hand with hers. "So very, very understanding."

"That's me, all right. Of course, this means you don't get your Christmas present now."

"*What?*"

It was a shawl-collared cardigan sweater made out of eight-ply oyster gray cashmere. A men's size forty-two. My size. I'd picked it up in the Burlington Arcade one afternoon, knowing it would look like a million bucks on her.

I wore it home on the plane. I figured I may as well start breaking it in right away, so it would be good and ready for her when our time came again.

The plane was nearly empty. Not many people fly on Christmas Day. Lulu didn't stop whimpering during the whole damned flight, even though I let her eat my seafood cocktail.

About the Author

David Handler was born and raised in Los Angeles and published two highly acclaimed novels about growing up there, *Kiddo* and *Boss*, before resorting to a life of crime fiction. He has written eight novels featuring the witty and dapper celebrity ghostwriter Stewart Hoag, including the Edgar-Award-winning *The Man Who Would Be F. Scott Fitzgerald*. He has also written five novels featuring the beloved duo off pudgy New York film critic Mitch Berger and alluring Connecticut State Trooper Des Mitry, including the Dilys Award-nominated *The Cold Blue Blood*. He has written extensively for television and films on both coasts and co-authored the international best-selling thriller *Gideon* under the pseudonym Russell Andrews. He is a graduate of the Columbia Graduate School of Journalism and began his career in New York City as a television and theater critic. He also served a stint as a ghostwriter. Mr. Handler currently lives in a 1790s carriage house in Old Lyme, Connecticut.

Visit David Handler online at www.davidhandlerbooks.com

About the Illustrator

Colin Cotterill was born in London in 1952. He trained as a teacher and worked in Israel, Australia, the U.S., and Japan before training teachers in Thailand and on the Burmese border. He spent several years in Laos, initially with UNESCO and wrote and produced a forty-programme language teaching series; English By Accident, for Thai national television. Ten years ago, Colin became involved in child protection in the region.

All the while, Colin continued with his two other passions; cartooning and writing. His work with trafficked children stimulated him to put together his first novel, *The Night Bastard* (Suk's Editions, 2000). Since October 2001 he has written seven more books: *Evil in the Land Without* (Asia Books, 03), *The Role of Pool in Asian Communism* (Asia Books, 05), *The Coroner's Lunch* (Soho, 05), *Thirty Three Teeth* (Soho, 05) and *Disco for the Departed* (Soho, 06), set in Laos in the 1970's. The fourth book, *Anarchy and Old Dogs*, has just been completed.

Since 1990, Colin has been a regular cartoonist for national publications and produced a Thai language translation of his cartoon scrapbook, *Ethel and Joan Go to Phuket* (Matichon, 04) and an anthology of his bilingual magazine column 'Cycle Logical' (Matichon, 06). Colin is married and lives in Chiang Mai in the north of Thailand where he lectures part time on the MA programme and rides his bicycle through the mountains.

Coming in Spring 2007
from
Busted Flush Press

The Man Who Would Be F. Scott Fitzgerald & The Woman Who Fell from Grace

by
David Handler

Trade paperback omnibus, $18.
Original cover and interior art by Dilys Winn Award-winning crime novelist Colin Cotterill.

The Man Who Would Be F. Scott Fitzgerald

Winner of the Edgar Award for Best Paperback Original!

"A wickedly amusing tale." – *Publishers Weekly*

The Woman Who Fell from Grace

"[An] awfully clever comic mystery . . . A mean plot, full of crises that ingeniously spoof the melodramatic events of the original pot-boiler saga." – *The New York Times Book Review*

"[A] hilarious spoof of bestsellers and the people who write them."
– *Mystery News*

Available Spring 2007 from your favorite bookseller.

Available now from **Busted Flush Press**

DAMN NEAR DEAD:
AN ANTHOLOGY OF GEEZER NOIR
edited by Duane Swierczynski; introduction by James Crumley

Trade paperback original; $18.
ISBN 0-9767157-5-9; July 2006.

Hard-boiled story collection, featuring original "geezer noir" tales by Jeff Abbott, Megan Abbott, Charles Ardai, Ray Banks, Mark Billingham, Steve Brewer, Ken Bruen, Milton Burton, Reed Farrel Coleman, Colin Cotterill, Bill Crider, Sean Doolittle, Victor Gischler, Allan Guthrie, John Harvey, Simon Kernick, Laura Lippman, Stuart MacBride, Donna Moore, Zoë Sharp, Jenny Siler, Jason Starr, Charlie Stella, Duane Swierczynski, Robert Ward, Sarah Weinman and Dave White.

"The best anthology I've read this year." – Jennifer Jordan, *Crimespree Magazine*

Available from your favorite bookseller.

Coming in 2007
from
Busted Flush Press

A Hell of a Woman: An Anthology of Female Noir,
edited by Megan Abbott

The Hackman Blues / London Boulevard, by Ken Bruen

Miami Purity, by Vicki Hendricks

Just Another Day in Paradise / The Frog and the Scorpion / Gatsby's Vineyard, by A. E. Maxwell

Noblesse Oblige / Impolite Society / Misleading Ladies / Silver and Guilt / Royals and Rogues, by Cynthia S. Smith

The Deep Six (limited edition), by Randy Wayne White, introduction by Tim Dorsey

And much more!

Visit www.bustedflushpress.com
and sign up for our free e-mail newsletter.

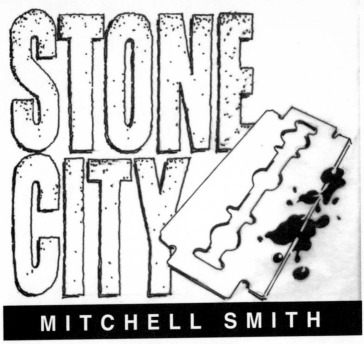

MITCHELL SMITH

Trade paperback; $18.
ISBN 0-9767157-7-5.

"I am asked frequently about my favorite books. *Stone City* is the best thriller I have ever read. Have you ever wondered how you would handle prison? *Stone City* answers that question in the context of a brilliant novel."

From the new introduction by Phillip Margolin.

Trade paperback reprint of the
classic prison crime novel.

Available Fall 2006
from
Busted Flush Press